I AM THE GREAT HORSE

I AM THE GREAT HORSE

BY
KATHERINE
ROBERTS

The Chicken House
SCHOLASTIC INC./NEW YORK

FOR BARRY

Published in the United Kingdom in 2006 by The Chicken House, 2 Palmer Street, Frome, Somerset BA11 1DS.
www.doublecluck.com

All rights reserved. Published by Scholastic Inc., *Publishers since 1920*,
by arrangement with The Chicken House. SCHOLASTIC, THE CHICKEN HOUSE,
and associated logos are trademarks and/or registered trademarks of Scholastic Inc.

Library of Congress Cataloging-in-Publication Data

Roberts, Katherine, 1962–
I am the Great Horse / by Katherine Roberts.
p. cm.
Summary: The war horse Bucephalas recounts his adventures from 344–323 B.C. with
Alexander the Great and his relationship with a groom who has prophetic dreams.

ISBN 0-439-82163-0

[1. Horses—Fiction. 2. Alexander the Great, 356–323 B.C.—Fiction. 3. Kings, queens, rulers, etc.
4. Generals—Fiction. 5. Greece—History—Macedonian Expansion, 359–323 B.C.—Fiction.] I. Title.
PZ7.R54325Iam 2006
[Fic]—dc22
                                   2005024559

10 9 8 7 6 5 4 3 2 1   06 07 08 09 10

Printed in the U.S.A.   23
First American edition, August 2006

The text type was set in Garamond Classico.
The display type was set in Skreech Caps, Trajan Pro, and P22 Acropolis.
Interior design by Leyah Jensen

Have you clothed his neck with thunder?

Can you make him leap like a grasshopper?

The glory of his nostrils is terrible.

He paws in the valley and rejoices in his strength.

He goes to meet the armed men,

He mocks at fear and is not afraid,

Neither does he turn back from the sword.

The quiver rattles against him,

The glittering spear and the shield.

He swallows the ground with fierceness and rage,

He is trained to charge at the sound of the trumpet —

He says among the trumpets, "Ha! Ha!"

And he smells the battle from afar,

The thunder of the captains, and the shouting.

JOB 39:19-25

CONTENTS

SCYTHIA

ALEXANDROPOLIS
MACEDONIA
R DANUBE
PELLA
BYZANTIUM
BLACK SEA
THEBES TROY
ATHENS
EPHESUS
ANCYRA
GORDIUM
HALICARNASSUS
CILICIAN GATES
ISSUS
ALEXANDRETTA
ALEXANDRIA
R TIGRIS
GAUGAM
CYPRUS
R EUPHRATES
TYRE DAMASCUS
GAZA
BABYLON
ALEXAND
MEDITERRANEAN SEA
ALEXANDRIA
SIWA ORACLE
MEMPHIS
EGYPT
ARABIA

BUCEPHALAS'S
HOOFPRINTS

RED SEA
R NILE

CASPIAN SEA

ARAL SEA

R. JAXARTES

SCYTHIA

R. OXUS

ALEXANDRIA ESCHATE

MARACANDA

SOGHDIANA

BALKH

BACTRIA

ALEXANDRIA UNDER CAUCASUS

TAXILA

R. COPHEN

BUCEPHALA

JHELUM

ZADRACARTA

ECBATANA

CASPIAN GATES

ALEXANDRIA HERAT

PERSIA

USA

PERSIAN GATES

KING CYRUS'S TOMB

PERSEPOLIS

LAKE SEISTAN

R. INDUS

ALEXANDRIA

INDIA

PERSIAN GULF

MILES

0   100   200   300   400   500

● BUCEPHALAS'S JOURNEY

⬤ ALEXANDER WITHOUT BUCEPHALAS

⚔ SITE OF BATTLE

INDIAN OCEAN

FROM THE
HORSE'S MOUTH

My name is Bucephalas, and you should know right away that I'm no black beauty.

My coat is the color of oil from the ground, but that's about as far as it goes. I have a big head, a white splotch between my eyes, battle scars, and a brand the shape of two horns burned into my backside. I am, however, very strong and worth my (considerable) weight in gold as a warhorse. At least I used to be, until I did the most shameful thing a horse can ever do. I killed my own rider.

I didn't mean to trample the poor man to death. All I remember is the enemy's pike, five times longer than a normal spear, hitting me in the eye. My rider fell off. The rest was a confusion of ghosts and screams. For half a year I lived in darkness. Once I could see again, the ghosts had not vanished like they usually do but lurked in the shadows of my damaged eye.

An inferior horse would have panicked. But I am a stallion trained for war, so I tried to fight them. Ha! It took me a while to realize no one can dominate a ghost, by which time I had gained my reputation for being unrideable. No one dared sit on me — until the day our trader took us north to the land of my enemy, where I met two remarkable humans who were not afraid of me:

ALEXANDER, *Crown Prince of Macedonia,*
CHARMEIA, *the only other person who could ride me.*

Forever after, our lives were joined by the invisible bond that links human to horse and can be escaped only by death. People may tell you some of this story isn't true. But Alexander's royal historian was paid to write lies, and he never ventured down to the horse lines, anyway, so what could he know?

Climb on my back, if you dare, and let me carry you into the battles that changed the world.

PELLA,
MACEDONIA
344 B.C.

ᛞOMINATING ᛞUNG

When we reach the river landing, I can't get off the ship fast enough. A storm hit us during our voyage up the coast, which is no fun if you're tethered in a dung-splattered hold with a hundred terrified horses slipping and neighing around you.

I gallop down the ramp, dragging with me the two strongest man-colts employed by our trader, Philonicus. The little curved spikes of the rough bit I'm wearing dig into the corners of my mouth as I fight against it, and they've attached a rein to each side of my bridle so I can't bite them. They haven't a hope of controlling me, of course. The only reason I'm going in the direction they want me to go is because I *never* abandon my herd.

The sand steams under our hooves as we are led onto the riding ground. It smells of strange horses, and I need to stop several times to dominate dung (lift tail over stranger's pile and drop own dung on top to show I'm boss). My grooms jerk my bit, so I rear up and fight them. By the time we catch up with the others at the far side of the ground, I am covered in white foam and the corners of my mouth are bleeding.

Philonicus squeals at my grooms, who mumble that I'm mad-fresh after being on the ship and that the state I'm in ain't their fault. Nothing ever is with man-colts, I've found. The Macedonians who have come to try us out give me wary looks.

"He's a bit excitable after the voyage," Philonicus tells them. "He's high-spirited, like all the best warhorses. He'll calm down in a moment."

Ha! Not unless he finds me a groom who knows what he's doing, I won't.

Philonicus gives the man-colts a glower that is the human form of flat ears, then hisses, "Take him over there and walk him around until he's cooled off. And for Zeus's sake, wipe that blood off his mouth before King Philip gets here! If you let this horse get worked up like that again, I'll take my whip to the pair of you when we get back to the ship."

The two grooms drag me away, complaining in low voices. All that kicking and neighing on the ship has taken more out of me than I thought, and I take a breather to listen. They assume just because we horses don't speak in words that we can't understand human language. But we're not as stupid as you think, and while they lead me around I learn a few things about this Macedonian king.

The battle that killed my rider and gave me my bad reputation wasn't the only one the Macedonian king has made. Soon, he's going to make a big battle in another world across the sea to the east, where the sun rises, because the king of that world stole some cities from our world. Many squealing threats have been issued by both kings, which is what stallions do before a battle. But humans make these threats by sending one another rolls of flattened grass with marks on them. Dominating dung would be easier, but you don't understand smells like we do.

That's why the Macedonian king wants to buy so many of us, because he needs horses to train as cavalry mounts for his battle in the other world. He's also looking for a horse to carry his son Alexander into his first battle. The king wants a quiet, well-trained mare. But the prince has his own ideas, because he is a man-colt and wants to be a hero. Ha! Sounds to me as if the king will soon have more than one battle to fight.

It is quiet at this end of the ground, and I've dominated all the dung within smelling distance. As my grooms talk, I relax a bit and my stride lengthens.

"I think he's cooling off at last," says one of them. "Get your mitten on and give him a bit of a polish. I'll hold him so he don't bite you."

The other groom eyes me warily. "Why bother? No one's goin' to buy him once they've tried to mount him."

"The Macedonian royal horsemaster is supposed to be a good rider."

"Ha! That's what they said about the horsemaster back in the last place, and look what happened to him!"

What happened was a ghost moved in the corner of my bad eye, and I panicked. The man fell off and rolled under my feet where I couldn't see him. I accidentally stamped on his arm and broke it.

"C'mon! If he looks the part, the Macedonians might buy him untried. Then at least we'll be rid of the brute."

"*You* polish him, then!" says the other groom, still eyeing me nervously. "I'll hold his head."

They take turns to run their grooming mittens down my neck and over my back, while the other one stands in front of me and hangs on to my reins tightly, as if I am acting wild, which I'm not because it's quite nice being groomed in those places. But they can't decide who is going to do my belly, which is where I sweat most. I give them flat ears to warn them not to try, and they jump clear. I have my second wind now, so I take advantage of my slack reins to drag them back across the ground. I want to see what the Macedonians are doing to my herd.

ALΣXANDΣR

By the time we reach the other horses, the king's family and friends have arrived from the palace along with a pack of dogs that run around our heels, barking loudly. They have enough brains to keep away from *me*, though. My herd is being trotted up and down, while the king's horsemaster checks their legs and teeth. Bridles are brought, and riding-cloths fastened on burnished backs. The men vault on and try out battle maneuvers. I keep a close eye on the horsemaster, because I don't like his smell.

The young Prince Alexander watches the others eagerly. I can't see him very well because most of his friends are taller than him. But I can see his energy, bathing everyone around him in its light. This fascinates me so much, I prick my ears and stand still. My grooms breathe a sigh of relief and even pluck up enough courage to wipe the blood off my mouth.

One of the king's eyes is a mess of scar tissue, but his good eye watches the horses with interest. Finally, he calls a dappled gray mare across and orders her rider to dismount so the prince can try her. She has big brown eyes and is gentle and kind. Her name's Aura, and I'd like to have her in my pasture. I give her a nicker, and she nickers back.

But Alexander tilts up his chin and says he wants to ride a stallion, not some soft mare. His friends laugh. The one-eyed king smiles and shakes his head. The king's horsemaster scowls. He says since none of the other horses are suitable for the prince he will have to wait for the next shipload.

Bags of gold change hands. Horses are led away toward unseen stables. My companions from the voyage, all going!

I neigh to them. Heads shoot up, and there are some whinnies in reply. I try to follow Aura. My grooms stop me with a jerk on my spiked bit and get another telling-off from Philonicus. He brushes aside their boasts of how they polished me, grabs my rein, and leads me toward the one-eyed king.

"Here's the perfect horse for Prince Alexander, Your Majesty!" he says. "He's called Bucephalas — after his brand. See? It's an ox head — very valuable type. He's as strong as an ox, extremely fast, and sound as a trumpet. Look at those high hooves! He's experienced, too. Twelve years old, the same age as your son. He'd make a fine warhorse to keep Prince Alexander out of trouble in his first few battles. Not *cheap*, of course . . . but I'm sure a man of Your Majesty's experience understands that quality comes at a price."

The king's gaze runs over me. He looks interested. So does his horsemaster, who runs his hands down my legs and looks at my teeth — though he doesn't get a very good look because he prods my sore mouth and I nearly bite off his finger.

The horsemaster's eyes narrow. "Put a riding-cloth on him," he orders. "I'll try him out."

My grooms glance at each other, and Philonicus goes a bit quiet. But the cloth is brought, and the girth and breast strap are tightened, making me shiver and sweat. For my last rider, I used to settle down (bend knees to lower my withers, so my rider can get on more easily if he's tired, wounded, or wearing armor). But I don't want this man on my back, so he is forced to vault onto me.

Like most humans who spend a lot of time around horses, he mounts from the left. It's my blind side, but he doesn't realize. When he reaches for a cavalry spear, it's all shadows, and my head whirls in panic.

I act WILD.

His weight is soon gone. I gallop off, scattering the crowd and leaving the ghosts behind me.

There is an outcry as everyone gives chase. The king's grooms vault onto the horses they were leading away and gallop around the far side of the ground to head me off. Philonicus's grooms race after me on foot, shouting for them to watch out and not to get too close in case I attack their horses.

As I wheel back toward the royal party, I hear the queen laughing.

"A fine warhorse, eh? He'll certainly be able to run away from a battle! . . . Horsemaster, aren't you always telling the boys to hold on to their reins if they fall off?"

Philonicus tries to explain that the storm has upset me, that I'm highly strung, and I've been trained to leap like that in battle. But the royal horsemaster does not appreciate being laughed at by the queen. He's like a stallion who wants to be boss of the herd but isn't, so is quick to take out his frustration on those who are weaker than him. He picks himself up, clouts a groom who is giggling at the queen's comment, and makes himself huge. He says I'm obviously unrideable, Philonicus is asking a crazy price for a rogue like me, and that I'm too old to retrain.

The king nods.

But the prince ducks under his arm and stares at me, his eyes shining with admiration. "He's the best of the lot, Father!" he says fiercely. "I bet I can ride him."

"That's a man's horse, Alexander," says the king sternly. "We're looking for an experienced mount for you so you can concentrate on your weapons training, not one you'll have to fight every step of the way. He's evil, you can see it in his eye."

"I want that horse."

The king sighs. "The last thing you want is a half-broken stallion you can't trust in battle! Besides, the price is a joke, ox-head brand or not. I wouldn't be surprised if old Philonicus didn't brand the horse himself — I see the brute has a fresh whip scar on his nose. What happened, horse-trader? He try to bite you?"

Philonicus flushes, because that is exactly what happened when he tried to stop me from kicking a hole in the ship during the storm.

But the prince hasn't given up. "If I prove I can ride him, Father, can I have him?"

The king looks angry. "I'm not shelling out good Macedonian gold for a rogue."

"If he throws me, I'll pay for him myself out of my allowance. Let the price of the horse be the bet." He gives the one-eyed king a calculating look. "That means if I stay on, you'll have to buy him for me, Father."

There is an uncomfortable pause. Everyone watches as the king and his young son glare at each other like challengers for the herd. The queen says Alexander is a better rider than most trained cavalrymen and should be allowed to try. The horsemaster whispers something in the king's ear while giving me a dark look.

The king grimaces and gives a reluctant nod. "*If* you stay on," he mutters, "I'll buy him. My horsemaster tells me there's a thing the Scythian tribes do to their colts to make them more manageable. We could always try it with this horse, though he's a bit old so it won't be easy on him."

The prince's friends whisper excitedly, betting on the outcome. The horsemaster, smirking at this mention of the unpleasant thing, seizes a rope from one of them and gives me another dark look. He starts to organize the grooms to drive me into a corner. But the prince ignores his warning shout and sprints across the riding ground toward me.

I flatten my ears and gallop straight at him. This usually frightens man-colts into jumping out of the way. But Prince Alexander does not move. He stands in front of me, his stocky legs planted firmly in the sand and his arms spread wide as if to catch me. An untidy pale mane flops into his eyes, which are fixed on mine. His chin tilts up to one side.

"Steady, Bucephalas!" he calls in a shrill voice. "Time to stop running now."

"Get out of the way, you fool!" yells one of Philonicus's grooms, not realizing it is the king's son he's shouting at. "That horse is a maniac! He'll kill you!"

But Alexander does not move a muscle. He keeps his odd eyes on mine. One is brown, the other flecked with blue. I've never seen a human with eyes like that. Nor have I seen a man-colt so determined and with such bright energy inside him.

Something shifts in my head. I forget the grooms chasing me, dig in my hooves, and come to a snorting stop, a whisker's length away from the prince.

One of Philonicus's grooms puffs up behind me. "Slowly," he says. "Grab his lead rein. Then we'll come and get him. He knows we won't stand for no nonsense."

Alexander grins. "Don't worry, I know how to handle horses. I could ride before I could walk." In one smooth movement, he steps forward and lifts the reins over my ears.

I can feel the blood pounding through his body, so I know I scared him. But he does not tremble like most man-colts when they hold my rein. While I am deciding whether to let him lead me back to the others without a fight, he squints up at the sun and turns me so that the light shines into my eyes and makes the ghosts disappear. Before I know what is happening, he has moved to my shoulder, gripped my withers, and vaulted softly onto my back.

Philonicus's groom takes an anxious step toward us but stops, not wanting to startle me. The king's horsemaster stops, too. He stands well back with his rope coiled and an expectant smile, giving me space to act wild, as I did with him.

I just stand there, I am so surprised. Alexander's legs reach only halfway down my flanks. I have no idea how he got up there on his own. His hand is still gripping my withers, and his other hand holds my reins loosely. He doesn't dig in his knees like the horsemaster did nor pull on the bit to hurt my sore mouth. He simply sits on my cloth, his heart still pounding, talking to me in his high voice as the whole Macedonian crowd comes running toward us.

The one-eyed king watches me closely, while the prince's friends call out advice.

"Be careful, Alex!" — "Keep his head up!" — "Watch that he doesn't bolt!"

Philonicus puffs after them, quick to take advantage of my apparent calmness. "See, Your Majesty? What did I tell you? He just needs the right handling, that's all."

The king's horsemaster scowls. He clears his throat and gives orders as to how I am to be tried out properly as a warhorse, including having blunt javelins thrown at me to test my reflexes.

Alexander gives the horsemaster a mischievous look. I feel his hands tighten on my rein as if he is going to ride me through the crowd to the gate. Then he changes his mind, clamps his heels into my sides, and heads me for the fence. "Come on, Bucephalas!" he says. "Let's get away from these idiots, shall we?"

I need no urging. I take three strides, clear the fence with a huge bound, and gallop across the plain toward the river. I throw a couple of bucks to let the man-colt on my back know I am boss. But he makes no attempt to stop me. He has the most amazing balance, and somehow he stays seated on my cloth.

Behind us, the king yells for someone to accompany the prince. I suppose I must look out of control. The horsemaster vaults onto a bay stallion and gives chase, but we soon leave him far behind.

It is a wild freedom to gallop so fast. I've done it before, sometimes with my rider's permission, sometimes not, but never with so young a man-colt perched on my back. Yet Alexander's hand is strong on my withers, and now that his fear has gone he holds my bit firmly enough with the reins so that I know he'll never let me fall if I stumble. It feels good.

On my back, Alexander must be feeling good, too. He shakes his mane out of his eyes and laughs. "Oh, my crazy, beautiful Bucephalas!" he shouts as he turns me along the riverbank, the wind whipping his words to pieces. "That showed them, didn't it? My fine, strong warhorse! You wouldn't throw me, would you? I was right. You're like Father. You can't see much out of your left eye, can you? Don't worry, it'll be our secret. I bet you're not afraid of anything. I'll ride you in my first battle, then together we'll conquer the world!"

I toss my head and gallop even faster, because his excitement infects me and he looks so happy.

You may think I was acting like some crazed youngster given the run of my first pasture, but it had been a long time since I'd galloped so fast with such a brave man-colt on my back. With some riders, you just know you will give your life for them.

A PLOT AGAINST THE PRINCE

Instead of bucking off Alexander when we returned to the riding ground, I arched my neck to accept the bit. Then I made myself huge so everyone stared at us.

The king's horsemaster scowled at me as if I were doing this deliberately to show him up, which I was. He tried to snatch my reins as we passed. I gave him flat ears and carried Alexander to safety. The queen clapped her hands in delight, smiling at her son as she called him clever and brave and all sorts of other things guaranteed to make his head swell.

The one-eyed king's fearful expression melted into one of pride. He gave me a wary look, then helped the prince down from my back and embraced him with tears in his eyes. "Alexander, you scared us!" he exclaimed. "If you're going to carry on like this, you'd better find yourself a larger kingdom, because Macedonia won't be big enough for you."

Alexander, his cheeks still flushed from our gallop, gave him that upward tilt of his chin and grinned boldly. "How about leaving Persia for me, Father? You've conquered just about everywhere else, and as you've just seen, my new horse Bucephalas likes to run east."

This set them all off laughing again. As they returned to the palace, the prince's friends crowded around to hear his account of how he'd "tamed" me. Some of them wanted to know if he was serious about Persia. The queen followed, still praising her son's bravery and skill.

But the one-eyed king remained on the riding ground, frowning after Alexander.

When the others were out of earshot, he took the horsemaster's arm and said, "I don't want to see my son riding that horse again. Put him in a back stable away from the others, and if he doesn't calm down in a few weeks find a Scythian who can do the deed. Before I leave on my next campaign, I'm going to make arrangements for Prince Alexander to go away to finish his schooling. He'll soon forget the horse, don't worry. In the meantime, find him another stallion more suited to his size and experience, and train it well so I don't have to be looking out for him when the time comes for him to join me on the battlefield."

The king's horsemaster smiled his dark smile and ordered his grooms to take me to the stables. I didn't make trouble, because I'd had a good gallop and was looking forward to my barley. But as we passed the crowd of onlookers at the edge of the ground, I caught a smell that reminded me of the time before the ghosts came, and saw a girl-filly clutching what looked like a mule's hoof. She was glaring at the one-eyed king with as much hatred as a colt that had just been driven out of the herd.

This was rather strange. But the horsemaster's grooms did not see her, because human eyes can't see all around like horses' eyes can, so I lowered my head and walked on.

Whatever the Scythian thing is, it can't be as bad as a spiked bit.

ROYAL STABLES, PELLA

344–340 B.C.

LIVING WITH MULES

I made an enemy that day on the riding ground, and the one-eyed king had delivered me into his hands.

Right away, the king's horsemaster set out to break my spirit. The stall he'd ordered the grooms to put me in was dark and airless, tucked away in a back corner where I couldn't see what was going on. It had thick iron bars that reached to the rafters, and my only stable companions were mules. MULES, I tell you! (To make a mule, shave off a mare's mane when she is in foal-season and put her with a male donkey. Her foal will turn out to be a mule, which has long donkey ears and a sticking-up mane, and is the lowest form of life. Mules cannot even sire more mules, because they are sterile. They are useful, though, for pulling heavy carts and carrying baggage.)

Even the mules have better stalls than mine, set in rows down each side of the stable block with windows in the back walls. Their doors do not have bars, so they can put their heads over and take a drink from the marble water trough in the passage whenever they want.

The muleteers who look after them are almost as bad. Rough, loud, and dirty, these men lurk like outcast stallions at the edge of the herd, causing trouble. They like to run their sticks along the bars of my stable, which makes me mad enough to kick the walls. Then they laugh at me, which makes me even madder. They say Alexander should have been made to stay here in Pella and ride me every day instead of being sent off to school. They say he'd learn a lot more by having me knock the stuffing out of him than he ever will from useless scrolls. Then they go off to drink magic made from our barley and snigger about the royal family. They say any fool can see Alexander looks nothing like King Philip, and that he's only heir to Macedonia because his older brother is a half-wit. They reckon King Philip would be better off staying at home to sire a legitimate son, and if he ever does get around to crossing the Hellespont the Persian king will thrash him like a mule and send him home with his tail between his legs.

Muleteers are even too stupid to know that kings don't have tails.

As well as muleteers, the royal stable employs horsemen to train the cavalry mounts and hundreds of scruffy man-colt slaves as grooms. The grooms are too afraid of me to come in and take out my dung, so I am forced to stand in a squelchy mess for days at a time. It's a miracle I haven't got hoof-rot, I can tell you. A muzzle of bronze wire hangs outside my stall for them to use when they lead me out for exercise. But they often leave it on me because they are so scared of me biting them. Then they forget to take it off, and I can't eat my hay.

Enough said. You've probably figured out by now that those first few months in the Macedonian king's stables were not much fun for me. The only good part was that the Scythian thing the horsemaster had threatened for me didn't happen. When he and a flat-faced stranger crept into the mule stables one night and opened my door, the flat-faced man took one look at me, threw down his knife, and fled. I acted wild, of course. But wouldn't you if your enemy and a knife-wielding stranger roused you from your bed in the middle of the night?

Apart from this, nothing happened to me in the royal stables of Macedonia that has not happened in all my previous stables. I am starting to think the routine is the same everywhere in the world:

Breakfast
Mucking out (in theory)
Exercise (lead-outs only — after the Scythian thing failed, the horsemaster
     forbade anyone to ride me until he got a chance to "sort me out")
Roll in the sand (if the grooms are feeling brave enough)
Lunch

Afternoon snooze
Mucking out
Grooming (*Ha! I'd be lucky!*)
Sleep

I got frustrated because I was not allowed to work off my energy with a good gallop. But I was still the boss, even if no one saw me. I could hear the others clopping past on the cobbles on their way to the riding ground, and every morning I whinnied loudly to remind them I was still around. Aura always whinnied back.

I was starting to think everyone had forgotten me, when something different happened.

CHARMIDES

I have finished my morning feed, kicked the wall to let the mule in the next stall know I'm boss, and whinnied to Aura and the others as they go out to exercise. It doesn't look as if anyone is coming to lead me out today. I am about to settle down to my usual morning entertainment of chewing the wood off the top of my door, when there's laughter and a lot of noise outside.

Some of the grooms come into the stable block, hustling a small groom between them. I think they're going to throw the small one into the water trough, which is something they often do to new grooms. I think it's a human form of dominating dung. But they push the small one past the water trough, right up to my stall. They're still making a lot of noise. So I give them flat ears, rear up, and smash my hooves against the door.

The older grooms grin at one another. One of them grabs a pitchfork and unlocks my door. Another one grabs the small groom. The mule-master, who is working nearby, spits on the floor and wanders up to see what's going on.

"New slave, ain't he?" explains one of the grooms, jerking his head at the new one. "Says he's worked in stables before, though no one seems to know where he's come from. Horsemaster says we're to give him a test on some horse that don't matter." They put the pitchfork into the small groom's hand and open my door a crack. "Here's your test, new boy! This horse's stall's not been cleaned out properly in ages. He needs a good currying, too. Make a good job of it!" Laughing, they push the small one through the gap and slam the door.

The new groom stumbles, and the pitchfork clatters to the floor on my blind side, bringing ghosts. I panic, forget I'm in my stall, and crash into the opposite wall. The mulemaster and the grooms push eager faces against the bars to see what's happening.

"Watch him, new boy!" one calls. "He's a bit wild. He killed the man who rode him in his last battle!"

"Killed hundreds!" says another. "He likes the taste of human flesh. We throw all the king's criminals in here so he can eat 'em!"

"He tried to trample the master to death, first day he was here, and no one's been on his back since!"

"Yeah, and he *ate* that Scythian the master brought in here to take away his spirit. Every last bone! The king paid thirteen whole talents for him, but he's less use than a mule."

Which is all lies, of course. And the groom they've thrown into my stall knows this as well as I do.

Once I realize the pitchfork is lying safely by the wall, my head calms and I recognize her smell. You, with your human nose, might be surprised, but we horses only have to smell someone once and we remember them for life. I know this girl-filly from the time before the battle that gave me my bad reputation, when she used to creep into my stable and feed me pastries stolen from the kitchens. It was her I saw watching from the edge of the riding ground on my first day, when the king told the horsemaster to put me in here. She's cut her long mane, and like the man-colts she's wearing a baggy brown tunic with a belt for grooming tools. But underneath she still smells like spring grass.

"Oh, poor Bucephalas!" she whispers, getting to her feet and moving close to my shoulder. Her fingers go to the base of my mane, find the itchy spot on my withers, and do mutual grooming (gently scratch teeth along another horse's mane and spine, concentrating on the withers, which get itchy because we can't reach them with our own teeth). She uses her fingernails for this, of course, not her teeth. But it is very nice and a long time since I've been allowed near enough to another horse to do it. I can't enjoy it with all those faces jammed up against my stall, though. I squeal and lunge at the bars, scraping the metal with my teeth to make them go away.

They leap clear, laughing. "Good luck, new boy!" they shout as they run off. "We'll be back for your corpse later!"

The mulemaster stays, chewing a stalk of hay and watching us with his wily eyes. "Not much point wasting time on that horse, lad," he says, when the girl-filly makes a chirruping sound with her tongue to soothe me. "He's a rogue, through and through, and I've seen a few in my time. Best get out of there, before he hurts you."

"Why's he in here with the mules?" asks the girl-filly, still mutual grooming me.

The mulemaster spits. "Best place for him. He'd only savage the other horses. Mules keep him in his place, at least. Old Philonicus pulled a fast one on the king with him, all right. Experienced warhorse, my foot! Only young Prince Alexander could ever sit on him, and he and his friends have been sent away to study philosophy and other useless stuff with that ponce Aristotle. King Philip's off fightin' again, and the royal horsemaster's far too busy to deal with him because he's trainin' up cavalry for the Persian campaign."

"He been out lately?"

"Are you jokin'? Grooms are all too scared of him, ain't they? Last time he went out, he got loose, and we had a devil of a time catchin' him. Took ten of us in the end. We had to drive him back into his stall with sticks. Makes a change to find someone who can quiet him, truth to tell. I wouldn't push your luck, though. Want me to let you out? Them cowards have shut the bottom latch on you."

"You can pass me a wet sponge," the girl-filly says softly, still scratching my withers. "And his halter, too."

"I suppose a good groomin' wouldn't hurt him." The mulemaster lifts down my muzzle. "Better put this on him, though, or he'll bite your arm off."

"I won't need that till I'm ready to take him out," the girl-filly says. "He'll be fine."

"Take him *out?*" The mulemaster shakes his head and shrugs. "Up to you, I suppose." He watches a bit longer as the girl-filly sets to work on my matted and dusty coat.

"What's your name, lad?" he asks.

She pauses, just slightly, then says, "Charmides."

"Charmides, huh? One of them fancy Greek names. What you doin' workin' here, then? King Philip capture your family on one of his raids down south?"

"Most people call me Charm," she says quickly, and I notice her accent has become rougher, more like the mulemaster's. "And I don't have a family anymore." She takes the wooden comb, scrapes it down my neck, and spits a mouthful of my dust on the floor.

The mulemaster regards her with narrow eyes, as if he thinks she might be doing this to make fun of him. Then he laughs.

"If you can keep that horse from upsettin' my mules, young Charmides, we'll be yer family and look after you. Them young grooms are useless, most of 'em. And the ones that are any good race around on their fine horses like they're in the royal cavalry or somethin'. Too stuck-up to talk to the likes of us." He spits again, watching her clean my head carefully with the sponge.

"You ever thought of becomin' a muleteer? We could do with more sensible lads like you."

A SECRET

That was how I got the girl-filly as my personal groom, and life improved. Although I still had my dark stall at the back of the mule stables, it was now cleaned properly every day so that I could feel the cobbles massaging my hooves again. I got proper grooming and exercise — long walks through the streets of Pella and along the riverbank with Charm at my head. I learned all the smells, until I knew I could find my way back to the stables from any part of my new home in Macedonia.

Now that I had an outlet for my energy, I grew much calmer in my stall. After a sharp talking-to by their mulemaster, the muleteers stopped banging their sticks on the bars to tease me, and the other grooms were relieved they didn't have to come near me anymore. They were so impressed when Charm led me out of the stable the first time and held on to me grimly while I plunged about in excitement, they never suspected she wasn't a man-colt like them. Most man-colts think girl-fillies can't do things like that. And Charm was clever. She smeared my dung on her face to hide her smooth girl-filly skin, which made her look a bit strange. But since she smelled so strongly of me, I didn't need to dominate her.

The royal horsemaster narrowed his eyes when he saw Charm leading me out, but he didn't bother us. Charm said he couldn't decide whether to be glad I was behaving myself or angry he didn't have an excuse to try the Scythian thing on me again. Summer turned to winter and back to summer again, and still Alexander did not return from his Aristotle school. I was starting to think he had forgotten me. But the horsemaster had not forgotten the one-eyed king's last order before he went away to fight — that his son was not to ride me again.

One day, when Charm leads me out to exercise, I see a strange horse being put through his paces on the riding ground with the rest.

He is bright red like the rising sun and very full of himself, although only half my age and size. When he sees me, he gives a bold squeal. So I squeal back to put him in his place. The red stallion loses concentration, and the horsemaster scowls at me.

"Quiet, Bucephalas!" Charm says, frowning. "We'd better go down to the river. That's a special horse the royal horsemaster is training for when Prince Alexander gets home."

This is bad news. Alexander is going to ride *me* when he returns, not some half-trained youngster who won't know the first thing about looking after such a headstrong man-colt.

There's only one thing to do. I go up on my hind legs, ripping the lead rein out of Charm's hand. I leap the fence from a standstill, find some of the red stallion's dung, and dominate it. Then I make myself huge and gallop straight for him, ears flat.

The red stallion isn't stupid. He spins out of range quicker than most, leaving the horsemaster sitting on air.

Charm catches up, breathless, and grabs my trailing lead rein. "Oh, I'm sorry, sir! I couldn't hold him —"

The horsemaster gets to his feet, yells for someone to catch the red stallion, and glares at her. "Take that brute out of here and don't bring him back until he's too tired to lift his head! You're lucky he didn't injure Petasios. The king paid a whole talent for this horse. If Bucephalas gets loose on the riding ground again, you'll feel my whip. The sooner King Philip gets back and we can get rid of the animal, the better."

Charm bows her head in submission and leads me away. The boys training the other horses straighten their faces as the horsemaster remounts. I find another of Petasios's dung piles and dominate it on our way to the gate. Then I dominate one of Aura's, too, to remind her she's part of my herd.

This makes me feel better. But Charm is strangely quiet as she leads me to the river.

"Oh, Bucephalas!" she says crossly. "What did you have to go and do that for? The horsemaster had almost forgotten about us, and now he'll be watching us again. That's the second time you've made him fall off in front of everyone. Another stupid walk's not going to calm you down, is it? What you need is a decent gallop to take the tickle out of your hooves."

As she talks, her fingers loosen my muzzle, which is unusual but nice. She hangs it carefully from a branch and checks that there are no boats in sight. Then she leads me to a rock, climbs up on it, and throws herself at my back. She chooses my left side, which startles me. I jump sideways, and she falls into the river. She gets up, wipes the fringe out of her eyes, and climbs back up onto the rock.

When I wouldn't settle down to be mounted by my previous riders, they used to get on me by vaulting from the ground or off their spear. So I don't know quite what she is up to, and it upsets me. Once, she gets herself lying across my back, but before she can swing her leg over I break into a gallop and she falls off again. This time, she stays sitting in the shallows and starts to cry.

I can't work it out. Charm never cries, even when I nip her.

I nibble the reeds around her for a bit, thinking she will get up out of the river and take me for my walk soon. But she sobs even louder.

"Oh, Bucephalas! You great big lump of a horse! Don't you see, you've got to behave, or the king will sell you for horsemeat when he gets back!

I'm sure you'd like a gallop along this nice, soft riverbank, wouldn't you? But first you've got to let me get on you, because if I let you loose out here, the horsemaster will beat me for sure. Then he'll find out I'm a girl, and I won't be able to look after you anymore."

When she finishes crying, she spends some time stroking me and talking to me. The next time she leads me to the boulder I am calmer, and she manages to slither onto my back. As soon as I feel she is balanced, I arch my neck and jump out of the water. Both her hands are twisted tightly in my mane. She laughs nervously. I prance, testing her seat. Then I give a small buck and break into a gallop.

Oh, the joy! Oh, it is wonderful! You have no idea how good it feels to stretch your legs after being restrained to human pace for so long. I throw several huge bucks in a row, forgetting it is Charm on my back and not a trained horseman.

And suddenly, I realize she isn't on my back anymore.

I pull up, a bit out of breath. There's nothing like standing in a stall all day to take the fitness off a horse. Charm is some way back along the riverbank, a crumpled heap of muddy brown tunic and dung-smeared flesh.

I trot back and sniff her to check that she isn't dead. She groans, rolls over, and blinks up at me. "Bucephalas? You came back for me!"

Well, of course. We warhorses are trained to do so, aren't we? Wouldn't do to go galloping off in the middle of a battle and leave your rider lying injured on the ground at the mercy of the enemy. I snort at her. Then I settle to my knees, as I have been taught to do.

She stares at me, surprised. "And you've been trained to settle down, as well! Oh, Bucephalas, you clever, clever horse!"

She climbs on my back (a lot easier than last time) and laughs as I lurch to my feet. I dance sideways, champing impatiently on my bit.

"All right, once more! But if I get caught riding you like this, I'm *really* going to be in for it with the horsemaster!"

This is a perfect example of what you humans do all the time. You pretend to submit, then you do what you want when the boss isn't looking.

After that, Charm rode me bareback whenever we were out of sight of the stables. But I didn't mind, because she never tried to dominate me. I knew I could throw her off whenever I liked, and she knew it, too. Sometimes I wished she would ride me more like Alexander did, because she didn't hold the reins very tightly, which meant I couldn't trust her not to let me stumble when I galloped fast. It was nice to have her on my bare back, though. She was always gentle, and she often mutual groomed me as she rode.

With proper exercise I grew fit again and my coat regained its black gleam. Charm grew taller and had to bind her teats tightly under her tunic so the other grooms wouldn't notice them. She learned the muleteers' rough language, how to spit, and how to drink magic without getting sick so they would think her one of them.

Aura went in and out of foal-season several times without mating. Petasios never squealed at me again. The youngsters who came with me on the ship were trained to gallop and turn quickly, not to startle at trumpets, and to carry a rider armed with javelins and a curved cavalry sword. The mules stayed as stupid as ever, though some went away to carry bags for the king's army, and others replaced them. I remained the boss, and Charm remained my special groom, sleeping in my stall so no one would discover her big secret.

Then Alexander returned from school, and all our lives got turned upside down.

THRACIAN BORDER

340 B.C.

PRINCE REGENT

I am eating my breakfast in nervous mouthfuls when Charm comes rushing into the stable. Her cheeks are flushed, and she is carrying an exercise-cloth with a bridle lying over the top. I start to sweat and shiver at the sight of it.

There has been much shouting and running around already this morning. Hooves clatter on the cobbles as horses are taken to the riding ground in greater numbers than usual. Men's excited voices ring out. They must be dressed for battle — I can smell the oil they put on the leather straps of their armor. I hear Aura whinny and send her a ringing reply. I am so worked up by now that I abandon my breakfast and press impatiently against the door. Charm has to dig her elbow into my chest before she can get in.

"You know as well as I do the horsemaster said he's got to be kept in today," says the old mulemaster, who has been looking out for Charm since her first day. "You'll be in for a beatin', if you're not careful."

Charm sets her jaw and doesn't reply. She's having trouble fastening my girths. The last time I wore a cloth was when Alexander rode me, four years ago at my trial. She gets it on eventually, pulls out her mitten, and rubs it over my neck. It's soon soaked with my sweat.

"Be sensible for once, Bucephalas!" she says. "If you don't behave yourself, Prince Alexander will ride Petasios into the battle instead of you."

This is not what I want to hear.

The mulemaster shakes his head. "So that's what you're up to, is it? Well, it's your funeral."

He opens my door and I barge out, knocking him against the trough and dragging Charm after me. The mules withdraw their heads quick. They've learned to keep out of the way whenever they see me coming. My neigh rings out as I emerge into the sunshine, and replies come from several horses I recognize. I prance beside Charm as she leads me to the riding ground.

Petasios is there already, wearing a quilted battle-cloth with a purple trim. I have to admit he looks magnificent, his red coat polished to perfection. He arches his neck and paws the sand while the horsemaster holds his lead rein. Other horses trot in circles, already mounted, their riders carrying spears and javelins.

Standing in the middle of the ground, frowning at the horsemaster, is Prince Alexander. I'd know his smell anywhere. It's slightly sweet, like sherbet.

He's not much taller than when I last saw him. But he's more muscular, has the same bright energy, and carries himself like a young boss-stallion who has just taken over the herd. The one-eyed king is not here, so maybe he has. His helmet is under one arm, so his untidy mane blows across his eyes. He is wearing a gleaming new breastplate bearing a design of a human head with snakes instead of hair. It glints and flashes as he moves. A purple cloak billows from his shoulders.

"Where's *my* horse?" he demands, his shrill voice carrying across the ground. "I'm not riding this one."

The horsemaster explains how wonderful Petasios is and how well trained.

Alexander cuts him off with a flick of his hand. "Put that little horse away and bring me Bucephalas. The Maedi tribe need a lesson in manners. If I'm going to give them one, I must be properly mounted."

An older man, standing at Alexander's shoulder, whispers something to the prince.

Alexander scowls at him. "No, Antipater, I'm *not* going to wait. My father's in Byzantium. If nothing's done about the Maedi, they and the other Thracian tribes will have overrun Macedonia by the time he gets home. We have to drive them back behind the border and show the others we mean business before it's too late. Father left me the royal seal, which means I'm in charge until he gets home, so it's my decision. Horsemaster, if you want to keep your job, have my horse Bucephalas brought out at once!"

At this point, Petasios spots me coming and whinnies nervously. I squeal at him and make myself huge. Charm clings grimly to my lead rein as she wrestles with the gate. The horsemaster sees us and curses under his breath.

Alexander has seen me, too. He narrows his eyes, taking in my sweaty neck and the old exercise-cloth. He frowns a little. "I suppose he looks fit enough. Bring him over here, boy!"

Charm dips her head as she does so, hiding her face under her fringe. I give Petasios flat ears to warn him to keep his distance.

Alexander hardly looks at Charm. He runs his hands down my legs and steps back to look me over again. He gives the horsemaster a strong glare. "Who's been riding him?"

The royal horsemaster bites his lip. "No one, sir."

"Someone has. There's a chunk missing from his mane where they've been holding on. You, boy, what's your name?"

Charm swallows, staring at her feet. "Charm . . . ides, Sir Prince."

"You're Bucephalas's groom?"

"Yes, sir."

"Do you ride him?"

Charm glances at the horsemaster. Her cheeks flush under the smears of dung.

But the horsemaster laughs. "Do you really think this slip of a groom could manage him, sir? The idiot boy can't even hang on to the horse when he's leading him out! This is quite ridiculous. Bucephalas has been standing in a stall for four years! He's nowhere near battle fit. Take the chestnut, sir, and you'll win your battle against the Maedi. Take this horse, and he'll dump you in the middle of the fight and probably expire from the strain. He must be sixteen, at least, by now, which is no small age for a horse. And his temper hasn't improved one bit since you went away to school."

Alexander's eyes narrow again. "Sixteen's a good age to be," he says. "Or are you trying to suggest your Prince Regent is past it, too?"

Some of his friends laugh.

The prince turns his back on the horsemaster's spluttered reply and questions Charm closely about where I've been stabled and my care and feeding. He says nothing more about her riding me, so she answers truthfully enough and tells him all about the mule stable.

Alexander frowns.

His friends — who are nearly grown like him and full of themselves like colts on the verge of becoming stallions — stop making jokes about the horsemaster and gather around to listen. Their horses champ their bits and paw the ground. Aura has a rider, but Petasios is still riderless. Ha! That'll teach him not to get above himself! Then Charm taps my shoulder, and I settle to my knees for Alexander to mount.

There is a collective intake of breath. The horsemaster stares at me in amazement.

"Temper not improved, huh?" Alexander says with a sudden laugh and springs onto my lowered back. "It looks good enough to me."

When Charm takes off the lead rein and steps clear I immediately prance to my feet. Feeling how firm Alexander is on my cloth, I give a little leap of celebration and flick my tail in Petasios's face.

Alexander laughs again, gathers up my reins, and looks down at the horsemaster. "I'll soon tell you if Bucephalas is fit for battle, when we thrash the Maedi! In the meantime, you'd better find yourself another position. As from today, you're no longer the royal horsemaster. I don't take kindly to people who keep my valuable warhorse in a mule stable, try a barbarian operation to ruin him for life, leave his feeding up to the grooms, and saddle him for battle with the oldest of cloths. I don't expect to see you here when I return."

The horsemaster's mouth drops open. He gives Charm an evil look and pushes back his shoulders in an attempt to make himself huge. "You've no right to do this to me! When King Philip gets back, he'll hear about this. I've trained Petasios personally and gotten him ready for you to ride in battle just as your father ordered. You're making a big mistake, sir — Antipater, tell him!"

The older man sighs and shakes his head. "I'm afraid it is Prince Alexander's right as Prince Regent to hire and dismiss staff in his father's absence. I'm very sorry. I'll make sure you are given a good reference."

Alexander has already forgotten the horsemaster. He puts on his helmet and tests my reflexes, making me gallop down the ground, turn, and charge the other way. It calms me to practice the old battle maneuvers I learned when I was young. I soon stop shivering and start to enjoy myself. It works Petasios up, though, since he still hasn't got a rider. The horsemaster is dragged unceremoniously around the ground as he tries to keep hold of him.

"Can I ride the chestnut stallion, Alex?" asks one of the man-colts who is not yet mounted. "He looks spirited. He might have a chance of keeping up with Bucephalas, so I can watch your back."

Alexander grins and strokes my damp neck. "You do that, Hephaestion, my friend! He's yours. I make you a present of him. Oh, and horsemaster . . . don't even think about dismissing my horse's groom before you leave, or when I get back from Thrace I swear by Zeus I'll hunt you down and have you executed for treason. You, boy . . . Charmides . . . while I'm gone, prepare the best stable for Bucephalas so it's ready for him when we get back." His grip on my reins tightens, and he looks suddenly serious and determined.

"Now, gentlemen, we've wasted enough time! Hand me my spear! We ride for Thrace!"

ALEXANDER'S GUARD

In the space of half a day, I was a warhorse again. But not just any old warhorse, oh no! I was the Prince Regent of Macedonia's mount, trotting at the head of his army with Petasios beside me and everyone else trotting along behind in a great jangling of shields and weapons. Also, my enemy the horsemaster had been dominated. Oh, it was a great day!

We traveled north into the mountains. We were nearly two hundred cavalry, with no hoplites (that's human for foot soldiers) to slow us down. The Thracian border, where the battle would be, was not far enough for Alexander to bother with baggage carts, so we took a few mules to carry the food and spare weapons and went as fast as we could.

There were eight horses in Alexander's Guard, all ridden by his friends. Alexander had obviously dominated Hephaestion and the other man-colts a long time ago, but it was the first time we had all been together in a herd. So there was a bit of tail-lashing, nipping, and squealing until we settled down. Here are their names and colors, because it's far too complicated to tell you their smells:

PETASIOS — *red stallion, carrying Hephaestion*

AURA — *dapple-gray mare,* very *beautiful, carrying Demetrius*

PSYLLA — *bay mare, quite sweet, carrying Hector*

HARPINNA — *speckled red (you humans say roan) mare, carrying Ptolemy*

APOLLO — *palomino stallion, carrying Perdiccas*

BOREALIS — *strong brown stallion, carrying Leonnatus*

ZEPHYR — *yellow mare, carrying Philotas*

HADES — *small dark bay stallion, carrying Iolaus*

As we go on they will all no doubt impress you with their bravery, so there's one thing I should add: They are all smaller than me, even Borealis with his massive crest, and leggy Harpinna, and only Aura is as well bred as me. That is why I am the boss.

ALEXANDROPOLIS

We find the enemy in the foothills near their scruffy little city. They are clearly surprised to see Alexander riding at the head of an army, and their scouts run back from the rocks, shouting the alarm. Alexander immediately puts his heels to my sides and urges me after them, and the whole of us cavalry break into a gallop. The enemy are on foot, so they cannot outrun us. But they scramble up the steep slope where we cannot follow, take cover behind boulders, and hurl their javelins at us.

Alexander gallops me out of range and throws up his hand to stop the others. The Guard close around me, dancing and snorting. I am trembling so much, it takes me a moment to realize Alexander is trembling, too.

"Steady, Bucephalas," he whispers, pulling my ear. "I am Achilles out of the *Iliad,* and you're my immortal horse, gifted to me by the gods. We're not going to die today. Don't let me down. I've *got* to win this battle."

That is when I realize his only experience of battle comes from stories like the *Iliad*, where the heroes never die. This is his first time in a real battle, ever.

Judging by their expressions, it is the first time for most of his friends, too. Only Philotas, who is a bit older than the others, seems to know what he's doing — but he is too busy looking down his nose at Alexander to be of much help.

My young rider's fear reminds me it is my job to look after him, and the panic leaves me. I nicker to Aura to tell her I'll look after her, too. Then I give the others flat ears to warn them to pay attention because the man-colts will need our experience today.

Perhaps I should explain here how important we horses are in a battle. At this stage of the fight, our riders are each armed with:

2 javelins for throwing at the enemy as we charge
1 spear for stabbing the enemy when we get close enough
1 curved sword for when the spear breaks or gets stuck in a dead body
1 shield, for emergencies

But humans have only two hands. So you tell me how many hands they have to spare for holding our reins?

In the end, it was a small battle. When human squealing matches become a fight, the army with the most men and horses usually wins. The Maedi had about the same number of men as us but fewer horses. We were obviously much better trained, and they were not prepared for us.

Alexander didn't waste time squealing. He sent some men to flush out the enemy hiding in the rocks, while we led a cavalry charge on those defending the city. One of them threw a javelin on my blind side, but Petasios whinnied to warn me, and I leaped to avoid it. Alexander barely moved on my cloth as it scratched my flank. I expected him to gallop me out of range, but instead he gave a shout of anger that one of the enemy had dared injure me, cast aside his spear, and drew his curved sword. With a wild war cry, "ALALALAI!," he dug his heels into my sides. His sword flashed down, again and again, sending Maedi ghosts rippling into the air. The rest of the enemy fled.

I feel so powerful with Alexander on my back, I would gladly have carried him until I collapsed. But just as I am starting to feel my lack of fitness, the Maedi city surrenders.

The gates open, and a man mounted on the scruffiest horse I have ever seen trots out to meet us. Alexander pulls off his helmet to free his mane, which is plastered to his forehead with sweat. He is shining with victory, and his breastplate reflects a shaft of sunlight breaking through the mountain mists. It has a spatter of enemy blood across it, and there's more blood on his face. None of it is his. I did my job well today.

The Maedi boss has an old scar across his forehead. He looks about three times Alexander's age, and the ghosts of his people cling to him as they are sucked away. Although he can't see them, I think he must feel something, because he shivers.

For a moment, Alexander seems unsure what to say. Then he sets his jaw, tilts up his chin, and says in a tough voice, "You broke your agreement with my father, King Philip of Macedon. As Prince Regent, I have his full authority to execute every last man, woman, and child in your city and wipe the Maedi from the face of the earth." He pauses to let this sink in, and there is a horrified hush among the enemy. "On the other hand," Alexander continues smoothly, "my father is not here, so if you surrender you can negotiate terms with me."

He holds his breath. Behind us, Philotas shakes his head.

But the Maedi boss knows a good deal when he hears one. He looks at his dead tribesmen strewn across the plateau, eyes the grim-faced Macedonians and their frightened prisoners, and gives Alexander's breastplate a sideways look. He bows his head. "Prince Alexander, please spare our families. The Maedi will serve you for the rest of your life. We'll do anything you ask."

Alexander's hand relaxes on my rein. He thinks a moment. Then he says, "You'll bring a hundred of your best javelin-throwers to Pella when I send for you. In the meantime, I'll leave a hundred of my father's men here to keep an eye on things in your city, which will from now on be called . . ."

"Philippopolis?" suggests the Maedi boss, relieved to have escaped the legendary Macedonian wrath and keen to cooperate.

Alexander looks up at the walls and gives a boyish grin. "Alexandropolis!"

That's typical human arrogance for you. Really, it should be *my* city. Who was it kept Prince Alexander out of trouble in his first battle, carried him to victory, and intimidated the enemy in the bargain?

I bite the scruffy Maedi horse on the neck, and he drops dung in terror. As he carries his master back into the city that is now a Macedonian garrison, I lift my tail and dominate his pile.

A NEW STALL

We trotted home with two dead cavalrymen, each one tied across his horse's back. A few others were wounded, but they would live to fight again. That's not bad for a human battle. All us horses were fine. Alexander's friends were in high spirits, laughing and telling stories of their own bravery. While Alexander discussed the battle with Hephaestion, planning how next time he would do better to avoid unnecessary Macedonian deaths, I blew gently at Petasios to tell him I forgave him for squealing at me the first time we met. His whinnied warning quite possibly saved me and Alexander from injury today.

Charm was waiting for us at the stable gates, sitting on a rock with her head in her hands. When she saw us coming, she jumped up and ran into the road to take my rein. She smelled of strange dung, which I did not like. Her groom's tunic was torn, and one of her eyes had a big purple bruise around it. I snorted at her, while she tried to see if I was sound.

Hephaestion chuckled. "Looks like your groom found a battle of his own while we were off conquering the Maedi, Alex!"

Alexander frowned but said nothing about Charm's eye. He ordered her to tend my wound, and said he'd be down to check on me later.

My new stall was big and airy, right next to the door with a grand view of the yard and the palace gates. There were marble pillars around the water trough. Borealis was solid and comforting in the stall next to mine. My new friend Petasios was across the passage, and — joy, oh joy — I could see Aura's gray head looking out of her window at me from the mares' stable! A pile of sweet-smelling hay was waiting for me in the corner, and Charm tipped a warm barley mash smelling of herbs into my manger. Best of all, there were no mules.

I was so hungry that at first I did not notice Alexander come into the passage. He watched Charm tending my javelin scratch with warm water and salve. She obviously hadn't noticed him, either, because she nearly jumped out of her skin when he asked, "Who did that to your eye?"

"N-no one, Sir Prince!" she stammered, letting her fringe flop over her face. "I fell off a horse at exercise."

Alexander's eyes narrowed. "If you're going to be Bucephalas's groom, you're going to have to start telling me the truth. I know you're a good rider. You must be, if you've been riding my horse."

Charm stopped sponging my wound and stood frozen.

"How many times has he thrown you?" Alexander insisted, opening my door.

"Hundreds," she whispered. "But he always comes back for me. I ride him bareback by the river. No one else knows. Please, Sir Prince, don't send me away! I only did it to calm him down. He was going crazy in his stall, and the horsemaster said —"

Alexander held up a hand to silence her. "I'm not angry. I was starting to wonder who I'd find to exercise him when I can't do it. My father's old horsemaster has gone as I ordered, hasn't he?"

"Yes, Sir Prince."

"And your eye?"

Charm dipped her head and mumbled, "The horsemaster said he'd teach me a lesson. But the mulemaster called some of his muleteers to stop it. They were a bit rough. I think they broke his knee. They chased him off."

Alexander grimaced. "Good. Some people only understand rough-ness. I don't think he'll bother you again now that I'm back, but if there's any more trouble you let me know right away." He considered me while I ate. "Bucephalas is to rest for a few days, slow lead-outs only, and then I'll be exercising him myself. So there'll be no more falling off him for a while, Charmides. Understood?"

Charm gave him a flash of her eye, fighting a smile. "Yes, Sir Prince!"

He studied her in much the same way he had studied me earlier. He frowned. "Bucephalas can't have a groom who looks like a muleteer. Clean yourself up a bit, then go and ask the new horsemaster for a spare tunic so you can wash that one. Tell him I sent you. I think you're hiding quite a handsome face under all that muck, and you've got brains, which some haven't. But next time I ride into battle, I expect you to saddle my horse with a proper cloth. I won't have him injured again through that sort of carelessness."

"But it wasn't my fau —" Remembering who she was talking to, Charm broke off and looked at the floor.

Alexander gave her a curious look with his odd eyes. He waited a moment to see if she would say anything else. Then he patted my neck and hurried up to the palace, where his friends were busy celebrating their victory the way you humans like to do, with a lot of noise and magic drink.

With the one-eyed king away, there were many such parties up at the palace. Alexander exercised me whenever he could, battle training with the others on the riding ground, and on longer rides to inspect his father's kingdom. We nine of the Guard got to know one another and became an excellent herd.

If you ask me, that was a good winter. I had the best stall in the royal stables, the best groom, and the best rider. But we often saw the prince's adviser Antipater striding across the yard red-faced, muttering under his breath about Alexander's crazy ideas of running a kingdom. He and Alexander had lots of public squealing matches, and our grooms made bets on who would become the new boss of Macedonia if the one-eyed king got killed on campaign.

ALEXANDER — *favorite*

ANTIPATER — *second favorite*

PHILOTAS — *long odds outsider, but he's the son of the general of the Macedonian army, so would make a stronger king than Alexander's drooling half brother who can't even ride Aura without a lead rein.*

Ha! Antipater and Philotas don't stand a chance.

GREECE

339–338 B.C.

The one-eyed king did not die on campaign. He brought his army back from Byzantium and ordered Alexander and his friends to arm themselves in preparation to accompany him to Greece. He was in a rotten temper because:

> *the Athenian and Persian herds had joined forces against Macedonia.*
> *a rebel tribe had ambushed his troops on the way home through the hills and thrown a javelin through his thigh.*

Charm was in a strange mood the whole time the royal physician was treating the king's leg. While she rubbed me over with long slow strokes of her grooming glove, she kept glancing at the palace.

"Doesn't look like he's going to die of it," she muttered in the end. "Maybe I shouldn't have gotten rid of that mule's hoof? But if I'd used its contents on the king as I'd planned to when I first came here, I'd have been arrested and wouldn't have been able to look after you — Oh, Bucephalas, what shall I do? He's going to take Prince Alexander into battle, I know he is! It was bad enough when Alexander went off to fight the Maedi, but they were only a disorganized tribe. The Greeks have trained armies! I can't bear the thought of you in a real battle. You're all I have. If you get hurt, I'll never forgive myself."

But she was just a groom and had no choice but to obey when Alexander ordered her to get me ready for the march south.

When she led me out, resplendent in my new purple-tasseled battle-cloth, there was a short squealing match between the one-eyed king and Alexander. The king did not want his son to ride me in the battle against the Greeks. He said I was too big for him and couldn't be trusted. Charm stroked my nose, holding her breath in sudden hope. But when Alexander pointed out I'd already carried him to victory against the Maedi, he got his own way.

This time we took lots of mules and baggage carts, because we would camp many times en route to the battle. This meant no dry stall and having to eat our barley from a leather nosebag. The good thing was that Charm got to come, too, riding in a cart at the back of the army with the other grooms. There was quite a lot of kicking and squealing in the horse lines, because the excitement infected us all. We knew the battle would be a big one, since the one-eyed king and the Athenian boss did their version of dominating dung (sending marks to each other on rolls of flattened grass) for a very long time. But we couldn't attack the enemy yet, because they had blocked the passes through the mountains. Our grooms complained it would take forever to lure the cowardly Greeks out to fight a proper battle, and they were right, because we ended up camping all winter.

This was not as boring as it sounds. There were plenty of little battles in the hills to keep us occupied, like the one when we dominated the Maedi. Every time we returned flushed and triumphant from one of these skirmishes we found Charm waiting for us at the edge of the camp. Alexander laughed at her anxiety as he handed her my reins so she could take me for my roll.

Alexander was excited about fighting in his first major battle, of course. But he was frustrated that we were stuck in Greece rather than driving the Persians out of Anatolia.

"Father got it wrong," he told Charm during one of his visits to the horse lines. "So now we've got to fight Greeks before we even *think* about crossing the Hellespont! I could have told him the Athenians would make trouble if he went marching off to Byzantium without first taking care of things properly over here. People are saying he's losing his touch, getting old." He gave my neck an affectionate slap and eyed Charm over my withers. "What do you say, Charmides? Do *you* think my father should be retired and put out to pasture to make way for a younger horse?"

Charm pretended to groom my other side, but that was only so she could keep me between her and Alexander.

"I think you should retire Bucephalas, sir, before he gets hurt."

He chuckled. "Don't worry so! I won't let anything happen to Bucephalas. I give you my word as future king of Macedonia. After he's carried me in a few more battles, I'll let him breed with the best mares in the royal stable. That gray, Aura, for a start. And maybe the little bay, Psylla. Then I'll raise his foals to carry me to Persia. Bucephalas is far too valuable to let some barbarian kill him on the battlefield. Aren't you, my beautiful brave warhorse?"

He gave my ear a fond tug, and I gave him an equally fond nip, just to remind him who was boss around here. I wonder when he decided I am not his immortal horse, after all? Or maybe he was lying to Charm? (To tell a lie, say human words that mean one thing while holding body very still so no one can tell what you *really* think. Very confusing.)

Alexander rubbed my teeth marks from his arm with a tolerant smile. As he left, he pointed to my shoulder. "You missed a bit. I can see I'll have to stand on the other side next time, or my horse's coat will soon look as odd as his eyes."

This made Charm blush.

She started to polish the place on my shoulder Alexander had told her she'd missed, then closed her eyes and clutched my mane.

"Oh, Zeus," she whispered. "Why does he keep coming down here and teasing me like that? He's the *prince*. He's going to be king of Macedonia one day. Worse, he still thinks I'm a boy!"

When summer came, the one-eyed king got fed up with squealing and told a lie on flattened grass to make the enemy think we were going back home to deal with a rebel uprising in the north. This did the trick. The Greeks ventured out of their hills, thinking we were retreating. By the time they realized we were not leaving but coming after them instead, it was too late for them to run and hide.

A TEST OF KILLING

We have our big battle at dawn outside a little town called Chaeronea, between the mountains and the river. Mist hangs over the plain, making everyone look like ghosts. I can't stop trembling, and Alexander's hand is tense on my rein. The horses of the Guard chew their bits and snort. Apollo keeps rearing, which is very annoying.

The enemy form up to face us with their backs to the mountains — a solid line of men and spears, stretching across the plain from the walls of the town to the river. Their cavalry is behind them, which is a pretty useless place to be, if you ask me. They can't gallop to engage us without trampling their own men. Our hoplites are angled down the slope to our right, the whole line bristling with long Macedonian pikes. The one-eyed king and his officers are out of sight at the far end of our line.

The final squealing matches and prebattle sacrifices take *ages*. While we wait, Alexander's friends nervously tell one another stories about the enemy band directly opposite us — a grim and battle-scarred herd of foot soldiers from a city called Thebes. They were supposed to be on our side but joined the Greeks at the last moment. The one-eyed king is very angry about this and has ordered Alexander to dominate them thoroughly. Too right. With the Thebans on the enemy side, our two armies — Greek and Macedonian — are more or less the same size. This, as I explained before, is NOT GOOD.

The remains of a sacrificed goat are carried away behind our line, and a hush falls over the two armies. My heart is pounding so hard I think it might burst. A trumpet blast echoes in the mountains, and a great roar goes up from our men.

With much rattling and creaking of armor, our hoplites form into a phalanx (a solid mass of men, eight rows deep, longest pikes at the back so the points are like a wall of spears when they charge the enemy). Last time I was in a battle like this, I was facing that lethal wall of spikes. The memory makes me shiver. I toss my head, looking for ghosts, and Alexander runs a calming hand down my neck.

"Remember, I am Achilles and you are immortal," he whispers.

Looks like he's decided we're heroes again.

Our phalanx advances at a steady pace, and the whole enemy line ripples. Finally, the Greeks can stand it no longer, and their line breaks with bloodcurdling yells as they charge toward us. The horses of the Guard leap and plunge around me, fighting their reins.

"Wait for my order!" Alexander shouts. "Wait!"

The Greeks run at an angle to meet our phalanx. Only the battle-scarred Thebans opposite us stay put on their mound. They look nervous. They should be. A gap has opened between them and the rest of their army, and now our phalanx is retreating under the one-eyed king's order, luring the rest of their herd even farther away from them.

Alexander shifts his javelins under his arm so he can pull my ear. "This is it, Bucephalas, my brave horse," he says. "Our first real battle. Let's show Father what we can do!"

I snort and shake my head. He laughs, digs his heels into my sides, and waves his javelins in the air with a great shout:

"ALALALALAI! ALALALALAI!"

The bit slackens in my mouth, and I leap forward in a thunder of hooves. I feel Alexander take a firm hold to keep me from stumbling over the plain, but my head is so full of the excitement of galloping at the head of such a big herd, I've forgotten we are racing into danger. On my back, Alexander yells encouragement to the others in his shrill voice. He sounds confident and he is shining with excitement, but I can feel his terror. The horses of the Guard are flat out, trying to keep up with me as we stream through the gap in the Greek lines and gallop in an arc to trap the Thebans on their hill. The rest of our cavalry thunder in a cloud of dust behind us.

They must be very brave humans, to stand and face us galloping horses. Alexander throws one of his javelins and scores a direct hit. The enemy soldier falls under my hooves, and his ghost ripples past my nose. I check my mad gallop to jump over his body, and swerve before I impale my rider on a spear. Hephaestion cheers. "First blood to Alex! Hurrah!"

From then on, it is a confusion of flying javelins, flashing swords, blood, shouts, neighs, and the ghosts of men and horses vanishing through the dust to wherever they go when they leave this world. Alexander fights with wild energy, like he did in the hills, and the others of our herd see this and fight furiously, too. But the Thebans are a wiser enemy than the Maedi, and it takes us a lot longer to dominate them. Soon the mound is thick with enemy dead. I tread on their bodies, rolling my eyes.

There is a pause when no enemy is near enough to fight us. Alexander allows me to catch my breath, while he takes a look at what's happening to everyone else. The Greek line is breaking up as they flee into the mountains. Petasios joins me, black with sweat. Alexander mutters to Hephaestion, "This is awful! How many more of them do we have to kill before they give in? Father's routed the rest of the Greek army. Surely they must see they can't hope to win now?"

"They're the Theban Sacred Band," Hephaestion says. "It's said they never abandon their post — Look out!" He kills another of the enemy, who had just run up the hill and tried to spear Alexander.

Alexander curses and urges me back into the fight. Several times, he calls for the Thebans to surrender, but either they don't hear him or they refuse to listen. Finally, someone kills their boss, and the few Thebans who remain on their feet throw down their swords. Alexander flops forward onto my neck, his arms hanging limply. "Thank Zeus," he breathes.

Our cavalry forms a circle around the prisoners. Alexander's friends pull off their helmets, still panting, and silently survey the piles of dead. Most of our men and horses have minor injuries, and I realize I'm bleeding, too, as a hot trickle runs down my left foreleg. It's odd, but in the midst of a battle you never notice it happen. I am trembling again, this time with exhaustion.

Alexander dismounts to check my leg. Clinging to my mane, he stares at the dead Thebans.

"They fought bravely," he says. Then he bends over and is violently sick.

No one says anything.

He wipes his mouth on his sleeve. In a very controlled voice, he tells our cavalrymen they have fought well and orders Hephaestion to take charge of the prisoners. Then he leads me slowly back to camp across the blood-soaked plain, past all the bodies and the loose horses. He hands me over to Charm without a word, ignores an order to report to his father's tent, and walks off alone.

Charm fusses over my injured leg, so I snap at her. Petasios lifts a hoof at me, so I snap at him, too. Psylla and Zephyr both nicker softly, but I am not in the mood to talk to mares, so they get snaps from me as well.

I am in a snappy mood like my rider. Although we dominated the Thebans, the one-eyed king won the battle because he was boss. Some colts are content to be second in the herd — but not me, and not Alexander!

A PLOT AGAINST ALEXANDER

You humans are weird about your dead. It's as if you think the departed members of your herd will be pleased if you do special things to their bodies. Any horse could tell you that's a load of dung. Once a ghost is gone from the world, it never returns. On a battlefield, the bodies of dead horses are left to feed the crows.

There would have been a lot less trouble if the one-eyed king had left the dead Greeks for the crows, too. But no, he had to burn their bodies on an enormous pyre that darkened the sky and send their ashes home to the Athenians. Another form of human squealing, I suppose. Since my cut leg wasn't bad enough to make me lame, but the one-eyed king's leg had suffered in the battle, Alexander volunteered to lead the victory procession.

This sparked off another squealing match. The one-eyed king said his son was too young. Alexander said if he was old enough to dominate the Theban Sacred Band, then he was old enough to dominate a few soft-handed Athenians whose only weapons were words. In the end, Alexander got his own way, though we had to take Antipater along to keep an eye on us. Charm rode in a cart with the ashes, very quiet.

This was better, because we got to lead the herd again. The men cheered Alexander and called him their "young king," praising his bravery in the battle, which soon had him shining with his old energy again.

Athens is a fortress built on a hill by the sea. As we arrive, the setting sun stains its walls violet, which makes the city look very fine. We trot through the gates in a clatter of armor and hooves. I forget about my injured leg and make myself huge. Crowds fill the streets to see us. As soon as he dismounts, Alexander springs up the steps to the citadel to meet the Athenian bosses, his Guard following.

Frowning after the prince, Antipater comes with us to the stables. When Charm goes to fetch my barley, a man with a familiar smell limps out of the shadows, making me break into a sweat. He looks different. He's clipped off his beard and is wearing the dirty tunic of a groom. But I *never* forget a smell. It's the disgraced horsemaster who was dismissed by Alexander in Pella.

I kick the wall and squeal a challenge.

"Well?" Antipater whispers to the man, ignoring me. "What are the Athenians going to do now? King Philip's just thrashed the Greek army, and young Alexander's a hero. Listen to the fools cheering him out there! The boy's uncontrollable, and Philip just refuses to get himself killed in battle. Persian gold obviously isn't going to buy us victory. We'll have to think of something else."

The horsemaster glances around, checking that none of the grooms is close enough to overhear. He doesn't seem worried about nine sharp-eared horses. "I've persuaded the Athenians that the sooner you take over the throne of Macedonia, the better it'll be for Greece. They'll help us. Perhaps an unfortunate accident at the victory games?" He glances up at the citadel.

Antipater shakes his head. "We daren't touch Alexander yet. Philip would bring the entire Macedonian army after us. He must be made to reject the boy himself. There are already rumors about Prince Alexander's legitimacy. All we need is someone who will 'confess' to sleeping with the queen while King Philip was away on campaign. Then we can remove Philip, and with public opinion turning against Alexander I'll be the obvious choice for the throne." He gives the horsemaster a sly look. "You can have your old job back once I'm king, of course. And compensation. Philip might not believe us, and the queen will deny it, naturally. But Alexander did dismiss you while his father was away in Byzantium. I think that should seed enough doubt in the king's mind for our purposes."

The horsemaster scowls. "Are you suggesting I pretend Alexander could be *my* son? I'll be in a lot of trouble if something goes wrong!"

Antipater puts a finger to his lips and takes the horsemaster's arm, steering him away from me. "You've nothing to lose and everything to gain. You certainly had the opportunity, so King Philip will believe it once

I've had time to work on him. It might take some of the wind out of Alexander's sails if he thinks his father could be a commoner, rather than a king. Even if his mother insists on bringing the boy back to court, things will be different once Philip is dead. If the worst comes to the worst, and Alexander is still the popular choice for the throne, I'll simply present him to the army as their new commander and pack him off to Anatolia with General Parmenio. Let him amuse himself fighting the Persians, while I keep the throne warm for him over here. The boy's such a hot-head, he's bound to get himself killed eventually. I can't think how he's survived this long, though the men say no spear can touch him while he's riding his horse. They're saying the animal came from the gods, like Achilles' horses did in the *Iliad*."

The horsemaster looks at me, and a darkness flickers behind his eyes. "I'll have my old job back, you say?"

Antipater nods.

"And you'll give me a free hand to deal with Bucephalas however I see fit?"

Antipater nods again. "Of course. I'll head back to Pella and work on Philip as soon as I can get away, but we must make sure young Alexander isn't around to interfere. Perhaps you can arrange a small insurance to make sure our heroic prince stays in Athens long enough for me to convince the king of the queen's unfaithfulness?"

The horsemaster smiles coldly. He gives me the same dark look as when he brought the Scythian and his knife into my stall that night in the mule stable. "I understand his horse picked up a minor wound in the battle? A cut like that can swell up badly if it's not properly looked after. Alexander loves the brute. He's unlikely to leave him behind in enemy territory, no matter what rumors come from Pella. Don't worry! This is the last time you'll hear anyone call Prince Alexander 'king.'"

MACEDONIA

338–336 B.C.

RUNNING WITH MARES

If the horsemaster had tried to come into my stall, I would have killed him. But he was too clever for that. Instead, he sent one of the Athenian grooms to Charm with a paste to put on my leg. Believing it to be special Greek medicine, she thanked the groom. And because I know Charm would never hurt me I stood still for her, even though the paste smelled funny and stung a bit.

Overnight, my leg swelled as fat as a temple column. Charm fell to her knees, begging Alexander to forgive her. She promised she'd sleep in my stall every night until I was cured, which wasn't really a hard promise to make because she sleeps in my stall, anyway. Alexander ordered a citywide search for the treacherous Athenian groom. Then he took Charm aside and told her that in future if she didn't know what medicine to use on a horse she should ask him or one of his Guard, and that she deserved to be beaten for crippling me. Charm burst into tears.

The groom, of course, was nowhere to be found. Neither was the disgraced royal horsemaster, but Alexander didn't know he was supposed to be looking for him, anyway. Antipater took advantage of my lameness to head home early and "report the successful surrender of Athens." But I expect you know what he was *really* up to.

By the time we reached Pella, the damage was done. I was still lame, so Alexander had to ride some other stallion who didn't even know enough to make himself huge when we entered the city. No one cheered their prince, as they should have done after he'd helped to dominate the Greeks so well. There were even some boos and hisses, and someone threw an egg, which smelled bad when it broke.

When Alexander heard there were rumors about him not being King Philip's son but the son of a commoner, and that the queen had been deceiving the court for years because she wanted him to inherit the throne, he went pale. He told Charm to look after me. Then he took a deep breath, made himself huge, and strode off to the palace.

I knew he couldn't ride me because I was lame, but something must have been very wrong because Alexander did not come to see me for AGES. Charm said he'd gone off with his mother to visit his grandparents in a place called Epirus, which is beyond Macedonia's southwest border. She said they'd gone because he and his father had a fight at a party over the king's marriage to another woman, and the one-eyed king had drunk too much magic and nearly killed Alexander. I don't know how much of this is true, but when you humans drink magic, things do tend to get out of hand.

I didn't really understand what all the fuss was about. It's natural for a strong boss like the one-eyed king to breed with as many mares as possible so he can have lots of strong foals like Alexander. Then, if something happens to one of the foals before it is grown, the herd will still have a strong leader when the old boss dies. But I suppose you humans take a different view of things.

With the king taking a new wife and the rumors, started by Antipater, flying around that Alexander had dismissed the royal horsemaster so the king wouldn't find out the truth about him and the queen, groom-gossip was all about who Alexander's father REALLY was. The main suspects were:

> **the one-eyed king** — *still possible, though it's true Alexander does not look much like him.*
> **Antipater** — *unlikely after what I heard in Athens. Besides, he is the father of Iolaus, one of Alexander's Guard, and those two man-colts look nothing alike.*
> **King Darius of Persia** — *ridiculous, because we have just declared war on Persia.*
> **one of the queen's pet snakes, which is a demon in disguise** — *I have never seen a snake change into a demon, have you?*

the horsemaster — *ha, he couldn't sire a mule!*
a god — *this is what the queen claims. I do worry about you humans sometimes.*

Meanwhile, with Charm's excellent care, my leg healed. And in the spring — joy, oh joy! — the one-eyed king ordered me turned out in the mare pasture. I couldn't run with Aura, since she had gone away with Alexander to carry the queen. But since Alexander's friends had been sent away from court in disgrace and told to leave their horses behind, I got to run with Psylla.

Oh, it was a fine time out in that pasture with the sun on my back, the soft summer rains to bathe me, and the river to cool my legs. But you're going to have to use your imagination here, because the next bit is strictly CENSORED!

DOMINATING THE ONE-EYED KING

There were lots of new horses around that year, so I had my work cut out squealing challenges over the fence at them all. The new horsemaster was buying from every ship. The riding ground was permanently full of youngsters, bucking and rearing and playing at being in battles. Meanwhile, foot soldiers drilled on the parade ground with their battle-scarred bosses shouting at them in loud voices until my heart started to pound.

Charm said there would be another campaign soon. She said the one-eyed king was going to rejoin his general in Anatolia to fight the Persians, and Alexander would come back to ride me. Then people would forget about the quarrel, and everything would be all right again.

But the one-eyed king never got to lead his herd to Anatolia.

One night in the spring, there is a lot of commotion over at the palace. People have been drinking magic to celebrate the wedding of one of Alexander's sisters, so at first I don't realize what has happened. I am far more interested in Psylla, who chooses that night to drop her foal.

She is a beautiful, long-legged filly, black like me but with no white on her head. I make myself huge and prance up to introduce myself, full of fatherly pride. But Psylla squeals and gives me flat ears, so I leave them alone. It's the one time I let a mare get away with this sort of behavior, because all mares are willing to fight to the death to protect their foals.

Charm does not visit me in the pasture that night. But in the morning, before it is properly light, I see a lone figure standing on the riverbank, staring at me.

He's downwind, so I can't smell him from here. But something about the way he stands with his chin tilted upward and his pale curls blowing around his head makes me shiver all over. He's wearing a purple cloak, and there's a dagger in his belt. Apart from that, he is unarmed. He walks slowly toward me, and the mares' heads shoot up nervously as they catch his smell.

Another shiver goes through me. At first, remembering all the ghosts we made in Greece, I want to turn and gallop away. But he calls, "Bucephalas! My beautiful one, what are you doing out here in the mare pasture? Is that your foal?" His voice sends ripples down my legs, and I can almost feel his hand firm on my rein.

I whinny a greeting, make myself huge, and trot toward him.

His eyes narrow as he watches me approach. They are red around the edges, and he looks very serious and grown-up.

"Well, Charmides is right. You look sound enough." As his hands rub my forehead, pull my ears, and tease the burrs out of my mane, he relaxes a bit. "Have you missed me as much as everyone else seems to have done?"

I give him flat ears, and he laughs.

"Oh, horse . . . at least *you* don't change! But your holiday is over, I'm afraid. They've killed my father. From now on, you'll be ridden into battle by a king. . . ." His voice falters. He clutches my withers, and in a fierce whisper tells me everything that happened in the night.

During the wedding party, the one-eyed king was *assassinated*. (That's a Persian word that means to dominate a herd in a sneaky way by killing its boss. I use it here because most people claimed the Persians were behind the assassination plot.) Even though the man who stabbed the king was caught and tortured, he wouldn't say who had told him to do it.

"Antipater says the King's Guard were bribed with Persian gold to plot against my father," Alexander tells me in the same fierce tone. "But I'm sure he knows more than he lets on. Mother says I shouldn't trust Antipater to look after Macedonia for me. But I'm not staying here to let someone put a knife between *my* ribs! As soon as I can, I'm going to take the army down the coast and deal with the Persians in Anatolia — finish what Father started. And while I'm over there, I'll visit the famous Siwa Oracle in Egypt, ask it who my father was, to settle that for once and all." He pauses to stare at the palace, and his voice quietens. "I don't believe for a moment I'm the son of that vile old horsemaster! He's obviously still angry with me for dismissing him. But there's been plenty of gossip about other men, and the worst of it is, Mother won't tell me the truth. All she says is that she prayed to Zeus for a son who would have the power of a god, and he answered her prayer by making her pregnant with me, but I think she's just making that up. Some people are even saying I planned the king's assassination myself so I could lead them into Persia on some sort of crusade, which is just ridiculous. I know we argued a lot about the campaign, but I'd never hurt my father, *never*!"

Sounds about right to me. That's what happens when a strong young colt grows up and the boss-stallion gets old. It's perfectly natural and good for the herd. But Alexander smells very upset, so I expect it's like the mare thing and different for humans.

I push him with my nose, searching his pockets for apples, and he sighs. "Oh, horse! What if it's true, and I'm not really a prince? People threw eggs at me — *eggs*!"

That was before Psylla's foal, though. If he's the king now, they won't dare throw eggs anymore. Besides, he'll be riding *me* next time we enter a city, and I won't let him get hit by an egg or anything else.

Alexander stays a bit longer, telling me his plans and sniffing into my mane every time he mentions his father. A lot of it is boring, so don't ask me to tell you everything he said. His Guard eventually work out where he is and run across the mare pasture calling for him to hurry up and get ready, because Antipater wants to present him to the army.

He gives a shudder, wipes an arm across his face, and takes a deep breath. Then he pushes me away and turns to meet his friends with a bright smile. None of them realize he has been crying.

I think he is going to make a very good king.

THE NORTHWEST FRONTIER

335 B.C.

When an old boss dies, it is natural for all the neighboring herds to test the strength of the new boss to see if they can steal any mares or pastureland. So the first thing Alexander did was take the army south to make sure the Greeks knew he was strong enough to lead the Macedonian herd. Charm had orders to get me fit while he was away.

Having spent so long in the pasture, my muscles were flabby and my dung had become liquid grass. It was embarrassing, to say the least, leaving such a mess on top of other horses' piles in the riding ground. But after my long rest, I was as sound as ever. By the time Alexander and his friends returned, laughing and joking about how much they'd scared everyone down in Greece, I felt great. After all Charm's polishing and oiling, my coat gleamed like ebony as she proudly led me out for inspection.

Alexander looked nearly as good as I did. He was relaxed and smiling, his cheeks ruddy with southern sun. He wore a circlet of golden leaves in his mane, which made him look very handsome. Groom-gossip claimed he'd made all the Greek states sign a treaty that named him boss of something called the Hellenic League. He did this without a single blow being struck, which makes sense to me. Often flat ears or a loud squeal are enough to dominate the enemy, provided you are big enough.

We spent that winter on training exercises in the mountains. The Macedonian hoplites with their long pikes were joined by ragged bands of mercenaries with slings and bows, so we were a very fierce herd. In the spring, we collected the Maedi javelin-throwers from Alexandropolis and went north to try out our mountain skills by dominating some more rebel herds.

At first, it was easy. The enemy either ran away when they saw us coming or surrendered immediately. But one tribe tried to trap us in a narrow pass through the mountains. They lined up their carts at the top and hid behind them like foals hide behind the mares when something threatens the herd.

We horses were so fit by then, we could have galloped up the steep slope and jumped the blockade, no trouble. But Alexander halted the army at the bottom and squinted up the hill, muttering to himself. He ran a hand down my tense neck. "What are they up to, Bucephalas? They haven't got archers. They fight with swords, normally. Are they planning to throw rocks at us?"

Philotas thought Alexander was scared and rode Zephyr so close to me I had to lash my tail to stop her from treading on my heels. "Anyone can see they haven't a hope of holding us off!" he said in his haughty voice. "We've got far more men than they have. What are you waiting for? We should just charge them."

"Shut up and let me think!" Alexander snapped.

Philotas did the typical human trick of bowing his head and pretending to be dominated, while scowling at his boss's back. We horses pawed the ground nervously. Despite all our mountain training, we don't like steep-sided passes. Our hoofbeats echo in them. And if we whinny, it sounds as if strange horses are hiding behind the rocks and whinnying back. The hoplites with their long pikes were not very happy, either. The track was so narrow, they couldn't form their phalanx.

As Alexander hesitated, there was a commotion behind us, and Charm ran up. I whinnied to my groom, and Alexander looked around. He didn't seem very pleased to see Charm at such a critical moment, but he told the Guard to let her approach. She hurried to my shoulder and lowered her eyes. She was very out of breath. On a mountain road, it is a long trot from the baggage wagons to the front of our herd.

"What is it?" Alexander snapped. "Make it quick."

"Those carts up there, sir . . . you mustn't get below them!"

Alexander frowned and leaned down beside my neck to hear her frightened whisper. "*Please* don't ride Bucephalas up there, sir! I had a dream last night. Carts were lined up just like those along the top of a ridge, and they came rolling down the slope right into the army! The horses' legs broke, and our men were crushed to death."

"Nonsense," Philotas muttered.

Alexander gave Philotas a strong glare. He waited until Charm was safely out of the way, then turned to his officers and gave his orders in a calm tone. "It's a trick, but we can beat them at their own game. Send the phalanx up first. Tell the men at the front on the steepest part of the track to watch the carts carefully. When they see them start to move, they're to crouch down all together and put their shields over their heads. The ones behind must be ready to open ranks and let the carts through. No one is to panic. The carts will bounce over the men's heads if they lie low and don't run. All cavalry to stay well back until the last carts have come down. We can't risk the horses."

It turns out this is exactly what happens. Our men have been well trained and, because Alexander has warned them what to expect, they don't panic. We horses are *very* brave. We simply snort and dance back a bit as the whole crashing, snapping mass of wood and iron-rimmed wheels bounces down from the top of the pass toward us. As the echoes die away, I stand like a rock so Alexander can watch everything with his narrowed eyes.

When the carts have all come down, the stupid enemy have nothing left to hide behind. Our hoplites rush the top of the pass, and we horses of the Guard leap up the ridge and easily dominate them.

NOT BAD FOR A KITCHEN BOY

We camp that night on the plain north of the pass, next to a noisy river. Charm is very quiet as she rubs me down and gives me my nosebag. I know Alexander has been watching her for some time from the trees, because I can smell him. But humans can't smell as well as horses, so Charm jumps when he steps out of the shadows.

At first he doesn't say anything, just runs his hands down my legs to check for heat. I am hungry and tired after all the steep mountain roads, so I give him flat ears to let him know I want to be left alone.

He pushes my nose away and frowns at Charm. "So, you have prophetic dreams, do you?"

Charm whispers, "Sometimes, sir. Please don't tell anyone."

"Don't call me 'Sir,' Charmides. It makes me feel old. How long has this been going on?"

"Since I came to Pella, Your Majesty —"

"*Alexander*. That's an order."

She flushes. "But I can't call you that. You're the king now!"

Alexander smiles at her. "Sometimes I don't feel very much like a king, Charmides. Sometimes I wish I was more like you. Just a groom, with nothing to worry about except the horses you look after. But I want to know more about these dreams of yours. I want to know how you came to be looking after Bucephalas. I never seem to have enough time to thank you for what you've done for the horse. He's a credit to you."

She relaxes a little. "Thank you, sir — Alexander. I ran away from home when my mother died. I was too upset to think straight. I didn't know what I was going to do, but I ended up in Pella, and . . . er . . . thought I might find work in the palace kitchens. Then I saw Bucephalas on your riding ground and recognized him as a horse I used to know when I was small. He's older, of course, and he never used to be so wild, but he's so big and proud there's no mistaking him. When I saw you ride him, I knew for sure he was the same horse. I still meant to go to the kitchens, but that night I dreamed Bucephalas was in danger, so I asked for work at the stables instead."

"Interesting." Alexander is watching her closely. "So where's home? By law, as a runaway slave you can be executed, you know."

She shudders. "Methone. I used to work with my mother in the kitchens there, but I was always sneaking down to the stables to see the horses. My old master wouldn't let me groom them because I was a g —" She breaks off, flushing. "I mean, I'd rather clean horses than clean pots, sir."

Alexander laughs. "Methone, huh? A spirited people. You might be too young to remember, but that's where my father lost his eye in battle, subduing the town. I was only a baby at the time, of course, but so many people have told me the story I feel as if I were there. And here you are, grooming the king's horse! Not bad for a kitchen boy!" He grows serious again. "As soon as we get back, I'll see to it the garrison commander at Methone is compensated for losing you. In the meantime, if you have any other dreams like that one, be sure to tell me, won't you? A bit *before* we meet the enemy would be good, next time."

She flushes again. "Of course, sir. Um . . . are we going home now that we've beaten the rebels?"

He gives me a pat and gazes at the river with a gleam in his eye. "Not yet, Charmides. In three days, we should reach the Danube. I've ordered General Parmenio to send ships from Byzantium to meet us there with some rather interesting siege engines my father was working on. We'll take them upriver and let all the tribes around these parts know I'm not going to stand for any nonsense while I'm away chasing the Persians out of Anatolia. We can head back through the mountains and check the western frontier on our way home. Should be easy enough. Then we'll call on those ships Athens promised me and take the army to the Hellespont to meet old Parmenio." He stares across the plain at the campfires and dark tents. "I'm finally going to see Troy, Charmides! The very city the great Achilles conquered in the *Iliad*!" His eyes glitter as he speaks, and I can feel his excitement running down his arm.

I stop eating. Charm bites her lip. She doesn't look nearly as excited as the king is about seeing this city called Troy.

Alexander doesn't notice. He grins and gives me a slap on the rump that makes me snort into my barley. "We'll soon take care of these mountain tribes, don't worry! Then when I cross the Hellespont and liberate Anatolia from the Persian yoke, no one will be able to say I'm not the son of a king."

At the Danube, the tribe across the river tried to join forces with the one we were dominating on our side and make a fight of it. But Alexander ordered the men to stuff their tent covers with our hay and make rafts. Then he used the rafts and the ships from Byzantium to ferry his entire herd across the Danube during the night and chased them away.

After that, the northern tribes couldn't surrender fast enough. They said we'd crossed the river by magic, and the story spread like fire. Lots of other bosses came to submit to Alexander as well. He didn't even have to use the siege engines to frighten them. He ordered his men to transfer the engines to our mule carts, reloaded the ships with the plunder we took from the enemy, and sent them home, then marched us west to secure his final border.

TYDEOS

Groom-gossip on our way through the mountains was all about the siege engines the mules were pulling along in pieces at the back of the army. Whenever we stopped for the night, an excited group of man-colts formed to discuss how they might work. Charm hovered at the edge of the group, pretending to be interested, but glancing around nervously as if she expected Alexander to appear at any moment. But the young king stayed in his tent talking to his officers. Our grooms said they were probably trying to work out how to use the siege engines, too.

"They throw stones," one groom claimed. "Like the slingers."

"I heard they throw boulders as big as houses!"

"Don't be stupid. How are boulders goin' to get in the engine in the first place, if they're that big? Even King Alexander couldn't lift one."

"Mules drag 'em, of course. Then they sit down on the engine, and the boulder rolls off their back into the throwing cup."

"Sit down? Don't be an idiot. How are you supposed to make a mule do that?"

"Maybe they throw mules!"

The grooms laughed, so I gave them flat ears. Mules are stupid, yes, but that's just bad taste.

"I bet Bucephalas could lift the rocks in with his teeth," one of the quieter grooms said, eyeing me. "Eh, Charm?"

Charm gave him a tense smile. His name was Tydeos, and he had been helping her with the Guard's horses, so he was part of our special herd.

"I don't see why we need the siege engines at all," she said. "The king told me there isn't going to be any more fighting — at least, not until he goes to Anatolia," she added, frowning.

"Ha!" One of the older grooms gave her a sly look. "You haven't heard the latest, have you?"

"What's that?"

"The Illyrians are rebelling now. Apparently, they've taken over a big fortress up in the mountains. We'll need our siege engines there, all right! I can't wait to see them in action."

Charm went pale. "But Alexander said we were just checking the border, then going home —"

"Oh," Tydeos said, teasing her. "*Alexander* now, is it? Other duties come with looking after his horse, do they?"

Charm blushed. "No!"

"I've seen him down here, sweet-talking you."

"Just talking."

By this time, they were all laughing at her. "Ha! Charm's soft on the king!" — "Better not tell anyone, or you'll make Hephaestion jealous!"

Tydeos smiled and said gently, "Don't waste your feelings on him, Charm. It's well known kings and princes don't bother with grooms. They don't even see us most of the time. We're like mule bags to them, or . . . pairs of boots! Just something useful to keep them from getting dirty. Then, when we're all old and used up with hard work, they throw us away and get new ones."

"Alexander's not like that," Charm said, defensive now. "He *does* care. He gave me gold before he went away with his mother."

"For his horse!" This set them all off laughing again. "I hope you didn't spend any on yourself?"

She shook her head. She didn't, knowing Charm. Both her tunics are patched, her grooming-belt is stitched together where it broke, and her sandals have holes in them from the mountain roads. I, however, have a nice new battle-cloth.

The grooms went back to arguing about the siege engines, and Tydeos went off with Charm to talk about something else. I don't think it will be very long before he figures out she's a girl-filly.

A TRAP

Alexander must have been as eager to try out his new siege engines as our grooms were to see them in action, because he made the army march extremely fast to reach the Illyrian fortress. It was an eerie place. Steep, wooded mountainsides loomed over our camp like shadowy walls. With the fortress perched at the top of the valley, the only way in or out was across a fast-flowing river and through a narrow pass. The cliffs were impossible for horses, and to climb them our riders would have been forced to leave their weapons behind.

We horses knew a trap when we saw one and laid back our ears. But Alexander stroked my neck and told me not to fret because this would only be a small battle. Then he led our entire herd straight in.

While our men hammered the siege engines together, winched back the arms, and sent rocks clattering against the fortress walls to frighten the Illyrians inside, the rest of the Illyrian herd was creeping up behind us. After squealing a few threats at Alexander, they left us to spend a miserable night without any food on the plain under their fortress. Our grooms huddled under their cloaks nibbling hard cheese and talking in whispers. They were very scared.

Alexander must have been worried, too, because a lamp burned all night in his tent, flickering through the leather. At dawn, he came down to the horse lines to ask Charm if she'd had any dreams.

Charm shook her head. "Your Majesty, I'm sorry. I haven't had a dream about this place."

Alexander sighed. "At least that means we're not going to die here — or is it just Bucephalas who survives? Of course the Illyrians will probably take the horses as spoils of war, so I expect he'll be all right."

Charm went still. "They won't *win*, will they?"

Alexander passed a hand across his eyes. "They have us in a bad place. The phalanx can't fight them effectively in the pass — it's too narrow. We'll thrash them if we meet them on the plain, of course, but they're too wily to face us in battle. Know-it-all Philotas says we should wait till they get bored and come out to fight. That's all very well, but we can't wait. We're running out of food. The Illyrians know that. And we can't continue our attack on the fortress with them at our backs. What do you think we should do, Charmides?"

Charm thought a moment. "Maybe you need a bucket and some barley, sir?" she said.

He gave her a distracted frown, as if he thought she was complaining about our lack of fodder. Then he looked thoughtful. "Something to lure them out, you mean? Yes, I've thought of that. But we haven't got anything they can't wait for. We certainly haven't got any spare barley. The poor horses are half starved."

Charm looked at the mud under her feet and said slowly, "When Bucephalas was in the mare pasture he didn't want to be caught, not even for a bucket of barley. So I gave up trying to catch him and sat down in the middle of the field. He got curious and came to see what I was doing. That's how I got him in."

Alexander gave her an amused look. "You sat down in the middle of the field? That's probably what the Illyrians are hoping we'll do! But it's an interesting idea. Maybe something else might do it, something they *don't* understand?" He looked at the damp tents and the gloomy men stirring in their bedrolls. The light returned to his face, and he grinned.

What Alexander did was order us all to form up for a parade.

The men polished their weapons and helmets and put on full armor. We horses wore our best cloths and bridles with all our trappings. The hoplites formed up the first pattern of their phalanx, and the cavalry made neat squares. I stood at the front and made myself huge so that Alexander could watch, and the eight horses of the Guard stood in a neat line behind me, champing on their bits. Petasios, Borealis, Aura, Apollo, Zephyr, Hades, Harpinna . . . even Psylla's replacement, a dark gray stallion called Arion, knew he was in superior company and arched his neck proudly. The cavalry practiced battle maneuvers in close formation at a trot, while the men did slow pike lowering and raising, changing the shape of their phalanx in response to signals from their officers. Usually, these are trumpet blasts. But that morning, they were silent signals given with hands.

Our parade was perfect. The only noise was the snorting of horses and the soft rhythm of our hooves in the dawn. Meanwhile, the mules had been harnessed up with the siege engines balanced on the baggage carts, and the grooms and muleteers waited with them near the river. They couldn't go anywhere with the Illyrians blocking the pass, of course. But as our parade continued, more and more Illyrians ventured out to watch. Soon they were sitting on the rocks with their spears over their knees, fascinated.

I am starting to get bored, when Alexander's weight suddenly shifts. He draws his sword and stabs the sky.

"ALALALALALAI!" he screams, startling me into a rear.

As if they have been waiting for this, the entire army breaks into the same cry.

"ALALALALAI! ALALALALALAI! ALALALALAI!"

The men beat their pikes on their shields, the cavalry turn as a herd, and the phalanx charges the unprepared enemy at the mouth of the pass. Half of them are still sitting down when we burst through their ranks.

The Illyrian boss is furious we tricked him. He yells after our retreating army, "That's right, Macedonian pup! Run back home with your tail between your legs! Better wait until you've grown a bit before you take on the men of Illyria again!"

Alexander flings him a vicious glare and hauls on my mouth to turn me back. But Hephaestion rides Petasios close to me and grabs my rein. "No, Alex!" he shouts. "He's angry we got past his men, that's all — don't let him provoke you into doing something stupid, after you got us out of that trap so cleverly."

Something flickers across Alexander's face, and his blade lowers. He urges me down the hillside beside Petasios, and we gallop to safety.

When we finally pull up, the Guard are quiet. Philotas mutters something about us being lucky to have escaped with our lives, and this time Alexander doesn't argue. But it could have been worse. We didn't dominate the Illyrians that day. But they didn't dominate us, either.

A WONDERFUL ROLL

Alexander did not take us home, of course. But it seemed he had learned a valuable lesson about dominating. We retreated a short way and made camp in a wide valley with lots of ways out, every route carefully watched by sentries.

After a few days, barley and other supplies arrived from a friendly garrison, and so did a roll of flattened grass with marks on it. This must have been some kind of squealing challenge, because it put Alexander into a wild rage. We heard him from the horse lines as he threw things around in his tent and yelled at his friends. The dogs began to bark, and the men jumped up and seized their weapons, looking for an enemy.

"Oh, what's up *now*?" Tydeos mutters. "I'm getting sick of these mountains. Look at this poor mare's foot." He lifted one of Aura's hooves. "Bruised half to death. Where's that paste we've been using?"

"All gone," Charm says, her voice tight. "I used the last of it on Bucephalas last night."

They go quiet, because they are still a bit scared of the Illyrians. Groom-gossip over the past few days has been about how close we all came to being killed on the plain under their fortress.

"Well, I hope it's done the trick," Tydeos says, nodding to the tent where Alexander is still raging. "Because it sounds like the king's in a bad enough mood already, without his horse going lame as well."

Charm makes a face at the king's tent, and — strangely for this time of day — decides to take me for a roll.

Usually we roll in sand, but there's no sand here so we're using a muddy patch by the river, and it's WONDERFUL. Why you humans don't try it more often, I don't know. Inferior horses can't flip over when they roll and have to get up and down again to do the other side. But I can keep going, over and back again, for as long as I feel like it. Charm holds the end of my lead rein and smiles. "Get as dirty as you like, Bucephalas," she murmurs. Which is strange, because usually she tells me off for getting too muddy.

I could have rolled in that mud for ages. But then I catch Alexander's sweet sherbet smell. I scramble to my feet and nudge Charm. She's standing in the mud, looking at me, when she ought to take me back to the lines and groom me.

Alexander strides toward us, buckling on his armor, a furious look on his face. "What are you doing down here?" he snaps. "I need my horse! I'm going to finish off those Illyrians, once and for all. We've been messing around in these mountains far too long."

Charm lowers her eyes. "I'm sorry, but he's just had a roll, Your Majesty."

Alexander sees the wet mud on me and swears under his breath. "Then get him clean. You can't put a battle-cloth on that. Give him a bath. Come on, get going, I haven't got all day."

Charm doesn't move. "And he's footsore."

"So are half the horses in the cavalry! I need Bucephalas ready for battle, *now*!"

"You could ride another horse today, sir." Charm's voice is barely a whisper.

Alexander has turned to rejoin his men. But when she says this, he whirls back. He clenches a fist and says in a dangerous voice, "*Get him clean!* Zeus, I have enough to worry about without grooms who can't do as they're told! You're going the right way about losing your job and getting sent back to the kitchens."

Charm's hand trembles on my rein. I get anxious and whinny. Some of the Guard come down to the rolling place to see what's wrong.

Hephaestion eyes the mud on me and Charm's determined mud-spattered face. He fights a smile and puts a hand on the king's arm. "Alex . . . why don't you give the old horse a rest? If the scouts are correct, it won't be much of a fight. The Illyrians haven't even dug any defenses. Their camp's wide open, and they're the ones in the trap this time. Give the lad a break. He didn't know."

Alexander looks hard at Charm. He sends Hephaestion and the others to mount up and takes a deep breath. When he next speaks, his voice is calmer. "All right, Charmides, you win this time. But while I'm gone, make sure you treat Bucephalas's feet. We've got a long way to go once I've finished with these Illyrians, and we're going to have to travel fast."

She starts to lead me away in relief, but he puts out an arm to stop her. His eyes narrow. "Why did you do it? Did you have another dream?"

Charm shakes her head, unable to meet his gaze.

Alexander frowns at her. Then he sighs. "Just as well. I wouldn't want to die twice in the same day."

This didn't make much sense to me at the time. But when Alexander had galloped off to deal with the Illyrians, the gossip filtered down to the horse lines.

A letter had come from his mother the queen, saying that someone (no prizes for guessing who!) had started a rumor that Alexander and his entire army had been killed fighting the border tribes. As a result, Thebes had thrown out their Macedonian garrison and declared themselves a free city again. Athens and the rest of Greece were ready to follow. Antipater was about to recall General Parmenio and the rest of the advance Macedonian troops from Anatolia.

This news made Alexander so angry, when the Illyrians saw him coming they burned down their own fortress and fled.

When he returned, he was in a much better mood. He should have been. With only a few hundred dead Macedonians and no dead horses, he and I have so far dominated:

the Maedi
the Theban Sacred Band
several Celtic herds
the Illyrians

Our grooms quickly forgot how afraid they'd been and said King Alexander would soon scare the Greeks back into submission. But dominating is a dangerous game, and it's never a good idea to turn your back on sly stallions like Antipater and the horsemaster.

THEBES

SUMMER 335 B.C.

A MESSAGE

You should have seen their faces when the Thebans realized Alexander was still alive! We reached their big, proud city just two weeks after leaving Illyria and camped outside their thick walls to remind them who was boss. They took one look at Alexander, mounted on me at the front of the army with his head bare and his untidy mane blowing around his face, and slammed their gates shut in terror.

Alexander sent a message to the city before he'd even dismounted. He told the messenger to say four things:

> As they could see, the rumors of his death were greatly exaggerated.
> They were breaking their promise to him, made under the terms of the Hellenic League.
> They must open their gates at once and let him reinstate the Macedonian garrison.
> If they did as he asked, he would pardon them — since their mistake had been easy enough to make — and take his army home.

Then he handed my rein to Charm, stretched the kinks out of his shoulders, and strode off to his tent. His friends followed, congratulating one another on having marched so fast out of the mountains that the Thebans never knew they were coming. No one else, they said, could have made it from Illyria to Thebes in just thirteen days.

TROUBLE IN THE HORSE LINES

That night Petasios and the others who have been to Thebes before munch their hay as happily as they would have at home. I am more alert. I've already dominated several piles of enemy dung, but I still need to keep throwing up my head to check for ghosts.

Our grooms sit on a pile of our cloths, rubbing oil into our bridles, while Tydeos tells Charm this is exactly how King Alexander frightened the citizens of Thebes into surrendering to him last time he came here. He says not to worry, because the same thing will happen now, and we'll soon be home. Charm does not look convinced.

Our campfires burn lower. The grooms finish their work and curl up in their cloaks. The sentry at the end of the horse lines dozes off, exhausted from the march. I am about to relax, too, when I smell the disgraced horse-master who I last saw in Athens, before my leg went bad.

I break into a sweat and give a loud whinny to wake Charm. The sentry jerks awake, reaches for his spear — and gasps as a shadowy figure puts a thong around his neck and pulls him over backward. His ghost struggles to stay, then floats quietly away into the night. There are shouts of alarm as shadowy figures run through the camp, swords in their hands. Sleepy Macedonians stagger out of their tents half dressed, and pairs of men stumble into the horse lines, fighting furiously.

From the darkness, a mule brays in fear. I whinny again, pulling at my halter. Petasios tries to rear up, gets a leg over the line, and falls over, causing the other horses to panic. The grooms come running to sort us out. But Charm cannot come to me, because the horsemaster has her trapped next to our fodder wagon. He's blackened his face with soot, and Charm is trying to fend him off with my metal grooming-comb.

He catches her wrist and twists it until she lets go.

"Well, well," he says. "So, you're still looking after Alexander's old horse? I'm surprised the brute hasn't collapsed on the battlefield by now."

"Let me go!" Charm yells, kicking him. "If I shout for help, thirty thousand men will come to arrest you."

"Not quite thirty thousand by now, I suspect," says the horsemaster, gripping her tightly. "I don't think young Alexander will find Thebes as easily frightened as those barbarian tribes up north. I want you to help me put the bridle on his horse. I'm taking the animal back to Thebes with me. Then we'll see how eager Alexander is to make demands."

"You're not taking Bucephalas anywhere!" Charm struggles furiously, yelling for help. Tydeos and some of the other grooms leave the horses and come running. But the horsemaster pulls out his dagger, puts it across Charm's throat, and glares at them.

"Keep out of it," he threatens. "You remember me, don't you? Remember the beatings I gave you all, back in Pella?"

Some of them obviously do, and back off warily.

"I'll fetch the sentries," Tydeos says. "Don't panic, Charm! He won't dare harm you. He'll never get out of the camp alive."

The horsemaster chuckles. "What sentries?"

Our grooms finally notice the dead sentry lying at the end of the horse lines. Charm goes limp with fear. It's just as well you humans don't have a horse's vision. It would only scare you if you could see as much as we can.

I rear up as the horsemaster limps closer, dragging Charm. But I've forgotten I'm still tethered to the stupid line and almost fall over like Petasios did earlier. I swing around and try to kick the horsemaster, but he is holding Charm in front of him, and he is too good a horseman to get behind me. He grabs a freshly oiled bridle and growls, "Put it on him!"

Charm drops it in the dust. "You do it. I'm not helping you steal Bucephalas!"

The horsemaster hisses in rage. He throws Charm to the ground, grabs the bridle and a whip, and approaches me with a determined scowl.

I act wild. He strikes me on the nose with his whip, so I rear up again. This time my tether breaks. One of my hooves catches him on the shoulder. He stumbles, suddenly pale, his bad knee giving way.

Charm picks herself up, blood pouring from her nose, and flings herself on top of the horsemaster with a cry of rage. This is stupid of her, because I can't dominate him properly with her in the way.

They roll on the ground like ferocious man-colts. Charm is strong and lean after the mountains and acting very fierce tonight. But the horsemaster is stronger. He pins her down and is just about to punch her in the face when his eyes go wide.

"You're a *girl*!" he gasps, lowering the fist in confusion.

Finally, someone's noticed.

Charm takes advantage of his hesitation to squirm out from under him. Tugging her tunic straight, she runs to me and scrambles up on my back. I don't need any encouragement. We wheel around and gallop through the dark lines of tents, dodging ropes and jumping the glowing embers of fires, until my enemy is left far behind us.

When I feel Charm begin to slip, I slow to a walk. She flops over my neck, sobbing, and buries her bloody nose in my mane. I stop and turn my head to nibble her sandal. By this time, the alarm has been raised, and the Macedonians are busy chasing off the Thebans. Dark figures race back toward the high walls of the city and vanish inside its gates.

I am too far away to smell if the horsemaster is among them. If he's got any sense, though, he'll be running as fast as he can. I mean, trying to kidnap the king's warhorse! What next?

DOMINATING THEBES

In the morning, Alexander orders the men to break camp. We stand outside the closed gate of Thebes with the breeze blowing our tails sideways and our banners snapping like whips. Alexander watches the walls with a calculating expression, his chin tilted up and his eyes narrow. There's a trumpeter standing beside us, keeping a safe distance away from my teeth. But Alexander doesn't tell him to blow the trumpet yet. He simply waits. Except to give orders, he hasn't spoken since Charm told him how the Thebans tried to kidnap me in the night. Behind us, the Guard and the rest of the army also wait.

At last, some Thebans appear on the tower above the gate. As soon as he sees them, Alexander makes himself huge and calls, "I've come to give you this message myself, since you seem to have ignored my previous one. Last night's raid on my camp will not go unpunished. But first, I'd like to extend the hand of friendship to any who still wish to keep the peace as agreed by the Hellenic League. Hand over the ringleaders of the rebellion and the man who tried to kidnap my horse last night, open your gates to me, and I'll deal with you lightly."

His voice is shrill and echoes slightly under the garrison rock. The other horses fidget and champ on their bits, but I do not move a muscle as

Alexander makes squealing threats at the Thebans. This is a very important time. We might not need an actual battle at all, if he squeals loudly enough.

But this enemy squeals back just as loudly.

"How about you hand over your regent Antipater, and General Parmenio's son Philotas, who we see sitting behind you on the yellow mare? Since it seems you are not King Philip's son, both of them have more of a claim than you to the throne of Macedonia. *Then* we might consider negotiating with you, Alexander, as a very distant third. May we also make it known to your men that if any of them wish to join us in overthrowing the tyrant who dares sit before the historic Electra Gate of Thebes on a broken-down old nag groomed by a *girl*, they are welcome to enter our city as friends."

There is a deathly silence as this insult sinks in. Some of the Guard whisper in consternation. Alexander's hand tightens on my rein. His face reddens. The tendons of his neck stand out, and he begins to breathe very fast. Out of the corner of my good eye, I see Hephaestion go pale and nudge Petasios forward with his knees, but it is too late.

With a terrible cry, Alexander whips out his sword and yells for his men to bring up the siege engines. "Destroy the city!" he cries. "Break down the walls! Give no quarter! Find the traitor who tried to kidnap my horse! Do not stop until every last man, woman, and child in Thebes is either dead or begging for mercy at my feet!"

It is a VERY fierce battle.

Alexander digs in his spurs and wrenches at my mouth until it bleeds as much as Charm's nose did the night before. The Thebans send out their army to meet ours on the plain, and Alexander lays about him with his sword, galloping with his Guard here, there, and everywhere in the thick of the fighting, until we horses are all foaming with sweat and as weary of the fighting as our riders.

Alexander is the only one who doesn't seem to get tired. Fueled by rage, he keeps on hacking at the enemy with his sword, grunting things like: "That'll show you who's the rightful King of Macedonia!" — "That'll teach you to call me a tyrant!" — "King Philip *was* my father, he *was*!"

All the while, stones are whistling overhead from our siege engines. But, although they frighten the enemy, they don't make much impression on the thick walls of Thebes.

Alexander eventually realizes this and pulls me up. He squints thoughtfully into the shadows beneath the wall. The others pull up around us, panting, their swords drooping from their hands and their horses' heads low. My legs are trembling with exhaustion from leaping out of the way of spear thrusts and arrows, and a hundred little places on my body sting where the enemy's weapons have scratched me. But I am still ready to fight.

Alexander's voice has an icy edge to it. "Do you see any guards watching the side gate?" he asks.

Hephaestion shakes his head. "No, Alex . . . they must have joined the struggle in the garrison."

My rider smiles for the first time since the squealing match outside the Electra Gate, and his brightness returns. "I need a volunteer to take a strike force through that gate. Organize whatever men you can find, go in through the garrison, and get the main gates open. We'll strike them where they least expect it, from the inside. It's dangerous, but whoever does it will be a hero."

Hephaestion frowns at the little gate and strokes Petasios's sweaty neck. He opens his mouth to volunteer. But Philotas hauls up Zephyr's head and coughs. "I'm rather embarrassed about what they said earlier, Alexander. Maybe I'd better —"

"I'll do it," Perdiccas says, raising his chin and wiping the blood off his breastplate. "Apollo's not as tired as Zephyr." He claps Philotas on the shoulder. "You're third in line to the throne, Philo. We've got to look after you in case anything happens to Alex. Your father would never forgive us if we got you killed over here in Greece before you even set foot in Anatolia."

Now the others are all quick to say they will do it, ashamed they didn't volunteer first. But there isn't time to argue. Apollo makes himself huge and gallops off, his pale tail rippling.

While we wait for Perdiccas and Apollo, Alexander rides me up a slope so he can survey the battle. He notices for the first time that my mouth is bleeding, leans forward, and wipes the bloody foam with his finger.

"Oh, I'm sorry, my brave horse! Sometimes they make me so angry I don't know what I'm doing. Charmides will soon make you better. . . ." He breaks off and curses under his breath. "Though I don't suppose that's her real name. A *girl*? No, it can't be true. Surely they were just trying to provoke me? Oh, Zeus! I don't have time to think about grooms now! I've got Thebes to worry about."

He looks around at Hephaestion. "Any sign of Perdiccas yet?"

Hephaestion shakes his head. "Not yet, but it looks like the Thebans are retreating."

Alexander watches the struggling crush of men near the wall, then grins. "Look, they're opening the Electra Gate! Perdiccas must have done it! Come on, gentlemen, one last effort. We'll get through after them, if we're quick."

That was how we got into Thebes. Another typical human trick. All night, the city was a confusion of screams and flames and horses galloping through the streets. Our army poured in through the gates, dragged out the Theban women and children, killed anyone who tried to stop them, and ransacked their houses. The mercenaries were the fiercest, taking revenge for something the Thebans had once done to their herds. I've no idea what, but it must have been bad because they dominated the Theban herd with more violence than I have seen in all my years of battle. Men died, and kept on dying, until the air was thick with ghosts. Alexander gave up trying to control them and led his Guard up to the garrison.

We found Perdiccas covered in blood, lying on a bench in the yard with an army physician treating his wound. Apollo stood nearby, still wearing his battle-cloth and caked in dried sweat. His proud head hung almost to the ground and his reins were broken. A sword cut had severed his breast girth and sliced into his chest. When he smelled us coming, he gave a forlorn little whinny.

Alexander flung himself off my back, raced to his friend's side, and clasped his hand. "Don't die," he said fiercely. "That's an order. You're not allowed to die, Perdiccas, do you hear?"

Perdiccas gave him a wan smile and croaked, "No chance. What's happening? I can hear screaming . . . are we winning?"

"Yes," Alexander said, his voice tight. "Don't worry about it. The city's ours."

While the Guard gathered around Perdiccas, I nipped Apollo to show him what I thought of him for letting his rider get hurt. But not too hard, because we were all pleased to find the vain little horse with his funny-colored mane and tail, alive.

A RUIN WITH NO NAME

We spent the remaining few hours of darkness in the garrison stables without our grooms, and in the morning Alexander bridled me and led his Guard through the smoldering streets. Two men from the garrison carried Perdiccas behind us on a stretcher, while Demetrius led Apollo with Aura at the back.

We went slowly because there were many bodies and much wreckage to avoid, stopping often so that Alexander could give orders to the officers. Our hooves echoed in the hush, and ash drifted around us, making us toss our heads and snort. I dominated a few piles of strange dung, but my heart wasn't in it. I badly needed a roll.

Outside the gates, we found men of both sides burying their dead. Flies buzzed around the piles of corpses, and smoke from the funeral pyres darkened the sun, masking all other smells. If you've never been in a battle, you should believe me when I tell you this is just as well.

Alexander ordered a tent to be set up outside the city and disappeared inside it with some important-looking men who had just turned up from Athens. Hephaestion took Perdiccas to the blood tent, and Iolaus was left outside to look after us horses. As he tied our reins to the line he'd set up, he grumbled about having to do a common groom's job and gave poor Hades a completely unnecessary whack on the nose. When he came near me, I bit him to let him know how it felt.

The talking in the king's tent went on for ages. Some of the other grooms came to tend their horses, and I started to wonder where Charm was. It's sometimes difficult to find people in an army the size of Alexander's, but she's usually the first to rush up and check me for injuries.

When Alexander finally came out of the tent and sent off his Guard to convey his orders to the men, there was still no sign of her.

He frowned at Iolaus. "Where's my groom?"

"How do I know?" Iolaus said, still grumpy. "Maybe the lad got fed up with your horse biting him." He seemed to have forgotten the squealing on the walls before the battle, but he hadn't forgotten the nip I gave him. Too right.

Alexander gave the smoking city and the lines of prisoners being escorted out of the Electra Gate a bleak look. "The Hellenic League says Thebes must be punished for rebelling. They want me to deport all the citizens as slaves and raze the city to the ground."

Iolaus's eyes widened slightly. "But we've already won. They're not going to give us any more trouble, not after last night. It'll only make the rest of Greece hate you."

"I know!" Alexander seized my reins, jerking my sore mouth as he untied me. "But what choice do I have? If I show any weakness now, we might as well forget the Anatolian campaign. I've tried peace talks, and they didn't work. The Greeks will follow me because they fear me. It's their own fault. Besides, Thebes insulted me before my men. Go help the others. I need a moment alone."

He led me through the camp, one hand pressed to his forehead. No one bothered us. I don't think many of the men even recognized their king, because both he and I were so dirty. Alexander was not acting much like the boss, either, walking with his head down and his shoulders slumped.

As soon as we reached the horse lines, he started calling for Charm. The grooms jumped at the sound of his voice and called for her, too. But I couldn't smell her anywhere. At last, we reached the place where Petasios was picketed with the other horses of the Guard. I whinnied to my friends in relief, and there were quite a few whinnies back. But Charm still didn't appear, which was *most* strange.

Tydeos was sponging Apollo's chest wound, while the silly horse flinched and made little snorting noises. But when Tydeos saw me with Alexander, he rushed out to meet us, looking concerned.

"Where's Charmides?" Alexander demanded.

Tydeos paled. "No one's seen him since yesterday, Your Majesty. We thought he was with you."

Alexander gave him the same bleak look he'd given Thebes. He said quietly, "Did *you* realize Charmides was a girl?"

Tydeos gave him a startled look. His lips moved a little, as if he couldn't work out if the king was making a joke. "A girl, Your Majesty? Of course not —" Then he broke off, frowned, and whispered, "Oh, Zeus, you're serious."

"Just tell me the truth!" Alexander shouted. "Is my groom Charmides a girl?"

By this time, all the grooms were staring. They whispered and muttered among themselves. "I always knew there was something strange about that boy." — "Always kept to himself, didn't he?" — "But he used to *ride* Bucephalas! How could a *girl* ever manage a horse like that?" They eyed me uncertainly, and I gave them flat ears to warn them to keep their distance.

Alexander took a final look around and shook his head. "So, she's gone, has she? Couldn't face me, I suppose. It's not the first time she's run away, if she was telling the truth about that — which I very much doubt." His hand tightened again on my rein. He picked out two unfortunate grooms at the front. "You and you! Take this horse and get him cleaned up! I can't waste any more of my time down here."

The grooms eyed my flat ears. One of them approached me from my blind side, and I struck out at him in reflex. He jumped back, whimpering and clutching his knee where my hoof had gotten him. Usually, the others would laugh if one of them had been careless enough to get kicked like that. But they didn't dare, not with the king standing among them.

Alexander gave my reins a jerk and the grooms an exasperated look. "Get a muzzle on him if you're frightened. The horse is twenty years old, for Zeus's sake! Come on, there must be someone who can handle him."

Tydeos ventured forward. Alexander threw my rein at him and stood on tiptoe to fasten the muzzle himself. The others watched, embarrassed but too afraid to help.

Alexander turned and eyed his audience. "See? All he needs is a firm hand. But if I hear that any of you has taken a whip to Bucephalas, or is not giving him the very best of care as befits a king's horse, you'll join the citizens of Thebes in chains. Understand?"

His voice was icy. Tydeos swallowed. The other grooms shuddered and stared at their feet. Even the muleteers who had gathered around to watch went pale, and it takes a lot to frighten them. Tydeos put a tentative hand on my neck. I tolerated this, because I knew his smell and I was very tired. He relaxed slightly and muttered something about taking me for a roll.

Alexander had already gone striding back through the camp. He was acting like the boss again, shouting orders as he went. I snorted at Tydeos and gave him a nudge with my nose to get him moving, because he was just standing there, looking around for Charm.

Eventually, Tydeos got me clean after a fashion and settled me in the horse lines in my usual spot between Petasios and Borealis. He gave me too much barley in my nosebag, but it was better than too little. I tucked in, listening to groom-gossip and hoping Charm would come back soon and groom me properly.

But all I discovered were the details of the domination of Thebes, which upset some of our grooms so much they shed tears.

Theban prisoners: 30,000

Theban dead: 6,000

Macedonian dead: 500

Horses dead: 8 (sad, sad, sad, sad, sad, sad, sad, sad)

Thebans spared: 3 poets, 24 priests, and the wife of the Theban boss

We didn't even get to rename the city. Instead of another Alexandropolis, Thebes became a ruin with no name.

TROY

SPRING 334 B.C.

CHARM'S SCENT

When we got home to Pella, Charm's scent was everywhere. It was in the corners of my stall where she used to sleep. It was on my grooming tools. And it was on the rakes and shovels she used to clean out my bedding.

I spent the first few days after we got back walking around and around my stable, licking all these places. I kept expecting her to open the door, chirrup to me, and do mutual grooming on my withers. But always it was one of the other grooms who came, usually Tydeos, who had gotten the job of looking after me after we'd dominated Thebes. I tolerated him because he was quiet around me. He didn't trust me enough to turn his back on me, though, and he was careful to put on my muzzle whenever he groomed me or took me out for my roll. Needless to say, I wouldn't let him get anywhere NEAR my back.

The only person who rode me during that winter was Alexander. I know the grooms thought this strange, because they gave Tydeos sideways looks and teased him about not being able to ride as well as a girl, but I noticed they kept well away from me themselves. Tydeos breathed a sigh of relief that he wasn't expected to exercise me and told me not to worry — Charm loved me too much to abandon me and would come back once things had settled down.

While he fed me apples, Alexander pulled my ears and poured out all his worries about the Anatolian campaign. Don't ask me to tell you everything he said, because most of it was very complicated. The things I understood were:

Alexander desperately wants to prove it was King Philip who sired him. This is understandable, because it's good to know what herd you belong to. That's why he wants to get to Siwa in Egypt as soon as possible, so he can ask the oracle (a place where gods answer your questions).

Antipater is eager for Alexander to go (you know why!), and General Parmenio is waiting for him at the Hellespont with the rest of the one-eyed king's herd. But, despite all the treasure and slaves he took from Thebes, Alexander has a definite lack of gold coins, which all humans, including the soldiers of the Macedonian army, seem to want before they will do anything. (In my opinion, you humans should get rid of these silly coins. It would make your lives a lot simpler.)

My life that winter was just as complicated. Psylla came back to the stables, having weaned our beautiful black filly, which the grooms named Electra in memory of the gate where we had squealed at Thebes. So I had four mares — Aura, Psylla, Harpinna, and Zephyr — to whinny at every morning and protect from the other stallions. Also, many youngsters were being broken on the riding ground. There were foolish displays of acting wild and squeal-challenges from the colts, which meant I had my work cut out, squealing and dominating dung, until the new generation learned I was boss.

Things did not settle down — far from it! Spring brought lots of strangers, who unloaded strange-shaped packs from their mule carts. They talked in excited voices about all the things they were going to discover on their way to Egypt and hung around the stables admiring us horses, until our grooms got fed up with them. Tydeos called them "stupid scientists," and they must have been stupid because they were going with us into enemy territory without so much as a dagger to defend themselves.

The army started to parade again in the mornings, and Alexander rode me down to watch them. A huge white tent arrived for the king, which the men set up on the riverbank. It held a hundred couches, and they filled it with fancy rugs and lamps, then carried in tables groaning with food. Alexander held a party inside it, which went on all night and kept us horses awake.

After the party, the tent was taken down and packed carefully, along with all its furniture and fittings, into carts. Then one bright dawn, with the smell of new grass in the air, Alexander came to the stables dressed in his armor and traveling cloak, and we all formed up and clattered out of Pella, going east toward the rising sun.

Nothing in the world compares to leading an army! I pranced like a four-year-old and made myself huge. On my back, Alexander sat equally proud, his mane freshly washed and shining in the sun, a huge grin on his face.

This was our complete herd, in marching order:

ME, BUCEPHALAS, carrying . . .
ALEXANDER, *King of Macedonia, Captain of the Hellenic League,*
        the reborn Achilles!
PETASIOS *carrying* HEPHAESTION
AURA *carrying* DEMETRIUS
ZEPHYR *carrying* PHILOTAS
APOLLO *carrying the battle-scarred* PERDICCAS
BOREALIS *carrying* LEONNATUS
HARPINNA *carrying* PTOLEMY
PSYLLA *carrying* HECTOR
HADES *carrying* IOLAUS
1,800 Macedonian cavalry
1,000 Thessalian cavalry
100 mounted scouts on scruffy ponies
600 Hellenic League cavalry on inferior Greek horses
12,000 Macedonians with their long pikes
2,000 Hellenic League hoplites
1,000 archers and slingers
2,000 troops from tribes we'd dominated in the mountains
5,000 mercenaries (the only ones who have been paid, but don't tell
        the men or there'll be grumbling in the ranks)
Baggage train and mules at the back, where they belong.

We didn't take many supplies, since General Parmenio had organized food for the first part of our march. But all the scientists came with us, bringing their equipment, and we also had Alexander's big white pavilion and our siege engines. So we had more baggage than last time, for half the number of men. The only bad part was leaving Charm's scent behind.

GENERAL PARMENIO

At the queen's urging, Alexander left the other half of the army to guard the borders while we were gone. I expect he knows what he is doing. The Persians probably don't have a very big herd.

When we reach the water that separates our world from the Anatolian world, we find the ships Athens promised us, ready and waiting to take us across. This proves that the Greeks have been well and truly dominated. We also find the one-eyed king's general and a herd of twelve thousand battle-scarred Macedonians camped on the shore, along with many horses I have never smelled before.

While I squeal a challenge to the strange stallions, Alexander orders the army to make camp and tells his Guard to follow him to General Parmenio's tent.

"You made good time, Alexander," the general says, coming out with his breakfast in his hand and making a rough count of our herd. He takes another bite of his bread and honey. Still chewing, he walks around Alexander and his Guard, giving them the kind of calculating stare you humans give horses when you're thinking about buying us. He pauses to adjust Zephyr's breast girth and greets his son Philotas with a slap on the thigh. Finally, he returns to Alexander, spits, and says, "Bit old to ride into battle, that nag of yours, isn't he?"

I don't like the way this old general smells, so I give him flat ears. He has almost as many battle scars as me, and he is not very clean. A dark beard, currently full of crumbs, has been allowed to sprout on his chin, and his unlaced tunic shows more hair on his chest. But he has big muscles, and he is quick. When his hand shoots out to grab my rein, it comes on my blind side. I rear up, striking out at him with my hooves. He lets go in surprise and steps back out of range.

Alexander's smile vanishes. His weight hardly shifted when I reared, and he runs a soothing hand down my neck.

"It's *King* Alexander in front of my men," he says. "And as you can see, there's nothing wrong with Bucephalas's battle sense. Take care, General, in case he thinks you're the enemy. He's not yet accustomed to your smell."

General Parmenio grunts. "I suppose he's the one all the grooms are scared of, the famous man-eater? Looks to me like he needs a man's firm hand. Better get him down to the horse lines and slap a muzzle on him. Then you can help me get these ships loaded, before King Darius sends his fleet up here to sink us all like stones in the Hellespont before we even get started."

The Guard give the water worried looks.

I feel Alexander stiffen a little on my back. But he shakes his head and laughs.

"I don't see any Persian ships, do you, General? And I'm quite sure a commander of your years and experience doesn't need my help to supervise the crossing. I'm going to visit Troy, so I'll need some horse transports sent down to ferry my men across the Hellespont from Elaeum. See to it, will you?"

He feels the bit and nudges me with his knees so that I make myself huge, then deliberately rides me past the general so close the older man has to step out of the way. From the corner of my good eye, I see him glare after Alexander. Philotas hesitates. But the rest of the Guard exchange grins as they follow us.

"That told him!" Leonnatus says, bringing Borealis up beside me. "Good for you, Alex."

"Are we still going to Troy?" Philotas asks. "Father knows what he's talking about. Maybe it would be as well to stay with the rest of the troops, in case the Persian fleet does turn up?"

But Alexander laughs again and waves a hand at the shimmering water and the hazy shoreline beyond. "He was trying to scare us, that's all. The Persian ships aren't here; even I can see that. Look! Over there lies Troy, the city of the *Iliad*! Don't you want to see the ancient ruins, Philo? Don't you want to stand where Achilles himself stood and gaze over the hills at the land of legend?"

"All the same, it might be worth taking some of the cavalry with us, Alex," Hephaestion says. "Just in case."

Alexander pulls me up, leans a hand on my hindquarters, and turns to look at their anxious faces. "Where's your sense of adventure, gentlemen? You're not turning weak-kneed on me before we've even set foot across the Hellespont, are you? Remember how we dealt with the Illyrians and the Thebans? We didn't need old Parmenio for that, did we? But I'm not stupid. I'll take three thousand . . . no, make that six thousand of the men with us. That make you feel better?"

Their faces relax, and they grin back at him. Even Philotas seems happier.

"Troy!" Iolaus breathes. "Are we really going there, Alex? I can't believe it's a real place."

Alexander gives the water a faraway look. "It's real, all right. Don't worry so, gentlemen! Troy is friendly these days. General Parmenio knows that, or he wouldn't let us go. This might be the last time we have to ourselves until we get to Egypt. We're allowed a little fun before the fighting starts."

SACRIFICES AT TROY

It was an easy march to Elaeum, with the members of the Guard laughing and joking as they used to do before Thebes. While we waited for the ships to arrive, Alexander made a sacrifice to Zeus on the shore and prayed for victory over the Persians. Then our grooms loaded us up, and we set sail for another world.

We horses of the Guard were tethered on the deck of Alexander's ship, so we saw the bull he sacrificed halfway across. Its dying bellow made Psylla and Aura tremble, and we all flared our nostrils. Bulls are not horses, so we weren't sad, but to see an animal as big as a horse killed like that is not nice. Over the hot tang of the bull's blood was the salt smell of the sea, and with the stiff wind blowing up the Hellespont the ship rolled under our hooves and spray hit us in the face.

Charm would have understood my fear. But she still hadn't turned up.

By the time we landed at Troy, I was sweating and trembling like a two-year-old. Alexander didn't notice. He was too busy putting on all his armor and throwing his spear into the sand. What for, I don't know. Maybe he thought he saw an enemy lurking there. I've suspected for some time that his eyesight is even worse than mine. But his friends cheered, anyway, and we were finally led off the ships on to the beach, while Alexander performed yet another sacrifice to the gods.

I've worked out that there are three reasons why you humans do this barbaric thing to animals. You spill their blood and send their ghosts to the other world because you are:

a priest and it is your job.
scared of something and want the gods on your side.
relieved to be alive after a battle, and want to say thank you.

Alexander was not a priest, and we had not been in a battle since Thebes. So you tell me why Alexander made so many sacrifices at Troy?

A MOUTHFUL OF CURLS

For a legendary city, Troy was rather disappointing. After everything Alexander had told me about it, while he pulled my ears and fed me apples back in Pella, I was expecting something more like Thebes (before we dominated it, that is). But the little town with its crumbling walls wasn't even as big as Alexander's first city, Alexandropolis, in the mountains of Thrace.

All the same, Alexander and his friends told our grooms to take us to the stables, then they rushed off to see the sights while the men posted sentries on the hills and made camp outside the walls. The men didn't seem too impressed with Troy, either. They grumbled about the detour and seemed worried someone might try to attack the king.

The stables were cramped and dark. There were no cobbles to massage our hooves, and the stall Tydeos put me in was filthy. I had to dominate several piles of stale dung before I could bear to take a single mouthful of my barley. The other horses were uneasy, too. They kept shooting up their heads and pricking their ears at the door, listening to the music and laughter coming from the town.

Tydeos and the other grooms settled us as best they could, then went off to find food for themselves. As it grew dark, there was still no sign of Alexander and his friends. Clearly, we were going to be here all night.

I used the doorpost to scratch my sweaty neck where Tydeos had not groomed me properly and resigned myself to sleeping standing up. I was thinking about Charm and missing her again, when two men crept into the passage and stopped outside my stall. At once, I recognized the disgraced horsemaster's smell coming from under the first one's dusty cloak. The other man had perfume in his beard and was holding his fancy robe up out of the dirt.

I gave them both flat ears to warn them not to touch me.

"That's the king's horse," whispered the horsemaster, keeping a wary distance from me. "An ugly brute, as you can see. Alexander rides him in every battle."

"I'll get a description off to the Persians," muttered the other. "General Memnon's in charge of the Greek mercenary forces here in Anatolia — he'll pass it on. Then, even if your King Alexander refuses our gift of the Achilles armor, they'll still be able to target him on the battlefield."

The horsemaster chuckled. "Alexander will accept your gift, Priest, don't you worry. It'll appeal to his vanity."

The priest smiled. "Is it true he sleeps with a copy of the *Iliad* under his pillow?"

"That and his dagger!" said the horsemaster with a frustrated look. "Seems our young Alexander isn't quite so confident of his invincibility as he likes us all to think. I'd take the horse with me now, but I don't have a hope of getting away with the animal if it plays me up like it did at Thebes. Alexander's brought a small army with him to Troy!"

"Yes, that's a shame. Without them, we might try sending an assassin to cut his throat in the night. But you've got to be careful when dealing with Persian honor. King Darius has heard of your young king's exploits and wants to defeat him in the field, which is probably just as well. I certainly wouldn't want to be the one caught creeping into King Alexander's tent with a knife."

The horsemaster drew his cloak closer and peered at the shadows. "Where's Alexander now?"

"Still playing at being Achilles conquering Troy!" the priest said with a look of contempt. "He'll soon find out real life isn't quite as easy as it seems in stories."

"The Achilles armor was supposed to be magic, though, wasn't it?"

The priest laughed. "All that stuff about it being made by the gods, you mean? It's been hanging in the temple of Troy for a thousand years, and it's as brittle as any other old armor, believe me. If your King Alexander is foolish enough to wear it in battle, the Persian spears will go through it as if it were papyrus. Does the horse have any markings on its legs?"

As the priest peered over my door I lunged at him and grabbed a mouthful of oiled curls before he stumbled back in alarm. "Athena's flashing spear!" he exclaimed. "The beast is crazy!"

The horsemaster pulled a face. "I warned you. That horse half killed me at Thebes, and it was responsible for me losing my job in Pella. When Alexander's no longer around, I'm going to teach the brute a lesson it won't forget. I have a score to settle with its little groom, too, if she ever turns up again."

They left quickly after that. They knew better than to try to touch me again.

I chewed the mouthful of curls to see if they were edible. But they tasted disgusting, so I spat them out. Then I lifted my tail and dropped dung to get rid of my enemy's smell.

THE ACHILLES ARMOR

I am so glad to leave the Trojan stables the next morning, I drag Tydeos out into the street. He stumbles over a fork in the narrow passage and lets go of me. The other grooms snigger, but the king and his Guard are coming, so they don't have time to tease him. Tydeos regains his feet, red-faced, brushes himself off, and hurries to catch me. He sorts out my reins just in time — and gapes at Alexander in amazement.

All the grooms are staring. So are the people of Troy, who have lined the streets to see the young king of Macedonia, who has come to drive the Persians out of their world. Our men hold them back with their pikes, but no one can stop them from cheering and waving and throwing flowers. I prick my ears and stare at Alexander, too. I have never seen him look quite so fine.

He is wearing new armor. It glitters and flashes in the morning sunshine, surrounding him with a golden glow. At his shoulder, Demetrius carries a great shield decorated with a gold-and-silver rim; the leather with its snake pattern is dark and scarred where ancient blades have scratched it. Alexander's shins and thighs are covered with glittering greaves, and his breastplate is beautifully polished. On his head, he wears a helmet with two huge horsehair plumes bouncing on top. They are the color of Apollo's mane and tail, a faded gold that shimmers white in the sun.

I look around to check that Apollo still has his mane and tail. Then I snort at Alexander, extending my nose to sniff the unfamiliar armor.

He laughs as he takes my rein from Tydeos. "See, gentlemen! Even Bucephalas thinks I look like Achilles!"

As he taps my shoulder to let me know he wants to get on my back, ghosts flicker in the shadows behind me. I give his new armor flat ears and dance backward.

He frowns at me and looks for Tydeos. "What's wrong with my horse this morning? You did stay with him last night as I ordered, didn't you?"

Tydeos turns red. "Of course, Your Majesty. He's probably upset by the strange stable. Er . . . do you want me to boost you up, Your Majesty?"

Alexander scowls. "Since when have I needed anyone to leg me up on my horse? Stand clear!"

He runs a hand down my neck and talks to me in a soothing voice, like he did the first time he rode me, until I lower my head and forget the ghosts. Then he holds out his hand for a spear, walks around onto my other side, and uses it to vault onto me in a gleam of gold and white. With the plumes of his helmet flaring behind him like wings, he flies.

The crowd gives a great cheer as he lands lightly astride my cloth. Alexander gathers up my reins, then takes the big shield from Demetrius and settles it on his knee. He punches the air as I prance forward. His friends laugh, take their horses from the grooms, and mount up as well. The people of Troy throw more flowers. The petals fall in our manes like snow. I toss my head and make myself huge.

It makes no difference to me if Alexander wants to wear the Achilles armor. I am strong enough to carry him, whatever he's wearing. I just hope Achilles' ghost has gone.

RIVER
GRANiCUS

SPRING 334 B.C.

LIBERATING OR DOMINATING?

Not even a strong young human like Alexander can wear armor and carry a shield all the time. He would soon begin to smell bad, and shields get in the way. They're supposed to, of course — that's the whole point of shields. But what is useful in a battle can be a real pain on a march, believe me.

As soon as we were out of sight of Troy, Alexander appointed Demetrius his official shield-bearer and stopped to take off the glittering Achilles armor and plumed helmet. He had them packed into the baggage cart with the spare weapons and put on his cloak and hat instead. Then we rejoined the rest of the army.

For a while, it was rather dull, just a long trek with no galloping. We dominated all the towns and cities on our route without a blow being struck. Alexander and General Parmenio claimed we were "liberating" them, but I can't see there was much difference, except that we didn't get to rename any of them, which was a pity, if you ask me.

PERCOTE — *already dominated by the one-eyed king, like Troy*
LAMPSACUS — *refused to let us in, but paid us to leave them alone*
COLONAE — *refused to let us in, didn't even pay*
PRIAPUS — *opened the gates to let us in, no fighting*
ZELEIA — *refused to let us in*

I'm not entirely sure that marching past the ones who wouldn't let us in without a fight counts as dominating them. But you humans have your own ideas, and Alexander was anxious to get on. After every town, he leaped on to my back and urged his Guard and the cavalry on the road again, leaving General Parmenio to follow with the rest of the army, and the baggage train trailing far behind.

"This is easy!" he said as we left Zeleia. "I can't think why my father had so much trouble."

Hephaestion smiled. "Maybe they've all heard what you did to Thebes."

But Philotas muttered, "Father says the Persians will try to stop us soon. They're probably waiting for us around the next bend."

The others laughed and said the Persians were obviously too scared to face us.

But Philotas was right this time.

WHEN THE PHALANX DID NOT FOLLOW

We find the Persian army on the other side of a deep river called the Granicus. Like most rivers at this time of the year, it is in full flood. The shadows under the bank are long in the afternoon sun. I can hear strange horses whinnying nearby. Sounds like a big herd.

Alexander's heart beats faster. Though it is late in the day, he orders his men to prepare for battle and rides me forward for a closer look. I arch my neck and play with my bit, while he squints at the fast-flowing river, the steep bank, and the line of enemy spears dark against the sky.

"Oh, Zeus, Bucephalas," he whispers, running a sweaty hand down my neck. "This isn't going to be easy." Then he shakes himself and smiles. "You'll just have to swim for me like you did at the Danube. Remember, I'm Achilles and you're my immortal horse. We're not going to die today."

General Parmenio, however, has a different view. When Alexander rides me back to the arms wagon and starts strapping on the glittering armor he took from Troy, the general strides across and seizes his wrist.

"What do you think you're doing, Alexander?" he growls. "What's with the fancy helmet? You're not seriously thinking of wearing that armor into battle, are you? It must be a thousand years old! It'll shatter at the first spear thrust."

Alexander snatches his wrist free and glowers at the general. "It's *Achilles'* armor. It was made by the gods, so it will never shatter. I must look my best when we meet the Persians."

"So, you're going to wear it all night, are you?" Parmenio snorts down his nose like a horse. "Up to you."

"I am not going to wear it all night," Alexander says with dangerous calm, "because we'll have beaten the Persians by then. We're going to attack across the river as soon as the men are ready."

General Parmenio gives him a disbelieving stare. "Are you crazy? It'll be dark soon! That river's a death trap. They'll massacre us before we even get up the bank. The phalanx is crippled in such situations, you know that. We have to meet the Persians on open ground. We need to wait for the baggage train to catch up, make camp, and decide on the best plan of attack for the morning. They won't come across here, don't you worry. And I can tell you right now what we should do. We should send out scouts to find another crossing place. Then when it's dark enough, we can leave our campfires burning and take the men quietly across the river out of sight of the Persians. Get behind them and engage them in battle tomorrow on the plain on the other side. *Then* we might have a chance of beating them."

"No," Alexander says, putting on his plumed helmet. "I'm going to finish the Persians now."

The general's face hardens, and he says in a low tone, "If you don't listen to me, Alexander, you're not going to be king for long. I've been commanding armies longer than you've been alive, and most of these men have been fighting at my side just as long. I'm warning you now, if you try to lead the army across that river tonight, they won't follow you."

Alexander's hands pause on the fastening of the helmet. He says, very quietly, "Is that a threat, General?"

The general shakes his head, impatient. "No, it's not a threat! It's the truth, and you know it as well as I do. Think a moment! We all know how brave you are. But the Persians will still be there in the morning and so will their treasure. Across the river on the plain, where we'll win the day with minimum losses."

Tydeos, who is holding me nearby and looking as if he would rather be somewhere else, shuffles his feet. But generals and kings ignore grooms like horses ignore mules. The argument continues, with Alexander's voice getting shriller and General Parmenio's face getting redder and redder.

Finally, Alexander marches across to me and snatches my rein from Tydeos. "Enough! I've already told the men we're going to attack. I can't suddenly change my mind now. While we stand here arguing, the light's going. Get the phalanx ready, General. Since you seem so scared of the enemy, I'll take the cavalry across first. They'll follow me."

General Parmenio looks alarmed. "Cavalry against an infantry block-ade? That's just *stupid* —"

Alexander is already up on my back, and we're galloping to join the others, his helmet plumes pale against the darkening sky. He mutters under his breath as we go. "Thinks he commands the army . . . I'll show him . . . Can't let the men think I'm scared — Oh, curses, Bucephalas, why does he have to be so *right*?" But no one hears this except me, and he is shining with energy as he always is before a battle.

The Guard cheer as he joins them, and the rest of the cavalry form up behind in a jangle of bits and spears. Alexander doesn't wait to see if General Parmenio is obeying his order but cries, "Follow me, gentlemen! King Darius is waiting!" and we lead our cheering herd at a gallop into the river.

The water isn't as cold as the Danube. But the current is worse. *Much* worse. I am struggling to keep straight, and some of the smaller horses get washed downstream. I see Aura swimming valiantly behind me, at an angle to the current, her dappled neck twisted with effort. Psylla's in trouble, and little Hades is in danger of whirling away into the shadows with Iolaus clinging pale-faced to his mane. Borealis sees this and swims beside him, pushing him back upstream with his bulk. Zephyr is all right, and so are Apollo and Harpinna. Petasios stays next to me all the way, his nostrils flaring and his eyes rolling. We nine are still together when we reach the shallows on the other side and splash out of the water in a huge spray, yelling the Macedonian war cry.

"ALALALAI! ALALALALAI! ALALALALAI!"

The enemy boss gives a shout, too, and javelins rain down on our heads from the overhanging bank, many finding their mark. Several men fall off their horses and splash into the water. Hephaestion gives an anguished cry.

"Hector's hit!"

I see Psylla struggling in the mud behind me, riderless. Hector floats in the river, facedown, blood swirling around him and a javelin stuck in his back. Iolaus urges Hades across, screaming for his friend to get up. But Psylla's rider will never sit on her back again. His ghost has already gone, and the current is carrying his body downstream. Poor Psylla! Frightened to be alone, she rolls her eyes and whinnies at us not to leave her behind.

"Keep together!" Philotas yells. "Iolaus! Get back here! Alex, we have to go back. *Now!* Father's right. This is a death trap. *The phalanx isn't following us!*"

Only one line of foot soldiers has ventured into the river, struggling to swim against the current. The rest of the army are still formed up in neat squares on the far bank, watching the fight from a safe distance. This is NOT GOOD. We are vastly outnumbered. We can't get up the bank because of the enemy's spears and the overhang, and our backs are to the river. That's the only way to go. Sometimes you have to run from a battle if you want to fight another day.

But Alexander is now close enough to see the designs on the enemy's shields, and his hand tightens on my rein. "Those are *Greeks* up there!" he hisses. "Greek mercenaries, fighting for the Persians against me! I'm not running from them!"

Philotas shakes his head. "If you want to get yourself killed, that's up to you. I'm taking the men back before we get massacred."

Alexander glares at him. But this is no time to divide our herd, and he knows it. I whinny to Psylla, warning her to stay close. As we begin the retreat, another volley of javelins comes down from the bank but I leap to avoid them.

Then I smell strange horses coming out of the shadows.

I squeal a challenge as they charge us from both sides. They are small and dainty, their bridles are decorated with silly tassels, and they carry their tails stupidly high. But they are fast and light-footed in the mud. One of the yellow-turbaned riders gallops straight at us. A javelin flies out of his hand toward Alexander's throat. I whirl out of the way. But my hooves slip on the steep bank. Demetrius raises the Achilles shield. The point goes right through it and pierces Alexander's glittering armor.

He gasps in shock and goes white. A wave of shame comes over me as I regain my balance. If he falls off me like Hector did off Psylla . . . But he plucks out the javelin, pushes Demetrius aside, and turns me to face the Persian who threw it. We horses squeal and snap at one another, while Alexander thrusts his spear into the enemy's chest with a cry of rage.

Hephaestion and Petasios are fighting at my side. I see Harpinna biting and kicking with the same fury she showed in Illyria, and another Persian takes a swipe at Aura's beautiful head with his spear as Demetrius struggles with the shield. She rears and knocks the weapon out of his hand with her neat hooves — Ha! That's my mare!

Our Persian is not yet dominated, though. The spear snapped on his breastplate, so he is only bruised. He draws his curved sword and bares his teeth. "You are going to die today, King Iskander," he shouts in a strange accent that makes Alexander's name sound different. "Your armor looks very splendid, but it seems remarkably old for a battle."

"This is Achilles' own armor, made by the gods!" Alexander shouts back. "It'll protect me even if it's broken. Where's your King Darius? Is he a coward, to hide behind his Greek mercenaries? Why doesn't he come down here and fight me himself?"

The Persian smiles. "The Great King sent us to finish you off. He's got more important things to do than cross spears with a half-grown boy playing at leading his father's army."

Alexander's face flushes, and his whole body trembles with anger. He ducks the long sword and jabs his broken spear shaft into the Persian's mocking smile. The silly Persian horse rears, and its rider falls off backward over its tail. I grab one of its stupid tassels in my teeth and it gallops away, snorting in fear.

Ha! Dominated!

But another Persian has sneaked up on my blind side. I don't see him until he brings his sword down on top of Alexander's plumed helmet. The shock goes right through me, and half the helmet splashes into the river behind us. I feel Alexander's weight sway dangerously and have to stand still until he regains his balance. He has his sword out now. There is a ringing of blades, before Alexander scores a cut to the Persian's throat and sends him thudding into the mud at our feet.

I don't even have time to dominate the enemy horse. Hephaestion yells, "Alex, *look out!*" And behind us, yet another Persian saber flashes down.

I leap forward, my hooves sliding in the mud. The blade misses Alexander's exposed head by a hair's breadth. One of the older cavalrymen, Commander Cleitus, bravely gets between us and chops off the Persian's arm.

Petasios gallops up beside us with flat ears. Hephaestion has lots of little cuts, and his sword drips with Persian blood. "We've got to get out of here, Alex!" he shouts above the noise of the battle. "Philo's right, this is crazy. It's getting dark. I can't see a thing under this bank. Alex — what's wrong? Oh, Zeus, you're wounded! Your head's bleeding —"

Alexander's hand loosens on my rein. I feel his weight slide again, but this time there is nothing I can do to keep him on my back. He slips over my shoulder and crumples, groaning, into the mud.

Philotas mutters a curse and yells for the surviving members of the Guard. They crowd around to keep the Persians away, while Hephaestion jumps off Petasios and tries to make the king get up. I immediately settle to my knees in the mud so my wounded rider can get on my back again. But there is such a fight going on around him, I can't even see him anymore. And while I am on my knees, two Persians ride their horses straight at me and drop a noose around my neck. Before I can get to my feet, one of them has the nerve to leap on my back and grab my reins!

I surge to my feet with an outraged squeal. But the noose tightens around my neck, half choking me. The man on my back clings tightly, and a third Persian rides his horse up behind me and brings the flat of his sword down across my hindquarters. It stings like crazy. I squeal again in anger and go up on my hind legs, striking out at their horses with my hooves and trying to bite their riders. Soon we are struggling as furiously as Alexander's Guard is around the groaning king. But whatever I do, the Persians keep forcing me farther away from Alexander.

We are struggling on the riverbank. It is so dark I can't see the edge. The rope tangles around my legs, and suddenly I am in the water, upside down. The Persian on my back slides off me with a curse and splashes toward the bank. But my legs are still tangled up in rope and leather, and though I fight like mad, the current takes me.

I whinny desperately to my herd. I hear Petasios whinny faintly in reply. But he has to keep Hephaestion alive, so he can't help me. It is all I can do to keep my head above the water. My heart bursts with shame when I think of Alexander lying in the mud.

My rider, hurt and helpless, without me.

At some stage, my cloth comes off. But I am too exhausted to break the ropes, and the river is very strong. As my struggles weaken, its current carries me farther and farther downstream, away from the battle into the night of a strange world.

GROOM IN A DRESS

In the end, the noose saves me. The rope snags around a tree root and holds me fast against the bank, where the river forms a pool. As I lie there with my nostrils just above the water and my breath wheezing against the tight rope, I smell our Macedonian army. The whole phalanx is moving downriver, a dark mass of men without lights, just as General Parmenio planned. I struggle afresh and whinny hopefully to my herd. But the only horses with them are Greek ones of the Hellenic League. They are too stupid to know it is me.

The last of them pass, and I lie half in and half out of the water, giving little hopeful whinnies into the night. Even a mule would be welcome, but there is no sign of the baggage train. I keep hoping Alexander will come and find me. Then the smell of the river reminds me of how I let him get wounded, and I feel shame all over again.

I grow shivery and cold. I think I hear more horses on the other side of the river, a huge herd of them going down the Persian side. But I am too exhausted to whinny very loudly, and they don't hear me. Everything fades away, and I drift in black clouds of ghosts.

I am about to go with them when a familiar smell tugs me back. It makes me remember being warm and clean and well fed. I can almost feel Charm's fingers mutual grooming my withers. At first, I can't figure out where I am. Then I feel the cold water around me and start to struggle again.

"Steady, Bucephalas, steady, it's me." Gentle hands loosen the noose.

It sounds so much like her voice whispering in my ear, a little nicker of greeting escapes me.

"Oh, Bucephalas," Charm chokes. "Oh, horse . . . Please wake up! I can't bear to lose you!"

I open my eyes. It is her. It IS!

Her hair has grown longer and is twisted in a scarf. She wears a cloak of patterned wool over a woman's dress with a muddy, torn hem. But she smells just the same. Sweet, like spring grass. She pulls a dagger from her girdle and cuts the tangle of rope and leather that is keeping me prisoner. I scramble up the bank, and she runs her hands all over me, laughing in relief.

"Oh, Bucephalas! If you knew how frightened I was for you! I came as fast as I could. But what have you done with Alexander? Did they kill him, like in my dream? Though you're still alive, so maybe Alexander is, too. In my dream, I saw you both fall together. . . . I promise I won't leave you again, no matter what the king does to me."

We find the baggage train camped near to where Alexander had squealed at General Parmenio before we crossed the river to meet the enemy. The scientists look up from their breakfast and stare at us. It is Charm they are staring at, sitting astride me in her dress. I am so bedraggled from my night in the river, they obviously don't recognize me.

She takes me to the horse lines, and my heart lifts as I recognize Aura's smell. Though my mare is not around, her dung is quite fresh. I trot around with my nose to the ground, sniffing other piles. Petasios, Borealis, Zephyr, Apollo . . . Harpinna . . . Hades . . . Psylla. I stop sniffing and snort in relief, which brings Tydeos rushing out to meet us.

"Bucephalas!" he gasps, so busy examining me for injury that he doesn't recognize Charm. "Wherever did you find him? Hey, how come you're riding him? He never usually lets anyone but King Alexander or his groom on his back —" As he looks properly at Charm for the first time, his mouth drops open.

Charm smiles. "Don't you recognize me, Tydeos?"

Tydeos's face goes slack with astonishment. "*Charmides!* Alexander wasn't joking, was he? You *are* a girl! And you're . . . you're beautiful."

"Don't be stupid," Charm says, flushing as she slides off me. "I'm just the same as I always was. Help me see to Bucephalas. He's had a bad time of it in the river. I think he's all right, but that cut on his hindquarters needs treating, and he'll want a warm barley mash and a good rubdown." She works on me as she speaks.

"B-but where have you *been* all this time? How did you get here? And how did you find Bucephalas? The king was so upset last night, you wouldn't believe! And he was so sick from that blow to his head, he could hardly walk straight. But he still rode off into battle this morning. . . . He'll be pleased you're back."

Charm mumbles something about helping the cooks in General Parmenio's camp and following the army in the baggage train. Then she frowns at the river. "You said he's fighting again?"

Tydeos finally stops staring at her and grins. "No one could stop him! Took the cavalry across as soon as it got light enough to see the water. The Persians decamped in the night, leaving their Greek mercenaries to hold us up here. They must have thought King Alexander was finished. When they realized he wasn't dead, they sent a herald across to beg for mercy, but King Alexander was so angry about them fighting on the Persian side, he wouldn't give them any. Did you see General Parmenio on your way upriver? He took the rest of the army off in the night."

Charm shakes her head. "Maybe he's found the Persians."

By now, the other grooms have noticed I am back. They crowd around, all talking at once. "Hey, Charmides! Is that really you?" — "Nice dress!" — "Where've you been all winter?" — "The king wasn't half furious with you at Thebes!" — "You'll be in trouble when he gets back, all right!" And a lot more garbage of the same sort. Grooms do so like to gossip.

Charm ignores them and carries on tending to my cut. She glances up at Tydeos, and he gives her a quick smile. "I'll get his mash ready," he says, and hurries off to boil water.

With Charm's gentle care I soon start to feel better, and give the other grooms flat ears until they drift back to their work. They keep glancing at Charm, though, and whispering about her being a girl.

I don't see what the problem is. Mares go into battle and still have healthy foals. But you humans seem to think your females are good for nothing but breeding and won't even let them be grooms. This is clearly stupid, because Charm is a good groom, and anyway she's not in foal.

CHARM'S DREAM COMES TRUE

I am digesting my mash and flicking flies away with my tail, when Charm comes rushing back to the horse lines. She has changed her dress for a groom's tunic, and in the daylight I see that her scarf, which she's used to tie back her mane, is red.

I nicker to her, hoping for some mutual grooming. But she pushes my nose away and starts to put on my bridle. Her hands are trembling. I throw my head up and begin to shiver. The sounds of the battle across the river are faint, but her tension upsets me.

"Oh, Bucephalas! Stop it. You know I can't reach when you do that." Charm makes another attempt to get the bit in, and this time I lower my head and open my mouth for her. "I'm sorry, horse," she whispers, doing up the straps. "But in my dream — when I saw the horse killed under Alexander, and he got killed, too — it wasn't dark, like the grooms say it was when Alexander fell off you last night. It was daylight! Oh, I hope we're not too late!"

She struggles up onto my back. She's lost a bit of fitness, but she is desperate enough to make it. Then she heads me out of the camp toward the river. A sentry calls after her. But she calls back, "Spare horse for the king!" and urges me into a gallop before he can send anyone after her.

She wants me to swim the river Granicus AGAIN.

I hesitate as I remember what happened last time. But Charm whispers to me and strokes my neck until I jump in. It is not so bad this time. Charm is lighter than Alexander, and there are no Greek spears coming down at us from the top of the far bank.

The screams and Macedonian war cries ahead of us fill me with nervous energy. I bound up a steep path and emerge in the sun on the enemy's side of the river, where the noise hits us.

The Greek mercenaries are trapped on a small hill in a defensive circle with their spears pointing outward, while our cavalry gallop around them. Alexander is leading a charge barely twenty strides away from us. He doesn't see me. He is riding Psylla. She looks very tired. But the little mare carries him valiantly into the hedge of spears, and the others close around her, fighting furiously. A lot of the Greeks seem to be dead, but the survivors are not giving up.

Charm tightens her hands on my reins. "Someone warn the king!" she shouts. "They're going to kill his horse!"

I prance and shake my head, impatient to join the herd. That should be *me* at the front carrying Alexander, not little Psylla.

Charm holds me back, still shouting warnings. But her voice is small in the noise of the battle. Everyone is fighting so hard, no one notices us. "We'll have to get closer," she mutters, and loosens my rein.

It is what I have been waiting for. My legs fly over the ground to catch up with the others. Charm clings to my mane. She's dropped the reins, so there is nothing to support me and I stumble slightly. But I soon find my feet again and gallop on. Oh, the joy! Oh, the excitement! I can see Aura up at the front of the herd, just behind Psylla, her rider Demetrius carrying the big shield of Achilles, which has been patched where it got pierced by the Persian spear. I flatten my ears as I pass the stragglers at the back, and one of the older cavalrymen finally notices Charm.

"What the —?"

"It's a crazy *girl*! Get back to camp, you idiot! Do you want to die?"

Charm is very pale. She hasn't a hope of stopping me now, and she knows it. I have the bit between my teeth, metal discs and all. I barge past more horses, and now it is just the Guard ahead of me. Zephyr's yellow tail whips my face as I whinny loudly to tell them I'm back.

Charm shouts at Philotas, "You have to tell the king to retreat! They're going to — *No!*"

A horse falls in front of us. It's Psylla. She's going so fast, she rolls right over, kicks once, and lies still. Her ghost ripples past my nose. I neigh at it, but it doesn't come back. Two spears are sticking out of her chest.

The others pull up in a confusion of shouts and flashing swords. We horses snort at poor Psylla, while their riders battle the Greeks. Alexander shakes his head, dazed, and gets to his feet. He was thrown clear, several paces behind where Psylla lies dead. But he's wearing a good helmet today, not the plumed one the Persians cracked last night. He looks more angry than hurt.

"Alex!" Hephaestion yells, springing off Petasios. "Take my horse. I'll find another."

With a huge whinny, I barge through the others, nipping them and giving them flat ears until I reach my rider. I settle down to my knees, forgetting Charm is still on my back, and whinny to him again.

The Greeks are fighting for their lives. But Alexander has eyes only for me and Charm. She has caught her balance and is leaning backward, her feet almost on the ground. She seems frozen with terror.

Then she steps off me, throws my reins to Alexander, and gasps, "I've brought your horse, Your Majesty!"

Hephaestion recovers first. "Don't just stand there, Alex!" he yells. Grabbing Charm's wrist, he throws her up onto Petasios's back and leaps up behind her. "I'll see your groom to safety."

Petasios gallops off toward the river, carrying his double burden easily.

Alexander does not hesitate. He springs onto my back and gathers up my reins with a firm hand. "Bucephalas . . ." he whispers in a choked voice as I rise to my feet. "Bucephalas, old horse, don't ever, *ever* scare me like that again." He gives my neck a quick, trembling stroke. Then he punches the air with his spear and shouts for his Guard.

We are together again. Alexander's energy flows into me, and mine into him, until we shine. I make myself huge with pride. But the battle is already over.

While Charm and Alexander were staring at each other, the boss of the Greeks broke out of the trap and fled with some of his men. It doesn't take the others long to throw down their weapons and surrender. Alexander gives poor Psylla a regretful look and leads the Guard back to the river.

We find Charm sitting on the bank, hugging her knees and shivering. When she sees us coming, she leaps to her feet, fists clenched.

Alexander dismounts, pulls off his helmet, and leads me across to her. The others hang back tactfully, keeping a good lookout for Persians. I nicker to Charm, and her lips tremble. But she doesn't move.

"Another dream, Charmides?" Alexander asks in a weary tone.

She bites her lip. "Yes, Your Majesty."

"I told you back in Thrace, you really should try to tell me *before* we meet the enemy. It would make things a lot easier for both of us."

She gives him an uncertain look and lowers her eyes. "I . . . Yes, Your Majesty. I'm sorry. I came as fast as I could. But I was in the baggage train, and you were already fighting before we got here."

"You were in my baggage train all this time? What were you doing?"

"Helping General Parmenio's cooks, Your Majesty." It is a whisper.

"Did he know you used to be my groom?"

She shakes her head.

"All right, I'll sort it out." He frowns, and asks in a softer tone, "What's your real name, Charmides?"

She goes rigid and whispers, "Charmeia."

"Charmeia, of course." He shakes his head and smiles. "It's no good, I just can't see you as a girl. I'll have to keep calling you Charmides. So you ran away at Thebes, but you came back to save my horse's life?"

"Yes, Your Majesty."

Even with my sharp ears, I can barely hear her.

He nods. "Good enough. But, I've told you before, if you're going to be Bucephalas's groom you'll have to learn to be less formal. I can't put up with 'Your Majesty' all the way to Egypt."

Charm looks up, her eyes bright. "I can still be your groom? You're not angry with me?"

Alexander glances at the Guard, who are watching him and Charm with little wondering smiles, and sighs. "No one else looks after Bucephalas as well as you do, and my official seer doesn't have dreams half as useful as yours. You're wasted as a cook. I need you. We can talk about this later. I've a lot to do. I've got to find old Parmenio, for one."

Charm fights a grin. She straightens her face and says, "The other grooms think he is downriver fighting the Persians, Alexander, sir!"

"Well, then, I expect he is." He looks at the line of Greek prisoners being escorted from the hillside littered with their dead and smiles again. "You grooms always seem to know more about what's going on than I do."

A SPLENDID VICTORY

Charm was sent back to the camp with an escort, while the foot soldiers who had stayed with Alexander remained behind to burn the Greek dead. We cavalry trotted down the Persian side of the river and found their camp guarded only by old men and boys. Persians travel with even more baggage than we do! Alexander paused to load up their carts with golden cups, fancy carpets, and glittering shields from the tents. Then we went to find the rest of our army.

Before long, we horses caught the unmistakable battle smell of sweat and blood. Small herds of Persians came galloping toward us, looking over their shoulders. They panicked when they saw us and scattered into the trees. Alexander smiled grimly and pressed on, not bothering to chase them.

We found General Parmenio striding through flattened, blood-spattered corn, barking out orders. But he was merely telling his men to collect up the dead and catch the loose horses. I squealed a challenge, and finally some of the men noticed us. They stared in amazement at our triumphant cavalry, the treasure piled in the Persian carts, and the line of Greek prisoners stumbling along behind us. Alexander took off his helmet to let his sweaty mane dry in the sun and sat up straighter. A hasty trumpet blared out, and someone called in a loud voice:

"The *king*! The king is back!"

The others dropped what they were doing and rushed to see if it was true. At once, they began cheering and calling to Alexander. Although I was getting a bit tired, I arched my neck and made myself huge.

General Parmenio looked around to see what all the fuss was about. He went quite still when he saw us. Alexander rode me right up to him, the Guard following — except Psylla and Hector, of course. Their absence was like a hole in my cloth. Not that I was wearing any kind of cloth that day, because Charm had not stopped to put one on me before she rode me into the battle.

Alexander halted me, and I champed at my bit while my rider looked down at the general. The men fell silent to hear what he would say.

"I see you've dealt admirably well with the Persians as I ordered, General," Alexander called out in a clear voice. "As you can see, we have dealt with the Greek mercenaries. These prisoners are to be put in chains and sent back to Macedonia to work the mines, as an example to all Greeks who think it's clever to join with the enemy and fight against me."

He looked at the Hellenic League troops, who were the only ones who didn't cheer when they saw us, and stared at General Parmenio in a very challenging way. If they were stallions, they would have been making squealing threats by now.

But the general was wise and said nothing.

Alexander nudged me with his knees until I took another step forward. He then leaned down and hissed so quietly that only General Parmenio and I could hear, "And if you *ever* leave me to face the enemy alone like that again, old man, you and all your officers will be joining them. Understand?"

The general went pale. He nodded, glanced at his son Philotas, and said in his loud voice, "I'm glad you approved of my battle plan, King Alexander. Your brave charge across the river last night won us time to cross and get behind them. Congratulations on your splendid victory over the Persians!"

Alexander nodded and smiled, and the army broke into wild cheering. They thought the king and the general had been working together all along. But before we left, I gave General Parmenio flat ears to remind him he had been dominated.

MOURNING PSYLLA

There were several changes after our first battle with the Persians in the other world. Charm being my personal groom again was by far the best, of course. But here's what else happened.

Zephyr and Philotas left the Guard to command another part of the army. Alexander said it was a promotion, but he told me he had sent Philotas away because he'd defied him at the Granicus. It is often better to let a troublesome rival lead his own little band. Then he will be too busy to challenge for leadership of the herd.

Two new horses joined us to replace Psylla and Zephyr: Arion, the gray stallion who had fought with us in Illyria, carrying Attalus; and Xanthus, a big stallion the color of ripe corn with dark legs. Xanthus dared to give me flat ears and a squeal, so I had to bite his nose to put him in his place. He might be big, but he's a very inferior breed. His rider was called Craterus.

All the cities that had closed their gates to us very quickly opened them and sent us treasure in apology, so we left the Hellenic League troops behind to look after them.

The men got paid out of the Persian gold. This meant another all-night party in the king's pavilion, much singing and drinking of magic in the camp, and no sleep for us horses.

Before we broke camp, Alexander ordered that all the horses of the Guard should have their manes cut off in mourning for Psylla and Hector. Silky hair fell to the ground in waves: white from Aura, pale gold from Apollo, red from Petasios and Harpinna, yellow from Zephyr, brown from Borealis, black from Hades. Apollo kicked up a bit of a fuss. But when I nipped him, he snorted and stood still.

Not even Charm dared touch *my* mane.

I don't know about General Parmenio's battle with the Persians, because I wasn't there. But our battle against the Greek mercenaries went like this:

Greek dead: 3,000

Greek prisoners in chains for the mines: 2,000

Macedonian dead from Alexander's command: 70, including
        Hector of the Guard

Horses dead: 3, including poor Psylla (SAD!!!)

It might have taken us two days and three battles, but in the end, the Persians and the Greek mercenaries who fought against us at the river Granicus were well and truly dominated. Ha!

HALICARNASSUS

334 B.C.

HONEY CAKES AT ALINDA

No one tried to stop us on our way south from the river Granicus, and the weather was good so we marched fast. Alexander wanted to dominate the boss of the Greek mercenaries, who had run away from the battle and taken refuge in a big city farther down the coast. Alexander knew very well the Greek boss was called General Memnon, but he called him a traitor, a Persian-slipper-licking slave, and a lot of less polite things besides. On the way, we dominated two smaller cities with no trouble:

> EPHESUS — *no fighting, since the Greek mercenaries defending the garrison ran away when they saw us coming. A pretty place, so Alexander and I had our portrait painted there, while General Parmenio went to liberate the surrounding towns.*
>
> MILETUS — *squealed a bit, but not strong enough to keep us out. Its Greek mercenaries changed sides and joined our herd when Alexander gave them the choice between death and dishonor. (That's mercenaries for you.)*

Hephaestion laughed and said at this rate we'd liberate Anatolia before winter.

But Alexander pulled a face. "We haven't achieved anything yet. Memnon's holed up in Halicarnassus with the Persian fleet, and King Darius won't come out and face me. By all reports, he's hiding in Persia. He pays Greeks to fight his battles, while he directs the war from the luxury of his own palace! And they call *him* 'Great King'? Yet I, who have fought in the front line of battle since I was sixteen years old, must struggle every single day to prove I'm good enough to lead my own army!"

His fist clenched on my rein, and Hephaestion laid a gentle hand over it.

"Alex, of course you're good enough. The men love you. They'll follow you anywhere. What happened back at the Granicus was just old Parmenio trying to assert his power. His troops hadn't seen you in battle, remember? They probably thought the news of your conquests in Greece was exaggerated. But they know now how brave and strong you are, and that you'll always be the first into the fight, no matter what the odds. That makes a difference to soldiers. You should have seen their faces when you cheated death at the Granicus, then rode onto the battlefield with your prisoners in chains and all that Persian treasure! They'll follow you against Memnon next time, don't you worry!"

"I did see their faces," Alexander said with a smile. "I was there, remember? But I've got an idea how we might capture Halicarnassus without another messy battle. Come on, my friend, we're going to visit a queen!"

Alexander's idea was to visit Queen Ada — who used to be boss of Halicarnassus before the Persians dominated her — and persuade her to give him detailed plans of the city together with all the weak points in its walls. He sent General Parmenio on ahead to start the siege, while we Guard and the rest of the cavalry took a detour into the mountains to visit her stronghold of Alinda.

He was clever enough to send Queen Ada some friendly nickers and whinnies on rolls of flattened grass, so by the time we arrived she was waiting eagerly to meet us at the gates of her fortress. Alexander's energy and smile did the rest.

The queen kissed Alexander on the cheek, called him her darling boy, and promised he would inherit her throne after her death if he chased Memnon and the Persians out of Halicarnassus for her. Meanwhile, Charm and Tydeos led us horses into the stables. They were rather cramped and dark, and I resigned myself to another uncomfortable night. But later, a girl-filly came down from the kitchens with a basket smelling of warm honey.

We pricked our ears in interest as she lugged it up to our grooms and pulled back the cloth.

"Queen Ada sent these cakes for you," she said. "King Alexander said to be sure to give one to his horse." She looked sideways at me and giggled. "I wouldn't, though, if I were you. They're much too good to waste on horses!" She snatched one from the top and crammed it into her mouth as she ran off.

Fortunately, Charm took no notice of the silly girl-filly and brought me a whole handful of honey cakes. They tasted as good as they smelled.

As Charm fed them to me, she whispered, "I like Queen Ada already, but Alexander's sure to rush off to Halicarnassus just as soon as he's got all the information he needs. . . . Oh, Bucephalas! How much farther? He says that after we've finished liberating all the cities here in Anatolia, we're going to Egypt. That's such a long way, I can't even *imagine* it. And the Persian army is still around somewhere. I couldn't bear it if he rode you into another big battle like the one at the river Granicus, I just couldn't."

I nudged her to give me the last cake, and she laughed as I licked her hand clean of sticky crumbs. "You silly brute! All you think of is your stomach. That, and fighting over mares! It must be nice to be a horse. You have no worries at all, do you?"

Which only goes to show how little you humans know about us.

Squealing at Halicarnassus

From the start, I suspect Halicarnassus will be no fun. As we draw rein at the top of the hill and look down on the city and its harbor, the wind blows hot and dry through my coat. A few yellow stalks under my hooves are all I can see to eat. The city has plenty of gardens inside, but out here is just white rock, sun-shriveled grass, and turquoise sea.

"Queen Ada wasn't joking about that ditch, Hephaestion," Alexander whispers, pointing to a deep, wide trench encircling the high walls. "It's going to be difficult to get our siege machines close enough. The men will have to fill it in, I suppose, and that'll take ages. Look at all those guard towers! Just as well she gave us the plans, or I wouldn't know where to start. And the Persian fleet's still in the harbor. I just hope old Parmenio's managed to get the transports through."

"I don't see any of our siege equipment, Alex." Hephaestion leans on Petasios's withers and studies General Parmenio's herd, which is camped outside the east gate of the city.

Alexander squints at the camp, too. He is in a good mood after Queen Ada's honey cakes, so he doesn't get angry. "Maybe he hasn't unloaded it yet. He's probably waiting for me to tell him what to do. Come on, gentlemen! Let's get a closer look at those walls. I want to know the worst!"

The Greek mercenaries defending Halicarnassus are not scared of us like the ones we dominated at Ephesus and Miletus. When they spot us trotting down the hill on the other side of their ditch, they throw spears at us from the walls. Then the city gate opens a crack, and a whole herd of them runs out, squealing threats and brandishing their swords.

Alexander tightens my rein in surprise. He's not even wearing his armor. His shield, javelin, and spear are still in the wagon, along with most of the Guard's weapons. Hephaestion draws his sword, drags Petasios around to face the Greeks, and yells, "Look out! Someone sound the alarm!"

A trumpet blares three times to call the rest of the cavalry. One of the Greeks rushes us. I leap at him, teeth bared. Alexander's sword is in his hand now. He cuts the Greek mercenary across the neck. Although his ghost does not leave his body our enemy falls to his knees, choking. Ha! All the Guard are fighting as the cavalry gallop across to join us, brandishing their spears.

"Quick!" Alexander yells at them, shining with energy. "That gate's open! Charge!"

But even as he turns me toward it and digs his heels into my ribs, the Greeks swarm back across the bridge and slam the gate shut. We pull up at a safe distance, surrounded by the cavalry, snorting from the sudden exertion.

"King Alexander!" shouts a herald from the wall. "General Memnon says that's just a taste of what you can expect if you attack Halicarnassus! Leave now and take your army with you, before we have to kill you."

Alexander whirls me back to face the city. He leans forward and shivers all over. I think for a moment he's going to make me gallop across the bridge and attack the gate anyway, even though it's shut. I make myself huge in anticipation. But Hephaestion says softly, "Alex, remember the Granicus. . . ." and my rider's weight shifts back again.

"Tell the *traitor* Memnon," Alexander calls, "that I will not go away until he is chained in my mines with the rest of his men, chipping gold out of Macedonian rocks!"

After giving them that good squeal, he wheels me around and we gallop back to the camp, where General Parmenio strides out to meet us.

Alexander doesn't even have time to dismount before the general starts another squealing match. "What did you think you were doing over there, Alexander?" he says. "Are you *trying* to get yourself killed?"

"They opened the gate! I saw an opportunity. It might have worked. Where's my siege equipment? Why haven't you started attacking the walls?"

That's when we learn the worst.

Our siege equipment and most of our supplies are stuck out at sea, prevented from landing by the Persian ships. Persian-slipper-licking Memnon has at least three thousand enemy troops inside Halicarnassus. He has stores enough for a long siege, and he has anti-siege machines ready to destroy our towers if we do ever manage to land them.

General Parmenio says it's Alexander's fault for sending the Athenian fleet home instead of having them protect the transports, and Alexander says it's General Parmenio's fault for transporting the equipment and stores by sea rather than by land under a decent guard.

Then Alexander squeals that he wants to move the camp north of the city, where Queen Ada's plans show the weakest defenses. But General Parmenio squeals back that his men have only just finished setting up their tents on hard rock and won't be very happy about being ordered to move them so soon.

The Guard glance at one another. We horses fidget, picking up the tension of our riders. Zephyr tosses her head, while Philotas stares from his father to Alexander as if he can't decide which herd he belongs to. That could be awkward if it comes to a battle.

But in the end, Alexander works out a cunning way to dominate General Parmenio without fighting him. He sends Philotas off with his band to secure a landing place for the transport ships and orders General Parmenio's men to start filling in the ditch on the side of the city where they are camped, ready for when the siege equipment gets through. Then he leads our half of the army back up the hill to make camp where he wanted to in the first place.

Petasios and I walk side by side, our necks stretched out in relief. Out of the corner of my good eye, I see Alexander run a hand through his hair. "Why can nothing ever be easy?" he grumbles to Hephaestion. "Could I really have a demon for a father, and that's why the gods hate me?"

Hephaestion is too sensible to answer. "I don't know, Alex. But if liberating the Anatolian cities were easy, King Philip would already have done it. You're the only one who has ever managed to get this far. You must be giving King Darius nightmares in his luxurious Persian bed."

Alexander smiles. "Good! Then when we've finished off Memnon, maybe he'll come out and fight me! I'm fed up with fighting Greeks. Bucephalas is as eager as I am to get his teeth into some Persian flesh. Aren't you, my brave horse?"

I toss my head and snort, because he knows very well I don't eat meat. I'd much rather have another bucket of Queen Ada's honey cakes.

Our siege equipment eventually arrived. But it didn't do us much good. As fast as our men filled in the ditch and dragged the towers up to the wall, the Persian-slipper-licking Greeks drove them back again and undid all our hard work. Whenever our siege engines made a hole in the wall big enough for our phalanx to climb through, the enemy fought so hard our men couldn't get in. Then, during the night when the fighting stopped, they built another wall across the gap to keep us out.

We horses got very bored and irritable, and our feeds began to get smaller again. The only good thing was that Harpinna came into foal-season, and I managed to break my halter and visit her in the night before Charm caught me. *That* showed Xanthus who was boss, all right.

Alexander spent a lot of time in his big white pavilion with his friends, poring over the plans Queen Ada had given him. But he still didn't lead an attack on the city, and the grooms grumbled that at this rate we'd be here ten years, like Achilles sitting outside the walls of Troy.

We might have been, too, if it hadn't been for Charm's dream.

A DREAM OF FLAMES

Charm is curled up in her cloak near me. I think she's asleep like the other grooms, when she suddenly sits up with a gasp. She stares at Alexander's pavilion, which is lit up as usual with some sort of party, then at the sleeping city, and pulls her cloak closer.

"Fire, Bucephalas," she whispers. "I saw Halicarnassus burning — Oh no, he can't do that again!"

Because she is so agitated, I check my blind side, but I can't see any ghosts. I nicker to her. She gives me a distracted look, scrambles to her feet, and rushes off toward the king's pavilion.

She's gone quite a long time. I start to worry that she's left me again. Then she comes back with Alexander and some of his Guard. Alexander has his hand on her elbow, and his friends are laughing and staggering a little. As they come closer, I smell magic drink on their breath. They stop near our lines, and Alexander points at the city, silver and quiet in the starlight.

"Look, Charmides! Do you see any flames?"

Charm is breathing hard. She tries to free her elbow, but he won't let go.

"It hasn't happened yet," she says. "But it's going to happen. I dreamed it. Please, Alexander, sir . . . *please* don't burn the city like you did to Thebes. Think of all those women and children who lost their homes and were sold as slaves! It wasn't fair."

His face hardens. "That wasn't my decision. The League wanted it done."

"But *your* men did it."

He frowns and lets her go so suddenly she stumbles. "And what will you do if Halicarnassus burns, Charmides? Run away again? Abandon me and poor old Bucephalas here, because you can't stomach the sight of a few children in chains? This is war. Better their children than ours."

"I didn't run away because of that! You don't understand!" Charm starts to cry. Alexander's friends go quiet, watching the king and his groom.

"How can I understand, if you refuse to talk about it?" His voice has risen. He takes a deep breath and shakes his head as Charm looks at her feet. "Oh, for Zeus's sake, you're only a groom. Why is it you disturb me so much? So! You saw the city burning, did you? Then let's see if we can't make your dream come true."

He turns to his friends and tilts up his chin. "Right, you've all seen Ada's plans. The wall has been breached at its weakest point. I want two volunteers to creep inside and open the north gate. I'll get the men ready."

"*Now*, Alex?" Hephaestion stares at him. "Tonight?"

"Yes, tonight!" Alexander gives Charm a thoughtful glance. "My groom's been right before, and they won't be expecting a night attack. If we don't do something soon, General Parmenio's going to say 'I told you so.' We have to lure Memnon out to fight." He grins a challenge, shining with the energy that infects people and horses alike. "It's dangerous."

His friends' eyes glitter with excitement.

"I'll go, Alex!" Demetrius offers, with a hiccup.

"And me," Leonnatus says. "We'll get our weapons!"

They rush off, and Alexander raises his eyebrows at Charm. "Well, girl? What are you waiting for? Get Bucephalas ready for me. Wake the other grooms. Quietly, though. We don't want to spoil the surprise."

Charm is agitated. She wakes Tydeos and some of the others and puts my battle-cloth on me with trembling hands. It's the middle of the night, which is a VERY strange time for a battle, but my heart starts to pound. Action, at last!

Alexander returns, wearing his armor and carrying a pair of javelins and his spear. He vaults onto me, and the reduced Guard form up behind. Borealis and Aura whinny from the horse lines, confused as to why their riders have gone into the city without them. Men stream out of our camp, armed and eager for action. Whispered orders pass along the ranks and we set off for the gate at a trot.

At first, the city seems just as quiet as it was before Demetrius and Leonnatus crept inside. Then a shout goes up from the guard tower, and a whole section of the wall flares with torches, showing the dark silhouettes of running men. Alexander looks at the closed gate and curses. "Over the wall!" he cries and rides me at the ditch toward the breach.

Our men had filled the ditch with rubble to get the siege engines close enough, but it is not easy ground. I gather myself for a jump, but at the last moment decide not to try it. It's a lot wider than I thought. Instead, I drop onto the rubble, stumble as my hooves hit the uneven surface, and feel something wrench in my left foreleg.

I'm so excited, there is no pain. I canter across and jump the remains of the wall on the other side. Petasios and Xanthus are still with me, but the other horses are floundering on the bridge of rubble. Alexander calls for Demetrius and Leonnatus, and their frightened shouts come back out of the night. I see them fighting a whole herd of Persian-slipper-licking Greeks with their backs to a wall the enemy has built inside the damaged one.

Alexander kills one of the Greeks with his first javelin, gives a great cry of "ALALALAI!" and shouts for the others to follow. My blood is up. I gallop through the enemy, scattering them with flat ears and snapping teeth, and Alexander's second javelin sends another Greek ghost rippling into the night.

Petasios and Hephaestion are fighting in the shadows nearby. Xanthus is kicking, leaping, and biting almost as brilliantly as me, while his rider Craterus hacks around him with his sword. The rest of the Guard and most of the men have made it across the rubble. But we are trapped between the old wall and the new one, with no way through. With triumphant cries, more enemy Greeks stream out of the guard towers at either side of us.

"Get the boy who thinks he's king!" calls one, and Alexander hauls me around to see who has insulted him.

"*Memnon!*" he hisses. He casts aside his spear, which is useless in our tight spot, and drags out his sword. He urges me into a gallop, straight at the Greek boss.

Several Greeks try to stop us and fall beneath my hooves. Their ghosts rise from their bodies and are lost. Hephaestion calls something after us, but Alexander is deaf and blind to all except Persian-slipper-licking Memnon, who watches me come with a smile that turns to panic as he realizes we are not going to stop. He starts to run for cover, but I am VERY fast. Alexander's sword slashes down and catches him on the shoulder. The night ripples as Memnon's ghost leaks out of the wound. But it clings on stubbornly and does not leave him. Memnon gives a cry of pain and stumbles behind his men, who close up around him. Even Alexander and I cannot get through.

That is when I smell smoke.

"Alex!" Hephaestion yells, pointing back the way we came. "The devils have sneaked out of the gate and are burning our siege towers!"

Alexander says some very bad words, gives the wounded Memnon a final glare, and leads the Guard back over the rubble to the ditch.

The Greeks outside the city are already running back inside with their flaming torches. The dark siege engine we passed on our way across the ditch is now a great tower of flame crackling fiercely ahead of us, flares of it falling through the darkness. They destroy my night sight, so I can't see the bridge. I stop dead, throw my head up, and blow at it in alarm.

Alexander hits me on the backside with the shaft of his spear, which hurts. "Get on, Bucephalas! It's only fire. This is no time to be scared!"

As I hesitate, something sharp comes flying out of my blind spot and bites me beside my tail. Shocked, I leap forward through the wall of flame and the others follow me, neighing in terror as the sparks singe their manes.

The whole of our camp is awake by now, and men are running up the hill from General Parmenio's camp. But the Greeks have retreated back behind their walls, and there is no one left to fight outside the city.

General Parmenio gallops up to us on a strange horse. I try to make myself huge. But now the excitement of the battle is over, my foreleg hurts where I wrenched it on the rubble, and my wound stings. I settle for giving the general's horse flat ears. Alexander plucks the spear out of me and snaps it over his knee, making the general's horse shy.

"What on earth's going on?" General Parmenio yells. "Did you try a night attack? Why wasn't I consulted?"

Alexander glares at him. "It's better than sitting out here all winter, as you seem happy to do! I wounded Memnon. Maybe they'll surrender now."

The general looks at the burning siege towers. Four of them are on fire. "Oh, well done, Alexander! And what are we going to use to get through their walls if they decide to stay inside until General Memnon recovers? At this rate, we're not only going to be here all winter but all next summer, too!"

"The men can easily build more towers!" Alexander snaps. "We'll talk about this later. I have to see to my horse. He's hurt." He jumps off me, turns his back on the furious general, and leads me back to the horse lines.

Charm races out to meet us, sees I am limping, and angrily grabs my rein from the king. Then she notices my spear wound and lets out a choked cry. "You let him get wounded!"

Alexander opens his mouth to squeal at her. Then he remembers she's not the enemy, and the anger runs out of him. He walks behind me (only Alexander would ever dare do that) and peers at my injury. "It's quite shallow. The cloth stopped it from going in too deep. Find the horse doctor. Takes more than a scratch like that to put Bucephalas out of action."

Charm feels my sore leg and frowns. "His leg's very hot. Did you gallop over any rough ground?"

Alexander gives her a distracted look. "Get the horse doctor to take a look at that as well. Charmides, I need to know. Did you . . . I mean, was your dream . . . ?"

She glances up.

Alexander clears his throat and crouches beside her. His voice softens. "I didn't mean to make fun of you, earlier this evening. You caught me at a bad time. Is this what you saw in your dream? The siege towers burning?"

Charm looks at the fires and bites her lip. "Maybe. I don't know. I thought it was the whole city, but I might have been remembering Thebes. That was a bad time for me."

Alexander nods and watches her examine my leg. Finally, he gives a sheepish smile. "Well, that wasn't much of a success, was it? I didn't kill Memnon, and Queen Ada's maps didn't allow for his men building emergency walls. I'd better go and see if I can get General Parmenio to calm down. We're obviously going to have to think of something else."

A BUCKET OF SEAWATER

I didn't see much of the fighting after that. I had to stand with my foot in a bucket of seawater, while Alexander rode Xanthus to supervise the siege. Then one morning, a messenger galloped back to camp, yelling that the Greeks had finally come out to face us. The cavalry mounted up and galloped off after Alexander with the phalanx racing after them. General

Parmenio's veterans shook their heads, muttered something about show-ing the king they still knew how to fight, and followed. With all the excitement, I kicked over my bucket and squashed it, so Charm had to fetch me another.

In the afternoon, the men began to stagger back to camp, tired and bleeding, but boasting about how they'd dominated the enemy. Xanthus came back to the horse lines with a small spear wound in his chest. It wasn't nearly as deep as mine, though you'd have thought he was dying from all the fuss he made when Tydeos bathed it.

Groom-gossip that evening was all about a monstrous tower the enemy had brought out of Halicarnassus, stuffed full of Greeks to throw spears at our men. They said it was as big as a mountain and could hold the whole Persian army. (Which was nonsense, because everyone knew their herd was still hiding in Persia with King Darius.) The grooms also said Alexander deliberately led some of the Macedonians into a trap so that Memnon would give the order to open the main gates and send out the rest of his troops. I don't know if that's true, either.

But one thing did come true. Charm's dream. That night, Halicarnassus burned.

Alexander didn't start the fire this time, though. Persian-slipper-licking Memnon set the armories alight before fleeing on his ships with the Persians who had been living in Queen Ada's palace, leaving our men to put out the fires and save as much of the city as we could.

It took us nearly two months, but in the end, we dominated Halicarnassus from all sides:

East — *General Parmenio was stupid and tried to attack the city without any siege equipment.*

North — *Alexander was stupid and tried to attack at night, after drink-ing too much magic at a party.*

West — *Persian-slipper-licking Memnon was stupid and tried to frighten us with a big tower stuffed full of Greeks.*

South — *the Persian fleet did the only sensible thing by running away.*

GORDIUM

SPRING 333 B.C.

WINTER LEAVE

When the fires were out, Queen Ada moved back into her palace, and our herd split up again. As a reward for fighting so well, Alexander let the married men go home to Pella for the winter so they could see their families. He sent General Parmenio and his veterans north with the baggage train to a place called Sardis, where we all planned to meet up again ready for the spring campaign. Then he mounted Xanthus and took his archers and slingers and what remained of the cavalry on a winter campaign to secure the rest of the Anatolian harbors so that the Persians would not be able to use them. I was stiff from my wound and too lame to travel, which meant Charm and I had to stay behind.

Once I'd gotten over the misery of neighing good-bye to my friends, it was not too bad. Alexander had left a garrison in Halicarnassus to help Queen Ada dominate the remaining Greek mercenaries who had holed up in the city's fortresses, and the queen's stables housed some nice Persian mares, so I wasn't lonely. We ate honey cakes every single day, and Charm devised an exercise program to get me fit. Soon, I could manage gentle trots through the streets.

A huge marble tomb stood at the crossroads in the center of the city. Our scientists called it the Mausoleum and were measuring it for their list of wonders of the world. I didn't like it. The place was haunted by the ghost of the king who was buried there, and I never knew when it might ripple out and chase me. I always pranced and snorted as we passed it, making Charm laugh and call me a big baby. But toward the end of the winter, it is not just the ghost that scares me. As we trot past the outer wall, I smell my enemy among the crowd around the gate.

I leap sideways in alarm. Charm, who was admiring the marble statues instead of paying attention to her riding, falls off over my shoulder.

The disgraced horsemaster limps across and sneers down at her. "So, you're still looking after the old horse? I must say I'm surprised at King Alexander, trusting his precious Bucephalas to a girl. But it seems young Alexander's full of surprises. He's survived a lot longer than anyone expected him to, but he won't get much further. I happen to know King Darius has sent General Memnon an army to get rid of him."

Charm recovers her wits and pulls out her dagger, which she wears all the time since Alexander left her here to look after me. "Leave us alone, or I'll have you arrested!"

The horsemaster laughs at her wavering blade. "Oh! You've got yourself a little knife, have you? Be careful not to cut yourself — be a shame to spoil that pretty face of yours. When King Darius kills Alexander, you'll be spending the rest of your days in a Persian harem, and the old horse will be mine."

Charm shouts for help.

The horsemaster casts a frustrated glance at the Macedonian sentries running toward us and hisses, "You might think you're safe here under King Alexander's protection, but I want you to know I'll get my revenge eventually, if I have to follow you to the ends of the earth. In war, things can change as easily as *that*." He snaps his fingers in Charm's face.

He's not watching me, and I catch his hand in my teeth. Small bones crunch. He yells in pain, gives me an evil look, and hurries off clutching his broken hand.

Ha, dominated!

The sentries gave chase, but the horsemaster had already vanished into the crowd. Grave-faced, they escorted Charm and me back to the palace, where they reported the incident to Queen Ada. She hurried down to the stables to find out what had happened.

"I hear a man attacked you up at the Mausoleum," the queen said as I sniffed her to see if she had brought any honey cakes. "Who was he?"

Charm burst into tears and told her all about the horsemaster. "It's my fault," she sniffed. "I told King Alexander how his father's old horsemaster had mistreated Bucephalas back in Pella, and now the man hates us. I think he's following us. He said King Darius has sent General Memnon an army to stop Alexander — That's not true, is it?"

Queen Ada looked thoughtful. "I expect Darius is worried that Alexander has gotten this far, so it's certainly possible. But an army marching all the way from Persia is unlikely to get here before next summer, and by all reports Alexander's winter campaign is going very well, so I don't think we need worry too much."

"The Persians wouldn't come if King Alexander didn't keep fighting," Charm said in a small voice.

"I know, my dear. But Alexander's young, and he's been hurt. His father publicly rejected him, and then there was the assassination. It must have been terribly upsetting for the poor boy. He needs to prove to the world that he's good enough to be king. He thinks he can do that by making war and winning battles. Maybe he can. He certainly has the gift for making men follow him. He's already a stronger king than Philip ever was."

"I hate war!" Charm sniffed. "I hate all the killing and burning and slave-taking. Alexander almost got Bucephalas killed at the Granicus. That's why I came back. I thought he'd be furious I'd pretended to be a boy, when he found out at Thebes. But all he said was he couldn't see me as a girl."

Queen Ada was silent a moment. Then she said, "I think that's a compliment, my dear. What he probably means is you're too good a groom to be a girl in his eyes."

Charm looked at her feet. "I'm not good. There's something I haven't told you. I didn't end up in Pella by chance. I went there to avenge my mother. I never knew my father. I thought he'd been killed in the fighting at Methone before I was born. But when she was dying, Mother told me she was raped when the Macedonians captured the city after the siege. That's how she got pregnant with me, and why she was never very well when I was growing up. I came to Pella with some poison in a mule's hoof. I meant to get work in the kitchens and put it in King Philip's food. But I recognized Bucephalas, fighting his grooms on the riding ground, and knew I had to help him. Then King Philip went away and I met Alexander, and things . . . changed. I never managed to get the poison into the kitchens, and poisoning the king wouldn't have been that simple anyway. In the end, one of his own Guard stabbed him."

Queen Ada studied Charm's face over my door. She sighed. "Ah, I begin to see. Perhaps the horse saved you, as much as you saved him. Does Alexander know all this?"

"No! I told him I ran away from Methone, but I didn't dare tell him about the poison, especially not after what happened to King Philip."

"Then don't tell him. You're not the first child to have a conquering soldier as a father, and you won't be the last." Queen Ada frowned at Charm. "You're going to have to stop torturing yourself like this, my dear. Follow Alexander, if you must, but don't expect any sympathy from him. Men like him, who have been touched by the gods, don't understand the concerns of us lesser mortals. Take the advice of an old woman, and make a life for yourself before it's too late."

"I can't leave Bucephalas, Your Majesty," Charm said, giving me a desperate look. "Not if there's going to be another battle."

"I know *that*, dear. I'm quite certain the horse wouldn't have gotten this far without your care, and I suspect Alexander wouldn't have gotten this far without the horse. There's something between the three of you. Some *power*. A bond, I don't know what. But I can sense it. It's like a light surrounding you — which is why we must get you reunited with the king as soon as possible, certainly before he reaches Gordium."

Charm looked up with renewed fear. "Why? Where's that? Is it in Egypt?"

The queen smiled. "It's near Sardis, and knowing Alexander, Gordium is where he plans to start his spring campaign. You'll find out why when you get there. And don't worry about your old horsemaster. He won't get into the palace; these stables are too well guarded. But Bucephalas is sound enough to travel now, so to be on the safe side I'm going to send you north to General Parmenio. Meanwhile, I'll order a search of the city, though if your horsemaster's got any sense he'll already have cleared out."

Charm managed a small smile. "Thank you, Your Majesty."

The queen smiled back. "The first step in becoming free, Charmeia my dear, is to stop thinking of yourself as a slave. Promise me you'll take that step when you rejoin Alexander?"

Charm straightened a tangle in my mane. This time, her smile was real. "I promise, Your Majesty!"

I remember Charm telling Alexander some of this, but I don't think it was quite the same story she told Queen Ada. This means one of three things:

Charm lied to Alexander.
Charm lied to Queen Ada.
Charm lied to them both.

As long as she stays to look after me, I don't mind if she lies to everyone.

A HUGE FILLY

We traveled to Sardis with the scientists who had stayed behind to measure the Mausoleum. Queen Ada sent honey cakes for Alexander and also some mares from the palace stables.

It was tremendously exciting to be back with my herd again. I carried Charm with my head high and my neck arched, swiveling my ears to catch the sounds of the mountains and flaring my nostrils. The air smelled of melting snow, which still lay in the shade of rocks beside the road.

We found General Parmenio's part of the army camped outside the town, together with the men back from their winter leave and new recruits from Macedonia. They had brought fresh horses with them, so there was a lot of excited whinnying going on in the horse lines.

I made myself huge and filled my lungs to let out one of my loudest neighs. Charm grabbed my mane as my whole body shuddered. The sound echoed across the rocks, and several of the horses threw their heads up and pricked their ears at me in admiration. One of the fillies whinnied back. I recognized her at once. It was Psylla's filly, from my winter in the mare pasture.

I neighed in delight and gathered myself to gallop down the hill. But Charm hauled on my reins. "No, Bucephalas, don't show me up, please! General Parmenio's coming. Behave yourself. You'll be seeing your friends soon enough."

I still wanted to gallop to the horse lines and say hello to little Electra. But the general's hand grabbed my rein, heavy and commanding. I restrained myself and sent Electra a whinny instead. Then I gave the general flat ears. His smell had not improved over the winter.

"I see the old horse is sound again," General Parmenio said, pulling a wry face at me. "I hope that'll cheer up the king, because he hasn't got much else to be cheerful about."

"Sir?" Charm said, still holding me tightly. "King Alexander's all right, isn't he?"

The general must have heard the fear in her voice, for he laughed. "Oh yes, young Alexander's fine! By all accounts he's waiting for us in Gordium, having trekked halfway around the snowbound mountains of Anatolia chasing robbers and capturing fortresses. Apparently, Gordium surrendered without a fight as soon as the defenders saw him coming. I didn't think he had it in him, but he's done what he said he would do and secured all the harbors as far as Phoenicia. Makes my efforts here in Sardis seem dull by comparison. But it might all be for nothing. That meddlesome Greek Memnon is undoing all our good work behind us, despite hardly being able to hold his sword after getting himself wounded at Halicarnassus. Alexander doesn't know it yet, but the men coming off leave say General Memnon's men have already captured several of the Aegean Islands, and now he's preparing to invade Macedonia! There's nothing else for it, we'll have to go back."

Charm's hands tightened in my mane. "Back home?" she breathed.

The officers around us nodded grimly. Some of them looked rather relieved.

"Back to deal with Memnon, anyway. Though it's King Alexander's decision, of course." The general coughed, as if he had just remembered he was talking to a mere groom. "Can you control this horse? Because I can't be looking out for you all the time."

Charm stiffened and took a better grip on my mane. "Of course, sir. I've already ridden him all the way here from Halicarnassus."

He grunted and let go of my rein.

I threw my head up and leaped forward, carrying Charm with me. She pretended she had given me the signal to do this and called back over her shoulder, "I'll just settle him in the horse lines, sir!" Then we were going where I wanted to go and she gave up trying to stop me, though she kept my rein tight so I couldn't break out of a canter.

Charm was still on my back when we reached the other horses, which shows how much she'd learned. When she first started riding me back in Pella, she wouldn't have stayed on nearly so long. I headed straight for Electra's familiar whinny and stopped dead in amazement, nearly throwing Charm over my shoulder.

Where had this huge black filly come from? She was almost as big as me, but she had Psylla's eyes and pretty head. Her tail was like smoke and looked as if it had been recently combed out by her groom. She was beautiful.

I nickered to tell her so. She stretched out her nose and nickered back, warm and soft.

"Careful!" said her groom, jumping up to separate us. "This is a filly, you know!"

But Charm had recognized Electra, too. She slipped off me on trembling legs to take my head. "Is that really Bucephalas's filly?" she said in wonder. "She's only a two-year-old. Look at the size of her!"

"Yeah, ain't she great?" Her groom puffed up with pride. "We taught her to carry a rider early, she grew so big and strong. The new horsemaster said it would be easier than leavin' her another year. But she's sweet and kind, not like her brute of a sire."

When I snapped at him, he jumped backward, and gave Charm a closer look. "You really are a girl, ain't you? I thought the other grooms were putting me on."

Charm smiled and gave me a pat. "Well, they weren't. What's wrong? Don't you think a girl can do a groom's job?"

"Um . . ." The young groom flushed. "I s'pose it must be all right if King Alexander lets you look after Bucephalas. Look at them sniffing each other! Do you think he recognizes her?"

"Of course he does! Bucephalas isn't stupid. Are you, old horse? Don't look so worried. Stallions don't mate with their own fillies." Charm pulled one of my ears and looked around. "I don't suppose Tydeos is here?"

The groom shook his head. "Afraid not. I think he's with the king."

Charm's face fell a bit. "I'll have to wait until we get to Gordium, then."

▷OMINATING THE GORDIAN KNOT

We leave the next day. General Parmenio is anxious to tell Alexander the news about Memnon and strides around the camp shouting at the men to hurry. But most of them have been here all winter and have to dismantle the huts they built, which takes AGES.

By the time we reach Gordium, Alexander's part of the army is already camped outside the town. I whinny in delight when I smell the horses. But only one familiar whinny comes back from the lines. It's Harpinna. Her belly is big with foal, which is obviously why she is here on her own. Confused, I prick my ears at the camp as the dogs jump around, barking excitedly to welcome us. Where is the rest of my herd?

Before the echoes of our trumpet have died away, a breathless soldier runs up to General Parmenio. "You're just in time!" he gasps out. "King Alexander's gone up to the Temple of Zeus to try his luck with the Gordian Knot! If he manages to untie it, he'll be lord of all Anatolia."

The men around us smile. "He already thinks he is," someone says.

General Parmenio frowns at the city, which is glowing in a burst of evening sunshine. On the acropolis hill, the Temple of Zeus stands against fiery clouds. Charm tenses. This makes me tense, too. Is there going to be a battle?

"Impetuous young fool," General Parmenio mutters under his breath. "I might have known Alexander wouldn't be able to resist it. Undoing some old knot is hardly going to drive Memnon out of Anatolia for us! But people are superstitious around these parts. If he's not careful, he'll undo everything we've achieved so far. I bet he never stopped to think what might happen if he fails."

I don't know what this Gordian Knot is. But it seems we are going to find out.

General Parmenio orders his men to make camp and seems about to order Charm to go with them. Then he sets his jaw and says, "Bring the king's horse up to the temple. Maybe it'll distract Alexander from this stupid test of kingship."

So Charm and I enter Gordium at the front of our herd where we belong, with General Parmenio beside us. We pass under a massive arch-way, its crumbling stone carved with bearded men dressed in long robes rather like Queen Ada's. Charm stares up at it and shivers. My hooves echo and I feel a bit nervous, too. Ghosts lurk under this arch. Once through, however, we find the usual streets, houses, and temples. People line our route to catch a glimpse of us, exactly as they did in all the other cities we dominated on the way here.

We head up the hill to the temple courtyard. I smell all my friends and give General Parmenio's horse flat ears until he lets me put my head in front. First, I see Petasios and Xanthus at the edge of the courtyard, being held by Iolaus. They both have new battle scars. When I whinny, they throw their heads up. Petasios whinnies back, but Xanthus has the nerve to give me a loud squeal. Carrying Alexander all winter has obviously gone to his head. I squeal back to remind him I'm boss, but this is not the place for a battle. Behind them, tethered in a line, are Arion, Hades, Apollo, Borealis, Zephyr, and last but far from least . . . AURA! I give my favorite mare a special nicker. She shoots up her white ears, whirls around on her tether, and nickers back at me.

"Keep a good hold of him," General Parmenio mutters to Charm, urging his horse into a trot. "I only hope we're not too late."

As we cross the courtyard, I catch Alexander's sherbet smell and let out another whinny. I can't see him yet, though. There are too many people crowded around what appears to be an old cart. The king is somewhere in the middle. Charm's fingers tighten on my mane, and she pushes one of her escaped curls back under her scarf.

The crowd parts when they see us coming. General Parmenio dismounts and jerks his head at Charm. She slides off me and takes hold of my bit. At last, I see Alexander. He has his back to us and is examining the yoke of the cart. He's wearing the glittering armor he took from Troy and the helmet with the white plumes, which has been mended and reinforced since being fished out of the river Granicus. Nearby, Demetrius holds the big shield of Achilles.

I give Alexander my special nicker. He swings around, and his whole face lights up. "Bucephalas!"

My heart pounds as he strides toward me. Hephaestion follows, as usual. There's a fresh scar on Alexander's cheek, but he's flushed with health and he walks with a bigger stride than he did at Halicarnassus.

As he approaches General Parmenio, he makes himself huge and says with a little smile, "I'm glad you finally made it, General. I was about to untie the Gordian Knot without you."

General Parmenio looks hard at Alexander. He shades his eyes against the sun reflecting off the Achilles armor and says carefully, "There isn't time for you to try the Gordian Knot now, King Alexander. We must talk about General Memnon. It's bad news, I'm afraid."

Alexander's chin tilts up. He considers the general with his odd eyes and says quietly, "I've already announced I'm going to undo it."

"In the morning, then. Memnon is much more important."

A lot of people are listening — not just Alexander's Guard and Parmenio's officers but also the people of Gordium and the priests of the temple in their long robes. Charm grips my bit as tightly as she held my mane earlier.

Alexander's eyes narrow. But he is in a very good mood and doesn't lose his temper. "I gave Memnon a fatal wound at Halicarnassus, remember? I've secured all the harbors and taken care of everything here. He won't bother us for much longer."

He turns his back on the seething general and smiles at me.

"Bucephalas," he murmurs, stroking my nose. "My beautiful horse! I've missed you. Xanthus tries hard, but he's not as good as you are at avoiding enemy spears. He looks well, Charmides. Bring him across so he can watch me untie this knot."

He is already walking back to the temple, one hand on my rein. Charm has no option but to come, too. General Parmenio hurries after us, dragging his horse and scowling.

When we reach the cart, I finally see what all the fuss is about. A big tangle of ancient rope is wound around the yoke. It looks like a groom's first efforts to tie a proper knot in a halter. But it's massive. More like a whole stable of novice grooms have tied halters around it and couldn't get them untied again. There are not even any ends sticking out to chew. I stretch out my nose, curious. The Gordian Knot smells FOUL. I curl my upper lip in disgust.

Alexander laughs. "See! That's what Bucephalas thinks of your famous knot, Priest! And you say that Zeus will bless whoever manages to untie it and make him Lord of Anatolia?"

The priest smiles. "No one has ever managed it, not even King Darius."

Alexander walks around the cart, considering the knot. "Did Memnon fail, too?"

"General Memnon hasn't tried. I hear he is very sick."

Alexander turns to General Parmenio. "See, General? I've prayed to Zeus to help me. If I undo this knot, we won't have to worry about Memnon anymore."

The general's face tightens. He mutters something about being realistic and says quietly, "And what'll happen if you fail to untie it, King Alexander? Have you thought of that?"

There is a hush as the crowd realize this is turning into a squealing match. Some of them push closer to hear better, but I give them flat ears, and they jump back again.

Alexander frowns slightly. Then he raises his chin and says in a strong voice, "I'm not going to fail, General. I've already conquered all the Anatolian cities, haven't I? Zeus will aid me in ending Memnon's life, you'll see."

General Parmenio rolls his eyes. "If you think Zeus is going to —"

He gets no further. A rumble of thunder on the horizon makes my mane stand on end. General Parmenio's horse throws its head up. Across the courtyard, Petasios and the others give little whinnies of unease. People glance around and pull their cloaks closer.

The priest looks up at the storm clouds and says, "King Alexander, the light's going and it looks like rain. It might be a good idea to hurry?"

Alexander nods. He walks slowly around the knot, rubbing his chin and frowning. He whispers to Charm, "Any dreams about this?" but she shakes her head. He scowls and mutters, "Oh, what difference does it make how I undo it?"

He moves so fast, the priest doesn't realize what he intends.

I jump in alarm as Alexander whips out his sword and slices through the Gordian Knot with as much force as if it were Persian-slipper-licking Memnon's head. Lightning zigzags across the sky, reflecting off the blade.

The tangle of rope falls apart in a blinding flash. There's a crack of thunder, and the earth under my hooves ripples like the sea.

Startled, I drag Charm back a few paces. A coldness goes through me as Memnon's ghost, which I last saw clinging to his body during the fighting at Halicarnassus, screams past my blind side and vanishes.

This is too much for General Parmenio's horse. It rips the reins from the general's hand and takes off across the courtyard. I want to follow it. But Charm clings desperately to my bridle, and eventually the sound of her voice calms me down. Still shivering, I check my blind side, but Memnon's ghost has gone. The ground is solid again. Big drops of rain start to fall, making cold spots on my back.

Alexander laughs. He lifts his sword to the storm, his armor glittering and the lightning flashing around him. The crowd — who went quiet when he cut the famous knot — lets out a great roar.

"Alex-an-der!" they chant. "Alexander, the reborn Achilles, King of Macedonia, Lord of Anatolia! HURRAH FOR KING ALEXANDER!"

The news travels fast. Those who were unable to get into the courtyard to watch take up the shout in the streets. Even with the rain hissing down and thunder rumbling overhead, people come out of their houses to cheer Alexander. When he puts away his sword and vaults onto me, my heart swells with pride. Although I hate thunder and lightning, and the rain is getting in my ears, I make myself huge.

Petasios, carrying Hephaestion, soon joins me, and the other horses of the Guard fall in behind. General Parmenio, who couldn't catch his horse, has to ride Xanthus at the back. Ha, that'll teach Xanthus to get above himself!

People are still cheering as we splash through the puddles and out of the city. They climb on walls and cling to statues to catch a glimpse of Alexander. They throw handfuls of tiny, wet spring flowers into our manes. Their clothes are soaked, but they don't seem to care. Alexander's legs grip my sides. Without my cloth, they feel hot and shivery against my coat. His excitement infects me in the same way it did back in Pella the first time he rode me, though he feels a lot more confident now.

"That showed old Parmenio, didn't it?" he shouts to Hephaestion between the rumbles of thunder. "Congratulations, gentlemen! We've successfully liberated Anatolia from Persian rule. Next, we ride for Egypt!"

12

TARSUS

SUMMER 333 B.C.

FAVORED BY THE GODS

The first part of our journey to Egypt lay through friendly territory, with plenty to eat and people who cheered us for liberating their land. The king was in such a confident mood, it made our whole herd happy from the officers down to our grooms. The Persian army didn't appear, and the men joked that King Darius was too scared to challenge us now that Alexander had proved he was favored by the gods.

Needless to say, General Parmenio wasn't convinced by Alexander's claim that Memnon would be no further threat to us. But I knew better, because I'd seen his ghost. And not long after Alexander dominated the Gordian Knot, news came that Memnon had died of his sickness, leaving his herd leaderless and frightened. Groom-gossip was full of it for a while. They could not decide whether:

> Memnon had gotten sick and died from the wound Alexander gave him during our night attack on Halicarnassus.
> Zeus had killed Memnon in answer to Alexander's prayers.

I don't see that it makes much difference. Dead is dead, horse or human. Besides, a much stranger thing happened the day Alexander cut the Gordian Knot.

He shook the world so powerfully, the veil between the living and the dead tore. Before the hole closed, a herd of female warriors rode through it and joined our army. The Greeks call them Amazons, and there are a lot of silly stories about them, such as that they live without men and are immortal. Though, if the first is true, it's just as well they never die, because without men they might have a hard time making more Amazon girl-fillies to replace the dead ones. Think about it!

Our grooms said, with little sniggers, that the Amazon queen had come to lie with King Alexander to make a strong girl-filly to lead their herd when she retired. I don't know if this was true. But when Charm saw the Amazons setting up their strange round tents at the edge of our camp, she grew very quiet.

"Do you think the Amazons really fight their own battles?" she asked Tydeos. "Alexander says they came to help Troy at the end of the *Iliad*, and they're supposed to be immortal. That can't be true, can it?"

Tydeos grunted. "Who knows? I never believed the Gordian Knot was magic until King Alexander cut it and made the world shake."

"That was just an earthquake, you dolt," Charm said. But she bit her lip and looked at the Amazon camp again. "Their horses look tough. People say they've got horns —"

"Forget them, Charm!" Tydeos said with a laugh. "We've got enough horses of our own to worry about. That roan mare's about to foal any day now, and we'll have to keep an eye on Bucephalas and Xanthus when the other mares come into season. The last thing we want is both of King Alexander's mounts getting injured in a stallion battle. When they get going, they're like Alexander and General Parmenio fighting over the command."

Charm was not really listening. "I wish Alexander wasn't the king," she said suddenly.

Tydeos gave her a startled look and began to laugh. "Oh, so *that's* it! And we all thought you came back for the horse!" He sobered. "It's not just you, Charm. King Alexander doesn't look at any woman, does he? I suppose he has other things to think about. That Amazon queen hasn't got a hope, either, if he's what she came for. Besides, it'd only end in tears, you know that. Alexander is King of Macedonia and Lord of Anatolia, and you're . . . a groom."

I don't know what he had been about to say, but Charm gave him a fierce look. "I did come back for Bucephalas," she said. "Of course I did. But Alexander's . . . oh, never mind."

Tydeos pushed one of her curls behind her ear. "I know," he said quietly. "King Alexander's like that, isn't he? He's not handsome like Hephaestion, and he's got a fierce temper on him. But no matter what he does, everyone seems to want to be near him. Maybe he really is the reborn Achilles. After what happened with the Gordian Knot, I wouldn't be surprised if he turned out to be the son of Zeus! If I were the Persian king, I'd take my army back home quick and keep running. All right now?"

Charm sniffed and smiled at him. "Yes, I expect you're right . . . that horsemaster was probably just trying to scare me, back in Halicarnassus. How could he know what the Persians are planning, anyway?"

Harpinna's colt was born black with white specks in its coat. It was healthy and strong and undoubtably MINE. (Remember when I broke my halter at Halicarnassus?) Charm named him Hoplite (foot soldier, remember?) because he had been born in the army.

She promised me that once we reached Egypt we'd be able to sail all the way back to Pella and give my poor legs a rest. She said I wouldn't have to fight in any more battles, because the Persians had obviously heard about Alexander cutting the Gordian Knot and gone home.

This only goes to show how little grooms know about dominating.

STILL HUMAN

General Parmenio thought the Persians might be planning to ambush us at the Cilician Gates, a pass through the mountains that was supposed to be so narrow only four men could walk through it abreast. Alexander told him not to worry, because Zeus would look after us just as he had finished off General Memnon. General Parmenio rolled his eyes and ordered the men to arm themselves and carry their shields.

Strangely, Alexander did not squeal at this. He felt a bit unsteady on my back. He kept wiping his forehead and running his hand down my neck, whispering, "Not far now, Bucephalas, I promise. When we get to Egypt, we can both have a rest."

The road got worse. Sharp stones lay in wait to bruise our hooves. The sun shimmered over the rocks. Mosquitoes bit us. There was not enough water. And it was HOT. We horses were dark with sweat the whole time. The men marched grimly, eyeing the high cliffs on both sides of us.

Something was definitely wrong with my rider. Beads of sweat glistened on his forehead, his cheeks were an unhealthy yellow, and he swayed over my shoulder.

But when Hephaestion suggested he should lie down in one of the baggage carts, he gripped my mane with sweaty hands and sat up straighter. "I'm not going to enter Tarsus in a mule cart! I'd never live it down. I'm the *king*, Hephaestion. I'm the reborn Achilles! I conquered the Gordian Knot. I can't be ill."

Since I carried him with extra care, Alexander managed to stay on my cloth until we reached the Cilician Gates. To keep General Parmenio quiet, he sent some men to check that there were no Persians hiding in the pass and asked Charm if she'd had any dreams about the place. When she said she hadn't, he wiped his brow and turned to General Parmenio with a smile.

"See, General? What did I tell you? There's nothing to fear. Zeus has made the pass safe for us."

The general muttered that we weren't through it yet, and the Persians were probably waiting for us on the other side. Alexander gave him a withering look. He said since the general seemed to be so scared, he himself would go first. Ignoring Hephaestion's whispered query after his health, he gathered up my reins and headed me into the pass.

He urged me into a trot and, as if to prove he wasn't ill, kept up the pace right through the Cilician Gates and all the way across the plain beyond with barely a pause to rest or eat. This was just as well, because someone had burned the crops on the other side. Our hooves raised a smoky cloud of ash that made our riders cough almost as much as Alexander.

The men defending Tarsus ran away when they saw us coming, and I made myself huge as we trotted through the city gates. But instead of parading through the streets as he usually did to show the citizens he was boss, Alexander galloped me straight for the river that flowed through the middle of the city. He leaped down from my back without waiting for me to stop, staggered a little, stripped off his armor, and threw himself head-first into the water.

I snorted at him in surprise. But he must have been as hot and thirsty as I was. I plunged my muzzle into the water and gulped without pausing for breath. The river was freezing. It chilled my stomach, but I didn't care. I could have drunk it dry.

"Alex!" Hephaestion cried as Petasios caught up. "What are you doing? That water's deep — *Alex!*"

The other horses saw me drinking and lunged toward the river as well, but their riders hauled up their heads. There was a lot of shouting and confusion as more of our men caught up. A curious crowd formed on the bank as Hephaestion dismounted and plunged into the river after Alexander.

I didn't realize what all the fuss was about, until I paused in my glorious drink and raised my head. Then I saw Alexander in midstream, white and shivering violently. He was thrashing and moaning like Harpinna when she gave birth to her foal.

By now, several of the Guard were in the water, swimming toward him. Hephaestion reached Alexander first and put an arm around his neck, lifting his face to the surface. The rest splashed across to help, and between them they dragged the unconscious king out onto the bank. Iolaus and some of the phalanx held their horses for them. No one dared try to catch me, though, and I got several more gulps of icy water before Charm finally rushed up and seized my reins.

"No, Bucephalas!" she scolded. "You're much too hot. You'll get a chill — *oh!*"

She had seen Alexander, lying motionless on the bank, surrounded by his friends. Hephaestion wrapped his cloak around him, and they lifted him onto the Achilles shield and carried him away.

Charm gave a funny little gasp and started to drag me after them. But Iolaus threw the tangle of reins at her and called as he ran after them, "Stay here, Groom, and look after the horses! I have to be with the king!"

I gave Xanthus flat ears. But I had a bellyache from the water, so my heart wasn't in it. Charm sorted out our reins, muttering to herself. "I *knew* he was ill! Oh, I hope he's all right! That water's so cold. He's such an idiot. Did he think Zeus was going to stop him from drowning? What are we all going to do if he dies?" She bit her lip and stared after Alexander.

Tydeos ran up, breathless, closely followed by our other grooms. Everyone was asking questions at once. They seemed to have forgotten we were hungry and thirsty and badly in need of a roll.

"Can't the king swim?" — "Is he sick?" — "Is he going to die?"
I could have told them the answers to all those questions:

No.

Yes.

Yes, of course, one day. *(You humans never ask the more helpful question: "When?")*

But they didn't think to ask me. They were too busy arguing about why the gods had let the king get ill. They said perhaps Zeus was angry with King Alexander for cutting the Gordian Knot instead of untying it. They said the Persians had tried to kill him by poisoning the river in Tarsus (which was silly, because no one else got sick from drinking the water). The only thing they could agree on was that King Darius's army must be nearby, because General Parmenio said the Persians had burned all the crops around Tarsus to stop our herd from using them for food.

Charm got very quiet when she heard this.

"Cheer up," Tydeos whispered. "At least if King Alexander dies, General Parmenio will take us all home."

Charm's hand clenched on my rein, and she shot him a fierce look. "You don't understand, do you? You don't understand *at all*!"

Later, Hephaestion emerged from the city and announced that since Alexander was favored by the gods we needn't worry because Zeus would make him better. But I knew my rider was suffering, because that night my bellyache got so bad, I lay down and rolled in the horse lines.

Tydeos rushed across to help Charm untangle me and get me to my feet. I was mad with pain for a while, so I don't remember how it happened, but in the morning she had a big, hoof-shaped bruise on her cheek. The horse doctor came and forced foul-tasting medicine down my throat. Then Charm led me around for the rest of the night, while the pain in my belly gradually eased.

CHARM VISITS THE AMAZONS

By the time the sun comes up, we are at the edge of the camp where the Amazons have pitched their round tents. The Amazons' horses are small and strong. They have blue circles painted on their necks and hindquarters and — yes, it's true! — little stubby horns in the middle of their foreheads. They throw their heads up as I get closer, and one or two squeal challenges at me. I am feeling a bit better, so I squeal back. A woman with braided hair, and wearing leather, is washing the circles off them. She has a deep scar across her cheek. When she sees me coming, she picks up an axe that was lying nearby.

Charm wrenches her gaze from the horses and halts me out of range, very tense. "You're the Amazon leader, aren't you?" she says.

The woman inclines her head. She isn't as young as Charm, but she is quite a bit taller than Alexander and as muscular as a man. "I am Queen Penthesilea, yes."

Charm bites her lip, eyeing the woman's scar. "I want to join you!" she blurts out. "I have a horse and a weapon. When are you going home?"

The Amazon queen frowns and says slowly, as if speaking Greek is difficult for her, "This is the first time we have been called from our land since the long war at Troy. When King Alexander cut the Gordian Knot, he opened the way. We must stay and fight for him until he opens the hole in the world again to release us." Her gaze sweeps over Charm, taking in her tangled curls, her dagger, and her grubby tunic. "You are one of King Alexander's grooms?"

Charm nods, still biting her lip. "My name's Charmeia. Please let me join you. I'm a woman, and I'm willing to fight."

Queen Penthesilea lowers the axe and gives her an amused look. "A woman, yes, just about. A fighter, I think not. You have never been in a battle, young Charmeia, I can tell."

Charm's lip trembles. "I have! I rode Bucephalas into battle at the river Granicus to save the king's life, when the mare he was riding got killed under him!"

Queen Penthesilea's frown returns. "This is King Alexander's famous horse?" She puts down her axe and rubs my forehead thoughtfully with her callused hand.

That is when I see her ghost is outside her body, rather than inside it like other people's. I give her flat ears and scrabble back in terror, but she takes my rein in her strong hand, unafraid. I try to bite her, but she laughs and knocks my muzzle away with her fist. Even in my weak state I could have dominated her easily, of course, but her ghost confuses me.

"Hmm, he certainly has spirit. And you ride him? Maybe you are more of a fighter than you look, young Charmeia. But I think we will be in a lot of trouble if we take King Alexander's horse and his groom away from him. He might try to follow us home."

"He won't invade your land," Charm says softly, glancing around to make sure none of the Macedonian sentries are close enough to hear. "He doesn't even know where it is, and he hasn't got time. He's taking the army to Egypt so he can ask the oracle about his father. General Parmenio says we've done most of what we came to do, liberating Anatolia, and there won't be another battle unless the Persians try to stop us. So, you see, King Alexander won't need you, and he won't need his horse, either."

Penthesilea gives Charm a narrow-eyed look. "Maybe. And maybe King Alexander sent you here to test us? Should I tell him we passed the test?"

"No! Don't tell him what I said, *please*!"

Charm sounds so frightened, the Amazon queen's expression softens. She lets go of my rein and steps out of range of my teeth.

"Take the king's horse back, Charmeia. I shall not tell. The Persians are going to try to stop Alexander, as I think you know very well. You have yet to see us in battle. You might change your mind about joining us, once you do. But when we go home, I will ask if you still want to come with us. It may not be possible to bring the horse. We do not harbor thieves." She looks at me pointedly.

Charm bows her head. "It doesn't matter about me. I only want Bucephalas to be safe, but I daren't run away with him on my own. Alexander would be furious and send his Guard after us. Also, there's a man hunting us — oh, you don't want to hear this! You're right, I could never join you. I'm too much of a coward! I'm sorry. I shouldn't have come." She vaults onto me and turns me back toward the horse lines, tears glistening in her eyes.

Queen Penthesilea puts a hand on Charm's knee and looks up into her face. "I do not think you are a coward, young Charmeia. Bravery is doing what scares you, and often fighting is not the most frightening thing. That is the first lesson an Amazon learns. I meant what I said. I will come to you before we leave. In the meantime, be very careful of King Alexander. The Gordian Knot is a test of kingship in more ways than one. Unraveling it would have required imagination, skill, and patience — three of the qualities a man needs to rule wisely. Alexander cut it with his sword. I do not know what that means for us, but men like Alexander do not have easy lives nor easy deaths, and neither do those who get too close to them."

WHICH PASS?

Alexander and his Guard remained in the city for three whole days, while General Parmenio took part of the army south to find out what the Persians were up to. The camp was gloomily quiet. Then, on the fourth morning, the gates opened, and a chariot rumbled out, drawn by two captured Persian horses.

The men at the edge of the camp started cheering, and everyone rushed out of their tent to see what was happening. Charm, who had been sitting on a pile of cloths oiling my bridle, jumped up onto the nearest cart to get a better view. She didn't seem to know whether to laugh or cry, and ended up doing both at once, which was a bit confusing.

"It's *him*!" someone shouted. "It's the *king*!"

By now the camp was so noisy you'd think we had just won a battle. Alexander's chariot drove slowly up and down the lines of tents to let everyone see him and stopped at the end of our horse line. The grooms hastily brushed off their tunics and tidied up our buckets. Charm fiddled with her mane and retied her scarf. I shivered all over as Alexander walked slowly toward me.

He smiled and opened his hand to reveal a honey cake. I licked his palm clean of crumbs and nudged him for more. Unusually, he staggered.

Hephaestion caught his elbow with a concerned look. "You shouldn't overdo it, Alex," he whispered.

Alexander shrugged off his friend and looked around for Charm. "How is the old horse, Charmides? I heard he had colic while I was sick."

Charm ducked her head to hide her bruise. "Yes, sir, but he's fine now." She chewed her lip. "Sir, is it true we're going to have to fight the Persian army before we get to Egypt? Maybe we could stay here and wait for them to go home? You shouldn't fight them until you're stronger, sir. Everyone thought you were going to die. . . ." Her voice trailed off.

Alexander gave Hephaestion an amused look. "What rumors have you been spreading about me?" He spread his arms and turned a circle. "As you can see, Charmides, I've never felt better! Do you think Zeus would let me die of a little chill after making me lord of all Anatolia? As for the Persians, General Parmenio's scouts say they're already on their way to meet us. So, you see, there's no question of anyone going home."

Charm glanced around in alarm, as if she expected the Persian army to appear there and then, and Alexander noticed the bruise on her cheek.

He lifted her curls away from her face and frowned. "Who did that to you? My father's old horsemaster hasn't been creeping around here, has he? Because if he has, I'll have him hunted down and punished. I'm getting very tired of him."

His tone had turned cold and dangerous. Hephaestion shook his head and tried to steer him back to the chariot. Alexander stood his ground.

"Charmides! I order you to tell me the truth."

She flushed. "Bucephalas kicked me, sir, when he was ill."

Alexander gave a sharp laugh and patted me again. "Oh, horse! Don't you dare kick my groom again, all right? It was careless of her to let you get sick, but I'm the one who gives out the punishments around here, and since she's made you well again I've decided to forgive her."

There was a big party that night to celebrate the king's recovery. The men feasted and ran races, while Alexander made sacrifices to Asclepius, the god of healing. His pavilion glimmered with torches, and the laughter and drinking continued all night, keeping us horses awake.

Our grooms got hold of some of the muleteers' magic drink and spent the night laying bets on which pass the Persian army would come through to meet us. There were only two choices, which ended up equal favorites because no one could agree:

The Syrian Gates
The Amanic Gates

Charm put her money on the Amanic Gates. Then she changed her mind and put it on the Syrian Gates. No prizes for guessing what sort of dream she had that night.

General Parmenio said the best thing we could do was wait for King Darius between the mountains and the sea, near a town called Issus (which we'd already dominated). He said the Persian army was bigger than ours, and at Issus we'd have less chance of being outflanked. If we went through one of the passes to meet them, we'd have to fight with the mountains at our back and enemy territory ahead. This would be bad for us, since the towns and villages in the south still supported the Persians and might send King Darius reinforcements.

For the first time ever, it looked as if Alexander was going to take General Parmenio's advice. But then Charm slipped away from the horse lines and ran off toward the king's pavilion. When she returned, she wore a determined little smile. Shortly afterward, Alexander announced that only the sick and the baggage train would stay camped at Issus. He then marched the rest of us fast down the coast to the Syrian Gates to lie in wait for the Persian army.

The plan is to attack them as they come through. They won't be able to make battle formation in the narrow pass, so we'll have the advantage, and King Darius will be history. Alexander seems very confident again. Even General Parmenio didn't squeal too much, since the latest reports from his scouts say that the Persians are indeed camped on the other side.

You should realize that this information is already half a day out of date, though. Only three of us know we came here on the strength of a dream: Charm, Alexander, and me. (And now you, of course.)

13

ISSUS

NOVEMBER 333 B.C.

CHARM'S MISTAKE

We made camp near the Syrian Gates but remained on full alert. The night had a prickly feel that made me tremble. My nerves were not helped by the fact that I was wearing my battle-cloth with the purple trim. Charm had my bridle ready to put on me at short notice. Alexander's javelins and spear waited beside it for her to pass up to him. The big shield of Achilles was propped nearby. Demetrius was going to carry it into battle to show that Alexander had the power of Achilles.

Alexander had sent scouts into the pass to keep watch for the Persians, and an expectant hush lay over the camp. Everyone listened for the trumpets that would signal the attack.

While we waited, Charm combed my mane. It didn't need combing, but her fingers felt nice so I didn't complain. Beside us, Tydeos fiddled with Petasios's girth. Petasios didn't think much of this and gave him flat ears and a little squeal.

Suddenly, Charm's comb stopped moving, and her fingers gripped my crest. "Do you think it's wrong to lie to save someone's life?" she said.

Tydeos gave her a puzzled look. "What do you mean?"

"Alexander wanted to know which pass the Persians will come through. It wasn't really a lie. I might have dreamed it wrong. These passes all look the same to me. It's hard to tell sometimes."

He saw her glance toward the Syrian Gates, and his eyes went wide.

"Are you saying what I think you're saying? Have you done something extremely stupid?"

She bit her lip and rested her forehead against my neck. "I only wanted to stop the battle," she said in a whisper. "If the Persian army goes through the other pass, then they'll miss us. We can carry on through the Syrian Gates and get to Egypt without having to fight them."

There was a silence — not even the sound of horses munching hay, because we hadn't been fed in case we had to gallop after the Persians. Charm lifted her face from my neck and looked at Tydeos with pleading eyes.

"Oh, Zeus," Tydeos whispered, glancing around to check that no one else had heard. "Do you mean you dreamed of them going through the *Amanic Gates*?"

Charm nodded miserably, and Tydeos paled.

"You little *idiot*! What do you think King Darius is going to do when he discovers he's gotten behind us? Do you think he'll just lead the Persians north on through the Cilician Gates and into Anatolia, leaving his enemies in the mountains? Do you really think King Alexander is going to just ride on toward Egypt without a fight? He's been looking forward to meeting the Persian king in battle for years! Probably ever since the day he jumped onto Bucephalas's back when he was twelve years old!"

His voice rose. Some of the grooms glanced our way. Tydeos put an arm around Charm and steered her away from the horse lines, whispering fiercely.

I wanted Charm to come back and continue combing my mane. Thunder rumbled over the mountains. Our grooms glanced up nervously. Xanthus shifted his big golden hindquarters sideways into Arion, and the two of them started a kicking match. I squealed at Xanthus to tell him to behave, but it made no difference. We were all far too tense.

A MESSAGE FROM KING DARIUS

The storm hits us in the night, and rain comes down so hard and violently that rivers of mud flow through the camp. Several tents are washed away. The men splash after their belongings, shouting and swearing. Charm and Tydeos and the other grooms have their work cut out rescuing our tack and fodder and our riders' weapons from the flood. We horses hate every moment of it. My quilted battle-cloth soon becomes sodden and clings to me as heavily as the horsemaster did on my first day in Pella. It makes my back so cold, I start to shiver. Thankfully, Charm notices this and takes off my cloth to wring it out.

The other grooms are following her example, when urgent shouts and trumpet blasts come from the side of the camp farthest from the pass. The dogs go crazy, barking and whining in a horrible way that makes my hair stand on end. The men look up from their rescue work in alarm.

They are right to be worried. The sky is paling behind the clouds, and dawn is a favorite time to attack an enemy camp.

The officers yell orders. The men strap on their armor and grab their weapons. The grooms hastily put our wet cloths back on us and tighten our girths. Charm gives Tydeos a wild-eyed look.

"Don't just stand there, then!" says Tydeos. "Your dream about the Amanic Gates must have come true. The Persians are going to attack us from behind, just like I said they would! I wouldn't want to be in your sandals when the king gets down here."

Charm shakes her head, very pale. "They can't have had time to go through the Amanic Gates and bring their army all the way up here after us. It can't be them . . . it *can't!*" But she is breathing hard, and I can feel the fear coming off her in waves.

She tries to put my cloth back on me, but it's still wet and even colder than before. Her hands are trembling, which makes me nervous, too. I give her flat ears and rear up to tell her I don't want it on my back yet. She ducks to avoid my hooves, and my cloth drops into the muddy stream running past the horse lines. Charm picks it up and says a bad word she learned from the muleteers.

Into this chaos strides Alexander, followed by an alarmed Hephaestion. The king's face is flushed with anger. He is dragging a man with him by the elbow.

I come down to earth and snort as I recognize the man's smell. It brings memories of the mule stable back in Pella, for it is the old mulemaster who helped Charm on her first day. We left him with the baggage train and the mares and foals at the camp in Issus. Blood is running from a cut on his head, and his face is blank with shock. There is something wrong with his hands. His arms end too early, and the stumps of his wrists are covered in a sticky black mess that smells horrible.

One of the younger grooms gives a strangled gasp and is sick in the mud. Alexander lifts the mulemaster's arm and waves the blackened stump at Charm. "See this?" he shouts in his shrill voice. "See? This poor man has just ridden all the way from Issus without his *hands*. King Darius took his army through the Amanic Gates in the night and attacked our base camp. He cut the hands off anyone strong enough to sit on a mule and sent them up here as a warning to me. He murdered the ones who couldn't ride. All my sick and wounded, butchered by the Persians! Now tell me again, Charmides, which pass the Persians were going to come through in the night?"

All the blood has drained from Charm's face. My cloth slips from her hands. She stares at the mulemaster's blackened stumps in horror. "I'm sorry," she whispers. "Oh . . . I'm *sorry*."

It's not clear whether she's apologizing to the king or to the mulemaster. But Alexander assumes her words are for him and in an icy voice he says, "You will be!"

"Alex, for Zeus's sake!" Hephaestion hisses, glancing at Charm's white face. "It was only a *dream*! Your official seer gets it wrong all the time. How was your groom to know? I thought we came up here because of General Parmenio's intelligence reports, not because of some silly dream. Let the poor man go to the blood tent with the others. Maybe the doctors can do something for him."

"Stick his hands back on, maybe?" Alexander shoves the mulemaster roughly away from him. "This man's useless to me now! How can he look after mules with no hands? I should have left my groom in the base camp instead."

Charm shudders but says nothing. I can see Tydeos out of the corner of my eye, standing nearby with his fists clenched. The other grooms are too afraid to say anything. We horses are upset by the king's anger and tug at our halters as we dance around in our lines.

"General Parmenio's coming," Hephaestion warns in a low voice, and Alexander shakes himself like a wet horse.

"Get out of my sight!" he yells at Charm. "Report to the garrison kitchen in Tarsus, and don't let me see you near my horses again. Think yourself lucky I haven't time now to deal with you as you deserve. You, Tydeos, or whatever your name is! Get that cloth back on my horse and get him ready for battle."

Charm sucks in her breath and flings herself at Alexander's feet. "Please, Your Majesty!" she gasps. "*Please* don't send me away! Punish me, whip me, anything! But let me stay and look after Bucephalas! He needs me."

Alexander's face twists as he looks down at her. "If you're here when I get back, being a girl won't save you. For the last time, *go!*"

"No. . ." Charm is sobbing now. "You don't understand, you can't send me away . . . *please.*" Alexander gives her tears a peculiar look, orders Hephaestion to make sure she leaves, and strides off to meet General Parmenio.

As the general and the young king approach each other, they both make themselves huge. This is a certain sign there will be a battle for the herd. But when General Parmenio says, "If we had waited at Issus as I advised, this wouldn't have happened —" Alexander shoulders him aside.

"Assemble the men, General!" he orders as he strides past. "I want to talk to them. We can't change what's happened, but King Darius is going to pay for what he did to my people. Tomorrow, Persian blood will run as deep as the floodwater Zeus sent down on our camp last night." His tone is chilling. His fists clench, and energy flickers around him. When he glares back down the slope, he looks twice as frightening as he did on the day we dominated Thebes. "I swear it on my father's name."

Charm went, as ordered. I don't know where. Tydeos stayed long enough to put my cloth back on, then followed her. Meanwhile, the damp tents were packed and the men assembled on the mountainside. Alexander stood on a rock above them, wearing his reinforced Troy helmet with the white plumes, and talked.

He said a lot of things about glory and honor in his loud, shrill voice. We horses soon got bored and nosed around in the mud for something to eat. But the men, who had been badly frightened by the mutilated captives King Darius had sent them, stopped muttering, stood up straighter, and gripped their weapons with fresh determination. When the king finally finished, they cheered wildly.

When Alexander came to mount me, there was still no sign of Tydeos or Charm, so he had to bridle me himself. He vaulted onto my back without a word, and we took our usual place at the front of the army.

At midnight, we saw the Persian fires glittering like stars below us. They filled the whole valley where we'd left Harpinna with little Hoplite and the baggage train. I flared my nostrils, but we were too far away to smell my mare.

Alexander rode on ahead with Hephaestion, halted me at the edge of the cliff, and squinted at the Persian camp. He was silent for a long while. Then he said, "Those poor men they sent back to us weren't exaggerating, my friend. I think they outnumber us, but not by much. It could be worse, but I must make the proper sacrifices tonight. We're going to need Zeus on our side tomorrow."

Hephaestion reined in Petasios beside me. He said softly, "Are you sure it was wise to dismiss your groom back there, Alex? The other grooms are all scared of Bucephalas, you know that."

Alexander frowned. "The last thing I need to worry about right now is who's going to look after my horse! Ask me again after we've beaten the Persians. Won't do the stupid girl any harm to spend a night in the hills. She'll soon come running back to us for protection when she sees King Darius's army down there."

When we rejoined the others, Tydeos still hadn't turned up, so Alexander removed my cloth and settled me himself. Then he vanished into the night with Hephaestion to make his sacrifices. No one noticed that the king didn't know the proper order for the horse lines and had tethered me next to Xanthus, instead of in my usual spot between Petasios and Borealis.

SPIES AND ASSASSINS

Our grooms are all curled up in their cloaks, asleep. The men sit in groups, talking quietly as they sharpen their swords and spearheads. There is the sound of happy munching in the horse lines. All the other horses have hay soaked in honeyed water, our usual last meal before a battle. But Petasios and I are hungry, because no one has thought to give us any.

I reach my nose across to take some of Xanthus's hay. He gives me flat ears and a brazen squeal. I give him flat ears and a squeal back, then snatch a mouthful anyway. I'm the boss, and he ought to let me have it. But the big fool goes up in the air, breaks his tether, and comes at me with bared teeth. So I break my tether, too, and fasten my teeth in his neck.

Xanthus shrieks. The grooms wake up but dare not come near my hooves and teeth. Some of the men run across and try to separate us by swinging their long pikes at our heads. It's like being back in the battle that half-blinded me, and I wheel away in panic. I have no rider to guide me, and no one around me smells familiar. Some of the grooms, arms outstretched, make a halfhearted attempt to block my way. But when I bare my teeth and gallop at them, they jump aside. Their shouts fade as I flee into the night.

By the time the ghosts stop chasing me, I am surrounded by black rocks. I slow to a trot and snort to clear my nose. One of my forelegs has a little nick from a sharp stone. I am high in the mountains, and the sky is paling over the mountaintops. I suck in the cool air and send a ringing whinny to my friends.

Very faintly, off to my right, a strange horse replies.

I sniff the ground, searching for familiar smells. But our army has not come this way. The strange horses have left dung, which I pause to dominate, and mixed with the smell of their herd is a familiar scent . . . CHARM! I whinny again, this time with joy, and set off at a trot with my nose to the ground and my broken halter lead trailing, following her spring-grass scent.

I find the herd of strangers hiding in a canyon. There must be a hundred of them, small with dainty hooves like the ones we dominated at the Granicus. They are carrying riders dressed in trousers with yellow scarves wrapped around spiked helmets. Tassels dangle from their bridles and cloths. Some of the men in the center of the herd have dismounted. One of them is holding a small human by the arm. I can't see her, but I catch another whiff of Charm's spring-grass smell. It's sharp with fear.

I whinny in delight and canter toward them.

The men look around in alarm and draw their long, curved swords. They smile when they see I am alone, and call out to their boss in a strange tongue. One of them rides up to me and tries to catch my halter lead. I squeal at his horse, give its rider flat ears, and barge through the herd to reach my groom.

Her face lights up. *"Bucephalas!"*

I open my mouth and charge the man holding her. His horse spins around, dragging the reins from his arm. I fasten my teeth in his wrist. He lets go of Charm with a startled yell, and she runs to me, grabs my mane, and makes a leap for my back.

She doesn't make it. I am still acting wild, because the strangers have surrounded us. They laugh at their boss and call to one another to catch me. Charm cowers by my shoulder and points her wavering dagger at the men.

"Stay away from me!" she says in a shrill, scared voice. "Or King Alexander will come up here and kill you all!"

The Persians laugh. Their boss calms his horse and says in good Greek, "I don't think so. We have your young Alexander exactly where we want him, trapped between our army and the mountains. Now be sensible, girl. Tell us his plans, and maybe we'll let you go back to him alive."

Charm shakes her head. "I wouldn't tell you anything, even if I knew! But I know he's going to make your horrid King Darius pay for chopping off our men's hands."

The Persian boss eyes her dagger and my snapping teeth. He says something to his herd in his own language and smiles at Charm. "We don't anticipate much trouble chasing your men back home. But if King Alexander has more women and horses in his army who fight like you two, maybe Great King Darius ought to be more worried!"

"King Darius should be *very* worried," calls a strong voice behind us. "Let the girl go. She is King Alexander's personal groom. If you harm a hair on her head, he will pursue you to the ends of the earth."

The Persians stop laughing at Charm and me and whirl in alarm to face this new threat. Charm gives a cry of relief.

"Queen Penthesilea!"

I smell the Amazon horses and whinny to them. They remember me and whinny back. In the dawn light, ghostly blue circles show on their coats, and their little horns glint. The Amazons have daubed their own cheeks with blood. Their hair is braided tightly, and their war axes rest across their knees. Bows and quivers full of arrows are slung over their shoulders.

The Persians stare in amazement at the Amazon herd.

The Persian boss smiles widely. "So, there *are* more of you! The Macedonian army is led by a boy, lets girls groom its horses, and sends women to fight its battles. . . . On second thought, Great King Darius doesn't have much to worry about, after all. But thank you for telling us who this girl is, warrior woman. We'd hoped simply for information. Now, perhaps, your king will negotiate a ransom for his pretty groom?"

With a wild warbling cry, Penthesilea sets her horse into a gallop, whirling her axe over her head. The other Amazons charge, too, and there are thuds and cries as they battle with the Persian herd. A spray of blood hits me on my blind side, and a ghost ripples into the dawn. The men who were still on foot leap onto their horses. One of them tries to grab Charm and pull her up in front of him. She grips her dagger in a tight fist and stabs him in the leg. I bite his horse on the neck, and it wheels away in terror.

A space opens around us. Charm finally struggles up onto my back, grabs my trailing halter lead, and drags my head around.

"Go with the others, Charmeia!" Queen Penthesilea shouts, axing another Persian.

Amazon horses surround me, and we are galloping again. It is very exciting. I charge through them, giving them flat ears. By the time we reach the rocks the queen had indicated, Charm and I are in the lead where we belong.

We pull up, dancing and snorting. There is still a lot of yelling behind us. Most of the Amazon herd stayed with their queen to fight the Persians. The ones who came with us stand guard around me, alert. Charm slides off my back and collapses in a little heap at my feet. I lower my head and snort into her mane. She is shaking all over. I graze a few stalks around her legs, and gradually she becomes calmer.

The sun rises, bringing color to the mountains, before the rest of the Amazon herd joins us. Persian ghosts are still whirling away. But none of the Amazon ghosts have left their bodies, because they are already on the outside. The scar on Queen Penthesilea's cheek pulses purple, and her face is spattered with blood. Her axe drips.

"Spies and assassins!" She spits on the rocks. "King Darius sent them to raid the Macedonian camp for the king's horse and ordered them to block the Syrian Gates in case King Alexander tried to retreat through them. I think they do not know King Alexander very well. They certainly did not expect to meet us!"

She hands the reins of her horse to one of her herd and kneels beside Charm. She's within reach of my teeth but I back away, disturbed by her inside-out ghost.

She puts her arms around Charm and holds her tightly. "They have gone," she murmurs. "You are safe now."

Charm bursts into tears.

Queen Penthesilea holds her until she stops crying. She pushes a curl out of Charm's eye, sighs, and says, "You have bloodied your weapon. You must wear the Amazon mark now." She wipes her finger through the wet blood on the blade of her axe and draws a red circle on Charm's cheek. "There! You are now a warrior!"

The other Amazons smile and give a cheer.

But Charm struggles to her feet and smudges the mark with her palm. She shakes her head. "I'm not a warrior! I could never kill anyone like you did just now. I felt sick when I stabbed that Persian . . . but I didn't have any choice. Oh, Queen Penthesilea, I was so *scared*. I thought they were going to chop off my hands, like they did to the poor mulemaster! But then Bucephalas came." She looks at me in wonder and whispers, "He came to find me."

The Amazon queen gives her a steady look. "You didn't steal him, then? You weren't running away?"

"No!" Charm's eyes go wide. "King Alexander *sent* me away. I was following the army, hiding in the rocks. That's when the Persians found me, and then Bucephalas . . ." She stares up at the sky. "It's morning! I have to get him back to the king before the battle! But he said he never wants to see me near his horse again. Queen Penthesilea, what am I going to do?"

The queen looks at my broken halter rope. She nods. "I believe you, and I think King Alexander will have to reconsider. I think you share the horse bond with Bucephalas as strongly as your king does, though I have never seen it work between a horse and two humans before — no wonder there is such power when the three of you are together! Those Persian spies could have done a lot of damage if they had captured you both. But it is too late. King Alexander has already begun his battle formation. He sent us up here because the scouts reported seeing Persian troops behind his line."

Charm stares at her in horror. "But he has to be properly mounted when he meets King Darius! He told me so himself." Then she looks at me, and her face relaxes as she realizes I am going to miss the battle, after all. "Who's he riding?"

Queen Penthesilea smiles. "Let us go and see, shall we, young Charmeia?"

GHOSTS AND RUMORS

Charm rides me at the front of the Amazon herd next to Queen Penthesilea's horse with its blue circles. As we descend through the clouds into the valley where the Persian fires burned last night, a great noise rises to meet us — war cries, shouts, screams, and the frightened neighs of horses. We flick our ears back and forth and flare our nostrils. We can smell the blood. Then a trumpet echoes from the mountainsides, and the sound makes me shiver all over. Charm winds her fingers into my mane and tightens my halter lead.

"Steady, Bucephalas," she whispers. "Steady."

Queen Penthesilea gives me a sideways look. "I think this is close enough. We shall wait here."

"No," Charm says, gripping my mane tighter. "I can manage him. I have to see Alexander. I have to see if he's . . . winning."

The Amazon queen looks hard at her, then dismounts with a sigh and takes the bridle off her own horse. "Swap!" she orders, handing it to Charm. "I am not going to be responsible for losing you on the battlefield because I let you ride Bucephalas in a halter."

I don't like the Amazon bit because it tastes of strange horse. But Queen Penthesilea pulls my ear, and between them they get the bridle on me. Charm remounts, and we follow a gully with a stream running down it. The rocks block our view of the battle. But I can smell that my herd went this way and take hold of the strange bit impatiently. I should be at the front, not the back. I wish Charm would let me gallop.

Finally, we emerge onto a plateau near the coast and see the battle below us. It looks like the usual chaos. In the center, our phalanx is struggling against the Persian line. Our cavalry seems to be mixed in with the enemy, and there is a thick knot of fighting around the Persian chariots. Dead and dying men and horses lie everywhere, their ghosts escaping through the dust. Down by the beach, there is more fierce fighting.

"Where's Alexander?" says Charm, frantically searching the field. "Can anyone see the king? Are we winning?"

Penthesilea smiles. "Looks like it. The Persians are running away. See?" She points to the mountains, where small groups of men in yellow scarves are fleeing for their lives.

"But where's the *king*?" Charm looks at the knot of men and horses around the chariots. "I can't see him. He might have been killed!"

"Not a chance!" Penthesilea says, giving her a frown. "If King Alexander were dead, the Macedonians would have stopped fighting. Come. I think we can risk going down now."

As we get closer to the valley floor, a herd of blood-spattered Persians run up the slope toward us, looking over their shoulders. They don't notice us until we are upon them. The Amazons cut them down with their axes, and their ghosts ripple past us. Charm grips my mane and watches with a sick expression. Farther down, bodies fill the gullies. I have to tread carefully to avoid stepping on them. Loose horses join us. I give them flat ears and send them to the back so they are not in the way. None of them put up a fight. They have all lost their riders, so they are ashamed.

At the river, we find a detachment of Macedonians with their long pikes, weary but grinning. They are standing on a makeshift bridge. In the dusk, it takes me a moment to realize the bridge is made of Persian dead. Nearby, a horse lies in the water, spears sticking out of it. We snort sadly as we pass it.

Queen Penthesilea questions the men about Alexander's whereabouts. But they don't seem to know much more than we do.

"Last I saw, he was leadin' the charge on King Darius's royal guard," says one. "He's probably still up by the chariots."

"Nah, he went to help General Parmenio down by the beach."

"Don't be stupid! He was right here in the center, didn't you see? Cut down a hundred Persians before my very eyes!"

"Zeus was looking after him, all right. I saw lightnin' flashing around his head."

"That was when *you* got hit on the head, you fool! Look sharp! Here come more Persian deserters!"

Without seeing us, the Persians jump down a little cliff on the far side of the river only to find themselves trapped. Our men's long pikes soon release their ghosts, and the Amazons catch those who try to flee. I dance impatiently, trying to reach the enemy with my teeth and hooves as I have been trained to do. But the Amazon horses are in the way, and Charm holds me on a tight rein, flinching whenever another Persian dies.

"I reckon King Alexander must've killed King Darius," another Macedonian says, once they have finished off the Persians. "That's why they're all runnin' away, ain't it?"

"Yeah, I heard they had a duel, just like Achilles and Prince Hector did in the *Iliad*. King Darius wounded King Alexander, but King Alexander struggled up again and killed him."

Charm gives a little gasp.

"Nonsense!" says their officer, arriving on a mare covered in grime from the river. He gives me and Charm a frown, as if he thinks he should know us. I know who he is at once, because it's Zephyr under all that mud, who — if you remember — carries General Parmenio's son, Philotas. The little mare whinnies a weary greeting. I nicker to her in sympathy, because I can see she's had a hard battle.

"Alexander's gone chasing after King Darius," Philotas says. "The Persian coward left his chariot behind, jumped on a fresh horse, and fled into the hills. He abandoned his men, that's why they're running. We're to mop up here and meet the king at the Persian camp when he decides to return. Watch out in the dark for more deserters. They're sneaky fellows."

Queen Penthesilea nods and turns her horse. But Charm drags my head around and urges me after Zephyr. "Which horse is the king riding?"

Philotas gives her an irritated look. "How would I know? That big chestnut with a scar on its head, I think. Stupid grooms let his precious Bucephalas run off into the hills last night. The king wasn't too happy, I can tell you, especially after that business with the severed hands. Never seen him in such a mood as when he marched us all down here. I swear we could all feel his fury rippling right along the line. I wouldn't want to be in King Darius's slippers when Alexander catches up with him, that's for sure!" He drags Zephyr's head around and shouts at his men, who are leaning on their pikes discussing the battle. "Get moving, you lot! The sooner we finish up here, the sooner you can all get your hands on some Persian loot and start celebrating."

He still doesn't recognize me. I suppose I'm not looking my best. No one's groomed me since the Syrian Gates, and I'm wearing a scruffy Amazon bridle. Charm looks a bit like an Amazon, too, since the queen painted blood on her cheek.

"Xanthus!" she whispers to the queen, relieved. "He'll be all right on Xanthus — he's almost as big as Bucephalas."

Sometimes, I think my groom understands nothing at all.

ZOROASTER

The Persian camp was almost as chaotic as the battlefield. Blood-spattered Macedonians were raiding the tents and piling gold and jewels into great heaps that glittered in the firelight. They also found some Persian women, who screamed as our men invaded their tents. Some ran across our path, their dresses torn and their long manes flying. The Amazons gave them grim looks but did nothing to help. "Do not think about it," Queen Penthesilea advised Charm, when she opened her mouth to protest. "It is war. At least they will stay alive. King Alexander is sensible not to bring women with his army."

"What about us?" Charm whispered.

We passed an enormous pavilion, even fancier than King Alexander's. Macedonian guards stood with crossed pikes at the entrance, and soft weeping came from inside it. More guards stood around a huge chariot of gold, its shaft and footplate carved with pictures of monsters. Its wheel hubs glittered with huge red jewels. Queen Penthesilea rode across for a closer look, but a Macedonian pike blocked her way.

"Keep away!" the man shouted. "This is King Darius's tent. No one's to touch anything of his until King Alexander gets here!"

We found our grooms setting up the horse lines. I smelled Harpinna and whinnied in delight. Little Hoplite bounded out, tail flicking, to greet us. The lines were not yet full. The horses who had been in the battle were tired and sweaty, and some had wounds that their grooms were sponging clean. I couldn't smell any of the horses of the Guard and started to worry. But as we neared the lines, Tydeos came running toward us, grinning.

"You found Bucephalas!"

Queen Penthesilea smiled and tactfully led her herd away to find a space for the Amazon camp, while Charm slid down from my back and threw herself into Tydeos's arms.

"Where were you?" he said, embarrassed but smiling in a funny way. "I looked all over for you! We thought the Persians had captured you."

"They nearly did! But Bucephalas saved me, and then the Amazons came and killed the Persians who'd grabbed me. . . . I know Alexander will be furious when he finds me here, but I had to bring Bucephalas back. · Is he in the camp?" She stared around nervously.

But Tydeos shook his head. "Not yet. He's still off chasing King Darius. Come and have something to eat. The Persians have left enough food and treasure to feed and clothe all Macedonia and half of Greece for a hundred years!" He pushed Charm's mane behind her ear and touched the smudged circle of blood on her cheek. "Don't worry, we'll hide you when he comes back. No one will tell on you. It wasn't fair, what he said to you, even if you did lie to him about your dream. He's the king. It was his decision to take the army to the Syrian Gates, not yours. Come on, cheer up! We've found the most incredible horse. . . ."

I have already smelled him. He is tethered at the end of our horse line near my usual spot. He is white all over and nearly as big as me, though he is fat and soft, not hard and muscular like we warhorses. His mane has been braided with silver threads, and his tail has little bells in it that tinkle whenever he flicks away a fly.

He smells of flowers, and he looks ridiculous.

I make myself huge and squeal at him. Charm gives a little gasp and tugs on my rein. "No, Bucephalas — not another battle, please!"

But the white horse doesn't squeal back. He simply turns his big dark eyes on us, pricks his ears, and stares at me. Then he gives a big sigh and goes back to his hay.

This is MOST confusing! It is a male horse, but it acts more like a mare.

"It's supposed to be sacred to the sun," Tydeos whispers. "Part of King Darius's divine power or something. The Persian captives say he's never carried anyone on his back. But he'll have to learn. He's King Alexander's now!"

Charm strokes my nose. "Don't worry, Bucephalas. Alexander still loves you the most." But she is interested in the white horse, I can tell. All the time, as she settles and rubs me down, she's looking at it. "So gentle," she murmurs eventually. "I wonder why Bucephalas didn't fight? It's not like him."

Tydeos laughs. "You don't want to know the details. The Persians have taken his spirit away and given it to their god. It means he'll never be able to get a mare in foal. They do the same thing to their male slaves, apparently — and they call *us* barbarians!"

Charm stares at the white horse. "Oh, poor horse . . . I thought that was just a Scythian thing? And to think the old horsemaster tried to make Bucephalas fat and soft like that! What's his name?"

"We've called him Zoroaster, after the Persians' holy prophet."

So THAT is what happens to a horse after the Scythian thing? You get to wear ridiculous silver bells, go fat and soft, and lose interest in fighting.

It must be worse than a spiked bit, after all.

FORGIVENESS

Alexander did not catch the Persian king that night.

The horses of the Guard came back around midnight, their heads low and their coats caked in dried sweat and grime. Too tired to whinny, Petasios and Borealis blew at me as Tydeos tethered them beside me. Aura lay down immediately once her cloth was removed. Arion, Hades, and Apollo walked past the new horse without even noticing it and drank noisily from the buckets of water the grooms brought them from the river.

Xanthus, who had been carrying Alexander, was in the worst state of all. He limped to the horse lines, snorting with pain, and barely looked at me as he passed my swishing tail. He had a deep spear wound in his neck and dried blood all down his shoulder. I gave him a little squeal to let him know what I thought of him for challenging me in the hills earlier. But afterward, I sent him a low whinny of sympathy to show I had forgiven him.

I know what it is like after a big battle, when the excitement has worn off and you start to feel the pain of your wounds. Alexander would have caught King Darius easily if he had been riding ME, of course. But you can't blame Xanthus for being a bit slow.

Charm and Tydeos worked in silence until all the horses were watered, doctored, clean, fed, and settled. This took them the rest of the night, so Charm was dirty and tired by the time Alexander came to see us.

This time, he didn't come unannounced. Trumpets sounded, and the big golden chariot we had seen last night rumbled through the piles of Persian treasure glittering in the sunrise. Alexander stood in it, wearing a long purple cloak trimmed with gold. His mane had been freshly washed and was caught in a golden crown. Hephaestion drove the two Persian horses at a slow trot so all the men could cheer their king. Sitting in the chariot behind Alexander was a small man-colt with a long black mane, holding a wriggling puppy in his arms.

Charm wiped her hands on her filthy tunic and stood stiffly beside me. Tydeos squeezed her arm and stood between her and the chariot.

Alexander called for Hephaestion to stop. He took a good look at me, then turned his attention to Charm. "I see you caught Bucephalas," he called. "Come here."

Tydeos stiffened, but Charm took a deep breath and walked bravely up to the chariot, where she bowed her head.

Alexander looked down at her matted curls and her ragged scarf. He sighed and jumped down — rather stiffly — from the platform. His cloak billowed, and I saw he had a bandage around his thigh. Charm saw it, too, and her eyes flickered from the bandage to his face.

"It's nothing." Alexander waved a hand. "King Darius pricked me with his dagger, that's all. Here, Ochus!" He pulled the man-colt to the side of the chariot and pointed to me. "See that horse? He's not as friendly as my dog. You can play with Perita, but you're not to go near Bucephalas. Understand? Dangerous horse. Dangerous!"

He bared his teeth and mimed flat ears with his hands. The man-colt smiled. His eyes were black and curious. Alexander ruffled the man-colt's mane and sighed. "The boy doesn't understand a word, of course, but he'll soon learn Greek. Look out for him, Charmides. Don't let Bucephalas hurt him. He's a valuable hostage."

I didn't know what a hostage was, but it couldn't have been too bad because Ochus was happily playing with the puppy Perita in the chariot. They were having a tug-of-war with one of the silly tassels the Persian horses wear on their bridles. Perita was winning. Alexander smelled faintly of flowers, but it didn't hide his familiar sherbet sweetness when he ran his hand down my nose. He had a stale honey cake in his pocket. I licked the crumbs greedily from his palm, and he smiled again.

"Ah, Bucephalas, I missed you yesterday! Why did you have to run off like that? I wouldn't *really* dismiss your groom, you know."

Charm, who was hovering near me, sucked in her breath and gave the king a flash of her eye. "Aren't you angry with me for coming back, sir?"

Alexander laughed. "Angry? When you brought my Bucephalas back to me? How could anyone possibly be angry today? We won, didn't we?" His eyes shone. He patted my neck with a firm hand and spun around, arms spread wide, purple cloak flying. "Look at all this treasure! I bathed in King Darius's golden tub last night and ate off a golden plate. And this isn't even half of it. The main Persian baggage train is still in Damascus — I've sent General Parmenio on ahead to collect it. King Darius has fled back to Persia. There's no one to stop me from marching straight down the coast to Egypt. But I can't have my horse undressed, and my groom looking like a muleteer when we get there. This is for Bucephalas to wear on the march." He lifted a tasseled cloth out of the chariot and dumped it into Charm's arms. He hesitated, glanced at Hephaestion, then pulled from his pocket a length of purple silk embroidered with gold thread and draped it around her neck with a man-coltish grin. "And this scarf is for your hair! When you've cleaned yourself up, get Bucephalas ready for parade — we've a military funeral to take care of before we leave."

Charm's cheeks flared red. Before she could speak, Alexander climbed back into his chariot and ordered Hephaestion to drive him around the rest of the camp.

This was how we dominated the Persians at Issus:

Persian dead: 2,000

Macedonian dead: 450

Horses dead: 150 (VERY sad, but pulling a chariot is like being tethered in a battle so the poor Persian horses didn't stand a chance.)

Hostages: King Darius's mother, wife, two daughters, his son Ochus; and Persian-slipper-licking Memnon's wife, Lady Barsine

Before we left, Alexander renamed a little harbor town at the mouth of the river, Alexandretta. I assume that means we have stopped liberating and started dominating again. Ha!

14

PHOENICIA

333–332 B.C.

SQUEALING AT TYRE

With me prancing at the front of the battle-hardened army, wearing my new tasseled cloth and carrying Alexander in his white-plumed Troy helmet, we made a fine sight as we marched down the Phoenician coast. More mercenaries joined us, attracted (as you humans are) by the gold Alexander had captured from the Persians, so we were a big herd. News of our victory at Issus traveled ahead of us, and we dominated lots of towns without a fight:

Gabala, Paltos, Aradus, Marathus, Mariamne, Tripolis, Byblos, Sidon.

Since they all submitted quickly and brought gifts of golden crowns to Alexander, he let them keep their silly names. But he left a Macedonian garrison on the coast in case any of them changed their minds later. He called this new town Alexandria, which I'm sure you'll agree is a better name than Alexandropolis or Alexandretta. I didn't fight in the battle at Issus so I'm not *too* upset he didn't name it after me. At least he didn't name it after Xanthus.

We ignored King Darius's squeals that we go home (which he sent on flattened grass because he was still licking his wounds after the battle), and everything went well until we reached a place called Tyre, which made the mistake of closing its gates against us.

Tyre stands on an island off the Phoenician shore. It has high, rocky walls and several harbors crammed with warships. No one can get into the city without swimming or going on a ship. If this city were a horse, it would be Borealis — strong and steady, but not big enough to challenge the boss. If only someone had told them.

We horses stop on the beach and snort at the sea. The channel between the mainland and the island looks deep, and crests of white foam dance along it. The wind smells of salt.

At first, everything seems fine. Men row a boat across from the city, bringing the usual gold crown. Alexander smiles as he leans down from my back to accept the gift. I give the fat man who hands it up to him flat ears to warn him not to touch the king, and he retreats hurriedly.

"The city of Tyre congratulates King Alexander on his victory at Issus," announces the fat man in an important-sounding voice. "And begs that he accept an additional gift of provisions for his army, so that his men will not go hungry as they pass through our lands on their way to Egypt. Tyre will not oppose you. You may continue your march."

Alexander looks up from examining the glittering stars on the crown and frowns. "I may continue my march? That's generous of you."

His words are very quiet. The Tyrian envoys do not realize what a dangerous sign this is and smile in relief.

"We'll send them over to you at once so you won't need to linger here," says the fat man, still smiling. "Fresh supplies just in from Carthage, plenty of grain for your horses." He eyes me. "Your royal charger looks as if he has a good appetite."

I give a little squeal and shake my head at him. Alexander steadies me and passes the crown to Hephaestion.

He narrows his eyes at the fat Tyrian and says in the same dangerously quiet voice, "And why do you assume we want to continue our march so soon? My men are weary, my horses need rest, and I would like to make a sacrifice in your city's temple."

The envoys glance at one another. The fat man clears his throat. "Of course, Your Majesty! A sacrifice of thanks for your victory at Issus, of course! Please feel free to camp for as long as you want and use the temple in our old city on the shore."

"I want to sacrifice inside your city walls," Alexander says. "I'd like to take a look around. With some of my men, of course."

There is a longer pause. The envoys shuffle their feet in the sand. The fat man clears his throat again. "I assure you, Your Majesty, our god will hear you at the temple in the old city just as loudly as he will inside Tyre. We mean no offense, but I'm sure you understand that until this war is over we must preserve our neutrality. We can't afford to show favor to either side, Persian or Macedonian. We said the same to King Darius, and he in his royal wisdom respected our wishes." He gives Alexander a sly look. "Or is Darius, perhaps, more of a king than Alexander?"

WRONG thing to say.

Alexander's fist tightens on my rein. His entire body goes rigid. The blood rises to his cheeks, and his breathing quickens. Hephaestion urges Petasios forward, bringing the gold crown to remind Alexander of the gift. But it is too late.

Alexander snatches the crown, digs his heels into my sides, and rides me straight at the fat man. The envoy throws himself into the sand in terror. Alexander hurls the crown at him like a javelin, hitting him on the cheek. The other envoys scatter and stare in terror at the king.

Alexander has drawn his sword. It flashes in the winter sunlight as he holds it over his head. He looks as if he intends to cut the fat man in two, like he did the Gordian Knot. Sensing his fury, I make myself huge.

"Get out of my sight!" Alexander yells. "Go back and hide behind your walls! If you won't welcome me into your city as a king, then I'll force my way in. But you'll be sorry when I do. Yours won't be the first city my army has destroyed."

The fat man cowers with the other envoys, one palm pressed to his cheek, which is bleeding where the gold stars on the crown cut him. The crown dangles from his other hand. He doesn't seem to know what to do with it. Then one of the others nudges him, and he holds it out again with trembling fingers.

"Please, King Alexander . . . look at our defenses! You have no ships, and our city has never submitted to a siege. Please take the crown and reconsider? We merely ask to be allowed to remain neutral. I promise we won't oppose you if you leave us alone."

But Alexander is past listening. He wheels me around and jerks his head at his Guard. "Escort these men back to their boat," he orders in an icy voice. "And if any of them say another word about me being less of a king than Darius, kill them."

The envoys flee, taking the crown with them. They are not that stupid.

As their boat rows back through the choppy waves, there is silence on the shore. The Guard glance at one another with stricken faces. We horses stamp and snort, impatient for battle. But it doesn't look as if there will be one just yet.

Alexander puts away his sword, and Hephaestion rides Petasios up beside me. He says softly, "Was that wise, Alex? They're right. We don't have ships with us anymore, so we can't attack them from the sea. And aren't you anxious to reach Egypt to talk to the oracle? That island's too far from shore to use our catapults, and not even Zeus could roll siege towers through that channel!" He smiles ruefully and adds, "Though no doubt if you could find a way, you'd do it."

Alexander's breathing slows. The fierce light around him fades. He closes his eyes and presses his palm to his forehead. Then with a sigh he runs a hand down my neck. "Ah, horse, fools like that make me so angry. They shouldn't have suggested I wasn't a proper king. Why does everyone call Darius 'Great King,' anyway? He ran away from the battle and left his whole family behind in enemy hands! I'd never leave *my* mother in such danger."

"Which is why the queen mother is safe back in Pella," Hephaestion says smoothly. "And why you're a better king than Darius." He looks thoughtfully at Tyre. "What do you think? Shall we send them a formal demand for surrender, now that you've scared them? See what they say? If they've got any sense, they'll let us in this time. You were terrifying! I thought Bucephalas was going to eat that fat man alive."

Alexander chuckles. "Bucephalas has got more sense. He'd have choked on the Tyrian arrogance." He squints across the channel at the city. "Yes, I suppose that would be easiest. The last thing we need is another long siege like at Halicarnassus. Maybe they realize who they're dealing with now. Find me some heralds."

You might think this was amazingly calm and sensible of Alexander. Not many who dared suggest he wasn't a proper king got a second chance. They were lucky his good mood from Issus hadn't quite worn off.

But the Tyrians did something extremely stupid. Our heralds did not return with the answer Alexander wanted. Instead, their headless bodies came back over the walls of Tyre and splashed into the sea. Needless to say, their ghosts had already gone.

This time, not even Hephaestion could persuade Alexander to march past Tyre without a fight.

THE PERSIAN GOD'S CURSE

Alexander assembled the army and announced they would build a land bridge across the channel to Tyre strong enough for the siege engines and wide enough for the phalanx to attack. The men stared at him in horror. Some muttered that it was impossible. Alexander assured them it was not and claimed he'd had a prophetic dream in which the Greek hero Hercules had beckoned to him from the walls of Tyre. He ordered them to demolish the ruins of the old city for foundation stones and sent troops inland to secure a supply of timber and to conscript men from the local towns and villages to help. Then he put the scientists to work, designing the great bridge.

While the men and mules sweated at Tyre, the rest of us made camp on the banks of the nearest river, where we older horses had a holiday and the youngsters learned battle maneuvers. My huge filly Electra became quite fierce when Ptolemy charged the hay-stuffed targets with his spear. Although my colt Hoplite was still too young to carry a rider, Charm led him around the camp to get him used to the noise and smells. Most of the horses who had fought in the battle needed the rest, though Apollo used the tiniest scratch on his leg as an excuse to limp.

Then there was ridiculous Zoroaster.

When we had been camped at Tyre for a month, and everyone had realized the bridge wouldn't be finished for ages, Alexander ordered that the white horse be backed so he would be of some use. He gave the job to Charm and Tydeos, saying he wanted to prove Darius's "divine power" was so small it could be taken away by grooms. The truth was, no one wanted to waste their time training a horse who would be useless in battle, and none of the men could be spared from the building work.

Our grooms choose a cool bright morning before the breeze gets up. Charm puts Zoroaster's bridle on him and fastens an old exercise cloth over his back. He must have worn such things before on parades, because he doesn't mind. He turns his head to chew a corner of the cloth, which is not exactly the Persian finery he is used to. Charm fastens a lead rein to his noseband and spends ages fiddling with the straps to get the bit the right height in his mouth.

Tydeos calls out for her to hurry up because he still has four horses to exercise that morning. So does Charm, and one of them is me. But before they can lead Zoroaster out of the lines, Prince Ochus darts up to the white horse and starts tugging at his breast strap. Alexander's puppy, Perita, who is much bigger now, bounds around his feet, yapping. She thinks it is a game.

"Stop that, Ochus!" Charm says. "He has to be ridden today, do you understand? The king ordered it."

Ochus shakes his head and gabbles something in his own tongue. Zoroaster blows into the prince's dark mane, curious.

Tydeos shrugs at Charm. "Can you understand a word he's saying?"

She shakes her head. But I'd say it's obvious. The prince does not want them to ride Zoroaster. Meanwhile, an excited Perita yaps around Zoroaster's hooves. It's a good thing the Persians took away his spirit, I can tell you. If those were the hooves of any other horse, she'd have been kicked halfway back to Anatolia by now.

Before our grooms can decide what to do with the prince, a breathless Lady Barsine arrives. She, if you remember, is Persian-slipper-licking Memnon's widow, the woman General Parmenio sent to Alexander from Damascus after he'd captured the Persian baggage train. She smells of barley mash when she gets warm, which she is at the moment because she's just run from the center of our camp chasing Ochus and Perita.

"I'm sorry," Lady Barsine says, drawing the man-colt away from us. "I tried to keep him in the tent with his mother, but he's as slippery as an eel."

Charm bites her lip. "What's he saying?"

Lady Barsine smiles. "He says you mustn't ride the sacred horse — it would bring bad luck on his family, and you'll die of the curse. The Persians believe the sacred sun-horse is a bond between the royal family and their god."

Tydeos and Charm glance at each other.

"King Alexander thinks backing him will take King Darius's power away," Charm says. "Is that true?"

Lady Barsine smiles again as she straightens Ochus's tunic. "Who knows? Stranger things happen in this world. Who would have believed young Alexander would ever defeat Great King Darius in battle? The last time I saw Alexander, he was Ochus's age and playing with a wooden sword."

"You knew the king when he was small?" Charm says, a bit too sharply. "What was he like?"

"Like all small boys," Lady Barsine says. "He thought the world was his to conquer. Most of them soon realize they have to share it. Alexander still believes it's his, that's the difference. Boys like him don't come along very often, thank the gods." She sighs and stares across the camp. "General Parmenio didn't send me to Alexander by chance, you know. He hopes I will take the place of his mother, maybe calm his temper and take his mind off this burning desire he has to prove he is better than every other king in the world. But I think the damage has already been done. I heard how he cut the Gordian Knot and the sky cracked open. Maybe those rumors about him being fathered by a demon are truer than we think."

She gives Charm a steady look.

"You know the Amazon queen thinks there's a bond between you and Alexander, through Bucephalas? If that's true, then anything that happens to you will affect the king and his horse. I don't know if the Persian curse exists, but only a fool invites that kind of trouble."

Out of the corner of my eye, I see Tydeos shaking his head. But Charm stiffens. "Maybe we shouldn't back the sacred horse?" she whispers to Tydeos. "We could just pretend to have done it."

Tydeos frowns. "No, we couldn't! What'll happen when King Alexander tells one of his men to mount the horse, expecting him to be broken? Zoroaster might look quiet now, but he's big. If he decided to throw someone off, he could do it, no trouble! What if the king himself got on him?"

"Zoroaster couldn't throw Alexander," Charm says. "Perhaps I could tell him I had another prophetic dream."

"He won't fall for that again."

"*He* lied about his dream of Hercules standing on the walls of Tyre."

"How do you know?"

"Because if Alexander really did have prophetic dreams, he wouldn't need to keep asking me and his official seer, would he? And he'd have known about the Amanic Gates. . . ."

Lady Barsine is listening carefully. Ochus asks her something, but she shakes her head. "Speak Greek, Ochus," she says. "Ask them yourself."

Ochus straightens his shoulders and clenches small fists. "Me — ride — horse."

Charm looks surprised and her expression softens. "He wants to go for a ride? Is that allowed? Maybe we could put him up on Aura."

But Ochus shakes his head fiercely and points to Zoroaster.

Tydeos laughs. "Oh no, little prince, not that horse! He's not broken yet. You don't understand, do you? Can't you explain to him, Lady? I don't think he's allowed to go riding, anyway. Isn't he supposed to be King Alexander's hostage?"

Lady Barsine's lips tighten. She glances at the sentries, who are watching but don't interfere. She often brings Prince Ochus down to the horse lines to teach him the Greek words for things.

Ochus gabbles something to her — another question in Persian, though he uses the same word *hostage* that Tydeos used.

Lady Barsine smooths Ochus's mane and says softly, "The guards won't let his grandmother, mother, or his sisters out of their pavilion. He'll hardly run away on his own. He's only seven."

"We'll get into trouble if we let him go riding," Tydeos says with a stubborn look. "I'm sorry, Lady, but we can't take orders from you. You're a prisoner, too. You'll have to ask King Alexander."

Lady Barsine's eyes cloud in anger. Ochus is still asking her about "hostage," tugging at her sleeve. She snaps something in Persian at the boy, and his face goes still. He frowns at Zoroaster, then calls Perita and heads back toward King Darius's pavilion. His head is high and his back stiff, exactly like Alexander's when he strides away from someone who has just said something he doesn't like. Lady Barsine gives Tydeos a look that is the human equivalent of flat ears and hurries after the man-colt.

"What did I say?" Tydeos mutters to Charm as he unties Zoroaster from the horse lines. "Why's she so upset? Who does she think she is, anyway? Coming down here with the boy, expecting us to give him a ride on one of King Alexander's horses! What nerve."

"I don't think Prince Ochus knows he's supposed to be a hostage. He calls Alexander 'Uncle,' doesn't he? And Alexander's always nice to him."

"So? He'll still kill him if King Darius tries to fight us again."

Charm bites her lip. "Do you think it's true? That whoever rides Zoroaster will die?"

"Of course it's not true! Zoroaster's not Bucephalas. The worst he can do is buck us off, and it won't be the first time a horse has done that to me. Don't worry, I'll sit on him. You can lead him around. Here, hold him still so I can lean over his back to get him used to my weight."

"No, Tydeos!" Charm sounds more scared for Tydeos than she is for herself.

"I'll do it," says a rough voice on my blind side.

At first, I think it is a ghost standing there. I leap in alarm, nearly breaking my tether. Then I recognize his smell. It is the mulemaster whose hands were chopped off by the Persians at Issus. He had refused to stay with the other crippled men Alexander left behind.

"If that horse is cursed, there's no point two youngsters like you fallin' foul of it. What would Bucephalas do without you? Me, I'm no use to anyone now. What's the Persian god goin' to do to me that's worse than what Darius's men have already done? Let me sit on 'im."

Charm stares at his ruined wrists and starts to say, "No, you shouldn't have to —"

But Tydeos says with some relief, "Good idea! You won't need to hold the reins the first time. We should have thought of it before. We'll lead him around while you sit on his back and teach him to obey your legs and weight. Er . . . you do know how to ride a horse, don't you?"

The mulemaster spits. "I was backin' mules before you two were born! Horses are a piece of cake after them, believe me."

They lead Zoroaster away to a quiet spot and bring him back at a trot soon afterward, with Charm running beside his head and Tydeos flicking a whip behind his tail to keep him moving. Zoroaster seems perfectly happy, though he is sweating and breathless. Bouncing on his cloth is the old mulemaster, his ruined arms spread wide for balance, and an even bigger grin on his face than when he used to tease me back in Pella.

"No problem!" he announces as he slithers off the white horse. "King

Darius's divine power ain't worth nothin' now. Next time they meet, King Alexander will be able to kill him."

DOMINATING TYRE

By summer, Alexander's "impossible" bridge had reached the walls of Tyre. This is how he did it:

Our herd: *throw stones into the sea*
Tyrian herd: *laugh*
Our herd: *throw more stones into the sea and fix tree trunks on top*
Tyrian herd: *get worried and start making anti-siege equipment*
Our herd: *throw more stones into the sea*
Tyrian herd: *send out ships to kill the men working on the bridge*
Our herd: *call on dominated towns to send us some ships so we can fight back*
Tyrian herd: *panic!*

We horses didn't get to fight in the battle, though. Alexander told the grooms to keep us bridled in case we were needed in a hurry. Then he led his entire army to Tyre, even those injured during the building work, who were so furious with the Tyrians that they didn't want to miss the final fight.

With all the men except a handful of sentries gone off to Tyre, it is eerily quiet in the camp. Wearing our quilted battle-cloths, we horses sweat in the Phoenician heat. We have been given hay, but none of us has much appetite because Charm and Tydeos are weaning Hoplite, and Harpinna's distressed neighs upset us.

Charm tethers Hoplite securely to the other end of our horse line, while Tydeos and two other strong grooms take Harpinna along the riverbank out of sight. Their whinnies get louder and more frantic. Hoplite is still only a yearling, but he's *my* yearling. He fights very fiercely, and Charm calls for help. The remaining grooms and our sentries go to watch the fun.

None of them notice Zoroaster is loose, until a white flash passes behind our tails and disappears on my blind side. I whinny to warn the silly horse not to run off without his groom. But Zoroaster is not loose. Crouched on his back, clinging to his long white mane, is Prince Ochus. He's pounding Zoroaster's sides with his small heels to make him go faster.

The sentries sound the alarm. Charm leaves Hoplite in the care of the other grooms, drags off my cloth, and scrambles onto my back. I flatten my ears and gallop after Zoroaster. More hooves pound after us, and I see Harpinna out of the corner of my eye with Tydeos crouched over her neck, urging her on with a whip.

Zoroaster has a good start, and he's quite fit now that he's had some training. We chase him for a surprising distance before I manage to get my head in front. I give Zoroaster flat ears and a squeal. But he doesn't slow down to fight me, like a normal stallion would. Nor does he swerve like a mare. He merely sticks out his white neck and gallops on.

"Turn him, Charm!" Tydeos yells behind us. "Head him back to camp. Don't let him get to Tyre, whatever you do!"

We reach the beach where Alexander's bridge crosses over to Tyre, and the noise of the battle makes me shiver all over. The air is full of shouts, screams, war cries, the crack of our siege engines, and the splash of missiles falling into the sea. Our ships surround Tyre, bristling with men and siege equipment. A phalanx of Macedonian pikemen blocks the end of the bridge to catch those trying to escape from the city.

This must frighten Ochus, because he stops kicking Zoroaster. As the white horse slows, Charm leans across to grab the reins. Harpinna catches up, covered in foam and breathing hard. Tydeos takes hold of Ochus's ankle and tips him off into the sand.

Charm leads Zoroaster clear so he doesn't tread on the man-colt, and I bite the white horse on the nose to tell him what I think of him. He lowers his head and looks ashamed.

"You little idiot!" Tydeos yells, throwing himself off Harpinna and grabbing Ochus by the arm. "What did you think you were doing? You could have gotten yourself killed!" He shakes Ochus until tears glisten in the prince's eyes, turns him around, and points to the island with its massive land bridge. "See that? That's what King Alexander will do to your home when we get there, if you don't behave so your father will surrender to him."

"Don't, Tydeos. It's not his fault. If I were a hostage, I'd try to run away, too." Charm is panting nearly as much as Harpinna. "Ochus, you have to come back with us. Understand? Your mother and Lady Barsine will be worried about you, and you have to look after Perita for King Alexander."

Ochus glances quickly at her and turns his dark eyes on Tydeos. His chin juts out stubbornly. "My home not in sea," he says. "My father rescue me soon!"

"Ha! You'll be lucky. I heard that in his last letter, King Darius offered to leave you with King Alexander permanently if he'd take his army home." Tydeos misses the anguished look on the man-colt's face and stares at the walls of Tyre. "Charm, see there! Isn't that the king?"

She stiffens. I prick my ears at the city. It is too far away to catch individual smells in the confusion of sweat and smoke mingling with the sea breeze. But I see Alexander's Troy helmet flash on the highest platform of one of the siege ships as he leaps across the gap to the walls. The white plumes flare in the Phoenician sunshine, like the wings of a seabird. With his golden energy shining around him, he flies.

Charm puts her knuckles to her mouth.

A great roar goes up from the Macedonians as Alexander lands safely on the battlements and raises his sword to the sky. He shouts something, pushes three Tyrian soldiers off the wall, and disappears into the city. There are more screams, and a great coil of smoke rises from within the walls.

"Oh, Zeus," Charm whispers. "I can't watch this! It'll be just like Thebes, I know it will!" But she keeps staring at the battlements where the king disappeared.

Ochus watches with big eyes. He says nothing.

Finally, Tydeos shudders and says in a sick voice, "This is no place for us. Come on, let's go."

He lifts the prince onto Zoroaster's back, and I nip the white horse until he puts his muzzle behind Charm's knee, in the easiest place for her to lead him from my back. Tydeos vaults onto Harpinna and rides her on Zoroaster's other side so he can't get away. But Ochus has given up for now. He sits quietly on the white horse, his back straight and his short legs dangling halfway down the cloth. Harpinna has given up fighting, too, and walks with her head low. All the man-colt says during the return journey is, "Not tell Uncle Alexander I try escape, please?"

Charm and Tydeos glance at each other. Charm sighs. "Don't worry, Ochus, it'll be our secret. We'll say you just wanted to see the battle, if anyone asks."

Ochus gives her a little smile and strokes Zoroaster's withers. "Thank you, Charmeia."

She looks startled that he knows her name. But then she smiles, too.

One good thing came of that day: When Hoplite smelled his mother coming back and neighed to her from the horse lines, Harpinna was too tired to answer. She had obviously decided our colt was old enough to survive without her, so she was back in my herd again!

No longer an island

The Macedonians had six months of anger to work out that day, and Alexander did nothing to keep them under control. The city of Tyre, which had taken us so long to join to the shore, was ours by sunset.

Tyrian dead: 7,000

Tyrian soldiers crucified as a warning to others: 2,000

Tyrians sold as slaves: 30,000

Macedonian dead: 400

Horses dead: none (HURRAH!)

People spared: ambassadors from Carthage. Alexander was angry but not stupid — Carthage is on the other side of Egypt, and we are going that way.

We didn't get to rename the city. But we did rename their god. When Alexander finally made his sacrifice in the temple of Tyre, he made it to "Apollo Philalexander."

WHAT NERVE!

I was the one who brought his man-colt hostage and Zoroaster back to camp, with Harpinna's help. What did Apollo do to deserve a god named after him? Nothing, except limp around the camp, complaining of the battle wound he got at Issus.

Sometimes, life is just not fair.

15

GAZA

332 B.C.

AN UNEXPECTED ARROW

After the example Alexander made of Tyre, no one dared so much as squeal at us the rest of the way down the coast. General Parmenio rejoined us, so we were a huge, strong herd when we reached the Phoenician border. It looked as though we might ride straight into the Egyptian world with no more fighting. But at the last moment, a place called Gaza closed its gates to us.

Alexander laughed and said its boss must not yet have heard about Tyre. He ordered the army to make camp on the beach, and we led the Guard inland through the sand dunes to see if we could make Gaza change its mind.

I had some trouble in the desert. Size is not necessarily a good thing on soft sand. Also, I was thirsty and too hot from the march, so I was not quite as alert as usual. When Alexander halted me at the top of a dune to take a look at the city, a herd of strange horses with silly dished faces and ridiculously high tail carriages came galloping over the top, and a curtain of arrows hissed out of my blind side toward us.

I leaped in panic. But my hooves sank in the sand, and Alexander gasped as his weight jerked on my back. I'd carried riders in enough battles to know this was a bad sign and felt a stab of shame. Hephaestion whipped out his sword and yelled, "After them, then!" He urged Petasios after the strange horses. But of the Guard, only Hades and Aura could really handle the sand. The others were soon left behind as the enemy fled into the city, waving their bows over their heads and whooping. The loose horses followed their friends through the gates, which slammed shut behind them.

They left me alone on top of the dune. I wanted to gallop after my herd but knew I must stay with my rider. Alexander had fallen off me and lay in the sand near my hooves. Blood was spurting from his shoulder, where the arrow had found its way through a joint of his armor. I sniffed him to check that he was not dead, then settled to my knees beside him. The dry desert wind lifted my mane and fluttered the black feathers of the arrow.

Alexander struggled up on his good elbow, flopped back, and shut his eyes with a groan. He whispered, "Bucephalas, my faithful horse . . . don't leave me. This isn't meant to happen. I can't die! Zeus is supposed to be looking after me . . . oh, horse, it's all going dark. . . ."

"*Alex!*" cried an anguished voice as Petasios stopped in a spray of sand beside us.

I whinnied in relief to my red friend. Hephaestion leaped off him, kneeled beside Alexander, and put a hand on the king's forehead. He closed a fist around the arrow sticking out of his shoulder, shook his head, and with a grimace removed his hand.

"Get up, you big lump!" he said to me, sticking his elbow into my shoulder. "The king's too sick to ride you back to camp. We'll have to get a stretcher. Alex, hold on, do you hear? We won't let you die. It's only a scratch. You'll be fine." But his voice faltered, which meant this was probably a lie.

The others returned, out of breath, and stared at the king in horror. Hephaestion yelled at them to get moving, couldn't they see the king needed a doctor, and what were they playing at, letting the Arabs get so close to him? He squealed like a stallion who knew he had just done the wrong thing by leading them after the enemy, and was trying to remind everyone he was still boss.

But it was my fault. All mine. I was so deeply ashamed, I let Iolaus lead me back to the horse lines without making a fuss. Hades had done better than me, so when he gave me flat ears I didn't even nip him.

My riderless state scared Charm. She rushed up to take my rein from

Iolaus, her face as pale as Alexander's had been lying on the dune. "What happened?" she gasped. "Where's the king? Oh, Zeus, he's not —?"

Iolaus pulled a face. "Dead? No, not yet. But I'm not sure how much longer we'll be able to keep him alive if he keeps on taking risks like this. Why do we have to beat down the walls of every city that closes its gates to us? Why can't we just go after King Darius and finish this stupid war? The longer we stay here, the longer the Persians will have to raise another army. Father might like being Regent of Macedonia, but he won't keep the throne for long without us to defend it for him."

Realizing a circle of curious grooms had gathered, he muttered, "Yes, well . . . the king's wounded, but he'll live. He'll have plenty of time to recover, anyway. Would you believe, General Parmenio wants us to build a mound around the city, the same height as Gaza's hill? I didn't join the army to build bridges across the sea and mountains in the desert! I'm a cavalryman, not a common laborer! I've got to go. The king needs me."

Iolaus hurried off, still grumbling.

Charm stared at Zoroaster. "It was the curse," she whispered.

Tydeos made a face. "It was those Arabs! King Alexander wasn't careful enough. He seems to think he's immortal or something, since he cut the Gordian Knot. It's like when he jumped into that river at Tarsus, when he couldn't even swim! Maybe now he'll stop doing such stupid things."

Charm put her arms around my neck and squeezed tightly. "Oh, Bucephalas," she whispered. "At least *you're* all right. I suppose if Alexander's wounded, he can't do to Gaza what he did to Thebes and Tyre. That'll be a good thing, won't it?"

ALEXANDER COPIES ACHILLES

Charm ought to have known Alexander better than that. Both his body and his pride had been hurt. He swore to knock down Gaza's walls and teach its boss a lesson he would never forget.

Our siege engines soon got stuck in the soft sand. When even the mules couldn't move them, the old mulemaster waved the sticks he had tied to his arms and yelled at his muleteers to "get those mules out of range before the Gazians start shooting from the walls!"

Meanwhile the Arab mercenaries who had wounded Alexander galloped out, picked off some of our men, and fled back in again.

On hearing the reports, Alexander threw things around his tent and shouted at his doctors and his Guard, who were all trying to keep him in bed. They didn't have a hope. When the mound around the city was finished, Alexander insisted on leading the attack himself, even though his shoulder was only half healed. He was too dizzy to ride me and went off to Gaza in a chariot driven by Hephaestion. So once again, I had nothing to do.

I had to stay in the camp with the nervous grooms, until the men began to trail back with their wounded. That was when we learned that a rock from one of Gaza's anti-siege catapults had cracked Alexander's leg as he'd led the charge over the battlements.

Charm clutched my mane and whispered, "I don't care what Tydeos says! It's the Persian god's curse, I know it is. We should never have backed Zoroaster. Oh, Bucephalas, I think Alexander's going to get himself killed in this horrible place. . . ."

But Alexander did not die in Gaza.

When we finally smell the king's sherbet sweetness in the horse lines, it is so drenched in other smells from the battle that I hardly recognize him. He is in a foul mood: limping with his cracked leg, a hand pressed to the bloody bandage on his shoulder, filthy, sweating, and red in the face. Leonnatus and Philotas follow, hauling between them an enormously fat man with brown skin. The prisoner's arms have been bound behind him, blood trickles from the corner of his mouth, and one of his eyes is swollen shut. The rest of the Guard hurry after them, all as sweaty and dirty as their king. The grooms stop what they are doing to stare.

"Charmides!" Alexander calls. "Harness Bucephalas to a chariot! Put him with that big golden horse, Xanthus."

"Wait, Alexander!" calls General Parmenio, frowning at his son Philotas as he hurries past. His hairy legs are bleeding and crusted with sand. "This man ruled Gaza for the Persians. He deserves better treatment."

"He deserves to be treated like the animal he is," Alexander mutters through clenched teeth. "This ugly creature is no more a man than

Zoroaster is a stallion! He heard what happened to Tyre, yet he still dared to challenge me. Those Arabs of his nearly killed me in the desert with that arrow. He has condemned his city by refusing to acknowledge me as king, and he even dares to suggest I'm the son of a commoner! He won't admit it, but he can only have heard that rumor from my father's interfering old horsemaster. He probably knows who was behind my father's assassination, too. Gaza is the gateway to Egypt. *Someone* must have told him to stop me from reaching the Siwa Oracle." He scowls at the prisoner. "This is your last chance! Either tell me the truth or die!"

The dark man's bruised mouth laughs at the king. "You wouldn't see the truth, Alexander, if it hit you in the eye. If you carry on like you are, you'll come to the same bad end as that tyrant Philip you claim sired you."

"Shut him *up*!" Alexander yells. "Gag him."

Leonnatus and Philotas glance at each other. Philotas coughs and says, "But I thought you wanted him to talk?"

Alexander turns on them with a furious expression. "I've heard enough of his lies. *Do it!*"

Philotas glances at his father for confirmation. But Leonnatus tightens his lips, knots one of our bandages, puts it in the dark man's mouth, and ties it behind his head. The boss of Gaza grins around the gag, his one open eye fixed defiantly on Alexander.

Charm puts a trembling hand on my neck and lifts her chin. "I don't think Bucephalas has pulled a chariot before, sir," she whispers. "I don't know about Xanthus, but warhorses aren't usually trained to pull chariots."

Alexander clenches a fist. Charm shrinks closer to me, but he doesn't hit her. He presses his knuckles to his forehead and snaps, "Put two of those Persian horses in a chariot, then. It'll make no difference to this ugly creature. *Move!*"

Charm and Tydeos run off to prepare the chariot, so they don't see what Alexander orders done to the boss of Gaza. This is probably just as well. Few humans have the stomach for such things. Even our grooms go pale. One youngster faints.

When Charm and Tydeos return, leading the Persian horses yoked to the chariot, Alexander's Guard is looking almost as sick as our grooms. General Parmenio shakes his head, mutters something about needing a bath, and strides off to his tent, ordering his son to follow him. Philotas casts an apologetic look at Alexander and hurries after his father.

A lead rein has been attached to the prisoner's ankles, and Leonnatus fastens it to the back of the chariot. Alexander snatches up a whip and looks down at the former governor of Gaza, who is now quiet.

Alexander's breathing slows slightly as he crouches beside him. "I am the reborn Achilles. This is what Achilles did to his enemy Prince Hector outside the walls of Troy, so I am treating you a lot better than you deserve. I want you to know that before you die."

He climbs stiffly into the chariot and gathers up the reins in his good hand. He shouts at Charm and Tydeos to let go of the horses, grunts with the pain of raising his wounded arm, and lashes them with the whip. The horses take off immediately, as they've been trained to do. The prisoner's body jerks as the rein attached to his ankles tightens, and he bounces along behind the chariot in the dust and flying sand. The grooms run after it.

That is the last I see of the governor of Gaza, although a little later his ghost screams past the horse lines, lifting our manes and making us all shiver.

Tydeos puts his arm around Charm and whispers, "Don't watch. The king is angry because he got wounded. He'll calm down soon. This is war. That man was our enemy. At least he'll die quicker than those poor men Alexander had crucified at Tyre."

Charm shudders and stares after the cloud of dust. "No one deserves that," she says in a fierce little voice. "No one."

An uneasy hush falls over the horse lines. Alexander's friends look at one another. I hear some of them whisper that this isn't what they came for, that if he's going to keep doing things like this they'd rather go home than follow him any farther.

As for what made everyone so sick and faint, if you're squeamish, you'd better skip to the next chapter now. If not . . .

Alexander read the *Iliad* every night and merely copied what his hero Achilles did to his enemy. He pierced the dark man's ankles with a spear and threaded the rein through the holes so it would not come loose when he dragged the body along behind his chariot. The only difference being that when Achilles did it in the *Iliad*, his enemy was already dead.

EGYPT

332–331 B.C.

ALEXANDER BECOMES PHARAOH

The world of Egypt is strange. It is fertile and beautiful on the wide banks of its river, where big lilies the scientists call "lotus" grow. But not far back on either side lies desert. Close to the sea, the river spreads out into marshland, which is full of birds. The reeds are taller than Hoplite's head and hide monsters that make horrible noises at night. We can hear them from our camp outside the dazzling white walls of their main city of Memphis.

Soon after we arrived, the Egyptian priests met us with a crown — but not a flimsy one like those Alexander had been given in Phoenicia, oh no! The Egyptian crown had a golden snake's head with emerald eyes curling out of the front. There must have been some kind of magic in it, because when the priests placed it on Alexander's head, thunder rolled around the huge columns of their temple. The Amazons looked around, hoping the hole in the world might open again. But there were no angry Egyptian ghosts waiting to go through it, so it stayed shut.

I had to wait outside with the other horses, which meant I didn't see the ceremony. But we could hear the cheering as far away as the riverbank. "ALEX-AN-DER! ALEX-AN-DER! LONG LIVE PHARAOH ALEXANDER! KING OF MACEDONIA, LORD OF ANATOLIA, LIBERATOR OF EGYPT!" (This time it might actually be true, since the Egyptians welcomed us as friends, and we didn't have to dominate anyone.)

"Did you expect that?" Hephaestion whispered as they emerged, blinking, into the sunlight and mounted me and Petasios so we could parade through the streets. *"Pharaoh of all Egypt?"*

Alexander laughed. "No, but if it's their custom, why argue? Zeus must have been testing me back in Phoenicia. I have a good feeling about this oracle, my friend! And I'm thinking we should go after Darius, once we've finished here. I want to make sure the Persians don't simply recapture Anatolia and Egypt once my back is turned. Removing Darius will show them I mean business."

Hephaestion looked unsure. "You're holding his family hostage. He won't make trouble while he knows you're looking after them. If we go farther east, he'll fight to defend his land."

"So?" Alexander chuckled and slapped his friend on the thigh. "We've defeated his army once. We can do it again."

"Zeus might not want us to invade Persia," Hephaestion said in a low tone, glancing around to check that no one had heard.

"Then I'll ask the oracle what he wants me to do!" Alexander grinned as he brushed lotus petals out of my mane. "Will that satisfy you, my friend?"

As soon as the parties were over, Alexander set off for Siwa. By this time he had recovered from the wound he'd received at Gaza and was very cheerful when he came to the horse lines to say good-bye to me.

He fed me some Egyptian pastries, which were not quite as tasty as Queen Ada's honey cakes but still good. While I ate them greedily, he pulled my ears and whispered, "Charm and General Parmenio will look after you, Bucephalas. I wish I could take you with me, but it's a month's trek across desert, and I'm going to need your strength when I get back. You have a good holiday and stay sound for when we go after King Darius."

Then he mounted Xanthus and cantered off with his Guard, the cavalry, and the Amazons, while Charm and I had to stay behind in the camp with General Parmenio's veterans and the baggage train. Since Tydeos had gone with the other grooms, we were a bit lonely at first. But Charm did mutual grooming on my withers and talked to me in her soft voice until I settled. She said I needn't worry, because Alexander wasn't going to fight any more battles. She promised that once he had found out from the oracle who his father was, we'd go home — which seems unlikely, considering what he told me before he left.

The scientists rushed off upriver to see the pyramids and examine the strange way the Egyptians keep their dead, alive but not alive. Our grooms say that instead of burning a body, they take out its innards and keep them in a jar so they won't rot, then wrap the body in bandages. They do the same with their bulls and cats. If they try it on any of my herd, watch out! The men took the dogs hunting in the marshes and came back laden with geese and fish. The officers organized games to keep everyone occupied while they were waiting for Alexander to return, and the weather stayed warm even though it was winter. There was a good rolling place on the riverbank, and I spent a lot of my time covered in black mud.

It was great . . . until Prince Ochus turned up.

CHARM MAKES ANOTHER MISTAKE

With Alexander away, Prince Ochus often sneaks down to the horse lines to groom Zoroaster. Since being dominated by us at Tyre, he hasn't tried to run away again. But one day he blurts out, "Charmeia, will Uncle Alexander do Achilles' chariot thing to my father?"

"No!" Charm says firmly, putting an arm around the man-colt. "Of course not. That bad man at Gaza wasn't a king like your father, and King Alexander was sick from his wounds so he wasn't thinking properly. He's not like that normally. Anyway, after he gets back from the oracle we're going home."

Ochus bites his lip. "Lady Barsine say Uncle Alexander not go home yet."

Charm gives the prince a sharp look. "How does she know?"

"She go to his pavilion at night. She say he like to fight too much. I want to see my father again before Uncle Alexander kill him," he adds in a little voice.

Charm's face twists. She goes very quiet, like she did at Tarsus before she went to visit the Amazons. Then she grips the man-colt's hand and whispers, "I know you do, Ochus. Don't give up hope. I'll see what I can do."

What Charm does is very strange. She bridles both me and Zoroaster, sneaks a look around, and climbs onto my back. Then she unties Zoroaster so she can lead him beside me.

We trot along the riverbank until we're past the sentries. They wave to her. It's not unusual to see a groom exercising two horses at once, so they don't realize Charm NEVER exercises me with another horse. If the other horse weren't Zoroaster, there would have been trouble by now. But Zoroaster is far too meek to fight me. I give him a nip on the nose to warn him not to try anything, and prance sideways, itching to go faster. I hope we don't have to go at his slow pace the whole way.

Charm holds me firmly to a trot, scanning the reeds. She stiffens as a canoe noses into the bank. Ochus climbs out of it. He has a bundle, which she helps him tie across Zoroaster's withers. Then she boosts him up and, with a bit of struggle, vaults back onto me.

This is better. Now that I haven't got stupid Zoroaster's head by my flank we can go faster. And we do! We gallop across the fields through the sprouting corn until we reach the edge of the desert. Charm is breathing very fast and keeps looking back over her shoulder. This is a real problem for you humans. If you look behind, you can't keep an eye on the danger ahead.

As we go over the first dune a line of monsters appears. They're twice as big as a horse and have necks that look as if they've been put on backward. Men in long robes are perched on their humped backs. Zoroaster does not seem too bothered. But I squeal a challenge and go up on my hind legs in alarm. The monsters turn their funny heads toward us, and one of them makes a sound like a mule in pain.

I come down to earth and make myself huge, ready for battle. But Charm, who (amazingly) is still on my back, shouts, "Stop it, Bucephalas! They're only camels. Haven't you seen camels before? They won't hurt you, silly!"

One of these camels comes closer, and I give it flat ears. The man sitting on its back grins down at Charm with very white teeth. He looks at Ochus, who is sitting stiffly on Zoroaster, and says in a thick accent, "This is King Darius's son? He is younger than I expected."

Charm nods. "Just keep him safe, please." She urges me closer to Zoroaster and whispers to Ochus, "These men will take you across the desert to Persia. I can't come with you. I have to take the king's horse back to camp. Tell your father I'll do my best to persuade King Alexander to free your grandmother, mother, and sisters. I'll make sure he doesn't hurt them, don't worry."

The man on the camel grins some more and looks around. Another camel comes out from behind the dune, and I snort in alarm. Camels smell strong, and the second rider's face is wrapped in a cloth, but I'd know his smell anywhere. It is my enemy the old horsemaster.

"You're going to be in a lot of trouble for this, slave," he says with an evil chuckle.

Charm stares at him, unsure. But when he pulls his scarf aside to reveal his face she goes rigid with fear.

She quickly recovers her wits and pulls out her dagger. "Get out of here, Ochus!" she yells, tugging me around so abruptly I lose my hind legs in the sand. "Get back to the camp! It's a trick!"

But it is too late. Men armed with long pikes rise up from the dunes all around us. I recognize Macedonians from General Parmenio's command.

Ochus freezes. The leader of the camel men shakes his head at Charm. "I am sorry," he says. "But what else could I do? I have to make a living. If I helped King Alexander's prize hostage to escape, my caravan would be finished forever."

Charm glares at the horsemaster. "You —" she whispers. "You've been spying on me!"

The horsemaster sits casually on his camel and smiles. "Told you I'd follow you to the ends of the earth, didn't I? I must say, I underestimated your cunning, but did you really think it would be so easy to help the little Persian prince escape? What's the matter, slave? Can't you control that old nag of Alexander's yet?"

I am acting wild, worried by the pikes and strange animals surrounding me. But the camels don't seem very impressed by my flat ears and squealing. This is probably because they are bigger than me. When I feel Charm start to slip, I remember she is not Alexander. I calm down so she doesn't fall off but lash out at anyone who gets too close.

The Macedonians keep a wary distance. They signal that Charm should throw down her weapon. She clutches the dagger tightly and grips my reins in a determined way as if she means us to fight. Then she looks at Ochus and shakes her head.

She drops her dagger in the sand. A soldier picks it up and scuttles out of range of my teeth. One of the Macedonians takes Zoroaster's bridle and leads him back toward the camp. The others indicate with their pikes that

Charm should follow on me, which she does with tears in her eyes. The horsemaster rides his camel close behind. I lash my tail at the camel and go sideways so I can keep my good eye on it. The horsemaster watches Charm, smiling in his dark way.

"General Parmenio will arrest you if you come back to our camp!" Charm says in a brave voice.

"Really?" the horsemaster says. "And why is that?"

"You tried to kidnap Bucephalas at Thebes! And you attacked me in Halicarnassus. King Alexander wants you caught and punished."

"You're the one who's in trouble, slave, not me. General Parmenio and I go back a long way. He'll be more than grateful for my bringing Prince Ochus back."

I feel the hairs of Charm's legs prickle against my sides. "I'm the king's personal groom," she whispers. "If you touch me, he'll kill you. You know what he did to the governor of Gaza, don't you?"

"Yes, I heard about that. Seems his temper has grown as bad as his horse's. But our fierce young Alexander is on the other side of Egypt, talking to the gods. By the time he gets back here, I'll be long gone."

Charm shudders and grips my mane tighter. Ochus turns to look at her, his lip trembling. "Charmeia, the general won't hurt my mother because I tried to run away, will he?"

Charm flings the horsemaster a look that is the human equivalent of flat ears and says, "It was my idea, Ochus, not yours. I'm the one who'll be punished."

Behind us, the horsemaster's smile widens. I lash my tail at his camel's nose, and the animal shies, making him grab its hump.

The horsemaster won't get near Charm while she is on my back. Camels might be big, but they are obviously stupid. I'm still the boss around here.

BƐTRAYAL

General Parmenio is waiting for us at the horse lines. He sends Ochus back to Lady Barsine's tent with two of his men, while a third man leads Zoroaster away. He grabs my reins himself and orders Charm to dismount. She slides off me, and her legs buckle. A soldier takes her arm to steady her.

I squeal and shake my head at him, warning him to leave her alone, but the general gives my reins a hard jerk. "Stop that, Bucephalas!" he snaps. "I've had about enough of your temper."

The horsemaster's camel lurches to its knees with a grunt so he can get off. Afterward, it stays sitting down, chewing on a piece of hay. Stupid, as I said. Even a mule wouldn't sit in the dirt for very long by choice.

The general shakes his head at Charm. "You're more dangerous to this army than all of King Darius's Persians put together," he says. "What did you think you were trying to do?"

She stares at her feet. "Please don't punish Prince Ochus, sir," she whispers. "It was my idea."

"I know it was. An eight-year-old boy would never dream up anything so stupid." He frowns at her bowed head and presses his lips together. Then he nods at the soldier to let her go. "Here, do your job. Settle this horse back in the lines and put his muzzle on. Use two tethers so he won't get loose!"

Charm eyes the horsemaster, who is leaning against his camel with his ruined leg stuck out to one side and smiling darkly.

"Bucephalas needs a roll, sir," she stammers. "So does Zoroaster."

"Do what I told you!" the general barks. "The horses can have their roll later."

Charm bites her lip and obeys. The Macedonians watch her every move. Her hands tremble as she fastens my muzzle and doubles my tether as ordered. She keeps glancing up at the general and the horsemaster, who are speaking in low voices as if they are members of the same herd who know each other well. Which they are, because for many years they both served under the one-eyed king.

A soldier brings me a bucket of water. I am thirsty after my fright with the camels in the desert, so I suck it up through my muzzle. The water tastes strange. I expect it's dirty, because they are not grooms and know no better.

Charm holds on to my mane as I drink. "Can I groom Bucephalas now?" she asks the men.

They shake their heads. One tugs my tether to make sure it is securely tied. Another takes Charm's elbow and steers her back to the general. The other men stand to attention, keeping people away from our part of the horse lines.

Charm takes a deep breath. "I'm very sorry for what I did, sir," she whispers. "I only wanted to get Prince Ochus safely back to his father. Please don't tell King Alexander."

The general waves her to be quiet. He is looking at something the horsemaster has handed him. It is a piece of flattened grass with marks on it. He rolls it up, hands it back to him, and gives Charm a thoughtful look.

"This isn't the first time you've betrayed the king, is it, Charmeia? I know what you did at the Syrian Gates. If it weren't for young Alexander's amazing energy and luck, none of us would have gotten this far. Our bones would be rotting on the battlefield back at Issus, and you would be serving sherbet to the Great King's guests in a Persian palace."

She trembles and looks at her feet.

"This scroll is very interesting. It's a list of all the garrison slaves at Methone. I always thought there was something suspicious about a girl who does a boy's job. I should have looked into your background before, especially since Alexander seems to think such a lot of you. The king's got no idea who you are, has he? But you are far too close to him, so I'm afraid I have to get rid of you. As it happens, the horsemaster has solved the problem for me quite neatly."

He eyes me. I am feeling sleepy, and my legs feel like temple columns. It is hard to concentrate on what's happening to Charm, but she is so white I think she might faint.

"All right," the general says to the horsemaster. "You can take her. I don't care what you do with her. Just make sure she doesn't come near this army again. Alexander will be upset, but it can't be helped. There's one other groom who can manage the horse, and he'll be back soon enough."

Charm stares at the general in terror as she realizes how he intends to punish her. She starts to run, but she doesn't get far. The Macedonians catch her and bind her wrists. She kicks and struggles as they easily lift her between them and carry her over to the horsemaster's camel. They push her against the animal's flank, pinch her nose, and make her drink something from a leather flask.

She splutters and tries to spit it out.

"Help!" she screams, twisting her head. "*Bucephalas!*"

It is my name. I lift my head, which has drooped almost to the ground. But I am securely tied, and I feel very strange. I lose my balance and fall on my knees. It's too much effort to get up.

Charm stares at me in horror. "What have you done to Bucephalas?" she cries. "Let me go! He needs me. *Bucephalas!*"

"We put something in his water to calm him down. You'll feel the same way shortly. It's not harmful, just easier this way," says General Parmenio, frowning at her.

Charm is still screaming and sobbing. But after a moment her struggles cease, and she sags against the camel. The horsemaster looks triumphant as the Macedonians tie her across its hump. He climbs up behind her, hits the camel with a stick, and the animal lurches to its feet.

"Thank you for remembering our old friendship, General," he says. "I'm glad there's at least one sensible officer left in the Macedonian army —" He breaks off as someone approaches on my blind side and mutters a curse. "Oh, Zeus, is that crazy muleteer still alive?"

There's a struggle going on behind me. I smell the old mulemaster, the one who lost his hands at Issus. He's using the sticks he has lashed to his wrists like weapons.

"Let the girl go!" he growls, shoving General Parmenio's men aside. He glares at the general. "If you let that man take Bucephalas's groom, King Alexander's goin' to hear of it! He gave orders for him to be arrested if he ever turned up again."

General Parmenio frowns.

"That's the man who broke my knee back in Pella and ruined my career!" the horsemaster hisses, glaring at the mulemaster. "Don't look like his career's going too well, either. What happened, Mulemaster? Someone chop off your hands because they were so dirty?"

"Yeah, and you've been trying to get *your* dirty hands on King Alexander's groom for years, haven't you?" growls the mulemaster, raising his sticks again. "Let her go!"

General Parmenio sighs, and his sword flashes out.

The mulemaster grunts in surprise as blood spurts from his neck. Before his body hits the ground, his ghost whirls past me. I am so drowsy I hardly flinch. But the sky rumbles, and the men look around.

They do not know that the mulemaster defied the Persian curse by backing Zoroaster, the Persian sacred horse. Nor do they know about the horse bond. If they did, they might have thought twice about separating me and Charm.

"The man was no use to anyone crippled like that, anyway," the general mutters, wiping his blade. "No one's going to mourn him."

The horsemaster looks at the dead mulemaster, and his smile widens.

"What are you waiting for?" the general snaps. "Get that girl out of here fast, before any of the king's friends see you. These men are loyal to me. They won't talk. But you'd better stay away from this army in the future. Officially, Charmeia is only a groom, but I can't guarantee what King Alexander will do if he finds out you've taken her. I'll think of something so he won't come after you."

The horsemaster nods, eyes me, and turns his camel.

As the camel lopes away, I try a whinny. It comes out like Hoplite's used to when he was a tiny foal. Charm makes no sound. Her red curls hang down as if she were dead, although her ghost is still inside her body.

To make things worse, the camel left an ENORMOUS pile of dung steaming in the horse lines, and there were no grooms to take it away. The smell of it drove me crazy. But the magic General Parmenio's men had put in my water had stolen my strength, so I couldn't even dominate it with my own.

AN OUTRIGHT LIE

I don't know who looked after me during the next few days. My water was brought in a bucket, always with more magic in it. But even in my sleepy state, no one dared try to ride me, and I'm sure I bit several of the general's men when they removed my muzzle so I could eat my hay.

Then one morning my water tastes clean, and the clouds in my head begin to lift. By the time I hear the familiar whinnies of the other horses I am feeling more myself. I whinny in joy, greeting them one by one.

PETASIOS!

BOREALIS!

XANTHUS!

HARPINNA!

APOLLO!
ARION!
HADES!
ELECTRA!
AURA!

There was a lot of whinnying and rushing around as the horses who had gone with Alexander were taken for their rolls and settled in the lines. Their grooms gossiped nonstop about their journey to the oracle. They were dirty, sunburned, and excited.

Seeing me in the horse lines, Tydeos called out, "Charm? Charm! You'll never guess what happened on the way back from Siwa! The king found a wonderful piece of land between the river and the sea. He's planning to build a huge city there with great harbors so people can travel into Egypt more easily. He laid it all out with chalk and flour. It'll be the biggest city you've ever seen — with twelve villages inside it, and there'll be canals, and temples to all the gods, and . . ." He laughed. "Charm, come out! Where are you hiding? *Charm?*"

He tied Petasios and Borealis in their usual places, one on each side of me, still looking around for Charm. "What have you done with your groom, Bucephalas? She must have heard us come back. We made enough noise."

I was so pleased to smell someone familiar, I nickered to him softly. He gave me a startled look. "What's up with you, you great brute? Glad to see me, or something?" He rubbed my nose and frowned when his fingers came away covered in dirt. "You're filthy! What have you two been up to while we've been away?"

This time he sounded worried.

I nudged him again and snorted. He ran his hands down my legs, stood back, and looked at me, puzzled. "You're definitely not yourself. You're not ill, are you, Bucephalas? I suppose I'll just have to look after you till Charm gets back."

With me and Zoroaster to settle as well, it took Tydeos longer than the other grooms to finish his work. As he is giving us our hay, shouts come from the end of the horse line, and I smell Alexander's sherbet sweetness.

The king, smiling and suntanned like the grooms, strides easily toward us, all trace of his limp gone. He calls for Charm. Of course, she doesn't appear.

When questioned, Tydeos shakes his head and says, "I don't know, Your Majesty. I haven't seen her since we got back. Maybe she went to get some medicine for Bucephalas? He doesn't look quite himself."

Alexander gives me an appraising look as he feeds me a pastry. I lick his palm. He runs a hand down my neck, looks at the dust on it, and frowns like Tydeos did earlier.

"Find me Charmides!" he shouts.

Some of the grooms hurry off to obey. Tydeos stammers, "I'm sure she must have a good reason for not being here, Your Majesty."

That is when General Parmenio appears, carrying something in his hand. It smells faintly of Charm, and for a moment I think she is back. I swing around on my tether and nicker hopefully. But it is only her purple scarf, the one Alexander gave her at Issus. It's torn and covered in blood.

Alexander stares at it. His fists clench, and some of the light goes out of his eyes. But he raises his gaze to General Parmenio and tilts his chin. "What's this? Why is my horse unattended and dirty?"

"I'm sorry, Alexander, but my men found this scarf down by the river. They think your groom must have been attacked by a crocodile. I organized a search party, of course, but we didn't find her body. That's the trouble with a girl doing a boy's job. She must have gotten careless when she was washing. This Egyptian river is dangerous for those who don't know it. My men have done their best with Bucephalas, but he's a difficult horse to manage."

As you know, this is an OUTRIGHT LIE.

I lash my tail and give the general flat ears. He eyes me warily but keeps his attention on Alexander. He makes himself huge as if he expects a battle and holds out the bloodied scarf. "I'm sorry, but I'm sure you understand I can't be everywhere at once looking out for grooms. I hope the oracle gave you good news?"

Alexander takes the scarf and frowns. He looks hard at the general and says in a level tone, "Thank you for your efforts, General. That's the trouble with leaving my camp in the care of an old man. This wouldn't have happened if I had been here, but not even a son of Zeus-Ammon can be everywhere at once."

General Parmenio flushes. He says in a low tone, "It was your idea to go gallivanting off to Siwa, when you should have been here negotiating a peace treaty with King Darius! His last offer was very generous. All the lands west of the Euphrates, his daughter's hand in marriage, and his son as a permanent hostage. You are already Captain of the Hellenic League, Lord of Anatolia, and now Pharaoh of Egypt. No Macedonian king has ever ruled so great an empire. If I were you, Alexander, I'd accept. We've finished what we came to do. We've thrown the Persians out of Anatolia and liberated Egypt in the bargain. The men are ready to go home."

Alexander's face flushes, too. He snaps at the openmouthed grooms to find themselves something useful to do, and they melt away. But, being grooms, they hover behind the baggage carts to listen. Tydeos stares at Charm's bloody scarf, his face white.

Alexander rests a hand on my hindquarters and takes a deep breath. He is standing on my good side, so I can see him. He makes himself huge without seeming to try. Even in his dusty tunic with his head bare, he looks more of a boss than the general ever does.

"I'd accept Darius's offer, too, if I were you, General Parmenio," Alexander says quietly. "You're an old man, so it's understandable you should have an old man's fears. The Siwa Oracle told me I'm the son of Zeus-Ammon, who changed himself into a snake to visit my mother the night she conceived me. King Philip is my mortal father, and his old horsemaster is a liar and a traitor, as everyone knew all along. I'm not afraid of the Persians or their curses. Did King Darius conquer the Gordian Knot? No! I did. We've already beaten their army once, so we can beat it again. I could marry Darius's daughter right now if I so wished. I already have the lands Darius is offering me. Prince Ochus will soon learn to love me as a father. I'm the son of a god! What do I need with the ransom Darius is offering for the rest of his family? I don't want more gold. I don't want a frightened Persian wife back in Macedonia. The oracle told me the only way to avoid King Philip's fate is to claim all the lands as far as the eastern ocean in the name of my holy father, Zeus. I will be rewarded with immortality, and so will every man brave enough to follow me!" He looks at Charm's bloodied scarf, and a shadow crosses his face. "Tell the men to break camp, General. There'll be no more talk of going home. We're starting after Darius tomorrow."

General Parmenio stares at Alexander as if he is seeing him properly for the first time.

Alexander glares back. "Well?" he says softly. "Why are you still here? The gods spoke to me at Siwa. Do you dare question their authority?"

The general shudders slightly and hurries away.

SON OF ZEUS

After Alexander had gone, Tydeos stood frozen to the spot. The other grooms ventured out from their hiding places and glanced at one another. When I nudged Tydeos he gave a great shuddering gasp and turned to me with tears in his eyes. "No," he whispered. "She *can't* be dead. Eaten by a crocodile! It can't be true, it *can't*!"

I wanted to tell him she was alive. But he didn't understand horse talk, so I nickered and nudged him again. When he finally took a comb and started to groom the dirt out of my coat, it was such a relief that I acted as gentle as Aura and did not nip him even once.

Groom-gossip was subdued that night, because of what they thought had happened to Charm. But they had so much to talk about, they couldn't keep quiet for long. While Tydeos went off to be alone, they argued about what the oracle had *really* told Alexander. The main theories are:

> He is the son of Zeus, like he told everyone, and he is taking us all to the edge of the world.
> He is the son of the old horsemaster, and he has made up the story about being the son of Zeus as an excuse to go after King Darius.
> He is the mortal son of King Philip, and he is afraid to take us home in case someone assassinates him, too.

Oh, and guess what he's calling his fine new Egyptian city? Alexandria!

You'd think he might have named it after poor Charm.

MESOPOTAMIA

SUMMER 331 B.C.

MISSING CHARM

When we left Egypt, we took plenty of food with us in the mule carts. The men were in high spirits after Alexander told them what the oracle had said, and our nosebags were full every evening. But I was missing Charm and left most of my barley. It was worse than when she went away after Thebes, because then her smell had lingered in my stall. This time we were moving on every day, and I couldn't find her spring-grass scent anywhere as we retraced our hoofprints up the coast to Tyre and then set out east across the plain to look for King Darius.

As soon as we left the coast behind, it grew seriously HOT. There were no trees to shade us from the sun, only endless dust that made us cough. When we camped, Tydeos tried his best to groom the sweat off me. But he didn't have water to bathe me because we needed every drop we carried to drink, so he had to use his mitten, and I HATE my belly being cleaned that way. After I'd nipped him a few times he gave up, only to get shouted at by Alexander for not looking after me properly.

Poor Tydeos. I think he was missing Charm, too.

Alexander kept her bloodstained scarf twisted around his belt. He fingered it thoughtfully as Petasios and I walked side by side at the front of our huge herd. "Do you think my groom was really eaten by a crocodile in Egypt?" he asked Hephaestion.

His friend gave him a sharp look. "Alex! I do believe you're pining for Charmides as much as your horse is!"

"Don't be ridiculous. She was only a groom."

"So why do you keep looking behind you? Persia's that way!" Hephaestion pointed at the shimmering horizon ahead of us.

Alexander sighed and took a swig from his water-skin. "She's not dead, my friend, I *feel* it. Maybe she ran away again, though I never thought she'd leave Bucephalas — Oh, stop looking at me like that! I only want her back so my horse will start eating again. Look at him, he's wasting away in this heat. At this rate, I'll be riding a skeleton by the time we get to Persia."

Hephaestion laughed, making Petasios toss his head. "You've got King Darius's wife, who is supposed to be the most beautiful woman in all Persia, and her two marriageable daughters captive in your baggage train, yet you're worrying about a slip of a groom?" He gave Alexander an amused look. "I should have guessed. She's defied you every step of the way yet you've never really punished her, have you? Not even after that business with the passes at Issus. It's a good thing she's gone, if you ask me. Imagine the scandal! The great King Alexander, brought to his knees by a slave girl who dresses like a boy!"

"You of all people know it's not like that!" Alexander snapped. He paused and looked over his shoulder again. "How far do you think I can trust General Parmenio?"

Hephaestion sobered at once. "Are you worried the men won't follow you across the Euphrates? Old Parmenio won't try the same trick he did at the Granicus, Alex, don't worry. He knows if he does, the phalanx will follow *you* this time, and he'll be the one left on the riverbank with a hand-ful of men to face the enemy. Somehow, I doubt he'll come out of it as well as you did."

Alexander sat a bit straighter on my back and smiled. "You're right there. After all, General Parmenio isn't the son of a god."

We walked on a bit, with just the thudding of our hooves and the creak of the men's armor breaking the silence. Hephaestion gave Alexander a sideways look. "Did the Siwa Oracle *really* say you're the son of Zeus?"

Alexander's eyes glinted. "Do you think I'd make up something like that?"

Hephaestion looked unsure. "And is it true the oracle promised you'd defeat Darius, reach the edge of the world, and become immortal?"

Alexander rested a sweaty hand on my crest and squinted at the horizon. "Yes."

If you ask me, that was a stupid question. What did Hephaestion expect Alexander to say? No?

"What about your father's assassination?"

Alexander stiffened. "I need to speak to my mother about that. It was unclear."

"But you asked the oracle if all King Philip's murderers had been punished, didn't you?" Hephaestion pressed. "You still haven't told me what it said to that."

"It doesn't matter what the oracle said!" Alexander smiled to take the sting out of his words. "Don't worry. I'm not going to let anyone slip a knife between *my* ribs. I'm the reborn Achilles and the son of Zeus, remember? When I've won the Persian crown and reached the edge of the world, I'll be a god as well as a king. Then I won't have to worry about my father's murderers, Persian curses, General Parmenio, or anyone else for that matter."

He gathered up my reins determinedly.

"According to the Greek maps, we're getting close to the Euphrates. Take some men on ahead, my friend, and find some boats to bridge the river. I don't want any delay crossing it. We need to find some shade before the men melt. Macedonians are not made for these temperatures!"

THE LAND BETWEEN TWO RIVERS

Hephaestion's bridge of boats shifted under our hooves, upsetting Electra and the other youngsters, so there was a lot of snorting and shouting as we crossed the Euphrates. On the other side we caught some enemy spies, who had come north from their city of Babylon to see what we were up to.

They were a small herd, easily dominated, and the ones we didn't catch ran away. But Alexander was suspicious and didn't chase them. Threatened by my flat ears and the king's sword, the captured spies soon told us that King Darius's entire army was waiting downriver to trap us in a place where the Persians had once dominated the Greeks. The boss of Babylon had orders to retreat before us and burn all the crops so our men would be tired and hungry by the time we got there.

Ha! How stupid do they think we are?

General Parmenio favored making camp on the west bank. But Alexander sent an order to the Amazons, who rode at the back of our herd, to burn the bridge behind us so no one could retreat. Then he turned my head into the rising sun, and we continued northeast away from the river. General Parmenio squealed a bit but ordered his men to follow us because he didn't want to fight the Persians himself, with only half a herd.

The Babylonian herd watched us go in dismay.

The land on the east side of the Euphrates is called Mesopotamia, which means "the land between the rivers." Mostly it was farmland, with canals crisscrossing the fields to water the crops. There was wheat to fill our nosebags and trees to shade us from the fierce sun. Only small villages lay on our route. The people either ran away before we got there or begged us not to hurt them and gave us their goats and sheep to feed the men. Since King Darius had not expected us to come this way, there were no soldiers to protect the vulnerable members of his herd from us. Alexander didn't bother dominating them. He treated the people of Mesopotamia like young foals, showing them he was boss without hurting them, because he knew they were no threat.

The next river, the Tigris, was shallow enough to cross without swimming. Although the baggage carts got a bit wet, and some of the shorter men had to be helped through the deepest parts by their friends, no one minded very much because it was lovely and cool in the water. We caught some more enemy spies and discovered from them that King Darius's army was now camped only about half a day's march away, having rushed across from the Euphrates to stop us marching farther east into Persia. Alexander smiled grimly and ordered the men to dig a ditch around the camp and set spikes in it to stop the Persians from attacking us in the night. Then he retired to his pavilion to talk tactics with General Parmenio.

Groom-gossip for the next three days was all about the coming battle. King Darius's herd is supposed to be bigger than ours. The grooms claim he has a million men and horses! I hope this is not true. We have only 40,000 men and 7,000 horses, and that's a lot less than a million.

The Amazons say that because of the horse bond Charm's absence weakens Alexander. So if our grooms are right, we're in a HUGE amount of trouble.

WHEN THE MOON WENT OUT

On the third night, I am in my normal spot in the horse lines between Petasios and Borealis. Tydeos has gone off with the other grooms. Ever since Charm disappeared in Egypt, he has been drinking so much magic it makes him sick in the mornings. We horses have had no work for the past three days, only lead-outs to stretch our legs, so I am feeling a bit fresh. When Aura nickers to me from the mares' lines, a shiver goes through me. She's coming into foal-season again, and her dappled summer coat glows beautifully under the full moon.

While I am remembering the last time I managed to run with a mare — Harpinna, back at Halicarnassus! — the light fades from Aura. Even Zoroaster is getting difficult to see. My coat prickles. The sentries light torches, and one of the men points to the sky and cries, "Look! A monster is eating the moon!"

My coat stands on end. Petasios whinnies nervously. Borealis shifts his backside into me. The sentries stare at the sky and whisper uneasily. They say it is a bad omen before a battle.

None of them notice a dark-skinned man run across from the hostages' pavilion and steal a bridle. The thief creeps behind the horse lines, bent double to keep out of sight. I whinny a warning, but he keeps well away from me. He eyes Zoroaster, but does not dare pass my lashing tail. Instead, he darts over to the mares' lines, where Aura nickers to him like the gentle mare she is. He smiles and puts the bridle on her.

The moon has now been fully eaten. It is very dark when the thief scrambles onto Aura's back and heads her out of the lines. He guides her between two stakes (easy, because they are pointing the other way to keep enemies out), twists his fingers in her mane, and gallops her at the ditch.

"Hey!" shouts one of the sentries, finally realizing something is wrong. "One of the Persian queen's slaves is escaping!"

A trumpet blares the alert call but too late. Aura, being both well trained and brave, leaps the ditch and vanishes into the night with the thief. The sentry tosses his spear after her, but it falls short.

I whinny wildly after my mare and rear up to break my tether. But before I can gallop after her, Prince Ochus races out of the hostages' tent.

"Charmeia!" he sobs, his thin face streaked with tears. "Where Charmeia?"

I haven't seen Ochus since Egypt, and his smell reminds me of what happened to Charm, which makes me forget Aura.

Tydeos grabs the man-colt and shakes him. "Was that one of your slaves who just stole our mare? He was lucky not to get speared! What's your mother thinking of, letting him run off like that?"

The prince's face twists. He clenches his fists and bursts into tears. "My mother's dead!" he sobs.

Tydeos stares at him in confusion. The moon is coming back now, but their faces are still in shadow. "The Persian queen's dead?" Tydeos looks fearfully at the hostages' pavilion. "Oh, Zeus, Alexander didn't kill her, did he?"

Ochus shakes his head again. "She get sick on journey. She die tonight. One of her slaves say he go to my father's camp with the news. I tell him to take Zoroaster, but he must get confused. Not hurt him, please. He only slave." He looks pleadingly at the sentries, who have gathered around to make sure Ochus does not escape as well. They seem embarrassed by the prince's tears.

"He's probably in the Persian camp by now, you little eel," grunts one of the sentries. "Galloped off on the gray mare like all the devils were after him."

Ochus sniffs. "He get away?" Some of the tension runs out of him. "Good! He will tell Father what happen. Then after the battle, Father will come and rescue me and my sisters and Granny Sisygambis and Auntie Barsine."

One of the sentries takes the prince's arm to escort him back to his pavilion, but Tydeos stops him. "No — wait!" He crouches down so he is level with the man-colt. "Charmeia's gone, Ochus. We haven't seen her since Egypt. General Parmenio thinks she was eaten by a crocodile, but I . . ." His voice cracks, and he continues in a harsher tone. "You were in the camp when she disappeared. Did you see her go to the river?"

Ochus bites his lip, glances at me, then whispers something to Tydeos.

Tydeos's breath comes faster. He grips the man-colt's shoulders and says, "What did General Parmenio do to her?"

But Ochus shakes his head. "I not see. His soldiers take me back to Lady Barsine. I get a spanking because running away not good behavior for a prince. Then Mother get sick, and Lady Barsine say it my fault because I make her worry so much. But Charmeia not get eaten by crocodile. She not that silly."

"No," Tydeos whispers, a little smile playing at the corners of his mouth. "I *knew* it couldn't be true. . . . Charm's still alive!"

I smell Alexander's sherbet sweetness and nicker to him. Tydoes looks around wildly, but there is no time to hide because the king is already striding down the horse lines toward us. The sentries rush back to their posts. The grooms quickly straighten their tunics and swill out their mouths with some of our water. Tydoes doesn't get a chance, because Ochus is clinging to his arm.

Alexander obviously hasn't slept. There are dark circles under his eyes. Perita, now quite grown-up, trots at his heels. But when she smells Ochus, she bounds past the king to lick the man-colt's face. Ochus puts his arms around the dog's neck and stares defiantly at Alexander.

"I'm very sorry to hear about your mother, Ochus," the king says quietly. "I've sent a message to your father myself. There was no need for your slave to risk his neck stealing one of our horses. Go back to Lady Barsine now. You can take Perita with you."

Alexander waits until the sentry has led the man-colt and the dog away. Then he glares at the men and grooms and snaps, "How did this happen?"

Tydeos stammers, "We're very sorry, Your Majesty. But we were asleep, and the moon —"

"*Drunk*, more like it!" Alexander shouts. He strides up and down the line of frightened grooms, sniffing their breath and shaking his head in disgust. "Don't any of you realize this is the battle we've been heading toward ever since we left Pella? All those cities we captured, all the men who have died . . . all that effort was so we could come *here*, to the very borders of Persia, and challenge King Darius on his home ground. He has every last fighting man in his empire camped half a day away. If we win this battle, the Persian army will never recover. Darius's crown will be

192

mine, and all his lands. There will be no one left to stop me from reaching the edge of the world!"

As the king speaks, his fists clench and unclench, and little shudders go through his body. The sentries fidget, uncomfortable. Tydeos looks at his feet and says nothing.

Alexander draws a final, shuddering breath and presses his knuckles to his forehead. The men and grooms tense. Tydeos closes his eyes.

But the king sighs and lowers his fist. When he next speaks, it is in a quieter tone. "You're only grooms. You can't be expected to understand. But you're lucky that slave took the mare. If he'd stolen Bucephalas, I'd have turned the lot of you out of this camp without your hands, like that old muleteer General Parmenio tells me killed himself in Egypt because he couldn't bear to live any longer as a cripple!"

He pauses to let this sink in, then orders everyone back to their posts with instructions to stay alert, because we are breaking camp tomorrow and going to meet Darius. "There's to be no more drinking until after we've won this battle," he continues, and his lips twitch up at one corner. "Then we can *all* celebrate."

Tydeos shivers at his lucky escape. He peers at the king and whispers, "Are we really going to win, sir? Everyone's saying King Darius's army is much bigger than ours, and the moon went out . . ."

The other grooms and sentries creep closer to hear the king's reply. Alexander flicks a hand at the moon and laughs. "My seer tells me the eclipse was a sign that Macedonia will darken the light of Persia before this month is out. It's a bad omen for Darius, but a good omen for us! As for these silly rumors about the size of King Darius's army, the prisoners we captured were probably exaggerating. Even if they weren't, one Macedonian is worth ten Persians. We'll get Demetrius's mare back again soon enough, don't you worry!"

A HUGE HERD

Alexander might have told our grooms not to worry, but next morning, in the cool time before sunrise, when he vaulted onto me the shadows around his eyes were even deeper. He called the Guard, and we galloped into the hills to take a look at the Persian army.

I could tell there were strange horses ahead long before we saw them. We could hear them whinnying as their grooms gave them breakfast. I flared my nostrils to catch the smells: sweat, smoke, barley, oil, men, stallions, LOTS of mares. As we crested the ridge, my skin tightened with excitement.

I filled my lungs and let out a shuddering neigh. Some of the Persian horses looked around, but most were too far away to hear me. The sun rose, huge and red out of the haze over the plain, bringing more and more of the enemy herd into view. Most seemed to be cavalry like us, but there were a few chariots, too. The sun flashed fire from their wheels as they drove up and down the lines and lines of horses, looking very tiny below us.

On my back, Alexander was silent. He raised a hand to shade his eyes against the sun. His other hand held my rein so tightly I had to toss my head to tell him he was hurting my mouth. He trembled slightly, moved his lips as if counting under his breath, and whispered, "Oh, Zeus, Hephaestion . . . have I made a very big mistake?"

Fortunately, the rest of the Guard did not hear this. They, too, were staring at the army, and whispering uneasily among themselves. Iolaus looked as pale as snow. Electra had joined the Guard to carry Aura's rider, Demetrius. My filly was being very well behaved, considering she had the big Achilles shield resting on her withers, but I missed my special mare.

Hephaestion nudged Petasios forward until his knee touched Alexander's. He said in a professional voice, "Nearly all cavalry, exactly as the Persian captives said. They have new weapons . . . longer spears . . . what looks like better armor . . . chariots, of course, with something on their wheels, I can't quite see . . . blades, I think." He glanced at Alexander. "We'll have to watch out for them, or they'll gash the horses' legs."

Alexander gave his friend a grateful look, sat up straighter, and took a deep breath. "Yes, it's going to be a cavalry battle — the best sort! I don't see any foot soldiers. Do you?"

"A few." Hephaestion pointed to the middle of the herd. "Not many. Probably only Darius's bodyguard." He glanced back at our army, which was still marching into position through the hills. "What do you think, Alex? The men are rested and eager to fight. Shall we attack before the Persians wake up?"

The Guard heard this and gathered up their reins, trying to look as if they weren't scared. Their horses had already sensed their nerves and danced closer to me. I trembled with excitement. My rider wasn't scared, of course, but he felt a bit less confident than usual.

Alexander shook his head and narrowed his eyes. "I'm going to have to think about this. They'll outflank us easily. Their cavalry outnumbers ours at least five to one. They've been camped here long enough to have set traps. You heard what those Persian spies we caught said about pits and hidden stakes. I want a closer look at the ground down there."

Hephaestion looked worried. "What about General Parmenio's idea of a night attack to target and kill Darius?"

Alexander shook his head and made himself huge. "No, my friend! No more assassinations. This battle must be won properly or not at all. I'd rather win tomorrow and have Darius escape again than kill him and leave all those Persians down there to fight me another day under another leader."

"But you have King Darius's only son and heir captive."

Alexander smiled. "Do you really think that matters to them? Since when has legitimacy had anything to do with power? How long do you think it'd take Antipater to seize the throne of Macedonia if I were to die here today? And General Parmenio's just waiting for someone to kill me, so his son Philotas can be king. Or maybe you want to lead the army, Hephaestion? Or *you*, Iolaus?"

He turned and made a playful jab at Iolaus's ribs with the shaft of his spear. The Guard looked a bit alarmed.

"No one's going to kill you, Alex, don't be silly!" Demetrius said.

"They won't get close enough, and they wouldn't dare," Ptolemy added. "Everyone knows you're favored by the gods."

"You're the son of Zeus, aren't you?" said Perdiccas.

"And it's different for you, anyway. The Persians respect their king's family. You don't have an official heir yet —"

Craterus should have known better than to mention that. Alexander's fist tightened on my rein, and his cheeks flushed. "Enough! We're wasting time. I need a cavalry escort. See to it, will you, Hephaestion. I'm going down there."

I lashed my tail in Xanthus's face as we cantered down the slope. But Alexander felt determined again and he had stopped trembling.

As we trotted around that plain under the burning sun, with half our cavalry as escort and the horses of the Guard close around me, Alexander grew more and more confident. We didn't find any pits with stakes — just a vast area of leveled ground with the stones removed, perfect for galloping over. I was impatient to try it out, but Alexander kept me on a tight rein and wouldn't let any of us out of a trot.

Meanwhile, a small herd of Persians trotted their horses up and down nearby and called out squealing threats.

"Where's your great army, King Iskander?"

"We only see a few boys not old enough to shave."

"Our Great King Darius say if you go home, he send you some golden toys to keep you amused. He say you should leave war to men, or we teach you a hard lesson tomorrow!"

Alexander ignored them. He told the Guard to pretend we were planning a night attack on the Persian camp as General Parmenio had advised, then he carried on surveying the plain, making notes on a piece of flattened grass balanced across my withers. Since he was obviously too busy to squeal back, I squealed at their horses to put them in their place. And every time I found a pile of Persian dung, I made sure I dominated it.

When we got back to camp, Alexander disappeared into his pavilion with his notes. He turned away everyone who tried to join him, even Hephaestion. He worked through the hot afternoon and most of the night. Finally, his lamp flickered out, so I knew my rider slept at last.

GAUGAMELA

AUTUMN 331 B.C.

ALEXANDER'S PLAN

After their telling-off the previous day, our grooms were up before dawn. They fed us our prebattle breakfast of barley soaked in honey (of which I managed only two mouthfuls) and groomed us until we shone. Tydeos combed out my tail almost as carefully as Charm would have done and checked my girth straps and bridle fastenings at least ten times. All this fuss put me on edge. I had to nip him on the arm to make him stop.

Every horse in the lines knew we were getting ready for battle. You could feel the tension rippling in the air. Off in the haze of smoke that hung over our camp, the men were putting on armor and checking their weapons. Trumpets sounded and officers shouted orders. Foot soldiers jogged past to form neat squares on the edge of the plain. Cavalrymen came for their horses, and the lines emptied. By the time the sun rose, only we horses of the Guard remained.

The Amazons cantered past on their little horned horses painted with blue circles, and the Guard came down with armfuls of spears and javelins. They propped these against a cart and stood nearby, talking in excited voices and looking over their shoulders. The grooms untied their horses and walked them up and down, ready for them to mount. Only Alexander had not yet arrived, so no one did.

Tydeos put a hand on my nose and whispered, "I'm sorry, old horse. I can't keep you out of this battle. If Charm were here, she'd find a way, but I'm not as brave as she is. I daren't defy the king. Just come back in one piece, in case Charm — just in case. Oh, where *is* the king? I can't stand this waiting!"

A man in battle-scarred armor strode toward us, and everyone stiffened. But it was only General Parmenio. He frowned at the Guard. "No sign of him yet?"

They shook their heads.

"One of you go and fetch him, then! The men are ready. If we wait much longer, there won't be time to finish this battle before dark. Tell him we want to know what his plans are. Zeus, if Alexander doesn't come and lead us today, this is going to be a massacre!"

That could have meant one of two things:

We were going to massacre the Persians.
The Persians were going to massacre us.

The Guard glanced at one another. Hephaestion cleared his throat and said, "Alex said we weren't to disturb him, sir. He hasn't slept for four days. I think he's still in bed. He needs his rest."

The general stared in disbelief at the king's pavilion. "You're telling me he's overslept, today of all days? Looks like I'll have to go and wake him up myself, then!" He strode off, grumbling under his breath.

Finally, after the sun has climbed much higher in the sky and even the Guard are beginning to get worried, I smell Alexander's sherbet sweetness. I let out a ringing neigh of welcome, and Tydeos clamps his hand over my nostrils in alarm. "Shh, Bucephalas! He'll be here —"

Before Tydeos can finish speaking the king arrives, smiling. The circles have faded from around his eyes. He is wearing his reinforced Troy helmet with its white plumes but has left the Achilles armor in the baggage train. He's chosen to wear his old snake-haired breastplate, which means this is going to be a serious battle. He runs straight up to me and offers me a pastry left over from his breakfast, which I am too excited to eat. I blow crumbs all over him. He laughs and springs onto my back in a great bound, like he used to do back in Macedonia.

I rear up high, catching his excitement, and Tydeos ducks.

"Don't just stand there, boy!" Alexander says. "I've a battle to win. Hand me my javelins!"

Tydeos hurries to obey. But as he passes up the javelins, he takes a deep breath and whispers, "Your Majesty, I've discovered something happened back at the camp while we were away visiting the Egyptian oracle. Charm might not have been eaten by a crocodile, after all. See, General Parmenio arrested her because she tried to help Prince Ochus escape, and —"

I am dancing around so much, Alexander doesn't hear properly. He frowns down at Tydeos. "What's that? Don't bother me with it now, boy. King Darius awaits!"

He gathers up my reins, tucks his spear and javelins under his arm, and trots me over to the Guard. "Hurry up, gentlemen!" he calls. "Mount up! Let's show these Persians what we Macedonians are made of."

"Do you have a plan, then, Alex?" Hephaestion asks, trotting Petasios beside me.

Alexander grins. "Yes, I've got a plan. Even old Parmenio couldn't fault it. Stick close to me, and ride as you have never ridden before. This is going to be the greatest battle of our lives!"

It takes some time to get everyone in position to Alexander's satisfaction. We trot up and down the ranks, while he checks every division from several angles. He doesn't seem interested in what the Persians are doing, although out of the corner of my good eye I can see the Guard casting worried glances at the far side of the plain, where the enemy is lining up.

They have reason to be worried. The Persian herd stretches across the entire horizon, and we can hear their horses whinnying in the distance. They might not have a million, but they have many thousands more men and horses than we do. As I've said before, this is NOT GOOD.

Finally, everyone is where Alexander wants him. I wonder if he's had too much sun. The phalanx is at the back, quite a long way behind everyone else. Most of our cavalry are on the wings, curving almost in a circle and facing the wrong way — sideways to rather than facing the Persians. There is a line of foot soldiers at the front with their long pikes, but not many. Some of the cavalry is with us, at the front where they should be, and the Amazons are hiding in the hills to pick off the enemy as they flee. But we're not nearly a big enough herd to dominate the Persians. We will have to be very fierce.

Nervous sweat gleams on our necks as I halt in front of the troops so

Alexander can make a speech. We chew our bits and arch our necks. Alexander hands his javelins and shield to Hephaestion and rides me a few steps forward to face his men. I make myself huge. Behind me, the Guard line up knee to knee as if they are on parade:

PETASIOS — *handsome, faithful, and my best friend* — *carrying Hephaestion*

BOREALIS — *a bit slow but comfortingly solid* — *carrying Leonnatus*

XANTHUS — *trouble in the lines, excellent in battle* — *carrying Craterus*

ARION — *quietly does his job* — *carrying Attalus*

HADES — *small, but quick on his feet* — *carrying Iolaus*

APOLLO — *still a bit vain but has learned how to fight* — *carrying Perdiccas*

HARPINNA — *an amazing fighter* — *carrying Ptolemy*

ELECTRA — *my beautiful filly, fighting her very first battle!* — *carrying Demetrius and the Achilles shield*

There is a hush. Even the Persians at the far side of the plain go quiet.

"We are going to win today!" Alexander begins, and there is a huge cheer from our herd. When it dies away, he says a lot of boring things about honor and glory, which make the men nod and look fierce. Then he prays to "his father Zeus," and draws his sword to personally make the prebattle sacrifice. I snort as goat's blood sprays across my nose.

The men give Alexander another great cheer as he retrieves his weapons from Hephaestion. When he whirls me around to take my place at the front of the army, all the men behind us ready their spears, and all the horses and foot soldiers make themselves huge.

A whole army, making itself huge at once!

I have never, in all my years of battle, seen that before.

DOMINATING THE PERSIANS

The excitement infects me. I begin to shiver, even though it is so hot, and every single one of my muscles goes tense. On my cloth, Alexander is tense, too. He holds me to a walk as we advance, but I am ready to gallop at the slightest shift of his weight. The Persian herd is getting slowly closer. We can hear their men calling insults across the plain. None of our herd replies. We advance in silence and with strict discipline. It is like a big parade.

The Persian horses kick up dust, which makes their herd seem even bigger. I suppose we are making dust, too, because some of the men in the phalanx behind us cough. But we don't make so much of it.

"Come on, come on," Alexander mutters as we get closer. "Charge, you Persian cowards. Why don't they charge?"

"There's King Darius," Hephaestion says, nodding toward the chariots in the center of the Persian line, their wheel blades flashing. "Hiding behind that group."

"Yes." Alexander still does not shift his weight. "We won't be able to see much once the charge starts. Remember where Darius is, gentlemen! Watch for my signal."

There are a few tense nods. The other horses are as ready to gallop as I am, but disciplined enough to obey their riders. The excitement is getting to Electra, though, who goes sideways in her eagerness to pass me. Demetrius is having trouble holding both her and the big Achilles shield. I swing my head at the filly and give her a little squeal. It makes all the horses jump.

Still, we walk. The Persians ahead of us are drifting sideways, trying to see how many troops we have behind us. Because our men are curved back in a circle, they can't see them properly. Maybe Alexander is cleverer than I thought.

"Your plan's working, Alex!" Hephaestion calls, excited. "If they keep this up, they'll soon be in the rough ground at the edge, and their horses and chariots will be in trouble."

The Persian herd is so close now, I can smell their horses. The enemy directly opposite us have spotted Alexander's helmet. They point at us and shout. Then one of their horses leaps forward, and a whole section of their herd at the end of their line breaks away and follows it. Trumpets blare in the distance.

A shudder goes through Alexander. He hisses, "*Yes!* They're falling for it, gentlemen. Be ready for my signal. . . ." A ripple of anticipation goes down our line. But Alexander's weight stays in the exact center of my back. He raises his first javelin and signals to the officers behind him. The enemy and their great cloud of dust have already gone around us to engage the troops behind us. Screams, shouts, and panicky sword clashes suggest they've found our phalanx and rather more men than they bargained for.

Still Alexander holds my rein tightly. He makes more signals, and the trumpets pass them on. Then Hephaestion shouts, "The chariots, Alex! Look out!"

Racing toward us are pairs of crazy Persian horses, completely out of control, dragging chariots with blades flashing on their wheels. As the dust billows around them, they head for our front line of foot soldiers, who melt out of their path and let them through to meet a phalanx hiding in the dust behind with a hedge of pikes. There are yells of alarm from the Persian drivers, who can't pull up in time, crashes and thuds, and the screams of dying horses. This is too much for Electra. She takes three huge leaps and breaks from the Guard into a wild gallop with her head in the air and the bit between her teeth. Demetrius drops his javelins and almost loses the Achilles shield, too.

Alexander curses, then shouts, "Follow me!" At last, he eases my rein and leans slightly forward. It is what I have been waiting for. I leap into a gallop, chasing my runaway filly.

"ALALALALALAI!" Alexander yells, putting his heels into my sides and heading me at the Persian line.

Behind us, the Guard echo the war cry.

"ALALALALALAI! ALALALALAI! ALALALALAI!"

And there is a great thunder of hooves as everyone follows us.

Oh, this is WILD! I can barely see. Dust is everywhere. The noise of battle is incredible. Ghosts whirl around me as men and horses die. But the plain is beautifully level, I have Alexander on my back, and I gallop through it all fearlessly. I catch up with Electra and bite her on the neck. She puts her head down and feels the bit again. Demetrius's relieved face flashes past us as he gets her back under control and takes his place behind us with the Achilles shield.

We form a tight wedge as we've been trained to do, with me at the front and the cavalry behind, so closely packed that I can hear the men's shields knocking together and feel the hot breath of the other horses on my hindquarters. There's going to be a few sore heels after this, but no one dares tread on mine. Petasios is beside me, Hephaestion's elbow brushing

Alexander's as they sight on the Persian line and balance their javelins for the throw. Our riders exchange coltish grins. Then they launch their javelins through the dust in perfect unison and make two more Persian ghosts.

"*Now*, gentlemen!" Alexander yells, and does a strange thing. Instead of urging me on through the Persian line to trample and kill more of the enemy, he digs his right knee hard into my ribs and clamps his right leg against my cloth, dragging my reins hard left against my neck. I swerve at once, feeling the wrench along my tendons, and head off at an angle along the startled enemy line. Petasios comes with me, tossing his head in surprise. The others make the turn behind, still in our wedge. It is perfect — until one of the blade-wheeled chariots without a driver appears out of the dust right beside me.

The Persian horses, wild-eyed and flat out, are on a collision course.

Hephaestion yells a bad word and hauls Petasios off to the side to give me room to maneuver. Alexander's weight shifts a little, and his knees turn me just in time. The nearest horse brushes my flank, and the blade on the wheel hisses past my blind spot. I leap to avoid it and feel a fierce sting like a mosquito bite on the side of my hind leg. Then it's gone, and I forget the pain. But there's a frantic neigh behind me, and a gray horse tumbles head over heels in the dust with a horrible crunch of bone.

"Attalus is down!" Hephaestion yells.

Attalus rolls clear and springs to his feet, but Arion is still thrashing on the ground behind us. As we race on, the chariot, now on one wheel, barges past the others and somehow gets through without hitting anyone else, the Persian horses dragging it on its side.

"His horse broke a leg!" Demetrius yells, catching up with us on foaming Electra. "Attalus is on his feet. . . . Do we go back for him, Alex?"

Alexander does not look around. "No. Stay with me. Close up! I'm going for Darius!"

He urges me even faster toward the dim shapes of the enemy chariots in the center, where the Persian line is breaking up because of everyone going sideways earlier. "Second javelins, gentlemen!" Alexander yells. "Make them count!"

He jerks on my cloth, and his javelin flies into a Persian chest, knocking the rider backward off his horse and releasing his ghost. I squeal in triumph. Now the Guard and the cavalry all throw their final javelins. There is a hissing like rain, and more Persians fall. Some of their horses get hit, too. But there is no time to be sad, because suddenly there are enemies all around us. Alexander is stabbing with his spear, Hephaestion and Petasios are fighting fiercely beside us, and I have to leap to avoid the long, curved, Persian blades.

The gap Arion left has been filled by another horse. Its rider is Laomedon, who rode Electra before Demetrius needed her. He flashes Alexander a quick grin and grimly stabs a Persian with his spear. I whinny at the little bay he is riding to get closer and leap to carry Alexander out of range of another scimitar.

I collect a few cuts. None of them hurt. That's what it's like in a battle, as if a small man-colt is slapping you from all sides. Irritating, but not painful. At least, not at the time. I look after my rider so well, no enemy blade or spear touches Alexander.

I have to keep snorting to clear my nose. The sweat pours off my sides. There is white foam on my neck. I cannot see more than five horses around me, though the noise and screams tell me there are thousands close by. Then another chariot comes into view, and I break into a fresh sweat as I remember what happened to Arion. But this chariot still has a driver, and there is an important-looking Persian standing behind him, gripping the sides and shouting orders. He is tall with dark skin and curly black whiskers. His helmet is wrapped in blue-and-white cloth. Gold glitters at his wrists and from the sides of the chariot. I can smell him from here. He smells of fear.

When Alexander sees him, he hauls my head around, hurting my mouth.

"King Darius!" he yells in his shrill voice, drawing his sword.

The man in the chariot turns his head, and his dark eyes widen in alarm. He shouts a warning, and his driver hauls the horses around and whips them into a gallop. Horns sound in the Persian line, and gaps open up around us with shouts of confusion. More trumpets blare — this time they're ours. Fierce shouting comes from the direction of our lines, and I see our phalanx with lowered pikes charging through the dust after a herd of fleeing Persian cavalry.

"The Persians are retreating, Alex!" Hephaestion shouts, turning Petasios to see better. "You've done it. I think you've actually done it!"

The Guard cheer.

Alexander shakes his head impatiently. "It's not over yet. Don't let Darius get away! Guard, follow me!" He urges me after the chariot.

I am tired, and so are the other horses. We try our best. But the Persians surrounding the chariot fight fiercely and keep getting in the way. Hephaestion gets left behind and yells as an enemy spear pierces his shoulder.

Alexander's head snaps around. "*Hephaestion!*" We have galloped no more than a few strides after the fleeing chariot, yet he turns me back at once to help.

But it is not yet time for Hephaestion's ghost to leave him. He grits his teeth, pulls out the spear, and keeps it, since he's already broken his own. "You go on, Alex!" he shouts, clasping his wound. "I'll be fine."

Alexander casts an anguished glance after Darius's fleeing chariot but stays to examine Hephaestion's shoulder. "Can you still fight, my friend?"

Hephaestion nods, while I nip Petasios on the nose for letting his rider get wounded.

"Good, then stay here and help General Parmenio clean up the stragglers. The rest of you, come with me!"

But as Alexander wheels me around to resume the chase after King Darius, Perdiccas yells, "Look out, gentlemen! Behind you!"

That's the trouble when the enemy is in retreat, and you have galloped so far through their lines. All those who charged past you during the battle then turn around and come back toward you, going the other way. We whirl as one to find ourselves facing a whole herd of Persians, their horses draped with bundles that spill golden coins and cups behind them in the dust.

One of them is leading a mule with a jeweled box strapped to its back. It is one of OUR mules — the nerve! Others have the Persian women we took captive at Issus sitting behind them on their horses, clinging to their waists. When they recognize Alexander, the Persians check their horses in dismay and stare around wildly. The women scream.

Alexander is already panting from the battle, but his breathing gets even faster. He casts a final frustrated look at Darius's vanishing chariot, gathers up my reins, and shouts, "Those men have been looting our camp! Don't let them get away! They've stolen my *Iliad*!"

The Guard, and those of the cavalry still with us, growl in their throats.

Alexander grips his sword tighter and heads me straight for the Persian leading the mule. The thief pales, drops the mule's rein, and turns his horse to flee, but I am too quick for it. I bite it on the neck to drive it back, and Alexander's sword flashes across the Persian's throat.

His ghost lurches from his body, while enemy blood sprays my ears and Alexander's cheek. The other Persians have recovered from the shock of coming face-to-face with the Macedonian king and are fighting furiously. They have the stolen captives in the middle of their group, and I can smell Prince Ochus among them. One of the Persians has the man-colt perched on his horse's withers.

I don't think Alexander has noticed the man-colt yet. But Ochus stares in horror as my rider kills Persian after Persian with his sword, until the blade is red and both he and I are soaked in enemy blood. Dust sticks to it and turns us both brown.

Some of our herd also give up their ghosts, because the Persian thieves know that surrendering won't save their lives. Finally, though, they are beaten, and the few survivors huddle with the stolen captives, ringed by our cavalry. Gold litters the plain like flowers. My hooves chink on it as Alexander walks me forward.

A dented cup rolls away as I kick it. He rides me right up to the Persian holding Ochus, wipes an arm across his face — which just smudges the dust and blood, making it look worse — and stares at the prince. The man-colt is very brave and meets his gaze.

"Leaving me already, Ochus?" Alexander says in his quiet, dangerous tone. "What's the matter? Don't I treat you well enough?"

"Not hurt our prince, please," says the Persian holding him. "We think Great King Darius win the battle. We take his children back to him, that is all."

"The 'Great King' *did* win the battle," Alexander snaps. "You're looking at him."

He gives the two sobbing princesses, who are still clinging to their rescuers' waists, a disgusted look. Then he turns his attention to Ochus. "Where are your grandmother and Lady Barsine?"

"Granny Sisygambis not come," Ochus says, sitting up very straight. "She say she too old for galloping around battlefields. She say she wait for Father to escort her back himself. Auntie Barsine stay to look after her."

Alexander shakes his head. "Is an old woman the only one with any sense around here?" he shouts. "You could all have been killed! Hephaestion, you take Prince Ochus back to camp. See him and the princesses safely back to their pavilion and double the guard — and someone catch that stupid mule before it trots off into the hills with my *Iliad*!"

One of the cavalrymen goes after the mule. Hephaestion takes Ochus up onto Petasios with him but hesitates, watching Alexander uneasily. The others put the Macedonian dead across the backs of the spare horses. They leave the Persian bodies where they lie because there are so many of them. A few loose horses are rounded up before they can get lost in the dust. Alexander shakes his head at the three Persian thieves left alive. They've been dragged off their horses and forced to their knees in front of me.

"Please, King Iskander," says the man who was caught with Ochus. "Spare us! We only do what we think best for our Great King's family. He very upset when his wife die. He worry about them."

Alexander scowls and rides me so close to the prisoners that my hooves stamp near their knees. They put their arms over their heads and cower away from my flat ears and snapping teeth. "You were stupid, and you've delayed me. If Darius gets away, it'll be your fault. You don't deserve to live. But since you've begged for your lives, and I am a greater king than Darius, I'll return the favor he showed my wounded at Issus. Then, if we don't catch King Darius tonight, maybe you can find your way back to him and give him a message from me."

The Persians turn a funny color as they realize what he means. The Macedonians seize them and stretch out their arms on the ground. Alexander backs me up to give them space. Then he gives a sharp nod. A sword flashes down, twice for each man. The Persian women cry out in protest. Ochus makes a small sound in his throat and buries his face in Hephaestion's shoulder. His sisters scream at Alexander in Persian. I don't know what they're saying, but it sounds to me like mares squealing.

The prisoners stare at their severed hands lying in the dust among the spilled gold, as if they can't believe what Alexander has just ordered done to them. Blood pours from their wrists. Even the Macedonians grimace as they tie rags around the bloody stumps to stop the mutilated men from bleeding to death before they reach their camp.

Alexander speaks to the three prisoners as if nothing has happened. "Tell Darius that I am the Great King of Persia now. Tell him that so far I have treated his family as my family, and his son as my son. But if he tries to raise another army against me, then I will give his daughters to my men to use as slaves and kill the boy. If Darius wants to live, he must surrender himself to me. Otherwise, I will hunt him to the ends of the earth. *Go!*"

The handless Persians stagger through the gap our cavalry makes for them and stumble off into the dust. Ochus stares in disbelief at Alexander, blinks rapidly, and is sick down Petasios's shoulder.

CHASING KING DARIUS

As the sun sank into the dust and turned everything around us red, I began to look forward to my roll. But Alexander turned my head to the east, pulled my ear, and whispered, "Come on, Bucephalas. I need your speed now." He put his bloody sword back into its scabbard, called the Guard to follow, and dug his heels into my sides.

We chased King Darius well into that night, overtaking some of his fleeing herd and passing his abandoned chariot. Alexander did not even pause to draw his sword, so it was just as well the frightened Persians took off across the fields when they saw us coming. I found my second wind and forgot my wounds as we galloped through the littered bodies of men and horses. I was determined to do better than Xanthus did after Issus. My hind leg was stiff where the chariot blade had cut me, and the other three felt as if they had boulders tied to them, but I did not slacken my pace. There were piles of dung smelling of Aura in the road, and every time I found one, a fresh surge of energy kept me galloping onward.

Eventually, though, my breath stopped coming so easily, and bubbles of something hot and bitter kept blocking my throat. If Alexander had asked me for more speed, I would have found it for him, but he finally noticed I was bleeding from the nose and pulled me back to a trot. There were some big, round-roofed huts near the river, and he turned me toward them. As soon as we stopped, my knees gave way, and Alexander had to pretend that he had told me to settle down.

He slipped off me, held on to my head while I drew shuddering breaths past the blood in my nose, and whispered, "Oh, Bucephalas . . . don't you dare die on me, horse! Even Darius isn't worth that."

Meanwhile, the other horses stood around me with drooping heads, heaving rib cages, and flaring nostrils. The men dismounted in relief, as wobbly-kneed as we were. Some of them went to investigate the huts, while the others led us to the river for a drink and found us some hay. Alexander tended me himself. He wiped the blood from my nose with his tunic and led me up and down until the stiffness went from my legs. Then he took the Guard into one of the huts, while the rest of the men curled up on the ground nearby.

Scenting another of Aura's dung piles nearby, I sent one last weary whinny into the night. But she did not reply.

How Aura Led the Persian Herd

It is still dark when Alexander mounts me again. We trot along the river road by moonlight, following Aura's trail. The blood has stopped coming out of my nose, though my hind leg is now very stiff so I am lame behind.

As the sun rises, we reach a town. Its garrison is deserted, so when Alexander and I lead our weary herd through the gates of Arbela, there is no one left for us to fight. This is just as well, because we are only a small herd now. We have not only fought a fierce battle, but have galloped through most of the night and must look a sight. The humans who live in this town are still scared of us, though. They run into their houses and slam their doors. Alexander stares wearily after them and trots me to the palace.

It is deserted. Our hooves echo in the marble courtyard. A fountain splashes into a pink marble bowl. The smell of water makes me thirsty. Doors bang in the wind. A few goats and dogs wander loose in the yard. Some women and old men creep out of the dark doorways and lie down in the dirt before me and Alexander, pressing their foreheads to the ground.

"Where's King Darius?" Alexander asks. But they don't seem to understand, so he calls Laomedon forward to translate.

"They say the Great King's gone, Alex," Laomedon says, after questioning the slaves. "He and the remains of his army headed into the mountains last night. Four, maybe five thousand men. We won't catch them now."

Alexander does not seem surprised. He sighs and rides me around the courtyard. My hooves echo in the silence and my stride is broken by lameness — clop, clop, clop-clop, clop, clop, clop-clop. I am so tired I can barely hold my head off the ground. But as we pass the stables, I catch a familiar scent inside. AURA! I summon the last of my strength and send her a ringing whinny.

A few of the cavalry horses who came with us on the chase whinny back. I fidget, wanting to sniff the dung piles I can see lying over by the entrance, but Alexander won't let me. Then I hear Aura whinny back, very faint. All the horses of the Guard flicker their ears. I whinny again and dance sideways, grabbing my bit in my teeth.

Alexander smooths my mane and frowns at the stables. He tells Iolaus, "Go and check inside."

Iolaus hands Hades' reins to Demetrius and stamps past us, grumbling that he's not a groom. All the Guard are tired and grumpy, so Alexander ignores this. We wait. The slaves stay quiet, with their faces still pressed to the ground. I manage to get my nose into the fountain bowl and gulp a few mouthfuls. The water is warm.

Then Iolaus comes back out of the stables, leading Aura. Her head hangs low. Her lovely dappled coat is crusted in dried sweat. Her flanks and sides are covered in whip marks, raw and bleeding. She is limping, too, with little snorts at the pain each time she puts her bad leg down. She looks twice my age, and that's a lot of years. If it weren't for her smell and her familiar whinny, I would not have recognized her.

"I think it's the mare the Persian queen's slave stole, Alex." But Iolaus sounds doubtful and looks to Demetrius for confirmation.

Demetrius leaps off Electra, abandoning my filly in the middle of the yard, and rushes across to take Aura's head. "Oh, my poor brave little mare. . . ." he says, stroking her nose and running his hand down her swollen leg. "What have those horrid Persians *done* to you?"

I nicker to Aura, who raises her head a little and manages a small nicker back.

One of the kneeling slaves says something, and Laomedon translates. "This man says King Darius was riding the gray mare when he arrived. He must have abandoned his chariot at his camp and changed horses again here. How about that, Alex? One of our own mares helped the Persian king get away!"

"Not without a fight, by the looks of it," Alexander mutters. "Bucephalas knew she was in there, didn't you, old horse? Was that why you nearly killed yourself last night, chasing after Darius, you silly horse? I should have guessed you were after a mare rather than the Persian king!"

He looks around the yard and sighs. "Laomedon, tell those Persian slaves to get up and make themselves useful. These horses need someone to look after them until our grooms get here, and I could do with a bath!"

The battle at Gaugamela was the dustiest I have ever been in, and the first time our herd has ever won against a much bigger herd. But many of our horses had their manes shaved in mourning for their lost riders, and Attalus — who had survived the battle on foot — cut off a lock of his mane in mourning for Arion, who never got up again.

Groom-gossip said the plain at Gaugamela stank of rotting Persian dead for days: because so many of them had died there was no one left from the enemy herd to collect up the bodies for their god. Even crows get full eventually.

This is how we dominated the Persians at Gaugamela:

Persian prisoners: none, except slaves found in their baggage train

Persian dead: 50,000, including Ochus's mother the night the moon went out

Macedonian dead: 1,500

Horses dead: 1,000, including Arion, who had to be put down after his leg was broken by the runaway chariot (VERY SAD)

Prisoners spared or rescued: Aura, the three Persians who had their hands chopped off, and Prince Ochus

But considering what Tydeos tried to tell Alexander before the battle, I think Prince Ochus could soon be in very big trouble.

ARBELA

WINTER 331 B.C.

WOUNDED

Even small battles are exhausting. Our last one was like being struck by a thousand thunderbolts, and that was before our midnight chase after King Darius.

The next day I was so stiff I could barely stand. My hind leg where the chariot clipped me had swelled to twice its normal size, and many smaller cuts I hadn't noticed during the fighting now began to HURT. I couldn't bear to be touched, so I kicked the wall whenever the Persian grooms came near. This meant I didn't get fresh water or barley, though they threw some hay into my stall to keep me quiet. Aura was in the next stall, but I couldn't bear even her soft nose questing through the bars. I nipped her (very gently, because she's still my favorite mare) until she left me alone.

When Tydeos finally arrived with the rest of the army, the Persian grooms pointed to my stall and tried to tell him how wild I was. Since they didn't speak Greek they mimed flat ears, just like Alexander had done to warn Ochus about me after the battle of Issus. One of them made a pathetic attempt at a squeal and kicked the wall, pretending to be me.

Tydeos straightened his tunic and pushed past them with a smile. "You've got to watch that horse," he told them. "Bucephalas has been trained to kill Persians. Let me through. I know how to handle him."

When he saw me tied to the manger where Alexander had left me the night before, he drew a shocked breath. "Zeus, you poor old horse! You're a walking skeleton. What has King Alexander *done* to you?" Then he

212

looked over the wall, saw the state of Aura, and whistled. "You two aren't going anywhere for a while, that's for sure."

Tydeos was right.

Aura and I had to stay behind in Arbela with General Parmenio's veterans to recover, while Alexander took the Amazons and the rest of the army south to "liberate" Babylon from the Persians. At least, that's what he told General Parmenio he was going to do — though it sounds more like dominating to me.

It was good to be with my favorite mare, but I missed Charm's fingers mutual grooming my withers. Every time I heard footsteps approach my stall, I flared my nostrils in the hope that it was her or Alexander. But when I did finally smell someone familiar, it was neither of my favorite humans.

HORSE THIEF

We have been in Arbela about a month when news comes of a raid by the Persian resistance on one of our new garrisons. General Parmenio's men gallop off at once to deal with it. Tydeos is out exercising Aura, and the Persian grooms have gone with him to exercise the spare horses. Although it is humiliating to be left behind, I am secretly relieved to be in my stall away from the flies, where I can lie down to rest my bad leg.

I am not expecting Aura back so soon, so the scrape in the next stall makes me jump. It's not her, of course. Even dozing, I would notice my favorite mare coming back in. But the smell coming over the partition is almost as familiar. It brings memories of Charm lying helpless across a camel's back. I scramble to my feet, snorting in alarm, and toss my head against the chain that fastens me to the manger.

The old horsemaster limps into my stall and chuckles at my wild eye and flat ears. He is wearing Persian-style trousers that cover his twisted leg and has grown his whiskers long. A dagger is thrust through his sash. I can smell fresh blood on the blade. He is carrying my bridle, my muzzle, and a long whip.

"Still up to your old tricks, I see," he mutters. "Don't expect any help this time, Bucephalas. The sentries have already felt my dagger between their ribs. General Parmenio's men are off dealing with a little diversion

my Persian friends arranged, and you'll never see your girl-groom again."
He chuckles nastily.

I lunge for him, but his whip slices across my nose. I rear back against
my tether, startled by the pain. He takes advantage of this to limp close to my
shoulder where I can't reach him with my teeth. His hand darts up on
my blind side. Before I know what he intends, he grabs my ear. He twists
hard until I lower my head, then he jams the bit between my snapping teeth.

"You don't scare me, horse," he says as he secures the straps and fastens my muzzle over the top. "I've had more experience of bad-tempered
stallions than you've had hot mashes, and I heard you were half dead after
the battle at Gaugamela. Give up the fight and make it easy on yourself."

He unchains me and tries to lead me out of the stall. I rear up and try
to get him with my hooves, but he ducks. When I come down he gives me
another slice on the nose with the whip. It hurts so much I barge out of the
stall backward, dragging him at the end of my reins. He doesn't try to stop
me, just leans back and lets me pull his weight out of the stable into the
courtyard.

After being inside, the Mesopotamian sunlight dazzles me. I instantly
feel the heat burning my black coat. The horsemaster drives me up against
the fountain with his whip and twists my ear again to force my head
around to my girth. He kicks me behind the fetlocks, trying to make me
settle down for him to mount. I fight him with all my strength. But my
hooves slip, and I crash onto my side.

It hurts. As I lie there, bruised, he climbs stiffly onto my back.

"Fight all you like, Bucephalas," he hisses, still holding my head at
that unnatural angle so I can't get up. "Wear yourself out. Then we'll go
for a good long gallop across the plain, see how long an old horse like you
can keep fighting in this heat."

I squeal in rage and snap at him inside my muzzle. The horsemaster
just laughs. Then I hear Aura's whinny in the distance. I whinny back as
loudly as I can. The horsemaster frowns at the gates. While he is distracted, I make a supreme effort and struggle to my feet.

I am really mad now and act wild. He wraps his legs around me, but
the one that was crippled by the mulemaster doesn't grip as well as when he
had tried to ride me in Pella. By the time Aura's hooves clatter into the yard,

and Tydeos yells, "Oy! You! What do you think you're doing with the king's horse?" the horsemaster's whip has gone and his weight is shifting.

I put my head between my forelegs and give a final buck that sends my enemy sprawling at Aura's feet. She shies, and Tydeos falls off over her shoulder. With an agile twist, he lands on his feet and finds himself face-to-face with his old boss.

"What are *you* doing here?" he demands, finally recognizing the horse-master. "What were you doing with Bucephalas?"

The horsemaster eyes me acting wild around the fountain and takes Aura's reins. "Nice mare, this," he says, changing the subject. "I remember her from Pella. Are those whip scars on her flanks? Alexander lose his temper with her, did he?"

"Never mind the mare," Tydeos says. "Bucephalas has whip marks, too, and I just saw you give him them! You're supposed to be put under arrest if you come near our horses. Everyone knows how you tried to kidnap the king's horse at Thebes. Stay where you are!"

He shouts for the sentries, but no one comes.

The horsemaster sighs, whips out his dagger, and points it at Tydeos. "Shut your mouth," he says, "or it won't just be the sentries I kill." He scrambles awkwardly onto Aura's back and heads her for the gate, where the Persian grooms are returning with the other horses.

"Stop him!" Tydeos calls. "He's stealing that mare!" But the Persian grooms don't understand his Greek words. As they hesitate, the old horse-master barges through them and urges Aura into a gallop.

My enemy is disappearing into the dust with my favorite mare, and they are just standing there! Tydeos tries in vain to catch me, but I swerve around him and gallop after Aura's white tail, my lameness forgotten, whinnying at the top of my lungs.

The horsemaster looks around in surprise, and a slow smile spreads across his face. "So all I needed was a mare in season? I wish I'd thought of that in the first place. It would have saved us both a lot of trouble." He looks back at Tydeos, giving chase on one of the other horses, and laughs out loud. "I think your stupid groom's going to be in a lot of trouble when Alexander finds out he let me take you *and* the mare. Come on, then, old horse! Catch us if you can!" And he urges Aura off the road and across the plain.

There are some fresh Persian dung piles nearby, but I don't have time to stop and dominate them. We gallop into the rising dust, Tydeos's shouts fading behind us.

GHOSTS ON THE OUTSIDE

When I catch up with Aura, I can hardly get my breath. I've lost a lot of fitness, and my hind leg is hurting. I still can't bite because of the muzzle, but I lean on Aura's neck to pull her up. She lowers her head and snorts dust from her nose. The horsemaster, chuckling at my heaving sides and the white foam on my flanks, leans down and takes my rein.

"Good," he says. "We're just in time to meet my friends who caused that little diversion in the Macedonian garrison. The Persians appreciate a man of my talents, unlike that young hothead Alexander. He's going to regret dismissing me back in Pella."

Aura pricks her ears, and I lift my head. A whole herd of horses is galloping toward us. They're raising a great deal of dust, so we can't yet see them, but I can smell the horses and recognize the Amazon herd. I neigh a welcome, while the horsemaster sits confidently on Aura's back, smiling. He can't recognize their smell like I can and still thinks they are his friends.

Ha, is he in for a shock!

The Amazons surround us in a whooping circle. By the time the horsemaster realizes they are not the Persian herd he was expecting, it is too late. He tries to make Aura flee, but I dance backward, almost dragging him off her back.

Queen Penthesilea rests her axe on her knee and bares her teeth at the old horsemaster. "Where are you going with the king's horse?" she demands.

The horsemaster stares in disbelief at the little horned horses with their blue circles. Then he raises his gaze to the Amazon queen, taking in her braided hair, her axe and bow, and her leather clothes. Seeing the others in her herd are all women, too, he relaxes slightly. "Out of my way, woman!" he says. "I'm exercising these horses."

"Oh yes? Then why is King Alexander's groom racing after you, shouting that you are a thief?"

The horsemaster's eyes narrow. He rests his hand on his dagger. While he is concentrating on the Amazons, I swing my head and knock him off Aura's back.

Queen Penthesilea laughs. She rides her horse close to him. "Bucephalas also seems to think you are a thief," she says. "What shall we do with him, sisters? Kill him? Or truss him up and deliver him to King Alexander?"

The horsemaster moves fast, despite his twisted leg. He grabs the Amazon queen's elbow and plunges his long Persian dagger up to the hilt into her body. The other Amazons hiss angrily.

A normal human would be dead from such a blow. But, as you already know, Queen Penthesilea's ghost is on the outside. My coat stands on end as her ghost whirls and thickens around the blade. There is no blood. The Amazon queen straightens up with a look of amusement, pulls out the dagger, and points it at the horsemaster's throat. The blade is cleaner than when it went in.

The horsemaster stares at it in confusion. His confidence is gone now, and he smells scared. "Who *are* you?" he whispers.

"Do you not know your legends, horse thief? How we fought at Troy and gained our immortality? I am Queen Penthesilea of the warrior women you call Amazons. King Alexander cut the Gordian Knot, which opened a hole in the world and summoned us. We must serve him until the hole opens again to let us go home. He sent us north to report on the successful surrender of Babylon. Fortunately, we arrived just in time to help General Parmenio put down your little Persian uprising."

"That's ridiculous! Amazons don't exist."

"Really? I wonder if my axe exists? Shall I test it on your neck, horse thief?"

Tydeos finally catches up with us. He looks relieved when he sees I am unharmed. "Thank Zeus you caught the thief!" he says to the queen. "Can you take him back to Arbela? General Parmenio will know what to do with him."

Queen Penthesilea shakes her head. "He just tried to kill me, so I think I will kill him."

The horsemaster pales. He is trapped in the center of the Amazon herd. But he speaks to Tydeos rather than to the women, his voice sly. "If you let these unnatural women kill me, boy, you'll never know what I did with your girlfriend."

Tydeos stiffens. He jumps off his horse, leaving its reins dangling, and pushes past the Amazon queen. "What do you know about Charm?" he demands. "*Where is she?*"

The Amazons glance at one another. Tydeos is breathing very fast.

Queen Penthesilea grabs the horsemaster's whiskers in her callused fist and says, "What did you do with Charmeia? Speak, thief, or you will feel the edge of my axe! If you tell us the truth, maybe I will let you live a little longer."

The horsemaster gives her a wary look. "Is that a promise?"

"On my horse's horn and the honor of my people. But I will know if you lie. There will be no second chances at life for you."

The horsemaster glances at Tydeos and chuckles. "What do you think I did with her? Alexander has hostages, so it's only fair the Persians should have one, too. Since Alexander hasn't got an heir yet, and his mother is safe at home in Pella, his groom was the closest thing to family I could find. I needed something to trade for my freedom, so I gave her to King Darius for his harem."

There is a shocked silence.

The Amazons growl like dogs. Queen Penthesilea narrows her eyes and tightens her fist on her axe. Tydeos flushes with anger and launches himself at the horsemaster.

"You sneaky son of a *snake*! If the Persian king so much as *touches* Charm, I'll . . . I'll . . ."

I don't hear what Tydeos wants to do to the horsemaster, because at that moment Aura lifts her tail and squirts at me. Her smell is glorious. The horsemaster spoke the truth about one thing: Though it is rather late in the year, Aura is definitely in foal-season! The heat must have confused her. When I nip her hindquarters to drive her away from the Amazon herd, she nickers at me, pleased.

Tydeos and the Amazons do not notice us. They are too busy arguing about what to do with their prisoner. They have two choices:

Take him to Babylon and hand him over to Alexander.
Take him back to Arbela and hand him over to General Parmenio.

I could have told them what they *should not* do, but I was with my mare. While the humans argued, Aura and I trotted into the shade of some trees beside a nearby canal and quietly made our first foal together. Ha!

20

SUSA

WINTER 331 B.C.

OUR HUGE HERD

The Amazons and Tydeos took their prisoner to General Parmenio. How were they to know? Back in Egypt, they were at Siwa with Alexander when the general gave Charm to the horsemaster and killed the mulemaster for trying to save her.

I'm sure you don't need me to tell you what happened next. My enemy mysteriously "escaped" and fled into the mountains. (Ha! If you believe that, you'll believe anything. Prisoners don't escape from the Macedonian army that easily, not unless someone leaves their door open accidentally-on-purpose.) General Parmenio said the man wasn't worth chasing, no harm had been done, and both he and Alexander had more important things to worry about than a horse thief.

I was a bit nervous in my stall after that, but Tydeos never again made the mistake of leaving me alone. As soon as I was sound again, we marched south with General Parmenio along the fertile bank of the Tigris to meet Alexander and the rest of the army on the road from Babylon.

The wind blew rain in our faces as we approached the crossroads, bringing smells from Alexander's camp long before we saw the tents and banners. I caught the familiar odors of horse dung, sweat, oil, leather, smoke from the campfires, fresh bread and olives, mixed with stranger ones of damp camel, spices, and musky lions. It smelled and sounded like a much bigger herd than the one Alexander took with him to liberate Babylon. After my long convalescence, it was *very* exciting. I arched my neck and danced impatiently at Aura's side, picking up my knees as high as a colt and tossing my mane.

Tydeos, who was riding Aura and leading me, cursed as my lead rein slipped through his fingers. "Steady, Bucephalas," he muttered. "Don't be stupid now, or you'll hurt your leg again. Then I'll be in even more trouble than I am already for letting that horsemaster nearly get you in Arbela — *Zeus!* Where did all those new men come from?"

As we reached the ford our riders saw what we horses had smelled long ago. The camp was HUGE. Tents spread across the entire plain, swamping the canals and fields. Alexander's white pavilion glowed like a sun in the middle, and King Darius's captured one sparkled beside it. On a mound beyond the camp the polished brick walls of a large city gleamed in the rain. Water glittered everywhere.

General Parmenio pulled up his horse and scowled at all the fluttering banners. "What does he think he's playing at now?" he muttered. "Those aren't just the reinforcements from Pella he told me about! I see Greek banners . . . Anatolian mercenaries . . . more horses . . . Babylonians . . . Egyptians . . . *camels*, for Zeus's sake! We've defeated the Persian army. We don't need all these men to capture a couple of undefended palaces."

He spun his horse around so roughly, the poor thing reared. He glared at Tydeos as if the size of Alexander's herd were his fault. "You, boy! Take Bucephalas to the king's lines before he gets loose again. I'm going to sort out this nonsense right now." He galloped off with his guard, kicking up lumps of earth, and leaving us with the Amazons.

As we made our way through the camp, the rain stopped and the sun came out. We glimpsed gold glittering under many of the tent flaps, even those of ordinary soldiers. The Macedonians wore new cloaks, and the officers' helmets had new plumes. We spotted many Greek-style helmets with nose-guards, and everywhere men were training for battle. A herd of cavalry trotted past us on strange horses, and one left a pile of steaming dung right under my nose. I paused to dominate it and almost pulled Tydeos over Aura's tail.

"What are you going to tell the king?" Queen Penthesilea asked, riding her little horned horse with its faded blue circles beside Aura.

"I don't know!" Tydeos grimaced and gave my lead rein a jerk, because

I was dancing around him to protect my mare from the lions in the cages we were passing.

Queen Penthesilea laughed as she reined her horse out of the way. "At least Bucephalas looks well! I think that is a good sign for Charmeia."

Tydeos gave her a sharp look. "What do you mean?"

"I mean the horse bond that links the three of them — Charmeia, Bucephalas, and Alexander. Bucephalas was injured and unhappy in Arbela, so one of those bonded to him must also have been injured and unhappy. But Alexander was flush with victory after winning his battle against the Persians, so it must have been poor Charmeia. But now the horse is recovered, I think Charmeia is also well. Do not worry, Tydeos. I am sure we will find her very soon."

Tydeos stopped Aura so he could sort out our reins. He stared at the Amazon queen. "You *knew* she wasn't dead?"

Queen Penthesilea nodded. "I suspected. So did King Alexander. He feels the bond, too."

"Why didn't you tell me? I thought she'd been attacked by a crocodile, until Prince Ochus told me about General Parmenio arresting her! Even then, I wasn't sure. Not until that wicked old horsemaster told us what he'd done with her."

"Would you have believed me?" Queen Penthesilea said gently. "You were drowning your sorrows in beer a lot of the time, and I did not wish to raise your hopes. You care for her, I can tell. It is good. But you should know she is a very mixed-up young woman. I am not sure she knows herself how much of her love for Alexander is due to the horse bond and how much is due to her own heart."

Tydeos made a face and let us walk on. "Where do you think King Darius is keeping her?"

"I suppose it depends how important he thinks she is to King Alexander. But whether or not Alexander cares for Charmeia, both he and Bucephalas depend on her for their power. So, I agree we must find her, and quickly, before the Persians decide she's no use as a hostage and get rid of her."

"I'll help find her!" Tydeos gripped my lead rein more firmly and gave the Amazon queen a determined look. "Are we going now?"

Queen Penthesilea chuckled. "Patience, Tydeos. You cannot leave

Bucephalas untended to chase the length of Persia after King Darius. His army might have been defeated at Gaugamela, but he still has more men with him than we Amazons could handle alone, despite our being unable to die. Let us see what King Alexander says first, shall we? We might find Charmeia in Susa. I actually doubt King Darius believes Alexander would care so much for a common groom. He probably left her behind in his palace with his other unimportant slaves."

"Or he might have taken her with him because he's so desperate now that he's lost his army, he's willing to try anything." I could feel Tydeos's anxiety vibrating along my lead rein.

Queen Penthesilea nodded gravely. "It is possible."

"What do you think the old horsemaster meant about her being the 'closest thing to family' Alexander had?"

The Amazon queen frowned. "I do not know. Maybe you should ask Charmeia when we find her? She might tell you what she will not tell anyone else. Speaking of which, you have not yet answered my question."

She gazed at Tydeos, waiting.

"I'll tell the king everything," he mumbled. "Even though I'll be in trouble for leaving Bucephalas alone in the stables, when he'd warned me not to. One of the other grooms could easily have exercised Aura for me that day, only I needed to do something to take my mind off Charm. . . ." He shook his head. "I'll tell him when the time's right."

"Good." The Amazon queen nodded again. "But be careful how much you say about Prince Ochus's part in it. It might be easier for the boy if the king does not realize Charmeia was kidnapped while helping him escape."

"Too late for that," Tydeos mumbled, obviously remembering what he'd said to Alexander before Gaugamela. But the queen didn't hear, because just then Aura and I smelled our friends.

I filled my lungs and let out a ringing neigh to announce my presence. Aura whinnied, too, almost as loudly. Petasios whinnied back at once. Then Electra's shrill neigh rang out. Xanthus answered Aura (he didn't know about our foal). Harpinna whinnied to me. Then Borealis, Apollo, and Hades neighed to us both, competing with Hoplite's high little squeal.

Zoroaster whinnied last of all, after a pause, as if he had politely waited for the others to finish.

Arion's whinny was missing, of course. But the others were all fine. And I was so happy to be back in the lines with my friends around me, I ate up every last grain of my barley, for the first time since leaving Egypt.

SQUEALING ON THE ROYAL ROAD

Alexander brings me a whole bag of honey cakes the next morning while I am dozing after breakfast. As soon as I smell him coming, I stop resting my hind leg and neigh a welcome.

His mane has grown lighter in the sun of this hot world. A golden collar gleams at his neck, and he is wearing a fancy new tunic that shows off his suntan and his muscles dented by sword cuts. Soon he'll have as many battle scars as me. Perita trots at his heels, also wearing a new collar that glitters in the sun.

Alexander's gaze darts along the horse lines, checking things. His hand flicks out, pointing to nosebags left in the dirt, unfolded cloths, overturned buckets . . . and the grooms leap to put things right. His stride is long and firm, like a stallion who knows he is the boss and does not expect a challenge.

Tydeos jumps to his feet, tugs his tunic straight, and wets his lips. But Alexander has eyes only for me. After looking closely at my hind leg, which was injured at Gaugamela, he comes to my head and holds my nose hard against his tunic.

"Bucephalas," he murmurs, rubbing the white patch between my eyes. "My faithful old horse! I'm sorry you missed Babylon. They threw rose petals over me, enough roses to fill your entire stable in Pella! There were so many people, it took two days for everyone to hear that I had arrived. I didn't ride Xanthus into the city, though. I entered Babylon in a chariot, so you needn't be jealous." I nudge him because I can smell the honey cakes in his pocket. He laughs and feeds me a handful. "There, you greedy thing! You're not pleased to see me at all, are you? You're just thinking of your belly, as usual."

This isn't true, because I'm also thinking of Aura and our unborn foal. But it is a long time since I've tasted honey cakes, so I make the most of them.

Out of the corner of my good eye, I see Tydeos creeping closer. He clears his throat. "Your Majesty, there's something I have to tell you —"

But before he can tell Alexander about the horsemaster, General Parmenio strides down to the horse lines, calling for the king. He sounds angry. The grooms point to me and make themselves scarce. Tydeos melts away behind a pile of our cloths. Perita growls low in her throat, and Alexander looks around with a grimace. "Never any peace," he mutters. "What do I have to do to get some time alone with my horse?"

He gives me a pat and steps out of the lines. He stands on my good side where I can see him and rests one hand on my hindquarters, daring General Parmenio to come any closer. Perita sits at his heel and fixes her yellow eyes on the general.

"I've just seen your plans for the army, Alexander!" the general says abruptly. "I don't agree with some of your promotions. Why have you split up the cavalry? And what's all this about youngsters getting pro- moted over the older officers who served under you and your father for years? The men won't like that at all."

Alexander smiles slightly. "As you pointed out to me yesterday, General, my army is bigger now than it has ever been. I have reorganized things to make it more efficient. The old ways were fine when the army was small and old men were in charge. But now *I'm* commander. . . ." He pauses to make sure the general doesn't miss this. "I have decided some new ideas are in order. It makes a lot more sense to promote young men for fighting well than it does to promote old men for getting grumpy and slow."

The general's face flushes. "And what are you planning to do with this great army of yours, Alexander? Your reinforcements arrived rather late for the battle. But no doubt they'll all have their greedy eyes on a share of the Persian treasure. How do you plan to share it out?"

"I plan to make them earn it," Alexander says smoothly. "There might be some fighting at Susa. And then we need to secure Persepolis, with all its treasure-houses and fire altars. We can hardly go home without giving the men their full reward."

"Yes, there might be fighting in the Persian cities — but it'll just be old men and women throwing stones! We both know King Darius's army was finished at Gaugamela. Even if you're planning to hunt down the remainder and finish off Darius, you won't need seventy thousand men to do it! If you want my advice, you'd best turn your attention to affairs back in Macedonia rather than push any farther east."

"I don't want your advice, General."

Tension crackles between them, prickling my coat like the air before a thunderstorm. I lash my tail. Beside me, Petasios and Borealis fidget and snort.

Alexander steps closer to the general and makes himself huge so he can tilt his chin and look him in the eye. Perita follows him, growling softly, her hackles raised.

"You have served me well, General," Alexander says softly. "I know I wouldn't have made it this far without you. But you are near the end of your life, and I am only at the start of mine. There are wonders out there none of us has ever seen! Babylon was just a taste. The scientists are still there, measuring the walls and trying to work out how the hanging garden is planted, arguing over which is the greatest wonder so they can add it to their list. I'd rather take seventy thousand men with me into Persia and finish this war quickly than head east with half the number and spend years fighting skirmishes in the mountains against the local tribes. Wouldn't you agree?"

His voice is still quiet, but you know as well as I do how dangerous that can be. The general glares a moment longer at Alexander, who stays huge before him, shining with energy and health.

Finally, this is too much for General Parmenio. He lowers his gaze and grunts.

"I agree it would be best to finish Darius as quickly as possible, grab his treasure from Persepolis, and head home rich and covered in glory. If you promise we'll go straight back to Macedonia once the Persian crown is yours, I'll do my best to explain your new policies to the men."

Alexander grins and slaps him on the shoulder. "I knew you'd approve, General! Tell the men to break camp. Let's show this fine army of ours the Royal Road to Susa!"

I should probably explain here about the Persian cities. King Darius is such a big boss, he doesn't just have one palace. He has two:

Susa for the winter
Persepolis for the summer

But Alexander already has four:

Pella in Macedonia
Halicarnassus (when Queen Ada dies) in Anatolia
Memphis in Egypt
Babylon in Mesopotamia

Soon he'll have Susa and Persepolis, too. This will make him the biggest boss there ever was.

DOMINATING SUSA

Can you imagine how it feels to lead a herd of seventy thousand men, nearly ten thousand horses, and a baggage train almost as long as our column of fighting men marching with their long pikes? Even without King Alexander sitting on my cloth, it would have been enough to make my head spin and my blood throb. With the king's hand firm on my rein, and him shining with energy and confidence, I was so proud that I arched my neck and pranced all the way along the Royal Road.

After the battle at Gaugamela and Alexander's shake-up of the army, we lost two from the Guard. Craterus got command of a cavalry division (probably because he made that remark about Alexander not having an heir), so Xanthus had to go to the back of the army with him. Ha! And Attalus got command of the archers and a scruffy pony to ride, because he had let Arion fall and break a leg in the battle. So my special herd was now down to seven:

PETASIOS *carrying* HEPHAESTION
BOREALIS *carrying* LEONNATUS
APOLLO *carrying* PERDICCAS
HADES *carrying* IOLAUS
ELECTRA *carrying* LAOMEDON
AURA *carrying* DEMETRIUS
HARPINNA *carrying* PTOLEMY

As soon as the boss of Susa saw our army approaching, he hurried out to surrender, bringing mule carts laden with treasure and a string of camels draped in Persian rugs.

Alexander accepted the gifts graciously, and we entered the city through a massive blue-and-gold gateway guarded by stone monsters twice the height of a horse. I made myself huge. Demetrius carried the big shield of Achilles beside us, and the white plumes of Alexander's helmet fluttered against the wide Persian sky.

At first, the Persian women clasped their children close, and old men with sun-darkened skin stared at us with hostile eyes. But Alexander rode me up the steps of King Darius's winter palace, ordered a herald to blow a trumpet, and announced that his army would not be allowed to loot or plunder the city because he was now their Great King and everything in it belonged to him.

A ripple of relief ran through the assembled people, and there was no trouble. No one threw flowers or cheered the king, but it didn't matter because their herd had already run away so they were well and truly dominated.

The royal stables were very grand. They had walls of blue brick with lines of gold-and-white patterns. The mangers were great blocks of blue marble licked smooth by hundreds of tongues. Zoroaster was excited to be back and kept sniffing things. He snorted when he recognized his old stall. But since it was the biggest one, surrounded by wooden columns with pearl decoration at the top, Tydeos led me into it and I passed water to make it mine.

Our grooms said we'd be home by next winter, rich as kings.

As I said before, you should never believe groom-gossip.

DEMON KING

It is a few days before we see Alexander again. He comes into the stables with Hephaestion, the two of them laughing like man-colts. Perita bounds ahead of them and runs into all the corners, sniffing at the interesting smells. Alexander is wearing a new helmet. It has two curly horns, like a ram's. When he reaches my fancy stall, he makes a horrible face and says, "Grrr, Bucephalas! See, they're calling me a demon king now!"

His voice echoes in the huge stable. When I give the horns flat ears, he laughs and pulls off the helmet. "Silly old horse! It's me. See?" He runs his hand over one of the patterns on the wall and stares up at the columns. "Look at this, Hephaestion!" he says. "Even King Darius's stables are full of treasure! But no treasure beats my Bucephalas. Don't you think he looks great? You wouldn't think he was twenty-five years old, would you? When we reach the edge of the world, he's going to live forever, just like me!"

"He's got dried sweat under his belly," Hephaestion points out, and Alexander frowns.

He runs his hand over my matted hair and mutters a curse. "Where's that good-for-nothing groom? *Tydeos!*"

Tydeos creeps out of Aura's stall. "I'm sorry, Your Majesty. I'll wash him at once! Only . . ." He looks around to check that none of the other grooms are near and glances at Hephaestion. "I need to talk to you alone, Your Majesty. It's very important."

Alexander fingers the horns of his demon helmet. "What is it? Something about Bucephalas? Hephaestion knows everything I do. Speak."

Tydeos swallows and lowers his voice. "Sir, please don't be angry with me, but it's about Charmeia . . . I mean, Charmides."

There is a heartbeat of silence. Hephaestion gives Tydeos a sharp look.

"What about her?" Alexander says in a rough voice. "She ran away in Egypt and Parmenio thinks a crocodile got her, the idiot girl."

"She didn't run away, sir! And she's not dead! Back in Arbela, we — that is, the Amazons and I — caught the man who kidnapped her from the camp in Egypt. He told us he'd sold her to King Darius for his harem. I'm really sorry. See, I made the mistake of leaving Bucephalas alone in the stables, and . . ." Tydeos's confession tumbles out, jumbled up with his worries about Charm.

Alexander's breath quickens. He silences Tydeos with an impatient hand. "Where is he?"

"King Darius, sir? I thought no one knew —"

"No, you fool! The man you caught in Arbela. The one who took Charmides!"

Tydeos swallows. "Er . . . he fled into the hills, Your Majesty, after he escaped from our prison in Arbela. The general said it wasn't worth chasing him."

A frown flickers across Alexander's face. He glances at Hephaestion and says softly, "And did you recognize the horse thief, Tydeos?"

Tydeos looks at his feet and mumbles, "It was the old horsemaster, sir. The one you dismissed from Pella."

Alexander throws his horned helmet out into the passage, making me and all the horses in the nearby stalls jump. Perita darts away with her tail between her legs. The king strides around my stall, one fist pressed to his forehead and his face turning red. Hephaestion watches him for a moment, then pushes Tydeos out of the door. "Make yourself scarce," he advises.

But Alexander darts out an arm to stop Tydeos from leaving. Breathing hard, he says between clenched teeth, "Before the battle at Gaugamela, you tried to tell me something about Prince Ochus. Was that also to do with Charmides?"

Tydeos bites his lip and whispers, "In a way."

"Well, out with it! And make sure it's the truth this time! I'm sick of people whispering and plotting behind my back."

"I —" Tydeos looks as if he wishes he hadn't said anything, but he dares not lie to the king. He whispers, "Charm was trying to help the prince escape in Egypt, sir. That's how the horsemaster got hold of her. I know I should have told you before, but there never seemed to be a good time, and I thought Charm was dead until Ochus told me what happened."

"Get out of my sight!" Alexander pushes Tydeos out of my door so hard that he stumbles. He closes his eyes and whispers, "Am I so terrible, Hephaestion, that Prince Ochus wants to run away so badly? Haven't I let him play with my dog and treated him like my own son?"

Hephaestion grimaces. "The boy's nearly nine and he speaks Greek well now. He knows why you're looking after him, Alex."

"But *Charmides*! How could she betray me like that? I trusted her!"

"I'm sure she was only doing what she thought was best for the boy. At least you know she's still alive."

"Alive and in Darius's power! You've seen how he treats my people. What possible use would a groom be without hands?"

Alexander beats his forehead against the blue wall. Hephaestion looks alarmed and rushes across to pull him away. There is blood on the king's face when he turns and a big smear of it on the bricks.

"Alex, for Zeus's sake!" Hephaestion dabs at the blood with a corner of his cloak. "She's only a groom. I don't expect Darius has harmed her. We might even find her in Persepolis when we go there in the spring." He smiles, trying to sound optimistic.

Alexander pushes away his friend's hands, breathing hard. "I want this palace searched! Turn it upside down. Question all the slaves. Ask if anyone's seen a girl answering Charmides' description. We're not spending the rest of the winter kicking our heels here! We'll set out for Persepolis in the morning."

Hephaestion frowns. "Through the mountains, Alex, in the snow? Is that wise? There are reports of a resistance force occupying the pass —"

Alexander punches his friend on the shoulder, making him wince and turn a funny color. "Since when have mountains and snow stopped us?" he says with a sharp laugh. "You're growing soft on Persian luxury, my friend, and you're not the only one. It's about time we had a good fight in the cold to wake us all up!" He gives Hephaestion an impatient look. "Oh, stop moaning! What's wrong? I didn't hit you that hard."

Hephaestion is clasping his shoulder, still pale. "Gaugamela . . ." he whispers, and Alexander's face crumples in remorse.

"Oh, Zeus, your wound? I'm sorry, I forgot. But I bet it doesn't hurt half as much as my head does when people make me angry like that fool of a groom did just now. At least we know the truth at last. I'll have to think what to do about General Parmenio — he's getting careless in his old age. Come on, we've work to do."

Hephaestion manages a smile. Alexander pats me, retrieves his demon helmet, and whistles to Perita. I snort in relief as they leave.

By the time Tydeos creeps back into my stall with a wet sponge to deal with the sweat on my belly, I am licking Alexander's blood off the wall. It tastes sweet, like it usually does, so I don't think he is a demon quite yet.

21

ZAGROS MOUNTAINs

WINTER 331 B.C.

ENEMIES IN THE PASS

We left Ochus's grandmother and sisters in the palace in Susa, along with most of the presents Alexander had been given by the cities we'd dominated so far. But before we set out, Ochus was marched out of the palace by two grave-faced Macedonians and lifted into one of the cages that used to contain lions. Lady Barsine flung a look at Alexander that was the equivalent of flat ears, hitched up her skirts, and ran to comfort the prince.

All the way across the plain to the mountains, the Guard whispered among themselves, afraid to raise their voices. Hephaestion kept looking over his shoulder and shaking his head. Alexander stared stonily between my ears and kept me to a brisk trot. He did not speak until we reached the foothills, where he halted me to let the others catch up.

"Well?" he said, his voice echoing in the steep rocks. "What's wrong, gentlemen? Let's have this out now, before we go any farther and I have to rely on you to watch my back."

The Guard glanced at one another. No one spoke.

"It's not the boy's fault, Alex," Hephaestion said at last. "You'd try to run away, too, if you were in the hands of your father's enemy, and your father was still alive. You should have left Prince Ochus with his grandmother and sisters in the palace. What's the point of dragging him along with us?"

Alexander sighed. "If I had left him in Susa, how long do you think it would be before some ambitious Persian satrap tried to use the boy to raise another army against me? It won't hurt him to travel in a cage for a while. I want to give him something to think about. It might make him appreciate how well I treat him, when I decide to let him out."

"Either that, or he'll hate you for it."

"He's my hostage. He has to learn to respect me one way or another. The Greeks learned the hard way. If necessary, Prince Ochus will learn the hard way, too."

Iolaus nudged Hades closer to me, frowning. "But, Alex, the boy's only nine! He's still too small to —"

We never find out what Iolaus was going to say, because just then a whole herd of tribesmen come sliding down the cliffs and block the road in front of us. They are wearing tattered robes over their trousers but are armed with bright spears. They grin boldly at Alexander.

The Guard immediately forget their quarrel with the king and draw their swords.

"Watch those cliffs!" Perdiccas shouts. "Someone ride back and warn General Parmenio there's trouble up here! Demetrius, bring that shield here and guard the king's back!"

Alexander squints at the men on the cliffs and eyes the ones in the road. He holds up his hand. "Wait, gentlemen. They're not Darius's men."

"Who are you?" he demands.

Their boss swaggers forward and makes a deep, mocking bow. In heavily accented Greek, he says, "We are Uxian people. This is our road. All travelers who pass this way must pay toll."

I give him flat ears, and he backs up a step. The Guard are still nervous, but Alexander smiles.

"Do you know who I am?"

"Yes, Your Majesty. You are King Iskander, the Macedonian demon with wild hair who flies through the air. But your men not fly. If you want to bring them through our pass, you have to pay toll. Great King Darius pays."

Alexander raises an eyebrow at Hephaestion. He is still smiling, but his eyes are like chips of stone. "And how much is this toll?"

The Uxian looks back down the road, sizing up our army. "One horse and five mules for every thousand men."

The Guard frown as they try to work this out.

"That's a lot of horses," Alexander says, still smiling. "I can't spare that many. And we're going to need all our mules for carrying the treasure away from Persepolis. Do you know how big my army is?"

His voice is quiet. The silly Uxian does not know how dangerous this is.

"It must be very large army if you defeat Great King Darius. Maybe hundred thousand men? That make one hundred horses and five hundred mules." He eyes me, puts his head on one side, and grins at Alexander. "Or perhaps we just take your big black horse and five hundred mules? People say you are Great King now, so you afford to pay. It only way you ever be as great as King Darius."

THAT was a mistake.

Alexander's hand tightens on my rein. He breathes faster. Hephaestion winces, draws his sword, and rides Petasios closer to me. Petasios's red ears flatten and he gives a little squeal, arching his neck, ready to fight.

But Alexander has grown a lot more confident since Tyre and controls his temper. He narrows his eyes at the Uxian boss. "Your guess is close, but I'll have to make a head count of my baggage train to make it fair. I lose count of my camp followers. Go wait for me up in the pass, and I'll come to you with my horse. Then I give you my word as a great king and son of Zeus that you'll receive the payment you deserve from my own hand."

The Uxian grins, bows again, then he and his men vanish back up the cliffs.

"You're not really going to give him Bucephalas?" Hephaestion says, horrified.

"Did you hear me say I would give him my horse?" Alexander runs a hand down my neck, while I dance and snort indignantly. "I'll certainly ride Bucephalas up there, but my hand will have a sword in it when I do. So will yours. It won't be my army that pays this toll. The Uxians will pay it — with their blood."

The Guard grin at one another and sit up straighter. But Hephaestion is less happy. "They might be able to hold the pass against us, Alex. We don't know how narrow it is yet. We'll force our way through eventually, of course, but they could kill a lot of our men first."

Alexander laughs, his eyes glittering with mischief. "That's why we're not going to use the pass, gentlemen! Go find me someone who knows these mountains and get Craterus up here. It's time for him to prove he can lead those men I gave him."

I shiver all over, sensing that there will be a battle soon. The nerve of it, expecting Alexander to give ME to them for passing through their mountains!

Alexander refused to pay the Uxian toll because he would never give me away. But five hundred mules would have been no great loss.

DOMINATING THE UXIANS

That night, Craterus's men climb up and hide on the heights above the pass, while we follow our guide around to the other side along a steep, stony track. It is cold at the top, and the cliffs fall away beneath us. But we had trained in the mountains of Macedonia, and not one of us put a foot wrong. Behind us, we have Attalus's archers, the Maedi javelin-throwers, the Amazons, and the pick of the cavalry.

As the sky pales, we gallop down through the sleepy Uxian villages. Alexander's sword cuts down tents, while I leap ropes and scatter their flocks of sheep with my teeth and heels. Their old men stagger out into the mist, wiping sleep from their eyes. Their women and children scream and flee. We don't bother chasing them.

We continue down to the far side of the pass, where we pause to regroup. The Uxian warriors who had squealed at us the previous day are just visible in the mist. Most of them are still rolled up in their cloaks, asleep. The rest sit on rocks with their spears across their knees, looking the wrong way. Alexander smiles, puts a finger to his lips, and sends Attalus with his archers up the cliffs to cover us. Then he walks me slowly forward.

When we are close enough, Alexander glances around at the Guard and grins. He raises his sword over his head, digs his heels into my ribs, and yells "ALALALALAI!" as if he has the entire army behind him.

The sleeping Uxians spring up in alarm and grab their spears. Those who are already awake shout in horror as we gallop out of the mist. They take one look at me, charging toward them with Alexander on my back, and run in all directions. Our arrows bring down a few. Some of them scramble up the rocks, where Craterus's men are hiding, and there is a confusion of screams and whirling ghosts as they run into the Macedonian javelins. The Uxian boss and the rest of his herd flee back down the pass.

Laughing in delight at the way his trick has worked, Alexander puts his heels in my sides and urges me after them. Hephaestion shouts for him to wait, but Alexander is glowing with the excitement of battle, and my blood is up. We catch up with the Uxian boss, and I knock him down with my shoulder as I gallop past.

Alexander leans down from my cloth and slices the boss's right arm with his sword. "That's for blocking my road!" he shouts. Then he wheels me around and slices the boss's left arm. "And that's for suggesting I am not as great a king as Darius!" He raises his sword a third time. "And *this* is for daring to demand that I give you my horse Bucephalas!"

The Uxian boss closes his eyes. "Please, King Iskander!" he shrieks. "Not kill me! I know where Persians hide in mountains to attack your army. I help you."

Alexander pauses. As the Guard pull up around us, panting, he lowers his sword and gives the prisoner a thoughtful look. "How many Persians?" he snaps.

The Uxian peers up at Alexander and says slyly, "We collect twenty-five horses and one hundred and twenty-five mules from one of the Great King's satraps, seven days ago."

Alexander's eyes narrow. He frowns at the cliffs. "There are twenty-five thousand Persians in these mountains? Are you lying to me?"

"No, Your Majesty! Why would I? They go into high mountains and not come out. They take old trade route through the Persian Gates to Persepolis. Let me live, and I show you secret paths, shortcut. Get you through mountains a lot quicker." The Uxian manages a grin through his pain. "Good trick with pass, King Iskander. Maybe you use same trick on Persians?"

Alexander puts away his sword and orders Leonnatus to take the Uxian boss up onto Borealis. As he stretches the kinks out of his shoulders, he eyes the snowcapped mountains with a challenging smile.

"You're not really thinking of taking the army up through the Persian

Gates, Alex?" Hephaestion whispers. "Twenty-five thousand men could hold that pass against us till next winter!"

"We can't leave twenty-five thousand Persians to cause trouble in these parts, my friend. Besides, if they learn we've taken the long way around, they'll simply head on through the pass and evacuate Persepolis before we get there. If Charmides *is* in their hateful city, I'm not going to let them keep her."

"It'll take forever to get the baggage train through in this weather, Alex," says Ptolemy, frowning at the white peaks.

"Then we won't take the baggage train."

"But —"

"But, but, but!" Alexander laughs and gives Ptolemy a playful slap on the arm. "Where's your sense of adventure gone, gentlemen? Remember what fun we had with the Thracians and the Illyrians back in Macedonia? Yet now you're scared to follow me into these tame mountains to deal with a few frightened Persians. You'll soon be advising me to turn around and go home, like General Parmenio always is!"

"We're not scared, Alex," Hephaestion says quietly. "You know we'd follow you to the ends of the earth. We're just looking out for you. It only takes one stray javelin or a lucky arrow. Remember what happened at Gaza. It'd be much safer to keep the army together, take the long route, and deal with the Persians when we get to Persepolis."

"That's why I command this army and not you!" Alexander is still flushed from dominating the Uxians. "The son of Zeus fears no earthly weapon. I have nearly eighty thousand men. I hardly need them all to assault a pass. We'll take the young men who still have an appetite for adventure, and General Parmenio can take the rest with the baggage train around the slow way."

Hephaestion sighs. "At least let poor Prince Ochus out of that cage first. I'm sure he's learned his lesson by now."

But Alexander shakes his head as he gathers up my reins. "With General Parmenio's record of letting prisoners escape? No, my friend. The boy stays safely locked up until we get to Persepolis — which won't be long now, gentlemen! The Persian crown is within our grasp."

Dominating the Persians

Surprisingly, General Parmenio hardly squealed at all when Alexander told him of his plans to divide the army so he could dominate the Persians in the mountains. But he glanced at the Uxian prisoners being sent back to Susa and said Ochus's grandmother would be upset because she had a soft spot for the tribe. Alexander said that's why he hadn't killed their boss and was instead paying him to guide them into the mountains.

This was, as you know, a lie. The Uxian boss didn't get any payment that I saw, unless you count a few extra days of life.

We marched over those icy mountain tracks for five days, leading a herd of twenty thousand men. Philotas, given the choice of coming with us or going with his father, wavered a bit but then came galloping after us on Zephyr with his little herd at his heels.

Alexander smiled grimly and patted my neck. "See, Bucephalas? Even Philo knows old Parmenio's days are numbered."

The road was narrow and stony, twisting up over steep ridges. It grew colder as we climbed. We trotted through patches of snow and splashed across icy fords, snorting particles of ice into the air. Above us, the peaks were white.

On the fifth day, we made camp at the mouth of the pass they call the Persian Gates. Since we didn't have our grooms, Alexander settled me himself and gave me my nosebag. It grew bitterly cold. We horses huddled up close in the horse lines, mares and stallions together, while flurries of snow drove down the pass and melted on our backs. There was no squealing, because we were all far too miserable to make trouble.

When it grew dark, the Guard came back with some little leather bags, clumsily sewn. Working by torchlight, Alexander picked up my feet, one by one, and tied a bag around each hoof. Then he bridled me and put on my cloth. Our riders extinguished their torches, and we set off up a steep, narrow path, following our Uxian guide. My legs ached from stepping high through snowdrifts. But the leather bags kept ice from balling in our hooves, so none of us slipped. We were a shadowy ghost herd, creeping though the starlit mountains, leaving bands of our warriors on the way:

The Amazons at the campsite, with instructions to burn enough fires for all of us
Attalus and 3,000 archers at the top, above the sleeping Persians
Philotas and 7,000 cavalry at the far side with orders to take the road to
*   Persepolis and secure the bridges*

By the time the sky paled, the rest of us were on the other side of the pass behind the Persian camp. We were tired, but we'd gotten around them in the night without them seeing us. Ha!

You can probably guess what comes next. It is the same trick Alexander played on the Uxians, and it works just as well on the Persians. They fight more fiercely than the Uxians did. But trapped between our three strong herds, they don't stand a chance. Eventually, the survivors flee, and Alexander gallops me along the road to Persepolis. The Guard follow, all still grinning at the way we dominated them.

We find Philotas's herd waiting for us at the river. In the distance, the city of Persepolis shimmers white and gold on the Persian plain. Alexander, who had let me ease back to a trot to catch my wind, gathers up my reins again and heads me straight for the bridge. But Zephyr is standing on it, blocking our way. Some of Philotas's men stand behind her. The rest of his herd form up on the bank, nervous but alert.

As we approach, Philotas takes a deep breath and says, "Alex, I'm very sorry, but the Persians you chased out of the mountains have forded the river farther north. Persepolis is their holy city. They're not going to give it up without a fight. I think we'd better wait for Father."

I nicker to Zephyr, pleased to see her. But Alexander scowls at her rider. "What are you playing at, Philo? I told you to secure the bridges so the Persians couldn't get across, not hold them against me! If we don't hurry, that troublesome satrap will have time to flee with Persepolis's treasure before we get there. Get out of my way!"

Philotas shakes his head. "We've just trekked through the Zagros Mountains in deep snow, negotiated an impossible mountain trail in the dark, and fought two battles. The men and horses are exhausted. I think we should camp here and wait for the rest of the army before we tackle Persepolis."

"When I want your advice, I'll ask for it," Alexander says in a dangerous tone, narrowing his eyes at Philotas. "Did your father put you up to this? I'm sure I don't need to remind you that I'm in command of this army, not General Parmenio. Move your men off that bridge at once, before Bucephalas tramples them. I'll deal with you later."

Philotas pales but holds Zephyr on a tight rein. The Guard stiffen. The men behind Philotas glance at one another and whisper uneasily. My legs feel too wobbly to trample anyone, but I make myself as huge as I can. On my cloth, Alexander tightens his lips and drops his hand to his sword.

"No, Alex!" Hephaestion hisses, squeezing Petasios beside me on the narrow bridge so that our riders' knees touch. He grips the king's arm and whispers, "Philo's an idiot to try to hold the bridge against us, but he's right. The men are tired, and poor Bucephalas looks spent. If there's going to be a battle for Persepolis, it makes sense to rest first. I don't mean we should wait for Parmenio and the baggage train. But it wouldn't hurt to let the horses graze and send a party out hunting so we can give the men a hot meal —"

Alexander might have listened, but just then our Uxian prisoner jeers that the Macedonian army has run out of people to fight so it is fighting against itself and makes a run for the bridge. I expect he thought Philotas would hold the bridge long enough for him to escape. But Alexander's legs clamp against my sides, and his sword catches the Uxian across the neck before he reaches the first span.

The king wheels me off the bridge and jumps me up on a flat rock so he can address the men. He pulls off his helmet so his wild mane blows in the sunlight. As he sweeps his blood-drenched sword toward the city on the other side of the river, he shines with the same power as he did when he cut the Gordian Knot.

"Over there is Persepolis, the most hateful city in the whole world!" he shouts in his shrill voice. "That is where the Persians worship demons on their fire altars. That is where the Persian kings make the world bring them treasure and force Greeks to scrape their foreheads on the floor before their proud feet! That city, gentlemen, is the heart of your enemy's power. Destroy it! Burn it to the ground! Seize all the slaves you want. Go take your reward, my friends, and wreak your revenge!"

A ripple goes through the men. They mutter at first, then shout and bang their shields.

"Revenge! Revenge for our people!"

Even the Macedonians seem to have forgotten they once fought against Greeks and join in the cry.

Philotas knows when he has been dominated. He rides Zephyr out of the way, shaking his head. "Father's not going to like this when he gets here," he warns as the cavalry mount up and take off across the bridge with a wild thudding of hooves. Foot soldiers seize their pikes and follow at a run. I plunge against my bit, impatient to follow my herd now that I have my second wind.

Hephaestion shouts, "Not the palaces, Alex! Remember Charm might be in one of them!"

Alexander flings Philotas a contemptuous look as he urges me after the others. "Don't touch the palaces!" he yells as we catch up with the others. "They're *mine!*"

22

PERSEPOLIS

SPRING 330 B.C.

SQUEALING AT PERSEPOLIS

The Persians who had fled from the pass made a final brave stand outside Persepolis. But they had very few men left, and after Alexander's speech our herd was WILD. We soon sent their ghosts whirling across the plain, and the city, which had no high walls to keep us out, was ours.

Alexander led the Guard straight to King Darius's summer palace, which was even bigger than the one at Susa. We trotted up the steps and through a forest of huge glittering columns. Leaning over my neck to pass through the doorways, Alexander tore down curtains with his sword and rode me across the marble floors and soft Persian carpets. Everywhere, statues of monsters glared at us, and strange creatures stared from the hangings on the walls. Slaves screamed and fled. I flared my nostrils, looking for Charm. But none of the women in their filmy dresses and tinkling jewelry smelled like spring grass.

Finally, we came to a huge room containing a plain white bowl of flickering fire, where Alexander let me clop to a halt. He sat panting on my cloth, his sword drooping from his hand, and stared at the fire. The flames reflected in his eyes. His mane stuck to his forehead with sweat, and he had smears of blood on his face.

Two priests ran out of the shadows and cursed him. They said he had defiled their holy city with his barbarian filth. It's true we were dirty, but we had marched all the way from Susa and fought two battles in the mountains on the way. Perdiccas and Leonnatus dismounted, seized the priests, and dragged them away from the king. Apollo and Borealis wandered off between the columns, nosing around for hay. They didn't find any, though. The fire room belonged to the Persian god, and gods don't eat hay.

Alexander sighed and dropped his sword with a clang that echoed through the halls. He pressed his knuckles to his forehead. "So tired, Hephaestion," he whispered. "So tired. Why does my head hurt so much?"

Hephaestion slid off Petasios, picked up the king's sword, and returned it to Alexander's scabbard. "You just need a rest, Alex," he said softly. "You did it. Persia is ours."

Alexander shrugged. "I suppose it is." He sighed again. "But I never expected to feel like this, my friend."

"Like what?" Hephaestion obviously did not understand. He grinned at the king and slapped him on the thigh. "Come on, you'll feel much better after a bath and something to eat. Let's go and inspect King Darius's treasure-houses before old Parmenio gets here, huh?"

This made Alexander sit a bit straighter on my cloth. "Yes, and Bucephalas can inspect the stables. I'm going to see if I can persuade those priests to crown me Great King of Persia before we go any farther."

"Farther?" Hephaestion said, frowning a little.

"We have to find Darius, my friend. And Bucephalas wants his groom back. She's obviously not here, or she'd have come running by now."

To please the Persian god, the crowning ceremony was supposed to take place at the Persian New Year Festival, so we stayed in Persepolis until the weather got warmer and crops started to grow on the river plain. The mules were kept busy carrying loads of treasure back to Susa, while we horses got a well-deserved rest in King Darius's huge stables.

"There's only Ecbatana left for the Persians to hide in," Tydeos told me as he combed my mane. "Everyone says we'll be heading up there, just as soon as King Alexander's been crowned Great King. Then we'll find Charm."

But the New Year came and went, and still we didn't leave Persepolis. There was no festival that I noticed, and none of the people cheered or threw flowers. Alexander strode around the stables, finding fault with everything. All the unbroken three-year-olds learned to carry a rider, including my colt Hoplite, and the men grumbled that at this rate King Darius would have time to raise another army against us. Our grooms even claimed, with nudges and winks, that the king had found a beautiful princess in the palace and wanted to spend more time with her — which proves how stupid they are. Alexander talked to me quite a bit that summer, and the only female on his mind was Charm.

Meanwhile, the little Amazon horses galloped north to Ecbatana and back again, carrying rolls of flattened grass. No one knew what they contained, though they were probably more squeals.

If you ask me, it was obvious why we were waiting. If members of a dominated herd refuse to obey you, like the Persian priests when they refused to crown Alexander, then you need to show them who is boss before they cause trouble. Alexander had to think of the best way to do this. He couldn't just kill them, because he still wanted to be crowned Great King.

GRUDGE ME NOT THIS SMALL PIECE OF EARTH

One morning, very early before our grooms are awake, I catch a familiar scent. I scramble to my feet, disturbed by the memories it brings. It is Prince Ochus. I haven't seen him since before the battle at the Persian Gates, when Alexander ordered him locked in a lion cage.

He has grown a bit taller, but his face is thinner and he has deeper shadows under his eyes. He walks tensely, surrounded by the Guard. The men are all wearing their armor. Alexander looks grim and has a dagger thrust through his belt. Perita trots at his heels. I whinny a welcome, confused by the armor. Ochus isn't old enough to fight. It would be like taking three-year-old Hoplite into battle.

Ochus has no weapon, though. He is dressed in a Macedonian tunic that is too big for him and waits silently as Alexander tells Tydeos to help the prince bridle Zoroaster. Alexander puts on my bridle and cloth himself, and the Guard do the same for their horses. Tydeos is sent to load a mule with packs of food. They seem anxious to get going, because they leave the rest of the grooms sleeping and lead us out themselves into the early morning haze over the plain.

Aura is not yet too big with foal to be left behind, so we are the same herd that climbed around the Persian Gates, though this time our road is much easier. We trot through the quiet streets, past the smashed remains of Persian statues and bloodstained bricks, snorting at the lingering ghosts. Tydeos stares after us in confusion. He dare not ask where we are going.

As we head out across the plain, Lady Barsine races out of the palace, her mane flying loose. "No, Alexander!" she cries, stumbling to her knees. "Please! He's only a child! Don't do this, *please*!"

Alexander tightens his lips. Ochus casts an anguished look over his shoulder at his nurse. But Zoroaster's reins are in Leonnatus's hands, so Ochus has no control over the big white horse. When Alexander urges me into a canter, the Guard follow, dragging Zoroaster with them. Lady Barsine's sobs are soon left behind.

We collect Craterus's cavalry and some empty carts from the main camp and ride north for two days. Perita runs ahead of us, panting and wagging her tail. The Guard chat among themselves, as usual, and seem to be treating the outing like a sightseeing trip. But Alexander barely speaks to anyone, and I can feel his tension rippling along my reins. It upsets me, so I toss my head and lash my tail at the other horses. Ochus doesn't speak at all. He sits straight-backed on Zoroaster, gazing out across the plain. Sometimes a tear glitters in his eye, and I see him quickly wipe it away before anyone notices.

We haven't brought Alexander's pavilion, so at night the Guard have to make do with sharing small tents. And we don't have our grooms, so they have to settle us in the lines themselves. I don't mind, because at least Alexander is not afraid to clean the sweat off my belly. I'd rather have Charm, though.

I can't think what there is to see out here. It is just a dusty plain with a distant line of mountains, and it's getting very hot now that summer is here. But on the evening of the second day, we come to another Persian city called Pasargadae, crossed by copper-colored shadows. Alexander leaves Craterus and his cavalry there with the mule carts, ordering him to collect all the treasure from Pasargadae and be ready for his signal. He says he's taking the prince to see the tomb of his ancestor, and we Guard ride on into the sunset with Zoroaster and Ochus between us, Perita bounding ahead.

A shadowy building rises from the plain. It has steps up all four sides and a little house on top. Torches planted around it flare in the dusk, making the winged monsters carved on its walls ripple and their golden scales glitter. My coat prickles. Inside the ring of torches I can see an ancient human ghost, so strong that it has lingered an unusual number of years in this place.

Alexander tenses as we get nearer to the tomb. He halts me and squints into the shadows as if he, too, can see the ghost. All the Guard fall silent. Ochus clutches Zoroaster's mane with tight fingers and stares at the torches.

Hephaestion rides Petasios up beside me and whispers, "The boy's terrified, Alex. Don't you think you should tell him why you brought him here?"

Alexander gives his friend a distracted look. "The less he knows, the better."

"It's not fair to him. What's he supposed to think? Secrecy was fine while you were negotiating, but now that we're here —"

Alexander jerks my rein, making me snort in protest. "All right!" he says. "I'll talk to the boy. Though I'm going to look pretty stupid if they don't come."

He trots me over to Zoroaster's side and frowns down at the man-colt. The white horse nickers to me, while the prince stares at Alexander with frightened eyes.

"Ochus, why do you think I brought you here?"

The man-colt bites his lip and whispers, "You're going to kill me, aren't you?"

Alexander stares at him in surprise. "*Kill you?* Why on earth would you think that?" His face flickers. "Just because I locked you in a lion cage for a few days doesn't mean you're no longer my adopted son. Did Lady Barsine tell you I was going to kill you? I'll have words with her when I get back."

"You said you would, if my father tried to raise another army against you." The prince's whisper is even fainter than before.

"You did, Alex," Hephaestion reminds him gently. "After Gaugamela, remember?"

Alexander waves an impatient hand. "I was angry. They stole my *Iliad*! You don't want to take too much notice of what I say when I'm angry, Ochus. Besides, King Darius isn't raising another army against me. These pockets of resistance are nothing to do with him, I know that. They're merely ambitious satraps, provincial governors trying to seize power for themselves now that Darius's army has been defeated. I'll soon deal with them as the traitors they are. I didn't just bring you here to see the tomb, Ochus. I brought you out here to send you back to your father."

Ochus trembles even more, staring at the tomb and its lurking ghost.

Hephaestion smiles. "The poor boy still thinks you're going to kill him, Alex. He obviously thinks you've already killed King Darius." He ruffles Ochus's mane. "Your father isn't dead, you silly thing. King Alexander has been writing to him secretly for months, and the Amazons have been galloping back and forth with messages. It'll be all right, you'll see. Your father has someone in his camp who the king wants back just as much as King Darius wants you, so we're going to trade you for her. That's only fair, isn't it? Cheer up! Your people will be here any moment."

The Guard glance at one another. They obviously didn't know all the details, either. But they smile fondly at Ochus, and the man-colt looks across the dark plain in sudden hope.

"My father is coming for me?" he says with a catch in his voice. "Truly?"

"He's sending someone," Alexander says with a little smile. "One of his officers. Seems I couldn't persuade King Darius to come himself."

Ochus's face falls a bit. But his eyes have renewed hope in them. "Thank you, Uncle Alexander," he says gravely in careful Greek. "I shall not forget this when I am Great King of Persia."

Alexander frowns and says in a sterner tone. "You realize I'll still be Great King of Persia, don't you? Darius has promised to surrender his crown to me once he gets you back safe. Remember, I still have your sisters and grandmother under Macedonian guard in Susa."

Ochus's forehead creases. "But you cannot be the true Great King, Uncle Alexander. Our priests say you cannot. Only one of royal Persian blood can make the bond with the god through the sacred white horse and slay the fire demon." He strokes Zoroaster's neck. "When I am old enough, I will take the spirit of a white colt so I may bond with the god like my father did. But I will not make war against you because you are my adopted uncle now," he adds quickly.

Hephaestion nods at this sensible remark.

But Alexander's hand tightens on my rein. "Your priests are fools!" he snaps. "They'll see sense soon enough. If they don't, I'll give them something to think about. Enough of this talk of royal blood, Ochus, or you'll make me angry again. Tell me what it says up there above the door of the tomb."

Ochus smiles. "It says, *Know, traveler, that I am Cyrus the Great who founded the Empire of the Persians. Grudge me not this small piece of earth that covers my body.*"

"Is the boy right, Laomedon? He didn't even look."

"Yes, Alex . . . I think so. It's quite archaic, isn't it?"

"Father brought me out here before the war started," Ochus explains. "He told me always to remember what the words on the tomb said, because no matter how great a king I become, my body will one day end up in a place like this. That is why I think you bring me here to kill me. I am ashamed." He hangs his head.

Alexander gives the writing above the tomb a funny, squinty look. I feel a shiver go through him. Then he looks around at the dusty plain and chuckles. "Your ancestor Cyrus is welcome to this patch of earth. It's not much good for anything else."

BESSUS

It grows darker, and the stars come out in a silver fizz that makes the sky seem huge. The members of the Guard sit on the steps of the tomb, holding the reins of their horses and talking in hushed voices. The ghost has hidden itself inside, so I am a bit calmer. But Alexander paces up and down, dragging me after him.

Suddenly, he stops and squints across the dark plain. "At last," he whispers as a dust cloud, kicked up by horses' hooves, comes out of the night.

I whinny, and one of the horses whinnies back. Alexander vaults onto me and reaches for the dagger in his belt. "How many do you see?" he says. "Have they kept to the terms? Get the trumpet ready. As soon as Charmides is safe, send the signal."

"Looks like there's only a handful of them," Hephaestion says, springing off the bottom step onto Petasios's back. "They have someone riding double on the second horse. It's a girl, Alex! Can't see her very well, but it looks like she has red hair."

"Good!" Alexander sits up straighter and smiles. "Everyone stay alert. If one of those Persians so much as looks at his weapon, take Prince Ochus back to the city and wait for me there. Laomedon, you come with me."

He takes a deep breath and trots me between the flaring torches. Electra follows me, shying at the flames and the dark door of the tomb where the ghost went. The Persian herd stops on the other side, eyeing us warily.

Into the shadows walks a black Persian stallion. When I squeal at him, he has the nerve to squeal back. His rider has a curly beard and holds himself like a boss. He watches Alexander carefully from eyes set very close together, and glances at Laomedon. He says something in Persian, which Laomedon translates.

"He says he's Bessus, the Great King's satrap in Bactria. He says it's good to meet the demon king Iskander at last, but you were supposed to come to this meeting alone." Laomedon doesn't use the Persian's tone, which sounded like squealing to me.

"This is my interpreter," Alexander snaps. "Where's my groom? I want to see her."

Laomedon translates this, and the Persian smiles. "She is ready to return to you. But first I bring my interpreter, also, in case of tricks."

He lifts a hand, and a small brown mare trots across from the Persian herd to join us. Her rider sits awkwardly on her cloth with one leg stuck out to the side. His smell makes me rear up and snap my teeth in fury. It is my enemy.

Laomedon stares at the newcomer. "Alex, isn't that —?"

Alexander goes for his dagger. But the horsemaster is careful to keep his mare behind Bessus, and we cannot reach him without first doing battle with the Persian boss.

Alexander grinds his teeth in frustration. "Traitor!" he hisses. "You're going to pay for what you've done."

"Alexander," the horsemaster says, baring his teeth in return. "You'd do well to remember you're a long way from home, and I doubt that brute of a horse you insist on riding will last the journey back to Macedonia. How old is he now? Twenty-five? Twenty-six? You once dismissed me for obeying your father's orders. Do you blame me for finding alternative employment?"

Bessus watches this exchange, his little eyes sly.

"You've done more than enough to make up for it! You made a mistake coming here. You won't escape this time." Alexander's hand tightens on his dagger.

"Alex," Laomedon whispers, his voice tense. "I think there are more Persians out there. We're too exposed in this place. Let's make it quick, huh?"

Alexander squints at the dark plain. "Let's get this over with," he says to Bessus in a rough tone.

Laomedon translates, and Bessus says, "First you send King Darius's son across to my men."

"Both together," Alexander snaps. "No tricks. They pass within sight of us, one on each side."

The Persian inclines his head and makes a signal with his hand. Alexander does the same, and Ochus rides Zoroaster slowly through the torches toward the Persian herd. His face is set, and he looks very tense. He keeps looking uneasily at Bessus. On my blind side, so I can't see her very well, the girl with the red hair slides off the Persian horse and walks toward us. She is about the same size as Charm, and in her long, dusty cloak in the dark she looks the same. But she doesn't smell anything like my favorite groom. She smells of burned bread and seems very frightened.

I stamp my foot, squeal at the horsemaster, and give the black stallion a nip on the nose. He nips me back.

Our riders haul on our reins to separate us. Alexander squints at the girl in the cloak, his heart beating hard and fast. Bessus smiles through his thick beard at Ochus. Laomedon whispers, "She looks unharmed, Alex, though it's difficult to tell for sure under that cloak. Do you want me to check?"

"No," Alexander says. "Secure the traitor first!" With a flick of his hand, he signals the Guard to arrest the horsemaster.

The horsemaster draws a long knife he was hiding under his robe and flings it at Alexander. At the same time, Bessus wheels his black stallion and seizes Zoroaster's reins. Ochus gives a little gasp and screams, "Uncle

Alexander! This man not take me back to Father! He bad man! Help!" Bessus growls something at the prince in Persian, and both horses break into a gallop. On the other side of the tomb, the girl runs for cover. I leap from a standstill, carrying Alexander out of the knife's path. It pierces my cloth and grazes my flank on its way to the ground.

With a furious yell, Alexander whips out his dagger and urges me after my enemy. Bessus is almost back with his Persian herd, dragging Zoroaster and Ochus after him. The horsemaster seizes a spear from the nearest man and aims it at the king. But before he can throw it, a dark streak launches itself off the steps of the tomb and fastens its teeth in the horsemaster's elbow. Brave Perita!

The horsemaster growls and thumps the dog between the eyes until she lets go and rolls under the mare's feet. He stabs downward with the spear, and Perita lets out a horrible howl. The mare kicks in panic, and there is a high-pitched yelp as Perita's body flies through the air and hits the steps of the tomb. Her ghost leaves her broken body in a long thin thread and blows away across the plain.

Alexander yells, "The signal! After them, you idiots!"

Our trumpet blares into the night. The Persians have split into two groups, one following the horsemaster, the other surrounding Bessus and the prince. The Guard don't seem to know which group to chase.

For a moment it looks as if we are going to lose both Ochus and the horsemaster. But then Ochus sees the motionless Perita and hauls on Zoroaster's reins.

"No! I not go with you!" he yells. "Uncle Alexander, Bessus want Persian crown for himself!"

Bessus slaps the prince's face and tries to pull him onto his black horse.

Alexander, furious and armed with only his jeweled dagger, gallops me straight at the struggling pair.

"No, Alex!" Hephaestion cries. "There's too many of them! Wait for Craterus!"

The Persians surround us, armed with scimitars they had hidden under their robes. Bessus laughs at Alexander's little dagger, then his eyes widen at the tomb behind us and he goes white. I feel something brush my tail and think it is one of the Guard catching up, but the wind that whirls past me is not a mortal wind. I shiver as the ancient ghost of Cyrus the Great blows through the Persian herd, making their horses rear and neigh in terror. The Persians back away from Alexander, take one look at our cavalry streaming out of Pasargadae, and flee.

"Don't let them get away, you fools!" Alexander shouts at Craterus. "Catch that treacherous horsemaster, and get me some prisoners! I need up-to-date information. Someone take this boy and keep him safe. Where's my groom Charmides? I want to talk to her. *Now!*"

Xanthus and the rest of the cavalry gallop past us, kicking up dust. I want to be at the front of the herd, where I belong, but Alexander won't let me go after them. He holds me on a tight rein and examines the graze the horsemaster's knife left on my flank, while yells and screams come out of the night as our cavalry catch some of the Persian stragglers.

I nip Zoroaster's nose to drive him back to our herd, and we horses of the Guard snort and dance around the shadowy tomb. Most of the torches went out when Cyrus's ghost rushed past, so it is quite spooky. Zoroaster looks thoroughly ashamed of himself. Ochus slides off his back and kneels beside poor Perita, stroking her motionless body and sniffing.

Alexander satisfies himself that my wound is just a scratch and stares down at the prince. "Oh, stop that," he says impatiently. "She's only a dog. She died doing her job, protecting me. What's all this about Bessus wanting the Persian crown? Does your father know? He must have trusted him if he sent him here to collect you."

Ochus gives Perita's body a final sad stroke. "He is bad man, but he has royal blood. I think he wait a long time, until my father is weak. Sometimes Mother" — he hesitates slightly — "and I heard him plotting in the palace, back at our New Year Festival when I am very young. He not think I understand, but I remember." Ochus gives Alexander a tight smile. "Bessus think I am still a child, but I am not stupid. I hate Bessus. He say many bad things about my father. I rather stay with you — and Charmeia."

He looks at the tomb, where the girl took refuge.

Ptolemy appears at the door, gripping her arm tightly. Her hood is down, and the one remaining torch lights up her terrified face. She is quite a bit older than Charm. Only the light skin and the red hair are the same. Ptolemy shakes his head. "I'm sorry, Alex. . . ."

Alexander finally realizes the full extent of the horsemaster's trick. As he stares at the woman, his breathing quickens and his face flushes. His fist clenches against my withers. With a furious yell, he throws his dagger at the steps.

Ptolemy jumps back in alarm as it clatters at his feet, and drags the woman with him to safety. "Alex, it's not the poor girl's fault! What shall I do with her?"

Ochus has stopped crying. He stares at the tomb. "It not Charmeia," he says sadly.

"No, it's not." Alexander's voice is icy. "That was a mistake. I don't care if King Darius sent Bessus to play that trick on me or if it was the horsemaster's idea. I'm going to show all these treacherous satraps with their eyes on the Persian crown who's in charge around here. We're going back to Persepolis, gentlemen, and we're going to finish this, once and for all. If those proud Persian priests love their holy fire so much, then they'll get holy fire. I'm the son of Zeus. I have no reason to be afraid of their curses."

The Guard glance at one another. Hephaestion whispers, "You can't mean to burn down the temples and palaces, Alex? You know what General Parmenio said. It's never a good idea to mess with the gods. Remember how you thought the Persian god cursed you, back in Phoenicia?"

Alexander glares at his friend. "Those palaces and temples are *mine* now, not General Parmenio's or the Persian god's! I can do what I like with them! Are you with me or not? Because anyone who isn't can go join that traitor of a horsemaster and his Persian friends and be hunted down as I will hunt them all down, once I have my faithful army at my back again. When I catch that satrap Bessus, I'm going to make an example of him. Will that please you, Ochus? Will it make me as great a king as your father? Do you think your god would approve of me *then?*"

Ochus does not answer. He is a very sensible man-colt.

Ptolemy puts his arm around the woman. "You're safe now," he says. "Do you understand? We'll take you back to Persepolis. It belongs to King Alexander now."

The woman breaks free, runs down the steps, and falls to her knees before Alexander in a mess of hair and filthy cloak.

"I'm sorry, King Alexander! They said I had to do it or they'd kill me.

I didn't know why, I swear! I'll tell you all I know. We hear things in the harems. Maybe I can help you find your girl?" She looks up, her eyes fierce. "I only ask that you let me be there when you burn the palace. I want to pay back the Persians for everything they've done to me. I was a little girl when they captured me. Now I am nothing. Their god's curse can't do anything worse to me than they have already done."

Alexander frowns down at her. Some of the fury trickles out of him. "What's your name?" he asks.

"Thais, Your Majesty. From Athens."

Alexander wheels me in a circle. "See, gentlemen?" he shouts. "This Greek woman has more guts than you do! She can ride back with the prince on Zoroaster, and I want no more talk of curses. Let's leave this tomb before all our bones rest here with those of Cyrus the Great!"

While the Guard boosts the woman and Ochus up onto Zoroaster's back, Alexander lifts Perita and lays her over my withers. I turn my head to snort at her, but her smell is fading fast, and she will never nip my heels again.

Alexander rests his hand on her bloodstained coat and stares across the dark plain. He whispers so quietly only I hear, "Oh, Perita, am I going to lose all those I love out here in Persia?"

I nudge him with my nose to remind him that I am wounded and need my groom. A dead dog is sad, but not as sad as a dead horse.

DOMINATING PERSEPOLIS

When we got back to Persepolis, Alexander left us in the camp outside the city and ordered that all the other horses from the royal stables, down to the smallest foals, be brought out to join us. Then he held a big party in his pavilion with plenty of magic for the men to drink.

Tydeos bathed my wound with a tight expression, muttering under his breath about Alexander taking too many risks. He didn't know about the failed attempt to get Charm back. Which was probably just as well.

Toward midnight, a procession of men and women wove their way through the camp to the city, wearing flowers around their necks and carrying torches. The women played flutes, and the men sang in their rough soldiers' voices. They disappeared through the palace gates, taking their noise and fire with them, and for a while it was quiet in the camp. I rested my leg and mutual groomed with Petasios.

Then we smelled smoke and saw flames leap above the walls. Soon, a fierce orange glow lit up the plain halfway to the mountains. Even in the horse lines we could feel its heat warm against our backsides. In the hottest part of the fire, where it crackled against the sky, an enormous monster with wings of flame flew up with a furious howl into the Persian night.

All the horses in the camp threw their heads up and plunged against their tethers, including placid Zoroaster. The men left behind in the camp snatched buckets, yelled at our grooms to help, and raced to collect water from the river. But they soon realized it was a waste of effort and stood watching silently as Persepolis burned.

In my experience, there are three reasons why you humans drink magic:

> *You want to forget something, like Tydeos when he thought Charm had been eaten by a crocodile.*
> *You are celebrating.*
> *You are terrified of something and need courage.*

Since the Guard had nothing to celebrate that night, I was a bit anxious for Alexander. But in the morning, he strode down to the horse lines in his armor, smelling of smoke and snapping out orders to break camp. He vaulted onto me, turned my head to the north, and put his heels into my sides. The Guard had to gallop to catch up.

Hephaestion called for him to be careful in case Bessus's men were still around, but Alexander laughed at his friend's worry. "So much for your Persian curses!" he shouted to the ash-heavy sky, spreading his arms and letting me gallop even faster. "See, proud Persian god, I am still alive! You might have killed my dog, but you can't touch me! I am the reborn Achilles and the son of Zeus-Ammon. I am *invincible*!"

23

CASPIAN
GATES
SUMMER 330 B.C.

SQUEALING AT ECBATANA

We marched slowly north for many days, going from oasis to oasis, our baggage train huge with Persian treasure and the mountains a shimmering line to our left. Each time we camped, more deserters from King Darius's army joined us and were hauled off at once to Alexander's pavilion so he could interrogate them. Groom-gossip said we were chasing King Darius, whose baggage train and harem had been sent east to a place called the Caspian Gates, which would take him out of Persia.

Tydeos bit his lip when he heard this and forgot he was supposed to be grooming me. "If King Darius has his harem with him, that means he may still have Charm! Oh, I wish King Alexander would hurry. We're going so *slowly*."

This was just as well for us horses, since it was very hot and Aura's foal was growing big inside her. Every time I looked out of the corner of my eye, I saw a flicker in the sky. It wasn't a ghost, though. The fire demon from Persepolis was following us, just waiting for an excuse to strike.

Eventually, we reach another city, the one called Ecbatana, which Tydeos had said was the last place the Persians had to hide. The gates open as soon as they see us coming. Alexander smiles and calls for his Troy armor. But before he can ride me into the city to accept its surrender, we hear hoofbeats drumming behind us, and I smell General Parmenio's horse.

The Guard look around, and Alexander sighs.

"Here it comes," he mutters.

General Parmenio scowls at Alexander. His horse dances on the spot, agitated by the general's angry grip on the reins.

"What's all this I hear about you trying to exchange Prince Ochus for your missing groom, Alexander?" he snaps. "That woman you brought back from the tomb at Pasargadae was at a party given by my son Philotas last night, and she told him what happened at the tomb of Cyrus the Great. Are you completely mad, exposing yourself to the enemy like that? Were you going to endanger our entire campaign for the sake of a single *slave*?"

"Philo, you traitor!" Hephaestion whispers as if Philotas is still in the Guard with us — which he hasn't been since Alexander threw him out of our special herd back in Anatolia and gave him a herd of his own to keep him out of mischief. Ptolemy, who took Thais to the party, flushes.

Alexander's fist tightens on my rein. His voice is icy. "You seem to be forgetting I am the son of Zeus and he watches over me. Part of the deal was that King Darius would surrender his crown to me in return for his son. As for Charmides, she is my groom and I want her back. You were wrong about her being eaten by a crocodile in Egypt. What's more, I've discovered that my father's old horsemaster, who has already insulted my mother and tried to discredit me with his treacherous lies, sneaked in and took Charmides from the camp *while you were in charge*, General."

This is definitely squealing, although not very loud.

The general's cheeks flush. He opens his mouth and closes it again. He looks carefully at Alexander and says, "So the girl's alive and King Darius has her? So what? I expect she's having an easier time of it in his harem than she ever had looking after your horse. If you want my advice, we should secure Ecbatana and wait. By all reports, Darius is little more than a fugitive in his own country, while his satraps are quarreling among themselves. It sounds as if this man Bessus was trying to get his hands on Prince Ochus to further his own ambitions and has taken most of the Persian forces with him. Darius is probably on his way back here right now to beg our protection. I know if I were the Great King, I'd swallow my pride and turn my attention to what really matters in this world — my son and heir. But it's not something you would understand, Alexander. You don't seem to have time between burning cities to take a wife, let alone sire an heir."

Alexander's breathing quickens. The Guard cringes.

Alexander says in a tough tone, "First, General, you are not the Great King. I am. Second, I don't need an heir because I don't plan to die. And believe me, the *last* thing I'd do is crawl to my enemy for protection from my own men. If my enemy held a son of mine captive, I would go after him with all my strength. And if I couldn't kill him, I'd die fighting! That's why I'm going after Darius to get back my groom. Then I'm going after Bessus and that traitor of a horsemaster to teach them both a lesson. If you don't like it, you can stay here. I don't need old men like you grumbling and moaning behind my back all the time. As from today, I'm disbanding the Hellenic League. Any man who wishes can go home. From this day on, I want only men I can trust in my army."

He looks pointedly at the Guard, and their horses fidget nervously, which is a sure indication of how their riders are feeling. Some of them can't meet Alexander's gaze. But Hephaestion brings Petasios close to me and rests a hand on the king's arm. "We're all with you, Alex, whatever you decide to do. You know that."

The general presses his lips together, and his sunburned face hardens. He says quietly, "Alexander, I have served you as faithfully as I served your father, King Philip. Everything I have done is for the good of Macedonia, this army, and the campaign. You wouldn't have gotten this far without me, despite what you say about being the son of Zeus, and you know it. Yet now you insult me by suggesting you can't trust me?"

Alexander meets his glare, chin tilted, and says smoothly, "You've proven yourself more than trustworthy since the Granicus, General." He leaves a little pause to make quite sure the general remembers what he did there. "But I am in command of this army, and I've made my decision. Go tell your men they can go home if they wish. I'll pay them each a bonus above their normal pay. Every man who leaves will receive one talent as a reward for his services so far. But any who want to stay with me can reenlist, and I'll pay them a mercenary's wage from now on plus two talents —" He smiles. "No, make that three talents each as danger money for their courage. I can afford to be generous these days, thanks to King Darius's treasure."

The general's jaw drops. The Guard draw a collective breath. That's three times the price of Petasios for every man in the army who stays, which is a *lot* of gold.

Alexander narrows his eyes at him. "From here on, we're going to be riding fast after King Darius. I need someone to stay behind in Ecbatana, to organize transportation of the treasure back to Pella, keep an eye on the local tribes, and to supervise the payoffs. That would be a good job for you, General, not too arduous for your old bones. And if King Darius does turn up here, as you seem to think he will, I'll need someone I can trust to deal with him. I'll pick you up on the way back and we can ride home together in triumph and glory."

"I might be old, but I can still ride fast —"

Alexander raises an eyebrow. "You want to come with us? Why?"

"No reason," the general mutters, avoiding the king's gaze. "So you're going after Bessus and the horsemaster after you've found King Darius?"

Alexander laughs. "I'm going to catch both the traitors *and* get my groom back. It's a task for young men. That's why I'm ordering you to stay here. Any more objections, General?"

What could General Parmenio say?

As to why he was so desperate to be there when we caught up with King Darius and his harem, I expect you've already guessed. I think General Parmenio's going to be in *big* trouble when Alexander finds out what really happened in Egypt.

Battles that are a long time coming are always the worst.

KISSING THE *ILIAD*

That evening, after we'd eaten and dozed through the hottest part of the day, Alexander ordered the Guard to form up. He mounted me, and I stood on a flat-topped rock as Hephaestion placed the box containing the king's copy of the *Iliad* in the dust below us. Then all the men filed past, choosing whether to stay or to leave the army. It worked like this:

Stay — *kiss the* Iliad *to show you are faithful to Alexander and take your three-talent bonus from a smiling Hephaestion. Cheers from everyone, plus you're rich beyond your wildest dreams.*

Leave — *walk past the box and take your one-talent payoff from General Parmenio. Boos and hisses from Alexander's friends, and you're not as rich as you would have been if you'd stayed.*

Alexander wore his Troy helmet, its plumes lifting on the evening breeze, and I made myself huge for the occasion. My rider felt tense at first, but slowly relaxed as man after man kissed the box. Some of the Macedonians went so far as to throw themselves on their knees before us and begged to be allowed to stay and fight even without payment.

Alexander watched the entire process with a stony expression. But as the last man kissed the box, he smiled slightly and lifted his sword into the cooling air. Energy shone around him, fiercer and brighter than ever before.

"Onward!" he cried in his shrill voice, jumping me off the highest side of the rock. "We ride after King Darius!"

The cheers must have been loud enough to hear back in Persepolis.

Well, what would *you* have done? Three talents is more than a soldier earns in twenty-four years on normal army pay. But that was not the only reason the men stayed. They'd have been almost as rich if they left. They stayed because they did not want to be parted from Alexander.

CROWS

Even though the older men stayed with General Parmenio, we were still a big herd when we set out east after King Darius. Ochus came with us, riding Zoroaster with our baggage train, though Alexander left Lady Barsine behind in Ecbatana, saying the prince wasn't a baby anymore and didn't need her to nursemaid him.

It was like the mountains back in Illyria all over again, only hotter. We marched through the nights and mornings while it was cool and camped in the afternoons. Our riders gave us mouthfuls of water from their own flasks. On our right shimmered a white seabed that smelled of salt but had no water in it and behind us flickered the fire demon. I think some of the men wished they'd chosen to go home, despite being rich beyond their wildest dreams. They, too, sensed the demon.

Hoplite, who Alexander had told Tydeos to ride to "give him some experience," soon stopped frisking around and plodded along as sensibly as an old horse. At least this spared Tydeos more bruises. During our march north from Persepolis, he'd fallen off every time Hoplite threw a coltish bucking fit, much to the amusement of the other grooms.

My eyes watered with the glare, and I kept stumbling over stones. Only Alexander's firm hand, holding up my head, kept me from falling. All the horses of the Guard were having a bad time, but Aura suffered most of all. I nickered to her whenever she staggered, to remind her that she was carrying my foal and must not give in. We swished the flies from one another's faces with our tails as we struggled on, but some of the cavalry horses were not so strong. They collapsed under their riders and had to be given water. Some struggled up again after drinking. Others, who were too far gone, stretched out on their side with a sigh, and their ghosts rippled past us on breaths of shivery wind. We left their bodies for the crows. There are always crows in horrible places like this, waiting for horses to die.

Eventually, after eleven terrible days of thirst and heat, we come to a narrow gorge between high cliffs. It looks very dark in there after the glare of the morning sun, but it seems quiet enough.

Alexander holds up his hand and lets me stagger to a halt. "What do you think, Hephaestion? Are the Persians in there, waiting to ambush us?"

Hephaestion looks back at the line of drooping men and horses behind us. "The men are in no condition to fight even if the Persians are in there, Alex. We need water and food. The horses are half dead. That poor mare Aura is carrying a foal, for Zeus's sake! We should have left her in Ecbatana."

Alexander sighs. "We have to get through the Caspian Gates and find the next oasis. If we stop here, we'll all be dead by morning. Loosen your swords, gentlemen, and stay alert. Tell Attalus to take his archers up the cliffs to cover me. I'm going in."

He walks me a few paces forward into the pass. It is eerie, and my hooves echo. I keep a good lookout for the fire demon. But nothing attacks us, except crows with their droppings. At least it is cooler between the cliffs. Something white trickles down the cliff-face. I stretch out my nose to lick it. It is salt and very good.

Alexander leans over my neck to scrape the salt from the cliff with his finger so he can lick some as well. "What do you think, Bucephalas? Do we trust those villagers who told us King Darius has already passed through the Gates?"

The crows are very bold here. They circle overhead, cawing and diving at one another. My hairs rise. I prick my ears and stare at them. Alexander stares up at them, too.

He pats my neck. "Clever horse! Something dead or dying up ahead. Let's go and see, shall we?"

The Guard whisper and stare around nervously as we walk deeper into the pass. My nose is so clogged up with dust, and the salt so strong, at first I cannot smell anything else. When we see a crumpled heap of cloak and red mane lying on the track ahead of us, I am as surprised as Alexander.

I shoot up my head and prick my ears, trying to focus on the small human and smell her at the same time. My heart beats faster as I catch a whiff of spring grass, bringing a surge of memory: gentle hands, comfort, relief from pain . . . I think it is . . . I KNOW it is —

"Alex!" Hephaestion whispers. "That looks like —"

"Silence!" Alexander says roughly, staring up at the cliffs, where our archers kneel with arrows on their bowstrings. "It might be a trick. Watch yourselves, gentlemen."

He sits rigidly on my cloth, staring from the crumpled form to the cliffs and the circling crows. One dives at the huddle of cloak. Charm — I KNOW IT IS HER! — stirs and moans. I let out a ringing neigh, paw the rock, and snatch at my bit impatiently.

"Stop that, Bucephalas!" Alexander hisses, still squinting at the cliffs. "If the Persians are here, you've just announced our presence."

I neigh again, the sound echoing around the cliffs.

Hephaestion looks at me and smiles. "Bucephalas recognizes her, too, Alex. If the Persians were here, they'd have attacked by now. Shall I go and check?"

"No, I'll go! She's my groom. Stay close to me, gentlemen. Be prepared for anything."

Finally, Alexander lets me walk forward. When we are nearly there, I drag the reins from his hand and lower my head to sniff Charm. She is not dead. Under the cloak, she is wearing a long red dress with a ragged hem and sandals with little jewels on them. She blinks at me and reaches out a trembling hand to touch my nose.

"Bucephalas?" she says in a cracked voice. "Clever horse . . . you found me!"

I snort at her and settle to my knees with a contented sigh.

Alexander slips off me. He kneels beside Charm and unstops his flask. Taking her head in his arm, he strokes the tangled curls out of her eyes and pours the last of his own water into her mouth. She swallows, still staring at me, her eyes full of joyful tears. I don't think she realizes it is the king holding her. Then she stiffens and focuses on his face.

"Your Majesty! I'm sorry —"

"Just answer my questions," Alexander says gruffly. "Are the Persians hiding up here?"

"No, Your Majesty. I haven't seen any soldiers since I left King Darius's camp."

"You're safe now, Charmides. But I want to know everything. What happened in Egypt, what you saw in Darius's camp, how you escaped — everything."

"Of course, Your Majesty," Charm whispers, stiffening again. "I'm sorry —"

"And don't keep saying 'sorry'! It's my fault this happened. General Parmenio's right about one thing. Sometimes I forget other people care about different things than me, and that's a mistake for a king. Can you walk?"

"I don't think so, Your Majesty, I'm sorry."

Alexander grunts. "We don't have any spare horses, but I'm not leaving you here to wait for the baggage train. Bucephalas is strong. You can ride with me."

"But you're the king!"

Charm's protests do no good. He lifts her onto my withers and jumps on behind her. Then he clamps his legs to my sides and says, "Up, Bucephalas! Let's go!"

Hephaestion and the Guard glance at one another with raised eyebrows. But Alexander doesn't notice. His arms are around Charm to stop her from falling off my back, and we are leading the herd again. It is the first time I have carried Charm on my cloth with Alexander, so it feels a bit strange. But she isn't heavy, and I am carrying my two favorite humans!

I am so proud and happy, I forget my thirst, lift my hooves, and arch my neck. Behind us, the Guard follow, still exchanging wondering smiles.

This is as it should be. The three of us, together.

CHARM'S STORY

Alexander took Charm off to his pavilion as soon as we had made camp, so Tydeos and the other grooms didn't realize she was back. They were busy in the horse lines, watering us and giving us salt in our barley to replace what we'd sweated during the march. After her nosebag, Aura lay down with a sigh of relief, and she wasn't the only horse to do so. Mares in foal should never be made to go on marches like that.

I lay down, too. Just for a bit. After all, I had been carrying a double load.

Tydeos is sponging Aura with water to cool her down when I smell Charm again. I scramble to my feet and whinny. She is still wearing her red dress and fancy sandals, though she has washed her face and looks much better. Alexander obviously fed and watered her while they were talking. The sun going down behind her gives her a red halo.

Tydeos stares at her, rigid. Maybe he thinks she is a ghost.

Charm hesitates. Then she sees Aura, stumbles to the mare's dappled side, and runs a hand over her distended belly. "How long has this mare been in foal?" she asks. "She looks half dead. What have you been doing with these poor horses while I've been away? Is that big speckled horse Bucephalas's colt? Have you backed him yet? And how did Bucephalas get that nasty scar on his hind leg? Looks like it went deep —"

"Hey, slow down!" Tydeos grins from ear to ear. He touches her hand, as if to check that it's real. "Charm, stop it! You come back after a whole *year* and already you're bossing us all around like nothing's happened! Never mind the horses. However did you get here? Does King Alexander know you're back?" He glances at the king's pavilion, stained pink by the sunset, its sheets fluttering in the hot wind.

Charm smiles tensely. "Where do you think I've been all day? He wanted to know everything, too."

Tydeos's grin fades slightly. He starts to ask something about

Alexander, but the other grooms notice Charm. They crowd around, staring at her dress and sandals.

"About time you came back, Charmides!" they call. "We've had to look after your horses as well as ours! Bucephalas has been pining for you. He went right off his food, didn't start eatin' again till after the big battle at Gaugamela. And you should've seen the trouble poor Tydeos had backin' Hoplite without your help. . . ."

"Leave her alone, you dolts!" Tydeos shoos them away with a laugh and moves around Aura so he can hug Charm. She stiffens a bit at first, then relaxes and gives him a little kiss on the lips. All the grooms whistle and cheer.

Finally, Charm and Tydeos come to see me.

Charm examines the scar the chariot made on my hind leg at Gaugamela, while Tydeos holds my head and watches her as if she might vanish again the moment he takes his eyes off her. "Don't panic, it's healed fine," he says. "He was lame for ages, but the king let me stay with him in Arbela. Actually, I'm glad Bucephalas got injured, 'cause that's where we caught the horsemaster and learned what he'd done with you."

"You caught the horsemaster?" Charm looks up sharply. "Alexander didn't tell me that."

"But he escaped," Tydeos says. "General Parmenio let him go."

Charm sighed. "Yes . . . he would, wouldn't he . . . they're old friends, aren't they. I could hardly believe it when he gave me to the horsemaster in Egypt."

It was Tydeos's turn to stare. "What do you mean, General Parmenio *gave* you to the horsemaster? We all assumed the horsemaster kidnapped you from the camp — Oh, Zeus, does the king know?"

"He does now," Charm says, resting her arm over my neck and mutual grooming my withers. "It's probably a good thing you left the general behind in Ecbatana. Alexander's absolutely furious with him, but he's not planning on going back there until after he's caught up with King Darius and got Bessus and the horsemaster in chains. Maybe by the time we get back, he'll have calmed down a bit." She sighs. "It was horrible, what General Parmenio did to me, but I don't think he deserves what Alexander is planning to do to him."

"Never mind General Parmenio! You still haven't told me how you got away. Did King Darius touch you? Because if he did . . ."

Charm smiles and takes his hand. "No, Tydeos, he didn't touch me. He didn't touch any of us, the whole time I was in his harem. He had a few other things on his mind — Alexander, mostly." She smiles again. "King Darius isn't the barbarian everyone says he is, you know. He cares deeply about his family, his country, and his god. He wept when he heard Alexander had burned Persepolis. I feel quite sorry for him. But at least he'll get to see Ochus again soon."

They sit on a pile of our cloths near my head, exchanging their news in low voices. This was how Charm got away:

King Darius's officers asked the king to give the Persian crown to Bessus.
King Darius refused, not very politely.
The Persian herd started fighting among themselves, and the harem guards
*   went to help their king.*
Charm escaped in the confusion.

"You ran all the way up here on your own?" Tydeos interrupts. "You might have been killed! How did you know we'd even be here?"

"I had a dream, of course." Charm smiles at me, then glances at Aura, who is sleeping on her side with her huge belly sticking up. "Now that Alexander knows where Bessus and King Darius are, I think we're going to rest here for a few days before going after them. He's sent some men off to find supplies."

Tydeos gives her a strange look. "You're nuts, Charm, you know that? Is it that horse-bond thing the Amazon queen's always going on about? Because if it is, the sooner you break it, the better. Alexander doesn't really care about any of us. He loves his horse more than any human being, and despite that he's going to get Bucephalas killed in battle one day — *Now* what's wrong?"

Charm stares at Alexander's pavilion and says in a tiny voice, "Nothing."

"Oh, I see. You still worship him, don't you, even after all the horrible things he's done? Well, let me tell you the rest. Since Egypt, he's had the hands cut off some poor Persians for trying to steal his *Iliad*, killed about ten thousand others, and burned their holy city Persepolis to the ground. I don't know what he did in Babylon, but he kept poor Prince Ochus locked in a lion cage all the way from Susa to Persepolis. And that's just what I know about. There's rumors of awful things happening to prisoners, like pouring oil from the ground over them and setting them alight to discover if they will burn."

Charm stays silent, biting her lip.

"You know it could never work, anyway, don't you?" Tydeos says gently, putting his arm around her again. "Alexander's a king and the son of Zeus. He's also Pharaoh of Egypt and Lord of Anatolia, and soon he'll be Great King of Persia, too. One day he'll marry a princess. If he shows you any attention, it's only as much as King Darius would show one of his harem slaves."

Charm gives him a startled look and laughs. "Is *that* what you're so upset about? That's not why we're so close. You are an idiot sometimes, Tydeos!"

Tydeos frowns. "What do you mean?"

Charm stares a bit longer at Alexander's pavilion. She says in a tight little voice, "Because it wasn't just any old Macedonian soldier who raped my mother after the battle at Methone, that's why!"

Before she can explain further, the dogs start barking and the sentries yell as two strange horses gallop out of the night through our boundary torches. Their riders' robes billowing against the flames reveal scimitars thrust through wide sashes. They get halfway to Alexander's pavilion before the sentries manage to disarm them.

"Those men!" Charm cries, jumping to her feet. "They were fighting for King Darius when Bessus tried to take over! Something awful must have happened."

A flap of the pavilion is thrown back, and Alexander hurries out. His mane is untidy and he is barefoot, but he has a dagger in his fist.

As soon as the Persians see him, they prostrate themselves at his feet. "King Iskander, we need your help! The traitor Bessus has declared himself Great King! He's taking our rightful king as his prisoner back to Bactria, where he plans to raise another army against you. We beg you to help us free King Darius before it is too late!"

The shouting wakes the men in the nearest tents, and the news travels fast through the camp. Some of the Macedonians mutter that Alexander is the demon, and it is already too late for the Persians. Others hiss at them to shut up.

Nine people wanted us to set out after Bessus and his prisoner immediately:

ALEXANDER, HEPHAESTION, PTOLEMY, PERDICCAS, LEONNATUS, LAOMEDON, *the two Persians, and* PRINCE OCHUS

About twenty thousand people said we should wait for our supplies and let the horses recover first:

CHARM, TYDEOS, *and the rest of our grooms*
DEMETRIUS *(thinking of Aura)*
IOLAUS *(thinking of his father, Antipater, back in Macedonia)*
PHILOTAS
*The cavalry, especially those who had lost horses to the fire demon on our
march from Ecbatana*
The foot soldiers, who had also lost many of their herd on the march

The Amazons did not vote but stroked their blue-painted horses and waited to see what would happen.

It was no contest. Alexander got his way, as usual.

HOPLITE LEADS THE HERD

While Alexander questioned the Persians about a shortcut that would get them ahead of Bessus, trumpets alerted the camp, and the men were ordered to assemble for parade. Alexander chose five hundred of the fittest foot soldiers and dismissed the rest. Then he and his Guard strode down the horse lines, picking out the fittest horses and ordering our grooms to get them ready.

Charm put her arms protectively around my neck and refused to let anyone near me with a bridle. But when Alexander reached us, he shook his head impatiently and said, "I'm not stupid, Charmides. Bucephalas stays here. Tydeos, go and put my battle-cloth on that colt you've been training. He's young and looks like he's got plenty of spirit. I'll ride him instead."

Aura stayed behind with me. So did all the horses who were lying down at the time, which made the choosing easy because that was most of them. This left only Petasios, Electra, Borealis, Apollo, Hades, and Harpinna for the Guard. So Zoroaster, who had carried only a light load this far, got the job of carrying Demetrius.

When Zoroaster was led out, Ochus ran across and tried to scramble up onto him, but Alexander chuckled and plucked the man-colt off by the ankle. "No, Ochus. You can't come with me this time. Wait here with Charmides."

It was a strange feeling to stand in the horse lines and watch Alexander trot Hoplite to the front of the column. My colt made himself huge, arched his neck, and gave a little squeal. When Alexander set his heels in his sides, he took off at such a fast gallop across the desert that even Petasios had a hard job keeping up with him. As the Guard gave chase, the five hundred mounted horses followed in excitement — which was just as well, because some of the foot soldiers Alexander had chosen to ride them obviously didn't know much about horsemanship. The Amazons galloped after them, and the fire demon followed.

When they had gone, the camp was very quiet. Charm put an arm around Ochus and said, "It'll be all right, Ochus. Alexander's going to catch the bad men and rescue your father. They'll be back in a few days with King Darius, you'll see."

My groom was correct about one thing. Three days later, Alexander did come back with King Darius. But things were far from "all right."

THE GREAT KING

After three days in Charm's care, I am feeling almost like my old self again. As soon as I hear Petasios's weary whinny, I shoot up my head and neigh a welcome to my friends. Their whinnies come back one by one: Electra, Hoplite, Borealis, Harpinna, Apollo, Hades . . . I am relieved to hear them. Our grooms run up the road more eagerly than usual to meet the returning horses.

Then I see Alexander is leading Hoplite at the front. My colt is limping badly and his head hangs low. He looks twice as old as me. I can see only six of the Guard. Directly behind them rumbles a covered wagon, driven by Demetrius and drawn by two oxen. A large dog follows with its tail drooping. Demetrius throws back the flaps as he stops. Stretched out on the floor is a man's body covered by Alexander's cloak.

"This doesn't look good," Charm breathes, looking around for Ochus. "Better keep the prince away."

Ochus gives a little cry, struggles away from a Macedonian sentry who tries to hold him back, and races to the wagon. None of the Guard stops him. The dog looks up and whines as Ochus drags off the cloak and throws himself onto the body.

"Father!" he wails. *"Father!"*

It is the tall, dark-bearded king I saw in the chariot at Gaugamela. His eyes are closed. Someone has washed his face, oiled his mane, and crossed his hands on his chest. A blue-and-white band encircles his head. He looks as if he is sleeping. But underneath the scent of oil and flowers, he smells like men who have been left lying on the battlefield too long. His ghost hovers above the wagon, but Ochus cannot see it.

The men shake their heads and silently hand their horses over to the grooms, who lead them away to the lines, looking back over their shoulders. Alexander tosses Hoplite's reins to Tydeos and mutters, "Look after him. He's a brave colt. He carried me well." Then he tilts his chin, puts a hand on the dog's collar, and says to Ochus, "I want you to know I didn't kill your father. We found him dying. He wouldn't cooperate with the Persian traitors, so that coward Bessus murdered him before he fled."

Ochus is crying. Charm doesn't seem to know whether to go and help Tydeos with Hoplite or stay to comfort the prince. More Macedonians emerge from their tents to stare at the dead king and his son.

"Hoplite's very lame," Tydeos mutters sadly, stroking my colt's speckled nose. "Poor colt. It's the baggage train for you, my lad."

Charm gives my colt a distracted look. "Where's Zoroaster?" she says suddenly, frowning at the returning horses. "I don't see him."

I had almost forgotten Zoroaster. I didn't hear his whinny with the others. As I neigh to find out where he is, there is a rush of flame in the sky and a horrible groan from the mares' lines as the fire demon we saw rise from the ashes at Persepolis strikes in all its terrible glory. The grooms shout for help and rush over that way. It's my Aura! She's on the ground, and I can smell blood.

I whinny desperately to her, pulling at my tether to save her from the demon. Charm races over and pushes through the grooms, ordering them to fetch warm water and cloths. But I know it is no good. Mares do not have their foals in the daytime by choice, especially not when there's so much else going on. The foal has come too early. My poor Aura!

It's over quite quickly. The fire demon takes the foal's ghost and flies away. I calm down a bit. Charm gets Aura on her feet and leads her out of the lines, while the grooms wrap the foal's body in an old cloth and carry it away from the disturbed mares. As they pass me, I see one of its long legs dangling out from the cloth. Beneath the blood, our foal is pure white.

Charm is stroking Aura and rubbing her ears, telling her she'll live to have another colt, and that albinos are often not very strong so it's no surprise she lost this one.

Tydeos is stroking Hoplite's neck and telling him his legs will get better soon.

Alexander is stroking Ochus's mane and promising him he'll avenge his father's death.

None of them has seen King Darius's ghost, which ripples closer to the wagon.

I let out a ringing neigh to warn them, and they look around. Ochus shrugs off Alexander's hand and wipes his tears on his sleeve. He kisses his father's folded hands and forehead and pats the whining dog. Then he eases the blue-and-white band from his father's head, stands on the seat of the wagon, and makes himself huge.

"My father is dead!" he says in Greek, holding up the crown. "I am Ochus of the royal bloodline, heir to the Persian Empire! Today, the crown of Persia is mine. But I surrender it to Uncle Alexander for him to wear until I am old enough to take the white colt's spirit and become king myself. Bessus is an evil man and a traitor. You must go after him and punish him."

There is a respectful silence as the prince climbs down from the cart and hands the blue-and-white band to Alexander. This done, the hugeness goes out of Ochus, and he kneels to hug the dog. It obviously knows his smell, because it licks his face and wags its tail a little. The men, who were loading up their tents for the return march to Ecbatana, look a bit ashamed.

Alexander smiles slightly.

"You heard the boy!" he shouts in his shrill voice. "Bessus has fled to Bactria. He's scared of us now, but if we turn around and go home as General Parmenio wants us to do, it'll be no time at all before the traitor Bessus raises an army and crosses the Hellespont to take his revenge on Macedonia and Greece. Only a few days more, and we'll finish him. So, who's with me? We have only to avenge King Darius's death by punishing the traitor, and Persia with all its riches is ours!"

As he puts on the blue-and-white crown, there is a flash in the sky above the mountains. Thunder rumbles as the barrier between our world and the world of ghosts tears, like it did back in Anatolia when Alexander cut the Gordian Knot.

The men shout and cheer.

"HURRAH FOR GREAT KING ALEXANDER! ALEX-AN-DER! ALEX-AN-DER! GREAT KING OF PERSIA!"

King Darius's ghost whirls away through the hole, along with the fire demon that took Aura's foal. The Amazons look up, their eyes alight with joy because the hole in the world is open again and they can go home. We horses flicker our ears and dance nervously.

Alexander ruffles Ochus's hair. "Well done," he says. "You can keep the dog. It was watching over your father's body. Dogs are more faithful than men."

Then, AT LAST, he comes to the lines to give me an apple.

I press my teeth against his palm, impatient for more, and he pulls my ear. His hands are trembling.

"Ah, Bucephalas," he sighs. "At least *you're* feeling better. Listen to the fools cheering me! At the next sign of hardship, they'll be moaning again about going home, you'll see. I'm not going to finish my life like Darius, left to die alone in an old wagon, murdered by my own men. If it can happen to a great king like him, it can happen to me. So before we go any farther, I'm going to have to deal with a few things I should have dealt with long ago." He glances around to check that no one is listening. "This isn't going to be easy, though. I just don't know who to trust anymore, horse! If General Parmenio can betray me like he did back in Egypt when he gave my groom to the horsemaster, how many of my officers might be ready to betray me by running a spear through my back? Oh, this isn't what it was meant to be like! I'm Great King of Persia, and my head still hurts."

I don't really know what he means by this. But I expect his head hurts because King Darius's crown is too small. Alexander's head, as you've probably realized by now, is almost as big as mine.

That was how we dominated the Persians at the Caspian Gates. It was a very strange battle — against a demon rather than spears and arrows. But we still won.

Persian dead: one (*King Darius*)

Macedonian dead: 30 killed by the Persian fire demon

Horses dead: 100, including Zoroaster and Aura's foal (VERY sad!)

People spared: Charm and the 365 women in King Darius's harem

---

The grooms say that is one for every day of the year, which is silly because it would mean King Darius could have made 365 new foals every year. So far, I have seen only Ochus and his two sisters, which is three.

It's just as well Prince Ochus doesn't know Aura's stillborn foal was a white colt. Had it lived, it would have been the next sacred horse of the sun. Alexander is Great King of Persia now, so I think the white colt's death is a very bad omen for the Persian royal bloodline.

24

ZADRACARTA

LATE SUMMER 330 B.C.

THE SEA AGAIN

Some places in the world are good for horses, and Zadracarta on the southern shore of the Caspian Sea is one of them.

When we came out of the mountains where so many horses had died and saw the water glittering ahead of us, hardly anyone could believe it was real. The men whooped like man-colts, threw down their weapons, and plunged in to scrub the caked battle grime from their bodies and manes. We horses did the same, pawing at the water and splashing our riders. Electra and several other youngsters got down to roll, making their riders yell and laugh as they got ducked.

I would have loved a roll, too, but I was carrying King Alexander, the reborn Achilles, son of Zeus, Lord of Anatolia, Pharaoh of Egypt, and Great King of Persia. So I just dipped my muzzle up to my eyes and snorted spray all over Petasios, who pushed his nose through the waves and did the same to me. The water was a bit salty but sweeter than the sea back home. The breeze from the sea was cool, and the earth green as far as we could see.

Everyone praised Alexander for bringing us here.

With food and rest, we horses soon recovered our strength. Although there were wolf and bear smells in the forest, they didn't bother us because we knew our grooms would not let them near us. Meanwhile, our herd swelled with officers and mercenaries from the Persian army, who hurried to join us once they heard about King Darius's death. It began to get difficult (at least for you humans, who can't smell the difference) to tell who was Persian and who was Macedonian, since Alexander and his friends took to striding around the camp in billowing Persian robes. Alexander even gave orders that we horses of the Guard were to wear Persian tassels on our bridles and cloths — which was pretty silly, if you ask me, because we are already beautiful. Then he took the cavalry on a raid in the hills to find more horses to replace those who had died. He took Tydeos and most of the other grooms with him. The Amazons went, too, so they could look for the hole in the world before it closed.

This meant the horse lines were almost deserted. But I didn't mind being left behind, because my favorite groom stayed to look after me and my favorite mare was tethered nearby. All three of us needed time to recover.

Me — *from battle injuries and the chase after King Darius*
Charm — *from her kidnapping ordeal*
Aura — *from losing her white foal*

But the men were getting nervous about Alexander's plans, and none of us got quite as much rest as the king intended.

A PLOT AGAINST THE KING

One morning, when Charm rides me back from my gentle exercise on the beach, I smell Demetrius in the horse lines. Since the Achilles shield was not needed on the raid, Alexander left him in charge of the camp. But Demetrius is not wearing his Persian cloak today, just his old Macedonian tunic, and he is alone. He strokes Aura's nose while Charm settles me. When she picks up my bridle and sits on a pile of cloths to finish sewing on the blue-and-white tassels that match the crown Alexander took from King Darius, he wanders over.

Charm scrambles to her feet, flustered. "I'm sorry, sir, I didn't see you there!"

"No, don't get up." Demetrius keeps a wary distance from my heels and crouches beside her. He glances around to check that the other grooms Alexander left in the camp are busy elsewhere. "I wanted to talk to you while the king isn't here."

Charm frowns. "What about, sir?"

"These tassels . . ." Demetrius says, touching her work. "What do you grooms think of them?"

Charm smiles and runs the blue silk threads through her fingers. "I think they're pretty. Bucephalas will probably eat them, though — he's not used to wearing Persian harness!"

"Nor are Macedonians," Demetrius says with a sigh. "Did you know Alex has given us permission to marry our captive Persian women and bring them along with the army? So far, the men have been allowed home on leave between campaigns to visit their families. Now Alex says it's getting too far for them to keep going back to Macedonia for holidays, and the women will help take their minds off their wives. Says it's only fair now that he has King Darius's harem." Demetrius doesn't notice Charm's sudden stillness. He makes a face. "Not that he's touched a single one of them, of course! Seems our Great King cares more for his groom than any Persian princess."

Charm flushes and puts down my bridle. "Please don't make fun of me, sir."

"I'm not," Demetrius says, watching her carefully. "You don't know how upset he was when he heard you might have been eaten by that crocodile. Once he found out you were alive and in Darius's hands, he was even willing to exchange Prince Ochus for you. Then, when that went wrong, he brought the army out here after you."

"After King Darius, you mean. He wanted the Persian crown!"

"Maybe. But he wanted you back just as much."

Charm looks angry. She starts to scramble to her feet again. But Demetrius puts a hand on her wrist. "No, please stay. I'm not making fun of you. I'm just telling you how it is. I don't even know if the king realizes how much he cares for you. It's hard to tell what he's thinking sometimes. Obviously, your dreams are useful to him, and you're the only other person who can ride Bucephalas. But we saw him give you his own water and take you up on Bucephalas in the Caspian Gates." He glances around again and lowers his voice to a whisper. "Some of us believe that, wherever you and the horse go, Alexander will follow. Even if it means turning back and heading home."

Now Charm is listening, her eyes wary.

"Most of the men have had enough," Demetrius continues. "We've done what we came to do. The Persian Empire will never have the same power again. If this man Bessus does ever raise another army and come across the Hellespont after us, we can fight him then. But we think it unlikely he'll dare venture past the Euphrates. However, back home, the Greeks, Thracians, and Illyrians are all chewing at our borders, and we're stuck out here unable to get back in a hurry if we need to defend our families. I know you don't like all the killing, and if Alexander turns back, Bucephalas won't have to fight in any more battles. We'd like you to help us."

It goes so quiet I can hear the other horses tearing grass with their teeth. I stop grazing so I can hear what Charm says.

She stares at my bridle with its blue-and-white tassels lying in her lap. "If I told Alexander what you just said, he'd execute you as a traitor," she whispers.

"I know that, but I'm willing to take the risk. Philotas said we should force you to come with us, but I'd like you to help us of your own accord. It'll make things much easier for all of us."

Charm gives him another wary look. She eyes her dagger, which is tucked into her bedroll, out of reach.

"Don't be alarmed," Demetrius says, following her gaze. "I know you don't want Bucephalas to get hurt, which is why you've defied Alexander so often. We're simply offering you a chance to get the old horse to safety. The local Mardian tribe is going to help us. They live to the west of here, and they're real horsemen who know these mountains well. They've promised to take you and the horse back to their village by a secret route through the forests, where they'll look after you for as long as it takes us to persuade Alexander to turn around and take us home. We'll tell him the Mardians kidnapped you, which should keep him from pressing any farther east until General Parmenio —"

Charm's face, which has started to look interested, closes at the mention of the general's name. "No!"

Demetrius puts a finger on her lips. "Shh, Charmeia! Listen to me a moment. Philotas told me what General Parmenio did to you in Egypt. It was horrible for you, I know. But you have to understand. He was doing what he believed was best for the army at the time. He thought you had too much influence over Alexander and were sabotaging our campaign by lying to the king about your dreams and trying to help Prince Ochus escape. He thought getting you out of the way was a good idea. The horse-master was just convenient, that's all. General Parmenio had no idea back then how much Alexander cared for you, or I doubt he'd have risked you falling into Persian hands. The horsemaster has nothing to do with this. We don't even know where he's gone to. If he fled east with Bessus, like Alex thinks, then I doubt he'll trouble any of us again. But we need Parmenio because he has the veterans on his side. You'll be well out of the way by the time he gets here."

"Who else is in on this plot?" Charm demands, her face tight.

"Philotas, of course. General Parmenio. Me —" He hesitates. "Others who think the same way. It's best if you don't know their names, in case something goes wrong." He gazes across the sea. "Alexander doesn't intend to stop when he catches Bessus, you know. He plans to take us on and on, until he finds the eastern edge of the world. Have you any idea how many more battles that'll mean? How long do you think it'll be before Bucephalas stops a spear like that poor mare Alex was riding at the Granicus?"

Charm is still shaking her head. But her face twists like Ochus's did when he saw the body of his father.

"Charmeia," Demetrius says gently, lifting her chin so he can see her eyes. "I won't lie to you. What we're doing is very dangerous. Alex will be furious when he realizes we tricked him. Some of us might get killed. But if it stops him from dragging us all with him to die in some Zeus-forsaken place on the other side of the world, it'll be worth it. I worship the king. We all do. We don't want to see him hurt, any more than you want to see Bucephalas hurt. But sometimes you have to be firm with someone you love, to keep them from harming themselves. Once we persuade him to turn back, we'll have won. Not even Alexander will be able to convince the men to come this far east again."

Charm blinks and whispers, "What are you going to do to Alexander?"

Demetrius smiles. "We'll simply disarm him and take him home with us. Philotas will probably assume command until we get back to Pella. Once we're there, I'm sure we'll be able to persuade Alex to see sense and stay to look after his own kingdom. He'll still be King of Macedonia. Bucephalas will get the retirement he deserves, and Alex won't touch you because we'll say the Mardians kidnapped you against your will."

I smell strange horses and neigh a challenge. Charm stiffens. A scruffy herd is trotting along the beach toward the camp, bows slung over their riders' shoulders. Demetrius glances up and smiles. "Ah, good, here they are! Come on, quietly. Get Bucephalas ready."

"Now?" Charm looks around, confused. "But Tydeos —"

"I'm sorry, we can't wait for your friend to get back. I'll tell him you're safe. I can't come with you, I'm afraid. I have to be here when Alex returns. Quickly, before the sentries notice something's up. We've taken care of the ones watching this side of the camp, but there's not a moment to lose."

Charm bows her head. She realizes she can't wait for Tydoes, because that would mean waiting for Alexander. But she refuses to put the bridle on me until Demetrius agrees to let her take Prince Ochus as well, to get him out of the way of Alexander's temper.

While Demetrius runs to the camp to collect Ochus, Charm rips the tassels off my and Aura's bridles and gets us ready.

Demetrius returns with the prince and boosts him up onto Aura. As we trot down to the beach, I am so happy to have my favorite groom on my back and my favorite mare at my side, I can put up with King Darius's old dog trotting along quietly behind us.

Charm smiles tightly at the man-colt and says, "Don't worry. I'll make sure you get safely back to your grandmother and sisters in Susa. I won't let Alexander hurt you."

Ochus bites his lip and strokes Aura's neck. "Uncle Alexander would never hurt me. He says I am his own son, now that my father is dead. I wanted to stay and wait for him to come back, but Demetrius says there might be fighting."

"There might be," Charm whispers. "Macedonians against Macedonians — Oh, Ochus, I hope I'm doing the right thing! What if there's a fight and Alexander gets hurt? He gets so mad sometimes, he doesn't stop fighting even when he's wounded. They might not realize, and —" Her voice breaks. "What if they kill King Alexander like Bessus's men killed King Darius?"

"No one will ever beat Uncle Alexander in a fight," Ochus says confidently. "He is much too strong."

Demetrius stays in the horse lines, watching us go. Out of the corner of my eye, I see him grip one of the posts and tremble all over, like we horses do before a battle.

AURA FINDS WHAT SHE HAD LOST

I don't know if Charm had second thoughts, because her hands are never as firm on my reins as Alexander's, which means her emotions don't travel as clearly along them. But as we came within smelling distance of the Mardians, I felt her weight shift on my back, and her hand dropped toward her dagger.

By then it was too late, because the Mardians had surrounded us with their little horses. The ones on the outside of the circle pulled the bows off their shoulders and put arrows to the strings.

"Who the boy and the dog?" growled their dark-maned boss. "Our friend say just you and black horse."

"He's just a captive we picked up on the way," Charm said quickly. "I'm looking after him because he lost his mother and father. The dog's his. It'll make no trouble."

The boss scowled at the big black-and-tan dog, which crouched on its belly in the sand and growled at him. Then he frowned and looked more closely at Ochus, who sat very straight on Aura's cloth. Wisely, the prince said nothing.

The Mardian boss shook his head and snapped an order to his men. One of them grabbed Aura's reins and dragged her into a gallop after his horse. But I bit the boss when he tried to grab mine.

"Leave him!" Charm said in a tight voice. "Don't worry, I'm coming with you. I want the fighting to stop more than anyone else."

The Mardian horses might have been small, but they had a terribly high opinion of themselves. I had to nip one who tried to lean on me, and kick another on the nose, before they saw sense and left me a decent space. Their riders eyed me warily as we entered the forest and headed up into the mountains.

We followed the Mardian herd along paths that didn't look like paths until we were on them. Aura carried Ochus under the low branches easily enough, but Charm had to lie along my neck as the tracks got narrower and gloomier. She didn't say anything, though, and after climbing all day we came out of the trees onto a high plateau, where huts crouched between the wind and the clouds. A huge herd grazed nearby, including lots of mares with foals. The Mardian horses whinnied to their friends and wandered across to greet us, since they were not tethered to lines.

The boss-stallion, a tough-looking bay with a white streak down his nose, made himself huge and squealed a challenge at me. I squealed one back.

Charm gripped my rein tightly and said, "No, Bucephalas! We'll be in enough trouble as it is, when King Alexander gets back."

Aura stared at the mares and foals, her beautiful ears pricked and her brown eyes sad. Then she did a very strange thing. She gave a little nicker, took hold of her bit, and trotted off to the village with Ochus hauling at her reins.

"Ochus!" Charm called, sounding worried. "Keep her away from that stallion!"

But Aura had the bit between her teeth, which was most unusual for her. Worried, I sent a whinny after her. She took no notice! I snatched at my reins and danced sideways, impatient to go after her before the Mardian stallion got to her.

Charm held me back and said to the Mardian boss, "I'm sorry, but our gray mare's a bit upset. She lost a foal recently."

Then I realized what Aura was up to! By one of the huts at the edge of the village, a goat stood tethered to a stake. A small golden foal lay in the grass nearby. The Mardian women were trying to make the foal get up and suckle from the goat, but it kept flopping back down again to stare at the herd with eyes as sad as Aura's.

Ochus slid off Aura. He put his arms around the foal and lifted it to its feet. Aura nudged it with her nose until it staggered around to her flank and found her milk. Soon its small tail was flicking and Aura was grazing happily.

The bay stallion stared at them and snorted. Then he gave me flat ears and lowered his head. He kept a wary eye on me, though. I kept an eye on him, too. He hadn't submitted to me, but we were like General Parmenio and Alexander. For the moment we needed each other, so I didn't fight him for his herd.

The women smiled at Aura and the foal.

Even the Mardian boss smiled. "Your mare lose foal? Our foal lose mother in fight against bear. Think they find each other, yes? That filly not like goat milk. We think she die of broken heart. Now your mare save her."

BATTLE FOR A MARE AND FOAL

At dawn, a curl of smoke rises from the forest below us. Charm is rolled tightly in her cloak beside me, so she doesn't notice it at first. She had a bad night, moaning and thrashing around in her sleep. I think she had another dream.

Ochus shakes her awake. "Fire, Charmeia!" he hisses into her ear. "You think Uncle Alexander comes after us?"

Charm leaps up and stares at the smoke, white-faced. The Mardian boss rushes out of his hut, bow in one hand, a quiver of arrows in the other. "Mount up!" he calls to Charm and Ochus. "We go. Now!"

Charm fumbles with my bridle. I throw my head up, disturbed by her panic, and she shouts at me, which is *most* unusual. Ochus starts to bridle Aura, but the Mardian boss drags over a small brown horse and tells him to mount that one instead. "Your mare stay with our foal," he reminds him, turning Aura loose and waving his arms to shoo her and the filly across to the bay stallion's herd.

I'm not letting the Mardian stallion have my special mare! I drag the bridle from Charm's hands and take off after Aura, making myself huge.

The bay stallion also makes himself huge when he sees me galloping toward his herd and comes to meet me with bared teeth and flat ears. I am twice his size (good), twice his weight (good), and twice his age (not so good). Also, he is surprisingly quick. Neither of us manage to do any real damage to the other before the Mardians gallop up with their whips and separate us.

All my attention was on the fight, so I don't realize we have been surrounded by another herd until Darius's dog barks a warning and a sentry yells, "King Alexander's men!" But the new arrivals smell familiar, and I calm down a bit as I recognize the Amazon herd.

"It's Queen Penthesilea!" Charm sobs in relief, grabbing my mane and pulling me away from the bay stallion.

The Mardians have arrows on their bowstrings, ready to fly. The Amazons raise their half-moon shields and grip their axes. But Charm wriggles up onto my back and urges me between the two herds, guiding me with her knees and voice because my bridle broke when I trod on the flapping reins. "No, don't fight!" she cries, raising her hands as if to catch the arrows. "They're friends!"

Finally, the Mardians realize the newcomers are not Alexander's Macedonians. They stare at the Amazon herd in amazement and lower their bows.

Charm sits tensely on my back as Queen Penthesilea gallops up to us. She eyes my bridleless state and says, "Thank our horses' horns we found you in time! King Alexander is furious! Did you really think you could hide from him? The horse bond lights your trail like a torch before his eyes! He is bringing the entire army up here after you, burning villages on the way. He is in a mighty rage. You must take Bucephalas back to him at once."

Charm closes her eyes. The Mardians who understood her words go pale and look to their families. The women and children cluster together, staring at us with accusing eyes.

The Mardian boss frowns at Queen Penthesilea. "You promise if we help you, King Iskander take his army back to Ecbatana and lead his wild-haired Macedonians home. You not tell us he burn our forests and villages!"

"That kidnap plan was nothing to do with us! King Darius's death reopened the hole in the world, so we are on our way home. King Alexander has more power now than any man ever had. We shall not fight for him anymore. He is becoming too dangerous to follow. I only came up here for Charmeia's sake. The army is less than half a day behind us, but it is not too late. I suggest you take his horse and the prince back to him and apologize. You could always say you kidnapped Bucephalas as a joke because he stole some of your horses on his raid. You might have to give him something valuable, though, to show you are sorry." She eyes the bay stallion's herd. "He still needs more cavalry mounts."

The Mardian boss scowls at Ochus. "I *know* that boy familiar! He grown a lot since I see him, but I recognize the dog from when the Great King's army pass this way. It belong to King Darius; it never leave his side." He turns his scowl on Charm. "You should not bring the Persian prince! You put our families in danger. I agree, we return him right away. But I not coward. We still take you and horse to next village, hide you there." He grins, baring white teeth.

Charm bows her head. "No," she whispers. "You don't understand. He wants me and Bucephalas back more than he wants Prince Ochus. That's how he followed us. It's the horse bond. We shouldn't have come. I've listened to the wrong people and put you all in terrible danger. I'm sorry."

CHARM'S CHOICE

While the Mardians got ready for the journey, cutting horses out of their herd to take with them as a peace offering, the Amazon queen helped Charm sort out my bridle.

"You do not have to go back, Charmeia," she said quietly. "I promised I would ask if you wanted to come with us, when we went home."

Charm looked up sharply. "You're leaving *now*?"

"The hole in the world opened again when Alexander took the Persian crown. We must go before it closes. We shall ride north across the steppe back to our own country." Queen Penthesilea hesitated. "It will not be possible for you to bring Bucephalas. The horse bond is too strong. King Alexander will chase us to the ends of the earth if we take his horse. You will be free of Alexander in our country. But if you really want to come with us, you must first break the bond between you and Bucephalas."

Charm's hand tightened on my rein. Her eyes searched the Amazon queen's. "I didn't know it was possible to break the horse bond."

"There is one way. Death."

Charm stared at her in horror.

Queen Penthesilea smiled. "Only one of you. The easiest thing would be to kill the horse. I know a quick, painless way that stops the heart. Bucephalas is old. King Alexander would not suspect if the Mardians told him he had died on his way up this mountain. Then you will be free to come with us, and King Alexander will be free to go his own way with those who are brave or stupid enough to follow him."

"*No!*" Charm's arms went around my neck, and she hugged me tightly. "No, *never!*"

The Amazon queen patted me and looked sadly at Charm. "I thought you would say that. But once the bond is broken, you might feel differently. You may even form another bond with a younger horse —"

"I won't!"

Queen Penthesilea sighed and lowered her voice. "The only other way is to kill King Alexander. That will be harder. But if you want to be free of him, Philotas and General Parmenio are already considering it as a last resort."

"*No!*" Charm looked utterly horrified. "*Kill King Alexander? No!*" Then she frowned. "But they can't kill him, can they? He's the son of Zeus, and soon he'll reach the edge of the world. Then he'll be immortal, like the oracle said."

The Amazon queen gave her a sad look. "Do you really believe that, Charmeia?"

"The grooms say *you're* immortal!" Charm set her jaw. "You don't die. You haven't lost a single warrior since you joined us, have you?"

The queen sighed again and touched her scarred cheek. "There was a time when I lost many warriors. This is not the edge of the world, Charmeia, and King Alexander is not immortal, believe me. There is a difference between legend and reality. Alexander might like to think he is his hero Achilles, but this is not the *Iliad*, and even Achilles was killed in the end. Think about it."

This upsets Charm again. "But Demetrius said they wouldn't hurt the king — oh, I knew something like this would happen! I should never have agreed to come up here in the first place. Everything I try to do ends up going *wrong*." She stared at the smoke in the valley, tears in her eyes.

"Again, it is horse bond that makes you care for Alexander so much," Queen Penthesilea said gently. "After his death, I promise you will feel differently. You'll come to love another, or maybe to live with us as a warrior without men."

Charm sobbed into my mane. "Just go. I told you, I'm not a warrior like you. I don't care if it is the horse bond making me feel like this. I won't let you kill Bucephalas, and I won't let anyone hurt Alexander. If there's no other way to break the bond between us, then I don't want to break it! Also, there's Tydeos . . . You don't understand. You're not human, are you? You belong in legends like the *Iliad.* Go home through your hole in the world. I don't care. Just leave me alone. Please . . ."

Queen Penthesilea rested a callused hand on Charm's shoulder. "Eventually, the bond will break of its own accord, Charmeia. No one lives forever — king, groom, or horse. When it happens, maybe one of you will find your way to us. I hope it is you. Good luck, and remember, the edge of the world is always farther than you think."

The Amazon herd trotted off into the forest, and that was the last anyone saw of their horned horses in this world.

Though we rode as fast as possible, we had with us half the mares and foals and all the colts old enough to be broken from the bay stallion's herd, which meant we couldn't take the narrow paths. After the fuss I'd made earlier, Ochus rode Aura with the golden filly trotting at her heels. We went the long way around and met some of Alexander's men fresh from burning villages en route.

Philotas was leading them. He pressed his lips together, exchanged a few whispered words with the Mardian boss, and brought Zephyr along-side me. While I nickered a greeting to the yellow mare, he frowned at Charm. "The king mustn't know any of us were involved, Groom," he said. "Understand?"

She nodded, her fingers playing with my mane. My reins were knot-ted on my withers where I'd broken them before my battle with the Mardian stallion, but they were just for show. Up on the plateau, Charm had learned how to transfer her wishes to me through fingertips and knees alone.

Philotas grunted. "Not a word to anyone! We're going to have to think of something else."

Charm took this very seriously. For the next few days, she hardly spoke at all — not even to Tydeos, who hugged her and said in his half-joking, half-sincere tone that it was about time she stopped getting herself kidnapped.

She wasn't the only one in the camp afraid to talk. Alexander was furious that the Amazons had left his army. He ordered his scouts to find their trail and stormed around his tent, hurling things to the ground. The tension in the air made us horses prickly, and our grooms shouted at us for stepping on their toes and nipping them. Meanwhile, the Mardian boss disappeared into Alexander's pavilion, and everyone held their breath.

The Mardian boss must have been a very clever talker. By the time Alexander emerged, dressed in his Persian cloak and wearing his blue-and-white crown, he had calmed down. He kept the youngest Mardians as hostages to ensure their tribe behaved itself in the future and sent their boss back to his forests with dire warnings not to touch his property again. Then our grooms led the new horses to the vacant places in our lines, and there was a lot of squealing and kicking until we all settled down.

THE WALL ACROSS THE WORLD

The next day, the trumpets sounded the order to break camp. While our grooms rushed around packing, Charm polished me carefully and spent a lot of time making sure I looked Persian enough for King Alexander — arranging the strings of blue-and-white tassels so they fluttered annoyingly whenever I tossed my head, and fastening so many of them to my cloth that they hung down my tail like Zoroaster's silly bells used to do.

She stiffened when Alexander came to the lines, but he just rested his hand briefly on her head and promised he would never leave her with people he couldn't trust again. Then he leaped onto my cloth and cantered me toward the rising sun, his Guard hurrying to catch up.

Demetrius was not with them.

We found Alexander's scouts waiting for us out on the steppe. But when we galloped across to them to see if they had found the Amazons' trail, they shook their heads and pointed to the ground. Alexander frowned at the hoofprints, which stopped in midstride as if the Amazon horses had taken off and flown away like birds.

While I sniffed the ground in confusion, Alexander stared at the sea of waving grass that stretched to the northern horizon. He rode me a short way ahead of the Guard until the grass tickled my knees. Clenching his fist on my withers, he muttered, "All women are crazy, warriors or not! Do you know what their proud queen said to me, Bucephalas? She dared tell me that a king is only a king for as long as he remembers who made him one! I'll come back and deal with their little country after I've punished Bessus and that treacherous old horsemaster of my father's. She'll be sorry she left me like this!"

Then his shoulders slumped, and he clutched my mane like Charm does sometimes. "Oh, Bucephalas, what am I doing wrong? Why did the Amazons leave? Didn't I give them a fair share of the spoils? There are more wonders out here in the east than a man can dream of, and we have the strength and power to defeat any army in the world! I just don't understand why everyone wants to go *home*."

But he let the Amazons go, because not even a horse could follow a trail that vanished so completely that even its smells had gone.

Before we marched east after Bessus and the horsemaster, Alexander sacrificed a goat to Zeus and ordered his men to build a strong wall to keep the wild northern tribes and their strange powers out of his empire.

So it seems the Amazon queen was right, and we are still looking for the edge of the world.

25

LAKE
SEIsTAN

AUTUMN 330 B.C.

WHAT ARE FENCES FOR?

Acting on information from Persian deserters, we went south in search of
Bessus and his herd. We reached a place called Lake Seistan, only to find
that they had lied to us, and Bessus had taken the fastest route back to
Bactria. This put Alexander in an even worse mood. The grooms said
we'd be on the march again by morning. But Alexander did an unexpected thing. He told his officers to take the best houses in the nearby
town, and ordered the men to build strong fences around the camp as if
we were going to stay all winter.

The camp remained on high alert for the rest of that month, and our
grooms were not allowed to exercise us out of sight of the guards. Alexander
said the increased security was because of the threat of an attack from
Bessus's herd. But we horses know all about fences. As well as keeping
your enemies out, fences keep you in.

One morning, when we returned from our exercise on the shores of
the lake, we found the number of sentries at the gates of the camp had
been doubled. Men were running back and forth between the camp and
the town, and there was a lot of excited shouting.

Charm tensed on my back, and Tydeos urged Hoplite up beside me.
My colt had come sound again during the march south, but of course he
pretended he'd forgotten most of what Tydeos had taught him. Tydeos
had fallen off three times that morning and was in a grumpy mood.

"What's going on *now?*" he says.

"I don't know. . . ."

"Do you think it's the Persian resistance?"

"Don't be stupid. They wouldn't dare attack our camp." But as we rode back to the horse lines, Charm kept looking over her shoulder.

"What's wrong?" Tydeos said.

"Nothing."

"Yes, there is! You've been acting like a scared foal ever since Zadracarta. Don't worry, Alexander's not about to let anyone kidnap you again."

Charm shook her head. Her hands trembled as she swapped my bridle for my halter and muzzle so she could take me for my roll.

I was rubbing my mane in the sand when I smelled Demetrius. He had been down to the horse lines to see Aura and the golden filly several times since we arrived. Normally, he let the filly — now named Caspia after the sea where we'd rescued her — lick his hands. But today he pushed Caspia's nose aside and hurried straight up to Charm. "You haven't said anything to the king about the Mardians, have you?" he whispered, glancing over his shoulder.

"Of course not, sir! Why?"

"Because he's just arrested Philotas!"

"Oh, Zeus!" Charm's hands flew to her mouth. She let go of my lead rein and seemed to forget me completely. I took advantage of this to get down for another roll — bliss!

Demetrius dodged my waving hooves and took her elbow. "I can't even get in to see him. Hephaestion and Craterus are interrogating poor Philo, and they're arresting people all over the place. Security's tight. No one can get in or out of the town or the camp without a pass. The king is in a terrible mood."

"He's found out about the plot, hasn't he?" Charm whispered, trembling like a foal.

"He must have. It's the only explanation. I can't stay. There are too many people around. I think I'm being watched. If something happens to me, remember to say the Mardians kidnapped you and the horse against your will. Whatever Philo says, I'll back you up." He cast a frightened look over his shoulder as some of Craterus's men pushed through the horse lines and marched our way. "They're coming! I've got to go before they see us together. I'm really sorry I got you into this, Charmeia. May Zeus help us all!"

I rolled over one more time and grunted with pleasure. Charm gave me a distracted look. By the time she pulled me to my feet and looked for Demetrius again, he had gone.

Groom-gossip at the time was wild. They said a hundred of Alexander's closest officers and friends had been stoned to death after being named by Philotas under torture, and that Alexander had sent some men on racing camels to Ecbatana to arrest General Parmenio.

I don't know how much of this was true. Knowing our grooms, they were probably exaggerating. But every day that Demetrius failed to turn up to see Aura, Charm grew more anxious. Alexander didn't ride me in all that time or even come down to the horse lines, which was probably just as well, considering the state Charm was in.

Then, ten days after Philotas was arrested, the order came to shave off Zephyr's mane.

Charm buried her face in her hands as the yellow hair fell to the ground. There was no surer sign that Philotas was dead. Our grooms breathed a sigh of relief and said that would be the end of it, because Alexander had now punished everyone involved in the plot. But Charm and I knew he had not.

A PRESENT FROM ECBATANA

The next morning, we see Alexander again. He is wearing his demon-horned helmet and his Persian cloak with the blue-and-white border, and he strides down to the horse lines as if he owns half the world — which he almost does, now. Hephaestion follows, dark shadows under his eyes. The rest of the Guard hurry behind, though there is still no sign of Demetrius. A new man called Peucestas carries the shield we took from Troy.

Alexander orders our grooms to get us ready for a parade. He taps his foot as Charm bridles me and puts on my cloth. His presence makes her hands shake, so it takes her twice as long as usual. She darts the king frightened glances as she adds the strings of silly tassels.

Alexander takes my rein from her without a word. He taps my shoulder until I settle on my knees for him. Then we lead the way to the parade ground. Out of the corner of my eye, I see Charm holding Tydeos's hand so tightly that her knuckles are white.

Some of the men are already assembled in their silent squares. Others hurry across to join them. It is a very big, impressive parade. Alexander rides me to my place at the front, and the Guard lines up behind me. Petasios, Electra, Borealis, Apollo, Harpinna, Hades — only Aura is missing. Instead of my favorite mare, Hoplite stands at the end of the line with the new man Peucestas on his back, nervously carrying the big shield of Achilles. My colt is dancing in excitement, so I nip him on the nose to tell him to behave.

Alexander jerks my rein. "Stop that, Bucephalas! Don't you let me down, as well."

I don't know what he means. I would *never* let him down. I chew my tassels, expecting the men to begin their maneuvers. But Alexander does not give the order, and the trumpets remain silent. The wind flutters the banners as everyone waits.

Finally, we see a puff of dust in the distance on the road from the west. Alexander grips my rein tighter and mutters, "At last! *This* will teach them all to plot behind my back."

I can smell the camel already. It comes galloping across the parade ground toward us, startling Hoplite into a rear. His young rider only just manages to keep hold of the Achilles shield. The camel's rider is carrying a round object wrapped in a cloak. Now that we are closer, I see the material is stiff with blood. Flies buzz around it as he throws it down in front of us. It bounces once, and a man's head rolls out.

I snort at the head in surprise. It STINKS. I can't tell whose it is, because its life smell has been replaced by the foul battlefield one. Its eyes are open, but its ghost has long gone. Alexander has been expecting my reaction and holds me firmly between his legs and hands, while I paw the ground in agitation.

The other horses of the Guard snort at the head, too. The men in the front ranks stir uneasily. Whispers pass back through the squares, rippling to the edge of the ground, where our grooms are standing on the baggage carts to see.

Alexander waits until everyone is silent again. He draws his sword and points it at the head and its swarm of flies. No one dares say a word.

"That is how I deal with traitors!" he calls in his shrill voice. "General Parmenio dared plot to assassinate me and put his son Philotas on the throne of Macedonia! I sent his death warrant to Ecbatana. Take a good look as you parade past, and satisfy yourselves this is really the general's head. Then go back to your tents and write letters to your families. We'll be pushing farther east soon, so this is the last chance you'll get to write home for a while. You need not worry. Philotas named everyone involved in the plot, and I have rooted out and punished all the traitors. I know the rest of you are faithful to me, so I will reward you by not charging the normal fee to mail your letters home. Every man who has left family or a loved one at home will, in addition, receive a one-talent bonus for continuing with me in pursuit of Bessus. Those in the baggage train who write to their families will receive half a talent each."

More uneasy whispers ripple through the assembled men, but they are too disciplined to break ranks or show more reaction than that. By the time Alexander backs me away from General Parmenio's head and takes the Guard to the side of the ground, the army is silent again.

The trumpets blare to start the parade.

Alexander twists my mane around his fingers and watches with a fixed expression as the men file past the general's head. It is like when we watched them kiss the *Iliad*, back in Ecbatana. Alexander is tense at first, then relaxes as more and more of his herd troop past the head without stopping. Some of the men glance down at it and quickly away. A few turn white and dart terrified glances at the king. One youngster trembles so much, he drops his pike. He picks it up, red-faced, and runs after his division. It is all very boring, and I chew off three of my tassels before they have finished.

Finally, Alexander rides me back to the horse lines and dismounts. As he hands my rein to Charm, he looks hard at her. "I want you to write a letter as well, Charmides," he says. "I don't want Bucephalas's groom to miss out on the bonus."

Charm bites her lip. She whispers, "But I haven't got any family to write to, sir."

"That doesn't matter. There must be someone you can write to. The Amazon queen, perhaps? I know you two were close."

Charm goes even paler, and her hands start to tremble again. "But I don't know where the Amazons live! How will the letter get to her, sir?"

Alexander gives her an impatient look. "Someone else, then! That's an order, Charmides."

"But, sir, I can't write. . . ."

Alexander does not hear her faint protest. He waves her away and calls Hephaestion across. "As of today, you're to take command of half Philotas's cavalry," he says. "I need someone I can trust in charge of them."

Hephaestion looks no happier about this than Charm did about writing a letter. "But I want to stay with you —"

"No arguments! I can easily find someone else keen to watch my back in exchange for a place at the king's table." Seeing Hephaestion's stricken expression, Alexander sighs and says in a gentler tone, "You've deserved this promotion for some time, my friend. I've been selfish keeping you at my side so long."

"But, Alex, I *want* to be at your side! I don't care about promotion."

"Nonsense. Every man cares about promotion. Look at that idiot Philo! I knew he had his greedy eyes on my throne, right from the start. He got what he deserved." Pressing a hand to his forehead, he strides back to his pavilion, his cloak billowing in the breeze.

Hephaestion stares after him, tears in his eyes.

Embarrassed, Charm slowly takes the remaining tassels and my cloth off me. She darts a glance at the new member of the Guard, who has propped the Achilles shield against a post so he can talk to Hoplite and rub his ears. Hoplite seems relieved someone loves him and is making the most of the attention. The other members of the Guard are also lingering with their horses, reluctant to go after the king.

Charm sidles up to Hephaestion and whispers in a tight voice, "Sir? What happened to Demetrius?"

Hephaestion presses his lips together and strokes Petasios, who is tethered next to me as usual. "This is bad business, Charmides, a very bad business," he says softly. "Demetrius wasn't tortured, I saw to that. Philo was a different matter. He plotted to kill the king! We had to find out who else was involved. Craterus did most of the rough stuff, but I had to be there because Alex said the son of Zeus-Ammon couldn't get involved in such things, and he needed me to watch in his place. I hope I never have to do anything like that again."

He takes a deep breath, as if remembering something very bad. Then he continues in a brighter tone, "Now that General Parmenio's gone, everything will be better, you'll see. Alex never liked sharing the command with him. You know how they were always arguing. Old Parmenio treated him like a little boy, and Alex never liked that, not even when we were small. Craterus is going to be his second-in-command now. This is a fresh start for us all, like when we were campaigning back on the Macedonian borders. That was a good time, wasn't it? You needn't be afraid, Charmeia. The bad stuff's over now. Just . . ." He glances at the king's pavilion. "Just be careful what you write in your letter."

Charm stiffens. Before she can say anything else, Hephaestion smiles at her, pats Petasios, and hurries after Alexander.

I nudge Charm to remind her I haven't had my roll yet, and she clutches my mane and presses her face to my neck. "Oh, Bucephalas! Alexander's *never* going to stop, is he? He's just going to go on and on fighting, until everyone is dead! Poor Demetrius! He'd never have gotten involved in a plot to kill the king! He only wanted to go home. And how could Alexander throw General Parmenio's head on the ground like that, in front of the whole army? Why does he have to keep killing everyone? *Why?*"

She ought to know by now. She's been around horses long enough.

When two stallions challenge each other for leadership of the herd, it is natural for the strongest horse to dominate the weakest. This battle had been a long time coming. General Parmenio was a strong boss. He would never submit to Alexander, so the battle had to be to the death. And all the other members of the herd had to see the result, so that they would think twice about challenging Alexander.

Sometimes, there is just no other way.

CHARM WRITES A LETTER

All the grooms are writing letters, even those who have no families and can't read. They all want their half-talent bonus, because if they save up enough money they'll be able to buy their freedom when they get back to Macedonia. Alexander knows most of them can't write, so he has sent one of the army scribes down to the horse lines to do it for them.

Charm and Tydeos sit on a pile of cloths near my head, where it is quieter. They have their pieces of flattened grass on their laps, but so far without marks because the scribe is busy.

"You could always write to Queen Ada back in Halicarnassus," Tydeos says. "She'd remember you. She might even send us some more of her honey cakes. That'd be good!"

Charm gives him a disgusted look. "I don't want that old scribe to write my letter for me. I don't trust him. Hephaestion said . . . never mind."

"I'll do it for you," Tydeos says.

She darts him a surprised look. "*You* can write?"

"I'm not as thick as I look!" Tydeos grins at her. "We all had to learn at my last place. Our master thought it would make us better grooms. Takes me ages, though, and it makes my hand hurt. So keep it short."

Charm looks a bit happier. "Is that who you're going to write to? Your old master?"

Tydeos makes a face. "No. I'm going to write to my mother back in Thessaly and tell her I'll be home soon with enough money to start my own horse farm! I'll buy a few cheap mares, sneak them in with someone else's stallion, and sell their foals to buy more mares." He looks sideways at Charm. "A whole talent would be even better. We might afford a stallion, then, too."

Charm's face closes. "Just help me with my letter. I'll tell you what to put."

Tydeos grins and picks up the stylus. "All right, but go slow. It's been ages since I did this."

This is what Charm told Tydeos to write:

DEAR QUEEN ADA,

WE ARE IN PERSIA. BUCEPHALAS IS FINE. HE HAS A THREE-YEAR-OLD COLT CALLED HOPLITE AND A FIVE-YEAR-OLD FILLY CALLED ELECTRA, WHO ARE BOTH IN THE GUARD. KING ALEXANDER IS FINE. GENERAL PARMENIO IS DEAD. I CAN'T STOP THINKING LIKE A SLAVE YET, BECAUSE THE HORSE BOND IS TOO STRONG, BUT ONE DAY I WILL.

LOVE, CHARMEIA

Tydeos gave her a funny look. But he kept making marks on the flattened grass until he had finished what she said. Then he frowned and added something else at the bottom. Charm did not notice, because she couldn't read.

I only know because of what happened afterward.

ALEXANDER READS SEVENTY THOUSAND LETTERS

The letters were collected and loaded into carts to start the long journey back through our string of garrisons to Anatolia, Greece, and Macedonia. I don't think any of them contained squealing threats like the ones Alexander and King Darius used to send each other. They were probably nickers and whinnies, like the letter Charm wrote to Queen Ada. Writing them seemed to calm the men. When Alexander announced we wouldn't be spending the winter here, after all, but would be marching on after Bessus to finish the campaign, they began to ready their weapons and pack without complaint.

But the trumpets didn't sound the order to break our lakeside camp for many days. Alexander moved out of the town and shut himself alone in his pavilion, where the lamps burned day and night.

When he finally emerged, he had dark rings around his eyes and squinted in the sunlight. He seemed much happier, though. He even smiled at some of the grooms as he brought a bag of apples down to the horse lines for us.

Alexander took my muzzle against his chest, and I inhaled his sweet sherbet smell. While I nudged him for apples, he said quietly without turning around, "Charmides, tell me everything you know about this horse bond."

Charm, who was standing tensely in the shadows nearby, started like a nervous filly. "H-horse bond, sir?"

"I read your letter."

She shivered all over and fiddled with my mane. I blew at her, happy to be with my two favorite humans.

Charm spoke without looking at Alexander. "It's a magic bond, sir. The Amazon queen told me it was called a horse bond, but Queen Ada saw it first, back in Halicarnassus. They say it's between me and Bucephalas and . . . you, sir. I'm sorry. I don't know how it happened."

Alexander frowned at her red curls, which she had tied up with a twist of blue-and-white cord left over from my tassels. "Magic? Are you sure?"

"I'm not sure of anything, sir. But the Amazons said it happens sometimes between a human and a horse. Queen Penthesilea said she'd never seen it work between a horse and two humans before, but she says it won't break until . . . one of us dies." It was a whisper.

Alexander laughed. "You don't want to take too much notice of what the Amazon queen said, Charmides! It's obvious she ran off home because she was afraid I might put her immortality to the test." He frowned, and his hand shot out and gripped her chin, forcing her to look at him. "Is it true what Demetrius said, that the Mardians forced you to go with them back in Zadracarta?"

Charm started to say yes, it was true, then burst into tears.

Alexander sighed. "Tell me the truth, Charmides," he said. "Don't you start lying to me, too."

"I'm sorry!" She sniffed. "I should never have gone with the Mardians. I shouldn't have let Demetrius talk me into it! Poor Demetrius, he was only upset about Aura losing her foal, he'd never have hurt you. . . . It's all my fault he's dead. And Philotas, and General Parmenio, and all those others . . ."

Alexander shook his head and let her go.

He said in a tough voice, "Philotas and General Parmenio were going to kill me and take my throne. They had to die. But Demetrius isn't dead, you silly girl. Do you really think I could give the order to have one of my closest friends stoned? He's merely under arrest. He's out of the Guard, of course. I can't trust him anymore to carry my shield. But for now he's alive, and so are most of the other idiots Philotas named."

She stared at him, her eyes still wet, but hope lighting up her face. "Really?"

"Don't you believe the word of your king? I've created a new division in my army called the Disciplinary Company. They'll serve in that until they prove their loyalty to me, or die trying."

Charm wet her lips and bowed her head. She said miserably, "Then you'd better put me in the Disciplinary Company, too."

Alexander narrowed his eyes. "Don't be silly, Charmides. You're my groom. You have to stay with me and Bucephalas. Besides, you came back of your own accord, didn't you? I forgive you."

Her gaze flew to his face. "I'll never try to leave you again, Alexander, sir," she whispered. "I promise."

Alexander nodded. He gave Charm another long look. Then his lips twisted up at one corner. "Ah, Charmides! Aren't you even a little bit angry I read your letter?"

"I . . . you're the king and the son of Zeus, sir. You can do anything you like."

He chuckled. "Hmm. I think some of the men might disagree. But I've sent your letter on to Queen Ada now, so the honey cakes you asked for will no doubt arrive eventually. When they do, I'll send them down here for Bucephalas."

It was Charm's turn to look surprised. "Honey cakes, sir? But I didn't ask for —" She broke off and looked at Tydeos, who was combing out Petasios's tail. He flushed.

Alexander frowned at Tydeos and ordered him to move Petasios to the other end of the line so Hoplite could join the horses of the Guard. As I whinnied after my red friend, Alexander told Charm she should never trust a scribe and promised he'd send Prince Ochus to teach her how to write her own letters, because the boy had more sense than all his men put together.

Obviously, Prince Ochus wrote only good things about Alexander in *his* letter to his grandmother and sisters in Susa.

THE DISCIPLINARY COMPANY

When we left Lake Seistan, things had changed. By executing General Parmenio and Philotas and punishing the others involved in the plot, Alexander had dominated all immediate challengers for the herd. As he mounted me to lead the army onward, his eyes gleamed with a new, cold power.

I was still the boss, of course. But with Hephaestion leading half of Philotas's old herd, Demetrius in the Disciplinary Company, and Aura still suckling Caspia, the Guard consisted of:

ELECTRA *carrying* LAOMEDON
BOREALIS *carrying* LEONNATUS
APOLLO *carrying* PERDICCAS
HADES *carrying* IOLAUS
HARPINNA *carrying* PTOLEMY
HOPLITE *carrying the new man,* PEUCESTAS, *with the Achilles shield*
A pretty gray Persian mare carrying King Darius's brother OXARTHES,
    who had joined us at Zadracarta to help look for Bessus

Alexander gave the other half of Philotas's cavalry to Cleitus, who, if you remember, saved Alexander's life at the Granicus. Cleitus mounted poor, short-maned Zephyr, who spent the whole of the first day searching the snow-covered rocks for Philotas's ghost. It is always sad to lose your rider and worrying to carry a new one until you know you can trust them. Mares worry about this more than stallions.

The new Disciplinary Company marched in the middle, made up of the men Philotas had named and those Alexander did not trust anymore after reading their letters. These men shuffled along on foot with their heads bowed in shame. Demetrius was among them, carrying a short spear and looking very small. One of the Persians who had joined us at Zadracarta had been promoted to be their boss. He rode a Persian horse and carried a long whip.

"Feel free to beat any man who steps out of line," Alexander told their Persian boss as we set out. "I want these men in the front line at every battle, and those who refuse to fight will get garrison duty at the farthest outposts of my empire. They can grumble about me all they like among themselves. But if any one of them so much as looks at a man from another company, you will report him to me and give him ten lashes. Understand?"

The Persian nodded gravely. "It will be exactly as you say, King Iskander."

Alexander frowned at Demetrius and wheeled me back with an

impatient jerk on my rein. He added, "And make sure you keep a careful record! Those who serve me faithfully and fight well can win transferral back to their old company. But they have to prove themselves worthy of my trust."

The Persian smiled. "You are truly a great king, Iskander."

Which, if you ask me, was a clever thing to say. It certainly made Alexander smile and sit straighter as I cantered past the long column of men and horses to take our place at the head of the army. He was wearing his Troy helmet again with the white plumes, and before we left he renamed the town on the shores of the lake where all the arrests had taken place.

For once, though, he didn't call it Alexandria.

From that day, the place where Alexander had gotten rid of all the challengers for his herd became known as Prophthasia — which, if your Greek is a bit rusty, means "anticipation" or "hope."

Different! But anticipation of WHAT?

BACTRIA

329 B.C.

ZEUS HIDES THE EDGE OF THE WORLD

To reach Bactria, King Darius's brother said we had two choices:

> *Go back the way we had come until we met the road from Zadracarta, and then turn due east (the easy route, but also the one Bessus expected us to take).*
>
> *Continue east through the mountains, turn north along the Kabul valley, and double back over the Caucasus range (supposed to be impossible in winter).*

No prizes for guessing which way Alexander chose.

We climbed high, right into the clouds. There was not much snow if we were careful to stay on the road, but it was *cold*. Every time we camped, we had to paw through the frozen crust for thin yellow stalks to graze. On all sides snowcapped peaks pierced the sky, while the wind cut through our winter coats.

At night I did my best to shield young Hoplite from the weather. Our grooms folded our cloths over our backs, and we all squeezed up close for warmth. But poor Borealis on the end of the line shivered through the nights with his tail tucked between his legs, and his ribs stuck out even more than mine. Charm sneaked extra handfuls of barley into his nose-bag, but it made little difference. Our riders were no happier, hunched in their cloaks with their bare legs shaking and their fingers too swollen to grip our reins. It was a good thing we didn't have to fight any battles on that march, I can tell you, because I'm not sure any of us could have moved faster than a trot, and the men could barely grip their spears. Lots of ghosts, human and horse, shivered into the freezing air during that march.

Besides wanting to catch the traitor Bessus unprepared by attacking him from the rear, there was another reason Alexander took the hardest route. But we horses only found out what it was when we stopped in the shadow of the mountains to dig the foundations for yet another Macedonian garrison: Alexandria-under-the-Caucasus. Ha, there's a surprise.

Our riders fell silent as they considered the line of jagged peaks that barred our way. We chewed our bits, and poor Borealis's ears flicked back in misery. But Alexander stared up at the snowbound mountains with the familiar light in his eyes that meant trouble.

He rode me forward a few paces and whispered, "Look, Bucephalas! The Caucasus Mountains! Aristotle says you can see the edge of the world from the highest pass! That's where Zeus chained immortal Prometheus to a rock as punishment for giving men the gift of fire and sent a vulture to peck out his liver every day for a thousand years. Prometheus grew a new liver overnight, so the torture could begin afresh. Maybe I'd better make the proper sacrifices before I go up there, eh?"

He pulled my ear, like he used to do back in Macedonia. Then his face took on the stony expression he'd worn most days since we left Lake Seistan, and he wheeled me back to join the Guard, shouting for someone to fetch Charm. The others all looked at Iolaus, who trotted off on Hades grumbling under his breath that he wasn't a messenger boy.

Perdiccas cleared his throat. "Alex, are we stopping here before we —?"

Alexander cut him off. "If I were Bessus, I'd set an ambush in one of these passes. We have seven routes to choose from. Which one would you take the army through, if you were commander?"

Perdiccas stared up at the snowy peaks and stroked Apollo's winter-furred neck. "I'd choose the lowest, Alex, with the easiest climb and the least snow. I know it'll be thawing soon, but the men are half starved and the horses are no better. They can't go on much longer without grazing."

Alexander nodded. "That's what I thought you'd say. If Bessus has heard we're coming this way he'll assume the same, so the lowest pass is out. But does he still have that treacherous horsemaster with him, whispering in his ear about me?"

"We could take one of the middle passes to confuse him," Laomedon ventured.

"Or split up the army, send the baggage train through the lowest pass, and take the cavalry over one of the others?" Ptolemy suggested.

Alexander gave Ptolemy a scathing look. "Don't be stupid! That's hostile territory over there. The last thing we want to do now is divide our men, when Bessus might be waiting on the other side to pick us off. Have you learned nothing? Where's Iolaus gotten to — ah, at last!"

Hades trotted up with Charm perched awkwardly on his withers in front of Iolaus. My groom gave me an anxious look. After satisfying herself that I was all right, she slithered off Hades and bowed her head to Alexander.

He frowned down at her. "Any dreams about these mountains, Charmides?"

She gazed up at the snowy peaks and shivered. "No, sir, no dreams. I'm sorry."

Alexander smiled. "Good! Then we'll take the highest pass. It's the most direct, and Darius's brother tells me the land on the other side of this range is fertile. The crops should be growing by the time we get down, so we'll be able to rest and eat before we fight. Someone bring me a sheep! I need to make a sacrifice to my father, Zeus." He glared at the members of his Guard, who were all looking at Iolaus again. "Why is everyone so slow to obey me lately? *Move!*"

The cooks used what little food remained to give the army a hot meal before tackling the pass, and we horses had double rations in our nosebags that night. In the morning, we set out on the long climb over the Caucasus Mountains. No one complained that we were taking the highest pass. In fact, those of the Guard who had been in the Aristotle school with Alexander seemed almost as excited about seeing the edge of the world as he was.

It was a long, slow, leg-trembling climb. The road from Lake Seistan had been bad enough for horses, but this was much steeper. Halfway up, our riders tied little leather bags over our hooves like they did back at the

Persian Gates, and we struggled on through knee-deep snow to the crest of the pass. We were so high up, and the air was so thin and cold, we could barely breathe. Poor Borealis staggered from one side of the path to the other, his flanks heaving and blood dripping from his nose.

Alexander urged me on with his strong legs every time I tried to slow down, so we reached the top ahead of everyone else. While I gulped the thin air and tried to turn my tail to the wind, Alexander shaded his eyes and squinted east for a long while, his heart beating very fast. The army was strung out below us like a snake, winding all the way back down to the newest Alexandria. Clouds filled the valleys behind us. I could not see anything under them.

As the Guard caught up, Alexander turned, frustrated. "Do you see it, gentlemen? Can anyone see the ocean at the edge of the world?"

"I just see clouds," Perdiccas said.

"I see water . . . I think," Ptolemy said.

"Maybe Zeus is hiding the edge of the world from us because he doesn't want us to go there?" Leonnatus suggested, stroking Borealis's sweaty neck. The brown stallion's legs were still trembling from the climb. "Alex, I don't think my horse is going to make it much farther without a rest —"

Alexander scowled. "We haven't time to rest! Zeus is hiding the ocean precisely because he *wants* us to go there and see it with our own eyes!"

Then Iolaus, who had been sulking at the back on Hades, looked the other way and groaned. "Forget the ocean . . . look what Bessus has done!"

Alexander rode me to the other side of the pass and uttered a curse. The rest of the Guard joined us and stared silently.

It was bad. Below us, in a shimmering haze, lay the valleys of Bactria and the fertile fields Darius's brother had promised. But instead of the crops that should have been growing in them, we could see only black earth and deserted villages. Through the haze of smoke, a river glimmered in the distance. Bessus had used the same trick the Persians had tried at Tarsus — he'd burned all the available food.

"Zeus help us all," Leonnatus whispered in dismay.

Alexander turned on him with a scowl. "Pull yourselves together, gentlemen! This isn't the first time we've been hungry. We'll just have to press on. At least it doesn't look as if he plans to fight us here. The plains on the banks of the Oxus will be much better for our phalanx and the cavalry. We'll soon finish him off when we get there."

The Guard stared at the distant river with hopeless eyes. They knew that what seems close from the top of a pass is a lot farther away than it looks. It was all too much for Borealis, who gave a horrible groan and crumpled into the snow. Even as Leonnatus leaped off him, Borealis's ghost rose slowly from his body and limped over to the rocks at the side of the trail.

I shivered all over.

My friend! My solid brown friend! DEAD!

I raised my head and let out a wild neigh that was answered back down the trail by Petasios and several other horses.

Alexander jerked my rein and shouted at the Guard to stop being so defeatist. He said they'd soon find more horses once they got out of the mountains, and Bessus was obviously scared of us or he wouldn't have burned all the crops and fled.

Poor Borealis didn't even get the next city named after him, because Alexander was in such a hurry to catch Bessus and the horsemaster that none of us stopped there. The most important city in Bactria kept its silly name of Balkh.

DESERTERS

Our enemy's trail led to the river we'd seen from the top of the pass, but first we had to cross a horrible desert, which was the last thing we needed after tackling snowbound mountains in winter. Alexander, however, made the men march day and night and kept pushing me into a trot when I would rather have walked. By the time we Guard reached the river Oxus and discovered Bessus had burned all the bridges to stop us from following him across, only Hephaestion's cavalry was still with us.

Alexander scowled at the smoking remains of a bridge and cursed under his breath. "This Bessus is getting seriously annoying," he muttered.

Hephaestion smiled. "You've got him on the run, Alex. We'll catch him. We've just crossed the Caucasus Mountains in winter with nothing to eat but our mules and marched across a desert with nothing to drink but wine. Nothing stops us. The men worship you, Alex. They'll do anything you tell them, because they know you'll always get them through the tough times, and you'll always be the first into battle. They might fear you sometimes, but they will always love you. I never realized before you gave me my command, but you're like a god to them."

Alexander cheered up a bit at this. "That's not surprising. The oracle said I'm the son of Zeus, after all."

He ordered the Guard to light fires as a guide for the rest of our herd, then rode me slowly beside Petasios while he and Hephaestion made plans to cross the river. As flames crackled to life along the riverbank, he squinted into the darkness and demanded, "Where's the rest of my army? They're so slow!"

"They'll be here, Alex," Hephaestion said. "They haven't got old Parmenio to lead them home now, have they?"

Alexander smiled grimly. "Only his ghost."

Men and horses appeared out of the night in a straggling line, exhausted, and finally the baggage train trailed in with our grooms. But not all our herd had followed us across the desert. The Thessalian cavalry had discovered there was a direct road west from Bessus's captured city and gone that way instead.

Alexander's hand trembled on my rein as Commander Cleitus brought him the bad news. Apparently, the Thessalians had requested that their final pay and bonuses be sent to Ecbatana so they could pick it up on their way back to Greece. While I stretched out my nose and nickered to Zephyr, pleased to see she had made it across the mountains and the desert, Alexander said to Cleitus in a dangerously quiet tone, "And you just let them go?"

"What else could I do?" The old cavalryman met his gaze. "They were volunteers, remember? General Parmenio's execution upset them. They'd had enough."

"And what about you, Cleitus?" Alexander said, still quietly. "You served under General Parmenio. Have *you* had enough?"

"My cavalry will follow you until we've finished what we came to do," Cleitus said carefully.

"And mine!" Hephaestion said. Putting a hand on Alexander's arm, he whispered, "Commander Cleitus saved your life at the Granicus, Alex.

You don't have to worry about his loyalty. Your army has followed you through snowbound mountains and across deserts to get here. We've lost a few thousand Greeks who didn't want to fight in the first place, that's all. Half their mounts were exhausted, anyway. We've plenty of men left to deal with Bessus."

Alexander closed his eyes and gripped my mane. He controlled his breathing and nodded to Cleitus, his face stony. "Thank you for the message. Hephaestion, go and arrange the necessary funds for the Thessalians. Tell your men to start making rafts with their tent covers. Use your horses' hay to stuff them so they'll float. We'll start the crossing tonight."

Cleitus gave him a sharp look. "Tonight, Alexander?"

"Yes, tonight! I've got to catch Bessus and that traitor of a horsemaster before the rest of my army decides to leave me."

He acted tough until Cleitus left. But when we were alone in the night with the black water of the Oxus sliding past us, the hugeness went out of him and he gripped my mane in confusion.

"I don't understand, Bucephalas! Why are they all so scared of following me these days? First the Amazons, then General Parmenio and that idiot Philo, and my shield-bearer Demetrius. And now the Thessalians. Who's going to be next? I can't stop now, when we're within sight of the edge of the world and immortality! Even if the oracle was wrong about that, how can I possibly go home to Pella and hunt lions after having all of Persia kneel at my feet?"

I nudged him to remind him I wanted my supper before someone stitched it into a raft, and he sighed. "Ah, my faithful horse! At least *you'll* never leave me. Come on, let's see if we can find your groom."

HARPINNA LEADS THE HERD

It took us five days to cross that river. We horses swam across with lines of rafts tied to our tails, then swam back again to collect more rafts, and back across again, until we had crossed the Oxus seven times. We saw some of Bessus's scouts on the other side, when we resumed our march. They took one look at us and fled across the plain. I don't think they were expecting to see us so soon — ha! Alexander let them go so they could take the bad news to their boss.

A few days afterward, a messenger arrived from the Persian resistance and told Alexander that they now had a new leader called Spitamenes, who would hand the traitor Bessus over to us so we could finish things here and take our men home. All Alexander had to do was send a Macedonian officer with a small escort to collect the prisoner.

"It's bound to be another trick!" Alexander muttered. "Look what happened last time I agreed to meet Bessus, back at the tomb of Cyrus the Great."

"But the message is from this new man, Spitamenes," Leonnatus pointed out. "If he's telling the truth, Bessus is a prisoner."

Since he'd lost Borealis, Leonnatus was now riding Aura, who kept neighing for the golden Mardian filly. I gave her a special nicker, because I knew what a sad time this was for her. It was even harder for Aura than usual, because she had lost her own foal.

Oxarthes looked a bit confused at the mention of Cyrus the Great's tomb. But he nodded and said, "I know Spitamenes. He is an excellent fighter who once fought in my brother Darius's army. He comes from this area, and he follows our prophet Zoroaster and worships the sacred flame. I believe he'll hand over the traitor as he promised."

Alexander gave King Darius's brother a narrow-eyed look. "Maybe. And maybe the message came from Bessus himself, in the hope of luring me to a remote place where he can kill me. I want a volunteer to take five thousand men and go to meet this Spitamenes to arrange the transfer of the prisoner. Once there, you'll leave most of the men in hiding and go on with a small escort as requested, but take a trumpeter with you in case there's trouble. The rest of us will make camp here. When you're satisfied it's not a trick, send a message to me." His eyes glinted, like they used to back in Greece whenever he dared his friends to volunteer for a special mission. "It's dangerous. Whoever goes will be a hero."

The Guard glanced at one another. No one looked very keen. Iolaus fiddled with Hades' mane, obviously hoping he wouldn't get the job.

Oxarthes said, "I'll happily do it, King Alexander. But they asked for a Macedonian and if I go Spitamenes will probably kill me. He does not understand your vision of Persians, Macedonians, and Greeks forming one nation."

"Nor, it seems, do most of my Macedonians," Alexander muttered. But if anyone heard, they kept quiet.

"I'll go," Ptolemy said.

The others breathed again, and Harpinna was soon trotting off proudly at the head of a herd of five thousand men and horses. As Ptolemy urged her into a canter, she made herself huge and arched her speckled neck.

Sometimes, Harpinna forgets she is only a mare. What next?

Over the next few days, I was lonely in the horse lines without Petasios or Borealis. Charm took pity on me and tethered Apollo next to me instead. He was not as solid as Borealis, nor as familiar as Petasios, and he wasn't my own colt like Hoplite. But I'd known him a long time, and he had not complained once going over the mountains or across the desert. After giving him flat ears to warn him not to steal any of my hay, I put my teeth gently on his withers and began to mutual groom. BLISS!

By the time Charm came back from settling Aura, who was still prone to fits of frantic neighing for Caspia, we had reached each other's rumps. She smiled at our half-shut eyes and scratching teeth. "There, Bucephalas," she said, patting my neck. "That's better, isn't it? Don't worry, Harpinna will be back soon. King Alexander's had a message from Ptolemy. It doesn't seem to be a trick, and I haven't had any bad dreams about it. We're going to collect Bessus tomorrow."

Groom-gossip was all about Bessus that night. They said Alexander had told Spitamenes to chain the traitor naked to a post at the side of the road with a slave collar around his neck. They said he was going to drag him to death behind his chariot, the same way he had killed the boss of Gaza. This was clearly stupid, because we didn't bring any of our chariots with us over the Oxus.

Also, the grooms didn't know about the trick at the tomb of Cyrus the Great when Bessus was supposed to have returned Charm in exchange for Prince Ochus but brought the horsemaster and his knife instead. If they had, they might have known Alexander wanted the traitor to have a much slower death.

THE PUNISHMENT FOR TRAITORS

In the morning, Alexander orders Tydeos to get Aura ready for Prince Ochus and tells Charm to put all my tassels and my best parade-cloth on me. Then we lead the army up the road to find Bessus, Ochus riding proudly on Aura beside his uncle Oxarthes.

The two gray mares make a good pair, but Aura's dapples are darkest and most beautiful. She neighed a few times to Caspia as we left the lines, but being up front with the Guard put her out of hearing distance of the filly, and she soon pricks her ears and relaxes her mouth to Ochus's gentle hands.

When we come to the chained Bessus, Alexander halts me and stares down at him with a funny expression. You humans always look strange without your clothes on, because we horses don't often see you undressed.

Bessus's muscular body is covered in black curly hair and lots of bruises. The heavy collar around his neck is made of wood and chained to a post at hock height, so he is on his knees. A deep cut across his forehead trickles blood down the side of his face where it forms a crust in his whiskers. Flies are feasting on it. His hands are bound tightly behind him, and he hasn't got a tail to flick them away.

His black eyes glitter with hatred as he stares up at Alexander. He bares his teeth at Oxarthes and Ochus and says, "I see Iskander has been forced to adopt King Darius's family because he is too young and irresponsible to have any of his own."

Alexander's eyes narrow. King Darius's brother rides his gray mare closer to the post and spits on the prisoner. "Silence! You'll speak only when you're spoken to."

But Bessus keeps grinning up at Alexander. "What are you waiting for, Macedonian midget? Kill me! I know you want to. Your precious little groom's dead, you know. She ran off back in the Caspian Gates. By now, her bones will have been pecked clean by the crows."

Alexander's fist clenches, but he keeps his hand away from his sword. Bessus obviously has no idea Charm found us.

Oxarthes snaps something in Persian, and an angry stream of squeals pass between them. Ochus listens silently, his face grave and his fist resting on the jeweled dagger in his belt.

Alexander motions Oxarthes back and rides me up to the post so I am nearly stepping on the prisoner's legs. He frowns down at Bessus and asks, "Why did you betray and kill your own king?"

Bessus bares his teeth. "To please you, Iskander! You wanted Darius dead. I saved you the trouble. You should reward me and set me free."

"I am Great King of Persia now, and you are a traitor! You'll die a traitor's death."

"You'll never be Great King of Persia," Bessus growls. "The priests wouldn't bless you, would they? Only those of the royal blood can rule Persia. You're a barbarian invader, nothing more. Kill me and have done with it."

Alexander's breathing quickens. This time his hand does go to his sword, and Bessus's gaze follows it. His eyes glitter.

But Oxarthes touches the king's elbow and says, "King Iskander, he killed my brother, who was the rightful Great King, and took the crown for himself. He must stand trial before a Persian court and be publicly executed in a painful manner. But first he must have his nose and ears cut off in the way of our people, to show he is a traitor."

Bessus tugs at his bonds and squeals something in Persian, which Oxarthes ignores, although it makes Ochus bite his lip.

Alexander narrows his eyes. He draws his sword and lowers it to Bessus's right ear. Bessus cringes, and his sweat sharpens. "I can do this quickly or slowly," Alexander says. "Tell me the truth! Where is my father's horsemaster?"

Bessus looks confused.

"You must remember! The Macedonian who was with you at the tomb of Cyrus the Great and tried to kill me. The one who killed my dog! He fled with you from the Caspian Gates. Where did he go? Is he with Spitamenes?"

The prisoner bursts out laughing. "How would I know? King Iskander conquers a hundred cities and defeats King Darius's immortal army, and he is worried about a lame barbarian from his own country who can hardly walk without his horse? Maybe you ought to look for him among the Scythians." He laughs so much, he coughs up blood.

Alexander stares down at him in disgust. He puts away his sword and backs me farther from the post. He looks thoughtfully at Prince Ochus and says, "This man killed your father. It's about time you bloodied that dagger I gave you. Cut off his ears and nose for me. Don't be afraid. He can't hurt you now."

Ochus swallows. He looks down at Bessus and shakes his head slightly.

"Let me have the honor, King Iskander," Oxarthes says quickly, drawing his own dagger.

But Alexander rides me between the gray mare and the post so Oxarthes can't reach the prisoner. "No," he says. "I want Prince Ochus to do it."

"The prince is only ten."

"When I was ten, I killed my first lion. When I was twelve, I tamed Bucephalas. When I was sixteen, I led an army into my first battle and killed my first man! I'm not asking the boy to kill him, merely to take off a couple of ears and a nose. It doesn't matter if he makes a mess of it, because Bessus doesn't deserve to be treated any better. It'll be good training for when the boy is older and ready to fight at my side. Take out your dagger, Ochus, get down off that mare, and do it. Come on. You're no coward, I know that."

Slowly, Ochus slips off Aura's back and draws his dagger. Bessus bares his teeth at him and rattles his chains. The prince hesitates. Bessus laughs and says something in Persian. Ochus's fist tightens on the dagger.

Alexander smiles coldly. "Go on!"

But Ochus cannot do it. He sets the dagger to Bessus's ear, makes a line of blood, and snatches back his hand. There are tears in his eyes when he turns to face us. "Please, Uncle Alexander . . . let Uncle Oxarthes do it."

Bessus laughs out loud. "You'd better hurry up and sire yourself a son who can stomach the sight of blood, King Iskander! This pretty pup of Darius's will never be strong enough to sit on your throne after you've gotten yourself killed."

Alexander leaps down off my back, seizes Ochus's hand, and forces the blade against the prisoner's ear. *"Do it!"* he shouts. "If you don't, I'll have you whipped for disobeying me in front of my men!"

Ochus shakes his head. "No, I cannot . . ."

"You can, and you will!" Alexander hisses. He drags his hand down, and Bessus's ear half comes off, messily. Bessus screams. Ochus struggles free, drops the dagger, grabs Aura's reins, and vaults onto her. He gallops back the way we came, past the long column of horses and men toward the tail of our army. I throw my head up and stare after them. No one is holding my rein, but I don't move. The bond with my rider is too strong.

Alexander is furious. All the men nearby are staring at him. His face flushes and his breathing quickens. He glares after Ochus and yells in his shrill voice, "Since no one else seems willing to do it, I'll teach this traitor a lesson myself!"

He strides down the road, pushing startled men aside until he finds one of the carts handing out water to the troops. He grabs a stick from the surprised muleteer and comes back with it at a run. In my blind spot, the stick turns into a long Macedonian pike, and suddenly I am surrounded by ghosts.

Sweat bathes me. I am already disturbed by Bessus's smell, but Alexander's shouting upsets me even more. When the king rains a flurry of blows on Bessus's back, grunting, "*That*'ll teach you to call me a barbarian midget! *That*'ll teach you to murder your rightful king! *That*'ll teach you to give sanctuary to my father's horsemaster. . . ." The bond between us loosens. I whirl around and gallop after Aura.

Alexander stops, his stick raised for another blow. "*Bucephalas!*" he shouts, a note of terrible fear in his voice.

Out of the corner of my good eye, I see him frown at the stick in his hand as if he doesn't remember how it got there. He drops it and backs away from the prisoner, clutching his wild mane with blood-spattered hands.

The Guard stares at him in horror and concern. No one says a word.

I hesitate, ashamed of my panic. But the blood is not Alexander's, and the only enemy in sight is chained to a post with a yoke around his neck. My rider does not need me. My favorite mare does.

I catch up with Aura at the baggage train, where we find Charm leading Caspia. Aura neighs to her adopted filly, but Caspia likes being with humans because the Mardians gave her goat's milk in the first few days of her life.

Charm stares at my empty cloth in horror. "What happened to the king? Oh, Zeus, Bessus didn't —?"

Ochus shakes his head. "Not to worry, Charmeia. Uncle Alexander is fine. Bucephalas got loose while he was dealing with the prisoner, that is all."

She gives the prince's face a closer look. I think she can tell he has been crying, but she doesn't mention it. "Bucephalas wouldn't just run off! What happened, Ochus? Did Alexander send you back?"

Ochus sits very straight and smiles. He hides his sore hand from her. "Everything is fine. Uncle Alexander and Uncle Oxarthes have Bessus prisoner now, and they are going to punish him for killing my father."

Tydeos hurries up and takes Caspia from Charm so she can check me over for injury. Satisfied I am not hurt, she strokes my nose. "Hear that, Tydeos? Alexander's caught Bessus! Maybe now he'll take us home."

Some of the muleteers and grooms riding in the carts overhear, and the news passes through the baggage train like one of Alexander's city fires. Men start to cheer. "We're going home! It's nearly over! We've caught Bessus, and we're going home!"

Which only goes to show how little grooms and muleteers know about dominating. Bessus was merely a beaten stallion turned out of his own herd. The herd was still at large with a new, stronger stallion, and our enemy the horsemaster had escaped to create more trouble. Alexander still needed to show Spitamenes, the new leader of the Persian resistance, that he was boss.

TWO KINDS OF PRISONERS

Before Alexander took the army north in search of Spitamenes, he sent Hephaestion's herd back to Balkh with the prisoner Bessus and instructions to collect the men we'd left at the River Oxus on the way. He sent Ochus, Charm, and me with them. He also sent Peucestas and the shield of Achilles, because he wanted to ride Hoplite himself. He told the Guard that since he was the son of a god and nearly immortal, he didn't need a shield-bearer anymore.

He told the men that my running off while he was interrogating the prisoner proved I needed a rest. He said the hard march had upset me and

I was, after all, twenty-seven years old. Ha! My age had nothing to do with it, as you know. Besides, Alexander used the same excuse for Prince Ochus, saying the boy was overtired, when he was only ten!

I don't know what he told Ochus in private. But when Alexander said good-bye to me in the lines, he stroked my nose, apologized for frightening me with the mule stick, and promised it would never happen again.

"Hephaestion will look after you and Charmides, Bucephalas," he whispered, pulling my ear. "It's time Hoplite saw some action, and this campaign is just the thing for him to cut his teeth on. Spitamenes is obviously scared, or he wouldn't have given me Bessus. It won't take me long to find my father's old horsemaster, then we can head back over the Caucasus and look for the edge of the world — only don't tell anyone, will you? I've still got to think of an excuse to persuade the army to follow me farther east."

Hoplite must have grown without me noticing. When Alexander vaulted onto him and my colt made himself huge, he looked like my reflection. We both had white hairs in our coats, though Hoplite's came from his mother and mine were where my coat had grown over battle scars. He gave a bold little squeal and a buck, and Alexander laughed.

As I watched my proud colt trot off at the head of the army carrying the king, a shiver went through me. Abandoning Alexander on the roadside with Bessus was the first time I had ever left my rider of my own will. I hung my head as Tydeos boosted Charm onto my back, and even her fingers mutual grooming my withers did not make me feel better.

On Alexander's orders, Bessus was forced to run all the way back to Balkh behind a mule cart, naked but for his wooden yoke. His back bled from the beating Alexander had given him, and maggots seethed in the wounds where his nose and ears used to be. By the time we got back to Balkh, the traitor who had murdered his king was truly dominated.

This was just as well, because it was the most dominating our herd did for a while.

27

BALKH

329–327 B.C.

DEFEAT

The stables in Balkh were cool and airy, built around courtyards filled with fountains and trees. They had the same smell as all other stables: horse sweat, dung, hay, and barley. But the shame of leaving Alexander at the roadside upset me so much that I could not settle and went off my feed. Despite Charm's care, my coat grew dull, and my ribs stuck out like Borealis's had before he collapsed.

Charm spent ages trying to make my coat shine again with the wooden comb and olive oil, walked me by the river like she used to do in Pella, and added different treats to my manger to tempt me into eating:

Herbs — *boring, boring, boring*
Apples — *sweet and crunchy, but boring*
Dates — *sticky, ugh*
Pomegranates — *suspicious, so I left that whole feed without touching it*
Camel's milk — *for foals!*

But nothing could replace Alexander's hands on my rein, his voice in my ear, and his strong legs trembling with excitement against my sides. I thought I would die if he never rode me again.

Prince Ochus missed Alexander, too. He wore a bandage around the two smallest fingers of his right hand, because Alexander had broken them when he tried to make him cut off Bessus's ear. But he kept asking Charm when the king would be back, until she lost her temper and shouted that she didn't know and she didn't care. If Alexander was stupid enough to keep fighting he deserved to get himself killed, and at least he couldn't get me killed under him this time.

This was a lie, because she told me she missed Alexander as much as I did.

One night when I was lying in my stall I felt a sharp pain in my leg, and the air around me sparkled, like when my eye got damaged in battle. I scrambled to my feet and neighed in terror. Charm woke up at once and sprang to my side. "What's wrong, Bucephalas?" she cried. "You're covered in sweat, you silly horse. . . ." She put a hand on her heart, stared at the door, and whispered, "It's Alexander, isn't it? Oh, Zeus, what trouble has he gotten himself into *now*?"

We found out a few days later, when Hephaestion came to the stables shouting for the grooms to get the horses ready for his men.

"A messenger got through from Soghdiana," he explained to Charm as he strapped a battle-cloth on Petasios. "There's been heavy fighting against Spitamenes and his resistance force. Don't spread it around, but I think we were defeated at Maracanda. Then the Scythians attacked the hill forts on the northern frontier, and Alex had to go up there and drive them back. He's been injured. The messenger says he was hit on the head by a large rock and went blind for a while. Seems a sniper shot an arrow through his leg as well, and then he drank some infected water. He's apparently very sick and can hardly speak or walk. . . . I don't know how much to believe, but I'm to take him more siege engines and his chariot. I knew I should never have let him go north without me."

Charm's hands flew to her mouth. She ran to fetch my bridle.

"No, Charmeia!" Hephaestion ordered. "You're to stay here with Prince Ochus."

"But, sir! Alexander needs Bucephalas if there's going to be more fighting. Hoplite doesn't know enough about battle yet. That's obviously why the king got hurt."

Hephaestion sighed, put a hand on her shoulder, and said, "If Alex can't walk or see straight, Charmeia, he certainly can't ride. That's why I'm taking him a chariot. He didn't ask for you. Try not to worry. If he's really as sick as the reports say, I'll bring him back with me. And if he isn't,

I'll help him finish off this Spitamenes, then I'll bring him back. If you're bored, you can always start training that Mardian filly."

That winter in Balkh was a lonely, tense time. Except for my stall and Caspia's, the stables stayed empty. Frost formed on the statues, and Charm had to break the ice on the water troughs so we could drink. With all the other grooms in Soghdiana with the army, there was no gossip. The Macedonian garrison left to look after us stared anxiously from the walls, blew on their hands, and gripped their spears tightly. If there was news from the north, we didn't hear it.

Huddled in Petasios's empty stall, Prince Ochus taught Charm more letters. When they got bored with that and the prince's fingers had healed, they taught Caspia how to settle on her knees for when she grew old enough to carry a rider. Caspia became so good at this, they taught the filly more tricks. Soon Caspia would stand on her hind legs on command or lie flat on her side and play dead.

If you ask me, it was all pretty silly. But I suppose there wasn't much else for them to do.

A PRESENT FROM SOGHDIANA

The spring rains make the desert bloom with flowers before we finally see a Macedonian column marching toward the city. Charm catches her breath and shades her eyes. I throw my head up and whinny in excitement to find out which horses are with them.

Only one whinny I recognize comes back — the gray Persian mare who carries Darius's brother. There are lots of strange whinnies, though, very fresh and full of themselves. In the middle of the column is a herd of big, strong-looking horses. Some are being ridden bareback by man-colts, laughing and chattering to one another in their own tongue. Part of the phalanx marches behind them.

Charm trots me to meet them, and the man-colts stare at her curiously. Her face falls when she sees it is only Darius's brother Oxarthes leading the herd. But she wets her lips and calls, "Sir, how is King Alexander?"

Oxarthes gives her a sharp frown. "Take that horse away, Groom! It looks sick. I don't want ours catching something from it."

"Bucephalas isn't ill, sir. He's just off his food."

"That's the *king's* horse?" Oxarthes takes a closer look at me. "I wouldn't have known it was the same animal! What on earth have you been doing to him?" He shakes his head. "Never mind, I'm glad you're here. I've a message for you. You'll be pleased to know King Iskander is back on his feet. He sent these horses and boys on ahead for training."

"Training for what?" It is Charm's turn to blink.

"For his army, naturally."

"But they're only boys —"

"Soghdian boys, yes. And these horses are Soghdian-bred. They'll make excellent cavalry when they're old enough, and there will be more recruits for the phalanx soon. Officially, they are hostages to ensure their fathers' good conduct. But I think they do not mind so much." He looks over his shoulder at a boy who is standing up on his horse's back with the reins in his teeth, and sighs. "I am supposed to teach them Greek. I just hope my Soghdian is up to it. King Iskander does not realize even we Persians sometimes cannot understand these people. Prince Ochus is to train with them. It'll do my nephew good to have something to occupy his body as well as his mind, perhaps help toughen him up a bit. These Soghdian boys are a fierce bunch."

"Is the fighting in the north over, then?" Charm glances at the men. "Is the king coming back?"

"Not yet." Oxarthes frowns a little. "As I explained to King Iskander, the Soghdians will fight over every handful of dust. Just conquering their cities is not enough. First, he has to build more fortresses. Then he has to hunt down Spitamenes and finish him. But he sent you a gift to cheer you up — it's back in the baggage train. Come and see."

Charm looks puzzled. But she turns me to follow the Persian mare.

We trot back down the column past the Soghdian man-colts (who are all attempting the standing-up trick now) and past the men with their long pikes, until we reach the mule carts.

I smell Alexander's gift at once and stop dead, nearly throwing Charm over my shoulder. Sweat breaks out all over me, and I tremble with bad memories. Charm grabs my mane in alarm. "Bucephalas, what's wrong?" Then she sees our gift, too, and pales.

It is our enemy, the horsemaster.

He smells twice as strong as usual, because he is filthy. He is tied behind the cart like Bessus was on our march back to Balkh, naked with a wooden yoke around his neck and his wrists bound. His lame leg looks as if it has been dragged most of the way along the ground. Both his knees are bruised. There are whip marks on his back. He looks like a broken-down horse, slumped over the tail of the cart, so relieved to have been allowed to stop that he does not look up.

Charm bites her lip and stares at the prisoner in silence.

Oxarthes watches her curiously. "King Iskander said to tell you this man will never hurt you again. He said, if you want, I am to allow you to help me torture him."

Charm shakes her head, looking sick.

"Well, I did not think it right for a girl."

"How did you catch him?" Charm whispers.

The horsemaster raises his head at the sound of her voice. His eyes are half shut with bruises and crusted with blood and flies. But they flicker open in recognition. He hisses, "You'd better watch out, slave! My Scythian friends know where you and that old nag are hiding —"

"Silence!" Oxarthes says, kicking him in the mouth.

Charm sucks in her breath. "Please don't!"

Oxarthes gives her a strange look. "King Iskander has ordered that his last days be made as uncomfortable as possible. Not only has he betrayed us to the enemy, but he shot the arrow that pierced the king's leg and roused the Scythian tribes against us. We chased them onto the steppe, which they didn't expect, and managed to capture him there. He is to share Bessus's fate, but not until King Iskander gets back."

Charm makes a choked sound, drags my head around with uncharacteristic savageness, and kicks her heels into my sides.

Relieved to be away from my enemy's smell, I break into a gallop. We thunder past the Soghdian herd flat out, Charm crouched over my mane with tears in her eyes. The Soghdian horses plunge and buck in excitement, and there is sudden laughter as the man-colt who was standing up with his reins in his teeth loses his balance and falls off.

The Soghdian horses filled the stables with excited squealing and neighing. I had to teach them who was boss, which wore me out. Charm was tired, too, because she had the job of teaching the Soghdian man-colts proper stable routine, and no colt likes being bossed around by a filly. Meanwhile, Ochus trained with them on the horse ground. The Macedonian officers were trying to teach them proper parades, so there was much shouting and laughter. The prince collected a lot of bruises from their blunt javelins, until Charm had the bright idea of training Caspia to carry him. The golden filly had not yet turned three, but the mountain roads had made her tough. She was so clever and quick that Ochus soon got his revenge, impressing the Soghdian man-colts with the silly tricks he'd taught her.

Soon after this, Charm brought a bulging bag into my stall. "That's Prince Ochus and the orphaned filly sorted out," she told me with a smile. "Now there's just you. This came from Queen Ada. I think you're going to eat today!" As she spoke, she emptied out my stale mash, replaced it with fresh barley, and added something from the bag.

I could hardly believe my luck. HONEY CAKES!

I gave a little nicker of joy, plunged in my nose, and ate up properly for the first time since abandoning Alexander.

PRINCESS ROXANNE

More of the army trickled back that winter, bringing with them more captives and treasure and also the news that Spitamenes was dead. After our herd chased them onto the steppe, the scared Scythians cut off his head and sent it to Alexander as a peace offering.

Zephyr came back with them, her head low and her mane shaved off *again*. Charm led the poor mare into Petasios's empty stall, patted her, and shook her head sadly. "Commander Cleitus," she said.

I nickered to Zephyr in sympathy. It is hard to lose a second rider so soon after the first.

Tydeos was still with Alexander, but we finally got to hear groom-gossip again.

It seemed I had not missed a big battle, after all, but lots of little ones. Alexander had divided his army into five columns, which had split up and played a game to see who could dominate the most Soghdians and Scythians. Afterward, they all met up in Maracanda and had a big party, at which Alexander had to dominate some of his own herd because they made themselves too huge. That was when Commander Cleitus died — at the end of Alexander's spear.

The grooms whispered that the king had been in an extremely bad mood because of the way the Soghdians kept attacking his men and then vanishing into their deserts and hills.

The results of the dominating game were:

Apollo and Perdiccas: 3,000 Soghdians

Harpinna and Ptolemy: 7,000 Soghdians

Xanthus and Craterus: 15,000 Soghdians and 800 Scythians

Petasios and Hephaestion: 20,000 Soghdians

Hoplite and Alexander: 65,000 Soghdians and 2,000 Scythians

As you can see, Alexander is still way ahead of everyone else, even though he almost died.

Charm went quiet when she heard how Alexander had killed Cleitus. Then she stroked my nose and whispered that she would look after me, and I wasn't to worry because the killing was nearly over. The grooms said the king had gone to finish off a few fortresses where the remaining Soghdian resistance had holed up, and that he would be back before spring.

But first, Alexander had one more surprise for us.

One morning, when Caspia and I return to the stables after a race along the riverbank carrying our riders (which I won), there is a strange smell in my stall. I stop dead. Charm's cheeks are flushed from our gallop, and our breath steams in the cold air. The sun is so bright I can't see inside. For a moment I am convinced there is a ghost in the corner and tremble all over.

Charm stiffens. "What's wrong, Bucephalas?"

Ochus stiffens, too. This makes Caspia stop and snort. Then she gives the soft nicker she reserves for greeting humans, and the panic leaves me.

It is only a girl-filly, crouched in the corner of my stall with her arms wrapped tightly around her knees. A long black mane falls over her frightened eyes. She is wearing a patterned dress with a stain on the skirt where she has been sitting in my dung. I don't know her smell, though, which is sharp with fear. So I am still wary.

"I think it's one of the Soghdian captives, Ochus," Charm says, her voice softening. "You'd better get her out of there before I take Bucephalas in. I'll hold Caspia."

"No need." Ochus takes the reins over the filly's head and puts the ends in her teeth. "Stay, Caspia," he says, and goes into my stall.

He tries speaking to the girl-filly, first in Persian, then in Greek. But she presses back against the wall and stares at him with frightened eyes. He makes a face at Charm and says something in stumbling Soghdian. The girl-filly takes a shuddering breath and gabbles back. Ochus gently lifts her mane out of her eyes, and his hand freezes. I see a shimmer in the air between them, like the light that surrounds Alexander when he is excited and happy.

Charm whispers, "Oh! She's beautiful!"

Ochus and the girl-filly are still gazing at each other. The girl raises her slender fingers to touch Ochus's hand. He smiles and rests his palm against her cheek, and she closes her eyes as the tension runs out of her.

I nudge Charm to remind her I want my hay.

"Bring her out, Ochus!" she calls. "Bucephalas is getting impatient."

Ochus takes the girl-filly's hand and leads her out into the sunlight. Her dress is thick wool in many shades of red. She and Ochus are about the same height, and they are in danger of getting soppy, so I stamp my foot and shake my head. The girl-filly eyes me warily. Then she sees Caspia holding her reins in her teeth and giggles.

While Charm settles me, Ochus and the girl-filly settle Caspia together, communicating with hand signals and glances. Finally, Ochus leaves her stroking Caspia and comes into my stall. He whispers in Greek, "She says she is a princess. Her name is Roxanne, and she says Alexander is going to marry her."

Charm's comb stops halfway through my tail. "That can't be right! She's too young."

"She's my age," Ochus says. "Eleven and a half. She's old enough."

"But Alexander can't *marry* her! He wouldn't come all this way to marry a Soghdian girl!" Charm stops pretending to comb my tail and rushes over to the partition to get a better look at Roxanne. She shakes her head. "You must have misunderstood, Ochus. Your uncle Oxarthes told me not even Persians understand Soghdian."

"I picked up some words from the other boys when we were training, so I think I am right. That is why she is so frightened. She says King Alexander is a demon sorcerer who gave his soldiers magic wings so they could fly up the cliffs to capture her father's fortress. Her father was so terrified when he saw them all standing up on the rock above him, he gave Roxanne to Alexander so he would not kill all the people like he did in the other Soghdian towns."

Charm smiles. "Then you must have gotten it wrong! Alexander's not a demon or a sorcerer. And our men can't fly, that's just silly!"

Ochus looks grave. "I do not think I am wrong, Charmeia. I think Roxanne is as beautiful as my mother was, and a great king like Alexander should have a beautiful wife." He stares at the girl-filly with a bleak expression.

Roxanne is still stroking and kissing Caspia, who enjoys such attention. Charm and Ochus have been whispering, so I don't think she can hear them. She wouldn't understand their Greek words, anyway. But when Ochus clenches a fist and says in a fierce tone, "I *hate* Uncle Alexander!" she must recognize Alexander's name, for her frightened look returns and she stares out into the yard.

"It's all right, Roxanne. King Alexander's not here." Charm shakes her head. "The poor girl's terrified. Tell her, Ochus. Tell her Alexander isn't back yet, and we'll look after her. I'll think of something. The king can't possibly mean to marry her. There must be something we can do."

Ochus nods and unclenches his fist. He goes back to Caspia's stall and whispers something in Roxanne's ear. Her face lights up like a dark sun.

"I've told her I will look after her," Ochus says, straightening his shoulders and resting a hand on his jeweled dagger. "I can fight now. I will ask Uncle Alexander to let Roxanne go free. Then, when I am old enough to be king, I will visit her father and ask him to let her marry *me*."

Charm stares at Ochus in growing horror as she realizes what he means. As you've probably guessed, Charm was thinking only of her own feelings for Alexander, not Ochus's feelings for Roxanne, which were blindingly obvious to me and Caspia.

"Oh, Ochus . . ." she whispers. "Be careful!"

"I will be very careful." Ochus smiles at Roxanne again. "We will wait until Uncle Alexander is in a good mood."

You humans make everything so complicated! To me, it is very simple:

Ochus loves Roxanne.
Roxanne loves Ochus.
Alexander doesn't love any woman, except maybe his mother.

So WHY is Alexander going to marry Roxanne?

A FINE PARADE

When the king finally returned, I barely recognized the big, battle-scarred young stallion who barged, stamping and snorting, into the stall next to mine. Hoplite had a scar across his chest and another scar down his left shoulder. His mouth was cracked at the corners, and there were whip marks on his backside. When I gave him a little squeal over the partition to tell him to behave himself, he reared and came at me with bared teeth.

Tydeos threw him some hay and leaned against the wall in relief. "He's even worse than Bucephalas used to be!" he muttered. "It's all King Alexander's fault. He rode him too hard and cut his poor mouth to bits. After he got injured, he swore he'd teach him how to be a proper war-horse. But Hoplite kept bucking, and King Alexander didn't like that one bit. Don't tell nobody, but he even threw the king off once!" Tydeos glanced around to check that no one was listening, and grinned. "It was pretty funny, really, and King Alexander's own fault for trying to ride before he was properly better. He was so dizzy he could hardly stand up, let alone keep his balance on a bucking horse. Except he was in such a rotten mood, no one dared tell him so."

His expression turned grave again. "Oh, Charm! You have no idea how bad it's been! The king kept flying into terrible rages — you know how he gets when his head hurts? But now he loses his temper a lot more often than before. Even his friends in the Guard are scared of him. I once forgot to put all of Hoplite's tassels on, and he had me thrashed for it. I've still got the scars — look."

He tugged up his tunic to show Charm his back, and she put a hand over her mouth. "Oh, Tydeos . . . I'm sorry. Where is he now? He usually comes straight to see Bucephalas."

Tydeos shrugged. "I told you. He's changed."

It is five whole days before Alexander comes to see me. There is a shout at the stable gate, and all the Soghdian boys and grooms run out into the yard, lie down in the dirt, and press their foreheads to the ground.

I snort in surprise. This is *very* strange behavior!

Charm is combing out my tail, and Tydeos is in the next stall putting olive oil on the corners of Hoplite's sore mouth, so they don't see what is happening at first. Then Tydeos looks out and gasps, "It's the king! Quick, Charm . . . we have to kneel before him, too, now."

Charm peers out into the yard at the Soghdian boys and gives a nervous laugh. "That's a Persian thing. I'm sure he doesn't mean us." She starts to use my comb on her own mane.

"He *does*!" Tydeos finishes with Hoplite and looks anxiously out into the yard. "Please, Charm! You don't understand how angry he gets. It takes the littlest thing these days."

Charm is still fiddling with her mane and smoothing down her tunic. Her cheeks and neck flush red. I can smell Alexander's sherbet sweetness now and push my head over the door in excitement. The smell stirs my blood and reminds me of battle. My heart thuds against my ribs.

The king is wearing a blue-bordered Persian cloak. The blue-and-white crown he took from King Darius holds his mane in place, and the Achilles breastplate glitters over the top of a new tunic. The Guard hurry behind him, all wearing their Persian cloaks, too. King Darius's brother Oxarthes is with them. Alexander ignores the kneeling man-colts and makes straight for my stall.

I neigh a joyful welcome.

"Charm!" Tydeos says in a strangled tone and hurries outside to lie facedown before the king.

Alexander ignores him, too, and stops at my stall to give me a long look. "Bucephalas," he says with a sigh, putting his hand on my nose.

I neigh again and search his pocket for honey cakes. He gives a quick laugh and pushes my nose away. "No, not now. Where's your groom gone?"

Charm ventures out, wiping her sweaty hands on her tunic, and bows her head to Alexander. The Guard glance at one another.

Hephaestion clears his throat. "Charmeia," he says softly. "You should do proskynesis before the king now. Like the others, see? Kneel and press your forehead to the ground, then put your fingers to your lips and blow him a kiss. . . ."

But Alexander waves Hephaestion back with an impatient hand. He gives Charm a long, hard look. "Is Bucephalas fit?" he asks.

Charm darts him a quick glance from under her fringe. "Yes, sir. He's well, but he's missed you."

Alexander smiles. "Good. Because I'm fed up with riding that colt. Get Bucephalas ready for a parade. Use his best cloth with all the tassels. And get that gray mare, Aura, ready for Princess Roxanne, tassels and best cloth as well. We're getting married today, so we must look good."

Charm sucks in her breath. "But, sir —"

Tydeos mouths something at her, shaking his head. Alexander, who was saying something to his Guard, swings back. His eyes narrow. "What is it, Charmides?"

"Princess Roxanne can't —" Charm loses her nerve and bows her head.

"Did you have a dream?" Alexander marches back and seizes her chin in his hand, forcing her to look at him. "Well? If you've had a prophetic dream about our marriage, Charmides, I want to hear it!"

There are tears in Charm's eyes. She has backed up so far her mane is close enough for me to touch it with my nose. I blow into it, and she jumps. "I — I haven't had any dreams about your marriage, sir. . . . I'm sorry." It is barely a whisper.

Alexander frowns, shakes his head, and releases her. "Good. It's a beautiful day! The sun is shining. The fighting's over. Anahita, goddess of the Oxus, is waiting to marry me to my beautiful young bride! But first, I want my young Successors to show me what they can do. Get them mounted, and someone go and find Prince Ochus. I want him to show me what he's learned, too. Let's leave these people with a spectacle they won't forget!"

Oh, that was a fine parade!

I carried Alexander proudly on my cloth, surrounded by a shimmering halo of white and blue. Aura carried Princess Roxanne, sitting sideways on her cloth, with a careful stride. Roxanne wore a long red dress encrusted with gold and a golden crown on her dark mane. Her eyes were lined in black, and her lips painted red. Tydeos had washed Aura's tail so that it floated like a white cloud in the sunlight. She was in foal-season again, so she looked even more beautiful than usual.

The statue of the local goddess, Anahita, was carried out of the city and placed on a platform in the middle of the parade ground. Her crown of stars glittered, and a robe of dead otters and strings of fresh flowers draped her body. Several sacrifices died in front of her: a white ox, a pale camel, and several lambs. Their ghosts whirled away reluctantly, because it was too soon for them. But nothing could scare me when I had Alexander on my back and my favorite mare beside me.

There were trumpet blasts and music, then the Soghdian boys demonstrated how well they had learned to be Macedonians by doing their parade. Alexander watched them with a stony expression, nodding when they performed their battle maneuvers well and scowling when they got it wrong. He picked out five boys who had made bad mistakes and ordered them taken away and beaten. Princess Roxanne sat very straight in her beautiful dress and crown, her eyes dry and her face expressionless. But she kept twisting her fingers in Aura's mane as she watched the maneuvers, and she smelled very afraid.

When it was Prince Ochus's turn, he and Caspia did so well that not even Alexander could find fault. He beamed at Ochus and told him to bring Caspia up with the Guard. Roxanne's eyes strayed sideways. She and Ochus exchanged a quick, desperate glance as he took his place. Neither of them dared say a word.

Finally, a loaf of bread was carried out and set at Anahita's feet. Alexander slipped off me and helped Roxanne down from Aura's back. Roxanne's legs gave way, so he had to catch her in his arms. Some of the men smiled, thinking this romantic. Out of the corner of my eye, I saw Caspia dance sideways as Ochus clenched his fist on her reins.

Alexander led Roxanne to the statue, where he let her sink to her knees. He drew his sword, took Roxanne's limp hand, and put it on the hilt. Then he covered her slender fingers with his own, raised the blade, and sliced through the loaf with as much force as he might have sliced off an enemy's head.

The sky above Anahita's crown crackled with sudden lightning. Every horse on the parade ground shot up its head. Caspia reared. Aura whinnied in fear, and my coat stood on end as all the ghosts Alexander had made in Soghdiana streamed past us with a furious howl.

Iolaus had been given the job of holding us. I ripped my reins out of his hand and nipped Aura until she did the same. I had only one thought — to drive my favorite mare away from the danger. With the lightning crackling above and the ghosts at our heels, we galloped from the parade ground, scattering men and onlookers before us.

But the ghosts soon vanished, the sky turned blue, and everyone whispered that Anahita had blessed the king's marriage. By the time Charm and Tydeos came running to catch us, Aura and I were grazing side by side, having made another foal together. Ha!

ALEXANDER'S WEDDING NIGHT

That night Charm cannot sleep. Alexander's pavilion is wreathed in orange flowers and glows with lamps. She cannot take her eyes off it. Eventually, she crawls out of my hay, whispers an apology to me, and goes to find Tydeos. All the other grooms have gone to one of the parties to celebrate the king's wedding night, so the stables are quiet when a lone figure staggers into the yard.

I whinny in delight, because it is Alexander.

He lets himself into my stall. He has been drinking magic, so his movements are rough and jerky. But I do not mind, because when he grips my mane and rests his arm over my neck, it feels very nice. I nibble his tunic, looking for honey cakes.

"Bucephalas," he whispers. "Oh, horse! Why do they make me so *angry*? That idiot historian of mine has been writing all sorts of terrible things about me. I pay him to make me into a hero, and he's turning me into a demon! I don't even remember doing half the things he claims I did in Soghdiana. And then he had the nerve to quote the *Iliad* at me, telling me Hephaestion would make a better king than me! And on my own wedding night!"

He groans and clutches my mane. "I can't go back to the party, and I can't go to my pavilion. That girl's there. Roxanne. Every time I see her, I remember why I had to marry her. If I hadn't done something, my men would still be dying out there in the deserts and hills. I've never lost a battle in my life, but these crazy Soghdians really will fight to the death over a handful of dust! It was all I could think of to get her father on my side and stop the fighting. . . . No one seems to understand it's much harder for me than it is for them. Things just keep getting more and more complicated, horse! And Demetrius . . . do you know what the crazy fool did? He ran to cover me with his own shield when I got hit by that rock in the fighting. Even though I had punished him by putting him in the Disciplinary Company, he still risked his own neck to save my life. Why did he *do* that, horse? Why? Was I wrong about him? What if I was wrong about the others, too? Philo, General Parmenio, all the rest — Oh, my head hurts! I thought I was going blind, up in the north. I saw things . . . horrible things . . ." His voice lowers, frightened. "Do you ever see ghosts, Bucephalas?"

Of course I see ghosts. I want to tell him it is normal, but I don't know how.

Alexander presses his knuckles to his forehead and slides down my shoulder into my hay. I am worried and sniff at him. But he is not dying. He keeps muttering to me. More stuff about the fighting in Soghdiana, the edge of the world, his stupid historian, the *Iliad*, how many people want to kill him, and how much his head hurts.

I get bored and blow into his mane.

Eventually, he stops muttering and staggers to his feet to throw up the magic drink in a corner of my stall. While he is doing this, the five Soghdian boys he ordered beaten earlier creep into the yard and start whispering over by the fountain. I have no idea what they are up to — in my experience, man-colts are always up to something — but one has a knife, and they run off toward the camp.

Alexander watches them from the shadows of my stall, and his eyes narrow. "I knew it!" he hisses. "See, Bucephalas? I can't trust anyone. Those boys are obviously plotting to kill me while they think I'm distracted by my little bride! Looks like I'm going to have to teach them a lesson, too. Oh, this is so tiresome. Why won't anyone just let me get *on* with things?"

Brushing the hay off his cloak, he gives me a quick pat and staggers off into the night, calling for his Guard.

A BETTER MAN THAN ALEXANDER?

Before we set off for India, the five Soghdian man-colts who were whispering in the night were tied to posts and stoned to death on the parade ground for plotting to kill the king. The other Successors watched the execution with frightened eyes and cast terrified glances at Alexander. It's going to be a while before any of them dare plot anything again.

Then the royal historian Alexander had been complaining about was dragged out. Two of the Guard tied him to a post and beat him, trying to make him admit it had all been his idea. Alexander sat astride me nearby, watching with narrowed eyes.

The historian would not admit anything of the sort. But he hissed at Alexander, "If you don't like what I write about you, King Alexander, you shouldn't do such things in the first place. It's no good saying you're the reborn Achilles. Even Achilles didn't massacre as many innocent people as you have done."

Alexander's fist tightened on my rein. His breathing quickened, and he gave the order for the poor historian to be stoned to death, too. But Hephaestion trotted Petasios out of formation, put a hand on the king's arm, and whispered, "Alex, please! Who's going to write the rest of your story if you kill your historian? It won't make any sense if you get someone else to finish it."

Alexander's face went bright red. He shook off his friend and yelled at him to get back in his place. But as he raised his arm to give the signal for the stoning to start, the historian shouted, "A better man than you by far is Hephaestion!"

Alexander leaned down from my back, grabbed a stone from the pile, and threw it himself. The stone hit the historian on the mouth. Alexander's aim is excellent, even when his head is hurting.

The historian spat out a bloody tooth and shouted louder, "A better man than you by far is Hephaestion, yet death will not spare him!"

A hail of stones hit him, thrown by Macedonians anxious to stop him from making the king's mood even worse.

"A better man than you by far is Hephaestion, yet death —!" yelled the prisoner one more time before a stone finally hit him on the head and knocked him out.

Hephaestion closed his eyes and clutched Petasios's mane. But Alexander's fury shuddered out of him when the prisoner stopped shouting. He pressed a fist to his forehead and ordered the Macedonians to lock the historian in one of the empty lion cages with his writing materials. "He'll finish my story whether he likes it or not," he said. "And from now on, he'll write exactly what I tell him to write."

Before we left the parade ground, Alexander trotted me forward a few paces and held up his hand for silence. A hush fell over the assembled men as the king announced:

"Today, I ride back over the Caucasus Mountains to find the edge of the world. Anyone who is too afraid to come with me can leave their weapons here and go back to Ecbatana with Oxarthes, who is taking the traitor Bessus there for execution before a Persian court. I will pick you up on our way back. But be warned, I will consider you under arrest for desertion, and I won't hesitate to act if you plot against me. Don't make the mistake of thinking I won't know what you're up to. I'm sure none of you has forgotten what happened to General Parmenio."

He paused to let this sink in.

The men glanced uneasily at one another and shuffled their feet.

Alexander's smile was like the sun breaking through clouds as he continued.

"If, however, you choose to follow me, I promise you treasure and wonders beyond your wildest dreams. In addition, I will give each man who comes with me a bonus of five talents. Grooms, scientists, and engineers will get another half talent each. Today is a new beginning. It is my wish that from now on, Macedonians, Greeks, and Persians will live together under one ruler and be known as Alexandrians. I have shown you the way by taking a Soghdian wife and training these Soghdian boys in my army. But war is only the first stage. When the fighting is over, there will be a thousand years of peace in my empire. Those who follow me to the edge of the world will be rewarded for their courage many times over. Just one small land called India lies between us and immortality. Let us go there, gentlemen, and show these Indians the glory of our new Alexandria!"

Thunderous cheers greeted these words.

Alexander punched the air and laughed. His white-and-blue cloak dazzled in the sunshine. He was wearing his Troy helmet with the white plumes and shining with his old energy again. I felt the power rippling through him and made myself huge.

We retraced our hoofprints to the mountains, accompanied by the familiar sound of jangling bits, thudding hooves, creaking carts, snorts and whinnies, braying mules, barking dogs, and the marching feet of eighty thousand men. The Soghdian Successors stayed behind to complete their training, but we were still a huge herd. And somewhere back in the baggage train, my enemy was locked in a cage, awaiting his execution. Ha!

That was how we dominated the Soghdians, who fight over every handful of dust.

Soghdian dead: 110,000, including Spitamenes (murdered by the frightened Scythians) and five man-colts (stoned to death by Alexander)

Scythian dead: 2,800

Macedonian dead: 24,500, including Cleitus

Horses dead: 200, including Borealis on the way over the Caucasus Mountains (VERY, VERY sad!)

Prisoners and hostages: Bessus, the old horsemaster, 30,000 Soghdian Successors, 10,000 Soghdian horses, Alexander's historian, and Princess Roxanne

We're getting close to the end of our journey, so I probably ought to tell you before we go any farther why Alexander got so worked up on the parade ground, and why Hephaestion was so upset. The lines the historian quoted were stolen from the *Iliad*. They referred to Achilles' best friend, who was killed in the fighting at Troy, after which Achilles (who, if you remember, was supposed to be invincible) went mad with grief and got himself killed, too. Hephaestion is Alexander's best friend. If he dies before we reach the edge of the world, I don't know what Alexander will do.

cHARSADDA

327 B.C.

FIGHTING ALEXANDER

Alexander sent messengers on ahead with squealing threats for the Indians, ordering their bosses to meet him in the Kabul valley to surrender their lands. Then he sent Hephaestion with the main army and baggage train through one of the lower passes of the Caucasus Mountains, while we led the Guard and half of the cavalry back over the highest pass, which we'd used before.

No one dared question the king. He claimed he needed to go to the top to make sacrifices to his father Zeus-Ammon for a successful campaign in India, but you can probably guess the real reason. The weather was a lot better than last time we'd crossed the mountains, and Alexander wanted another look at the edge of the world.

It is only the second time we have retraced our route since setting out from Pella. We keep coming across our herd's old dung piles, smashed wine jars, and bits of broken armor our men threw away on the march out. The climb is not as difficult this time, because most of the snow has melted. But the air is thin, and I am not yet fully fit after Balkh, so I jog up the slope, which is easier for horses than walking uphill.

This soon makes Alexander impatient. "Walk properly, can't you, Bucephalas?" he mutters, jerking my rein, which hurts my mouth. "You're worse than that colt of yours!"

This is not true. Behind me, Hoplite's dark coat is covered in foam, because he has been jogging nearly all the way from Balkh. Peucestas gave up trying to make him walk ages ago.

At the top of the pass, Alexander leans forward, eager for a glimpse of the edge of the world. But I stop dead and blow through my nostrils. At the side of the track is the skeleton of a large horse, its bones picked clean and bleached by the sun. And in the shadows under the crags, Borealis's ghost is waiting.

My whole body goes rigid with fear. I tremble and sweat. Alexander, who is still looking for the edge of the world and not paying attention to his riding, loses his balance and nearly falls over my head.

He pushes himself back onto my cloth and digs his heels angrily into my sides. "Get on with you, horse! What's wrong with you today?"

Behind me, the other horses of the Guard have stopped and are blowing through their nostrils, too. I am not sure they can see Borealis's ghost like I can, but they know I would not make such a fuss unless I had seen something dangerous.

Ptolemy draws his sword, glancing warily at the crags. "What's happening, Alex? Is it an ambush?"

Alexander scowls. "There's nothing there! It's this stupid horse of mine. He's been playing me up ever since we left Balkh! I don't know what my groom's been doing to him. Get on with you, Bucephalas!" He jerks my reins from side to side to make me unbrace my forelegs and brings his spear down across my hindquarters.

It hurts.

I give a small buck to warn him to stop hitting me, and he yells in rage. The spear is suddenly whirling on my blind side, and blows rain down on me out of the dark, bringing panicky memories. Alexander's heels dig into my sides, his legs clamp against my cloth, and his hands jerk at my sore mouth. It is as bad as when the horsemaster tried to "tame" me back in Pella.

I forget it is Alexander on my back and rear so high I am in danger of toppling over backward. He has to throw his arms around my neck to stay on. When I come down again, I whip around on my hocks and throw three huge bucks. Anyone else would have been off at the first. But Alexander barely shifts on my cloth. He grits his teeth, hauls up my head, and whacks me again. No matter what I do, I cannot dislodge him.

This is the first time I have ever fought Alexander, and it is HORRIBLE.

"Alex!" Leonnatus calls. He steadies Aura, who is trying to whip around and bolt back down the trail because I am upsetting her. "For Zeus's sake! That's Bucephalas you're riding, not some half-trained colt! If he's not going forward, you can be sure there's a good reason for it."

The other horses of the Guard are giving half rears, upset as well. Hoplite snorts at me in sympathy. If this is what happened to him in Soghdiana, then no wonder he was so bad-tempered when he came back.

I don't know how our battle would have ended, because both of us would rather die than be dominated. But Leonnatus's voice gets through to Alexander. He stops hitting me, closes his eyes, and gives a little shudder. I calm down a bit and stop acting wild.

"I think it's that skeleton," Leonnatus says, softer. "This is where Borealis died, remember? Maybe the horses remember, too."

Alexander squints at the crags. He pales and trembles all over, like I did earlier. He throws down his spear and presses a hand against my sweaty neck, chirruping to soothe me. "Whoa, Bucephalas, steady now. . . . I'm sorry, horse. . . . It's over."

I stand still, trembling, too. Borealis's ghost is watching us with pricked ears. Alexander squints at it again, shudders, and slips off me.

"All right," he whispers, retrieving his spear. "I know what's wrong now. I can see him, too. But we have to go past. If you don't go past, none of the other horses will. Come on, my brave Bucephalas. I'll go first, see?" He takes my reins gently over my head and walks forward, keeping the spear low so as not to startle me.

I trust him, so I follow.

Borealis's ghost stays where it is, watching us silently. My coat prickles as we pass it, but it doesn't attack us. The Guard follows, the other horses pricking their ears at the shadows. Alexander vaults onto me again and pats my damp neck. He looks back at the crags, laughs, and shakes his head.

"Horses!" he mutters to his Guard, and they smile in relief.

He made his sacrifice farther on, where the pass started its descent. We horses grazed at the side of the road with Iolaus and Leonnatus to watch us, while Alexander climbed the crags with the two sheep we'd driven up with us. I don't know if Zeus let him see the edge of the world this time, because he didn't say anything when he came down. But from where we were standing, it was hidden in a blue haze.

By the time we set off again, Alexander seemed his old self again. He rode me in his familiar, firm way, running an apologetic hand down my neck whenever he thought no one was watching. This made me calmer, too. But all the way down to Alexandria-under-the-Caucasus, he kept glancing over his shoulder, and I knew he could see what I saw.

Borealis's ghost was following us, lurking in the shadows of my damaged eye.

A DREAM OF MONSTERS

When we met up again in the Kabul valley, Charm went quiet as she ran her hand over the welts on my flanks. She rubbed ointment into the cuts at the corner of my mouth and groomed me very gently, whispering, "Poor old horse, what has he been doing to you?"

Tydeos whistled when he saw the state of me. "Alexander's getting worse, isn't he? If he can do that to his favorite horse, kill his friends, and stone young boys to death, what'll he do to *us* if we annoy him? Things are going bad, Charm. We've got money now. I'm getting out as soon as I can. I don't want to be dragged off to India as spoils, when the men decide they've had enough and abandon us all out here. If you've got any sense, you'll come with me."

Charm gave him an exasperated look. "The men aren't going to abandon Alexander! You heard them cheering him back in Balkh. They still worship him, whatever he does. And you know I can't leave Bucephalas, especially not now. If you want to go, I'll cover for you as long as I can. But Alexander doesn't like losing his grooms any more than he likes losing his battles, so you'd better be careful he doesn't see you."

"You could bring Bucephalas."

"After what happened last time? Don't be silly."

Tydeos sighed. "I'm not going anywhere without you."

"Then you're stuck, aren't you?" Charm pretended to treat my wounds. But her hands trembled, and she soon gave up pretending and hugged my nose. "I had another dream last night," she whispered.

Tydeos looked up from fixing Hoplite's tether. "What did you dream this time?"

She pressed her hand against my neck with a sigh. "Alexander and Bucephalas were fighting a battle against huge gray monsters. I saw Bucephalas fall in the mud with javelins sticking out of him, and . . . oh, Tydeos, he didn't get up again!"

Tydeos frowned. "Have you told anyone?"

"No, not yet. I have to be sure."

Tydeos shook his head. "I wouldn't tell the king, if I were you. He probably wouldn't believe you, anyway, not after what you did at Issus."

"But what if it's *true*?"

"I'm sure it isn't, Charm."

"I've been right before."

Tydeos chewed his lip. "What did these monsters look like?"

Charm sighed. "I didn't see them clearly, but they were as big as houses with feet like tree trunks. They made a terrible noise, and they had enormous curved teeth growing out of their faces. Each one had a long tentacle that could wrap itself around a horse, pick it right up off the ground, and crush it to death —" She gave a little laugh. "Oh, forget it! It sounds ridiculous now."

Tydeos grinned, too. "You've been listening to too much camp gossip! It's enough to give anyone nightmares. I'm sure there aren't any monsters like that in the world. And if there are, King Alexander will soon deal with them like he deals with everything else."

Charm smiled, too, because groom-gossip at that time was wild. Here are just a few of the things our grooms claimed we'd find in India:

Giant ants that dig up gold
People who have a tail and the head of a dog
Horned horses (you know where they got THAT idea from!)
The water of life
Wise men who wear no clothes and know the answer to every question

But I am a bit worried, because Charm's dreams have come true before.

ELEPHANTS

A few days later, the first of the Indian tribes arrived, bringing gifts for Alexander from their boss, Prince Ambhi. In the distance, advancing slowly through the smoke haze from our campfires, we saw a column of large gray animals with flapping ears and long noses, their backs and heads glittering with jewels. The wind was blowing the wrong way, so I could not smell them. But Charm's hands flew to her mouth, and she raced off with Tydeos at her heels. The other grooms hurried after them.

We horses were left unattended in the lines. I shifted my weight uneasily from one hind leg to the other. Beside me, Hoplite munched his hay, calmer now that he was being ridden by Peucestas rather than Alexander. On my other side, Apollo sniffed my mane and tried to mutual groom, but I was not in the mood. Borealis's ghost had trotted off when we made camp, but I kept expecting it to reappear, which made me more nervous than usual.

When Charm came back, she was very pale. "They're exactly like my dream, Bucephalas!" she whispered. "They each have a little hut on their back that the Indians ride in, and they're *huge*! Oh, horse, what should I do? Alexander's talking to the Indians. They've brought him gifts and treasure, but if my dream's true they'll fight us . . . yet how can it be true if they're surrendering? And now that the elephants have come to the camp and everyone's seen them, Alexander will say I made up my dream to protect you! I should have told him before they came. I'm such an idiot, listening to Tydeos. What does he know about India and the edge of the world? Not even Alexander knows what's out there!"

When the Indians left, the elephants stayed. We horses could smell them faintly when the wind changed. Their strong odor made us uneasy because we had never come across anything like it before. If one of them snorted through its long nose while we were dozing, it made us jump. Charm spent a lot of time in the lines, soothing us all. When the grooms took us out for exercise, they rode us in the opposite direction so we wouldn't have to pass the place where the elephants were tethered. Worse, Alexander spent more time with them than he did with us, training his men how to fight the gray monsters. Every day when we returned from our exercise, we saw the phalanx out on the plain beneath the mountains with an elephant stamping and whirling in their midst, making its horrible noise as our men attacked it with javelins and spears.

Charm tried to tell Alexander several times about her dream. But when he eventually came to the horse lines to see me, he told her not to bother him. His gaze slid sideways looking for Borealis's ghost. Then he snapped at the grooms to get us ready, because he wanted us to train against the elephants, too. He armed our riders with the phalanx's long pikes so they would be able reach the enemy in the little huts on the backs of the monsters.

This was a disaster from the start. The cavalrymen were not used to carrying the heavy pikes and kept dropping them. Every time the elephant made its horrible noise or stamped a foot and made the ground shake, a horse whipped around and someone fell off. Not me or Alexander, of course — elephants might be frightening, but you can't dominate an enemy if you run away.

Eventually, Alexander lost his temper. Ignoring Hephaestion's warning shout, he headed me straight for the elephant and gave me the order to leap as if we were on parade. While we were in the air, he lifted his pike like an enormous javelin and launched it into the little hut on the monster's back, exploding the hay-stuffed sacks we were using as targets.

"Is Bucephalas the only one in my army who's not afraid of the Indians' secret weapon?" he cried as we landed. "*That's* how to deal with these war elephants! I want five elephants with their tusks sawn off like this one for training, and the rest left intact so you can practice against the real thing. Prince Ambhi has offered us his city of Taxila to use as our military base across the Indus if we'll help him see off his troublesome neighbor, Prince Porus. Before we leave this valley, gentlemen, I want every man and every horse ready to face the worst the Indians can throw at us!"

The men muttered uneasily, and the horses snorted, sensing their riders' nerves. I could have shown them how to be brave, but that was the end of my elephant dominating. The monster had swung its trunk at us when we attacked it, causing me to land awkwardly from my high leap. By the time I got back to the horse lines, the tendon I'd injured at Halicarnassus had started to swell.

Charm patted me and promised she would stop Alexander from taking me into battle against the elephants if it was the last thing she did. This was brave of her but rather stupid. If it comes to a battle between Charm and Alexander, who do *you* think will win?

ANOTHER PLOT AGAINST THE KING

For the journey through the mountains to India, the army split into two. Alexander wanted to dominate all the local tribes that had refused to surrender and said the baggage train would only slow him down. So he sent Hephaestion and Perdiccas with the main force through the easiest pass to look after the wounded and anyone else who couldn't fight, while he mounted Electra and took the rest of the army, the Disciplinary Company (with Demetrius on probation after saving the king's life in Soghdiana), and the siege equipment into the hills.

This meant I got to stay with Aura, who was too big with foal to fight, and Prince Ochus got to stay with Roxanne. Charm was the only one of us who was unhappy, since Tydeos had to go with the horses of the Guard. Also, before he left, Alexander had told her to decide how she wanted him to punish the old horsemaster who, like the king's reluctant historian, was still trailing along in a cage at the back of the baggage train.

Only one city on our route had not sent Alexander any gifts, and we had orders to dominate it on our way. But the boss of Charsadda would not send out his army to meet us, and neither Hephaestion nor Perdiccas dared take the sort of risks Alexander would have done to force their way in, so it turned into a siege. This gave Prince Ochus time to make more trouble.

One cold, bright morning, the prince turns up in the horse lines with Roxanne just as Charm is about to take me for my walk. She seems glad of the company and lets them lead Caspia and Aura behind me. When we reach the river, they take off our muzzles and let us graze the yellow winter grass. It is rather tasteless but makes a change from hay. Ochus gets Caspia to do her play-dead trick, which makes Roxanne laugh.

The filly gets to her feet, shakes herself, and settles down to graze next to me. Roxanne watches Charm carefully, then wets her lips and says in her broken Greek, "Ochus tell me Alexander talk much to you. You have special relationship with him, maybe?"

Charm grips my withers tightly. "Sometimes he talks to me. Not very much, though."

"Do he tell you things about me?" Roxanne watches her closely.

Charm shakes her head. "No. We mostly talk about Bucephalas."

Roxanne sighs. "Ochus think —" She frowns and starts again. "Ochus say Alexander not love any woman. He not come to me on our wedding night. I would kill him that night, if he did. I ask the Successors to bring me a knife. But Alexander not come, so I not have to use it. He not come to me since, either. He say Ochus teach me talk Greek first, then when I grow up we can be properly married. But I think he not really love me."

Charm goes pale as Roxanne speaks. "Oh, Zeus!" she whispers. "You mean those poor boys in Balkh were stoned to death because of *you*?"

Roxanne raises her chin. "They know the risk when they bring me knife. They good Soghdian boys. Alexander kill very many of our people! I swear to kill him in revenge. But now Ochus think of a better way. He say I must wait until I old enough to have baby. Then we tell everyone my baby is King Alexander's. I am Alexander's queen, so when I have avenged my people's deaths I will be able to marry Ochus, and he will be king until our son grow up."

This is typical complicated human stuff.

While Charm is distracted, I take the opportunity to nibble Aura's lips. She nickers to me and snorts frost into the air. She has grown a furry white coat for the winter, and she looks very beautiful with her big foal-belly.

Charm pales as she works out what Roxanne has said. "No! Ochus, tell her! Alexander will be furious if he finds out you're plotting against him. You know what he does to people who anger him — Oh, Zeus, why are you telling me this?" She glances nervously at the sentries, but they are too far away to hear.

The prince regards Charm with his dark eyes. "You helped me before, when I was a hostage. If Uncle Alexander dies in battle, we won't have to kill him. We know about your dreams. He listens to you. You must continue to keep him alive until Roxanne is pregnant. Then we simply need you to stop warning him when you dream he will die."

Charm closes her eyes. "You silly things! I don't have dreams about

Alexander — I have dreams about his horse! And it's no good, anyway, because the king doesn't listen to me anymore."

They frown at each other, and Roxanne whispers something in Soghdian. Ochus whispers back.

"Please, Charmeia?" he says. "Help us."

"I can't help you. And you're crazy if you think you can get away with plotting to kill Alexander! You know what he did to Philotas and General Parmenio — do you imagine he'll think twice before doing the same to you?"

Her voice has risen, making the sentries look around. She drops my reins and grips Roxanne's arm.

"Listen to me!" she hisses. "I was about your age when I went to the palace in Pella to kill King Philip. I had poison in a mule's hoof. I was going to put it in the king's food. Bucephalas saved me. He saved me from doing something very stupid. I understand what you're feeling. I wanted to kill King Philip because he had attacked my home and ruined my mother's life. But later, I was glad I hadn't done it. Even if I'd gotten away with it, do you think I'd have been able to live with myself? Do you think I'd have been able to look Alexander in the eye, knowing I'd killed his father? Do you understand what I'm saying, Roxanne? Do you? Ochus, tell her!"

Roxanne looks angry, then frightened. She snatches her arm free and raises her chin. "I not scared of King Alexander."

"That's a lie. I saw you hiding like a frightened rabbit in Bucephalas's stable in Balkh."

"That was when he first capture me. I not scared of him anymore," Roxanne sniffs.

"Then you should be! You should be more scared than anyone else! How long do you think his generals and friends will let you and Prince Ochus live, if they find out what you are planning?"

"They won't find out, Charmeia," Ochus says, glancing at the sentries. "We'll be very careful."

"Ha!" Charm shakes her head. "As careful as telling me? I'm not just Alexander's groom, you know. When the Macedonians invaded Methone and made my mother pregnant with me, it wasn't just any soldier who raped her that night . . . it was King Philip himself, half-blinded by an arrow and crazy with the pain! He was my father as much as Alexander's, which makes me Alexander's half sister. *Now* do you understand?"

They stare at her in amazement. Ochus's mouth is slightly open. Roxanne goes pale. Suddenly, they both look very scared.

"Is that why Alexander talk to you?" Roxanne whispers.

Charm shakes her head, still angry. "No, don't be stupid! I haven't told him I know who raped my mother. How do you think he'd react? He's Great King of Persia, and I'm a groom! He talks to me because of Bucephalas . . . the horse bond . . . oh, you wouldn't understand."

Roxanne frowns.

"You won't tell Uncle Alexander what we said, will you?" Ochus says. "Please, Charmeia, don't! I couldn't bear it if he hurt Roxanne."

Charm snatches up the end of my reins and takes a shuddering breath. "Of course I won't tell him! Do you think I want to see any more people tortured and killed? It's bad enough I have to decide about the horse-master! Just don't tell me any more. I can't help you. I can't even help Bucephalas."

Ochus whispers something to Roxanne. The young queen smiles, pushes her hair behind her ears, and says, "But King Philip die, anyway, Charmeia. His own Guard assassinate him."

WEARING ELEPHANT SKIN

When we got back to the horse lines, we found Hephaestion waiting for us. He frowned at Ochus and Roxanne and sent them back to the camp, then nodded at a pile of wrinkled gray skins that the grooms were unloading from a nearby mule cart. The mule's long ears were flat with distaste, and we horses flared our nostrils in unease. But they were only like the dead lion skins Alexander wears after hunting. The ghosts of the elephants had fled back in the Kabul valley.

"We're going to try something," Hephaestion said to Charm. "Put these skins on the horses instead of their cloths at night. Start with Bucephalas, then Petasios and Apollo . . . that filly Caspia seems sensible enough, so you can try her, too. Best keep them away from Aura, though. I don't want her getting upset and losing her foal a second time. If this works, then at least we might have some horses that can bear the smell of elephants by the time we meet up with the king again."

"Is there definitely going to be a battle against the Indians, then, sir?" Charm asked, biting her lip.

Hephaestion smiled. "Not if we can help it. Alex is going to try for a peaceful settlement with Prince Porus. He's more worried about meeting war elephants in battle than he lets on."

The elephant skins were heavy, made us sweat, and they smelled foul. I bucked mine off several times. So did Petasios. Charm got fed up with replacing them and strapped them onto us with lead reins.

Caspia didn't buck. She simply lay down on her side and played dead, until Charm got so worried she took the skin off her. Then the filly scrambled to her feet again, raised her head, and curled her upper lip. Fillies and mares do this when they smell something peculiar, like stale elephant. All the grooms laughed at her, and she didn't have to wear the skin again.

INDUS

After about a month, the men finally broke through the walls of Charsadda with their catapults and killed its boss. We left a Macedonian garrison to look after the city, and we didn't bother renaming it. What would we have called it? Hephaestionia? Perdiccasia? Ha! I can think of better names for a city. But I had to stand in the horse lines wearing my elephant skin all through the battle, so I suppose it wouldn't have been fair to name it after me.

We reached the river Indus first and waited for Alexander. By this time, the weather was warm enough for the mares to foal. Aura hung stubbornly on to ours for several nights. Then, when Charm dozed off, she whinnied softly, lay down in the lines, and quietly gave birth to a colt as black as the Indus at night.

I nickered anxiously to my mare, remembering what had happened to our white foal at the Caspian Gates. But no tiny ghost rose from the black colt, and when Aura licked it clean, I could smell its new-foal scent.

By the time Charm stirred and rubbed her eyes, the colt was on its feet and suckling strongly with his black tail wagging. She laughed and stroked

Aura's nose, calling her clever and feeding her handfuls of barley. The other grooms gathered around to admire the colt.

"Is it Bucephalas's foal?" one of them asked.

Charm gave him an amused look. "Of course it's his! Look how big and strong he is already! I'm going to call him Indus, because he was born here at the edge of the world."

Aura had her foal just in time, because the next day there was much whinnying and excitement as the horses who had gone dominating with Alexander returned to the lines, footsore and weary. My filly, Electra, had suffered the most. Alexander was dragging her by one rein, which he's always telling our grooms not to do, walking very fast with a hand pressed to his upper arm. Electra jogged behind him, throwing up her head every time he jerked her mouth. There was foam on her neck, blood on her bit, and a deep scratch down her left shoulder.

"I hope Bucephalas is sound now!" he called. "Because I'm sick of riding young horses who don't know enough about battle to watch out for arrows."

Charm took Electra's reins and tried again to tell Alexander about her elephant dream. But sensing Borealis's ghost (which had followed us through the easy pass), Electra whirled and trod on her toe. Alexander squinted at the ghost, shivered, and hurried off to his pavilion, calling for Iolaus to bring him wine.

Later, Tydeos told us Electra had let the king get wounded twice — once with an arrow in the shoulder, and once on the ankle with a stone. That's why my filly was in disgrace. Even so, Alexander had dominated far more Indians than we had on our way through the mountains. He massacred an entire town after saying they could go free if they opened their gates, dominated a fortress even the legendary hero Hercules had failed to dominate, and nearly killed himself by drinking too much magic to take away the pain of his wounds. Here are the scores:

ALEXANDER:

Indian dead: 25,000

Macedonian dead: 250

Horses dead: 5

Prisoners: none *(Alexander massacred them all.)*

HEPHAESTION AND PERDICCAS:

Indian dead: 1,500

Macedonian dead: 50

Horses dead: none *(unless you count Caspia pretending)*

Prisoners: none *(Hephaestion and Perdiccas left the survivors at Charsadda to rebuild their homes.)*

As you can see, Alexander is still way ahead of everyone in the dominating game. If we were finished, he would be the biggest boss ever.

But I am not sure the river Indus is the edge of the world, like Charm thinks. I can see grass on the other side.

TAXILA

SPRING 326 B.C.

SQUEALING AT TAXILA

When Alexander has made all the proper sacrifices, we cross the bridge of boats Hephaestion's men had built while we were waiting. Then we march toward Prince Ambhi's city, which he has promised to surrender to us for our military base. But as we approach, the gates open and a whole herd of war elephants stamps out to meet us.

Each elephant has a hut swaying on its back, with yellow-and-orange flags fluttering overhead. Indians in glittering armor walk between them, blowing on long trumpets that make the whole plain vibrate. I flicker my ears uncertainly. Behind the elephants and the trumpeters, we can see yet more Indians advancing in a line across the plain, carrying spears that glint in the sunshine. The elephants are a long way off still, but they are noisy and very, very frightening.

As soon as he sees them, Alexander halts me and flings up a hand. "A trap, Bucephalas!" he hisses, his eyes gleaming with the challenge. "That treacherous Ambhi has led us into a trap with all his fine words and promises! I *knew* he was plotting something. Ha, so now he's going to find out what we Macedonians are made of!" His excitement at the prospect of battle makes me excited, too.

He shouts for our trumpeters to blow the battle call. The horses of the Guard flare their nostrils and dance on the spot as their riders tighten their reins. Everyone except Alexander looks rather pale. But we are a very well-trained herd. Behind us I hear shouts, the creak of armor, the rattle of weapons, and the pound of running feet as the phalanx fan out into position. Horses gallop everywhere as the cavalry hastily arm themselves with shields and javelins. Alexander jams on his Troy helmet and calls for someone to bring him a long pike.

As a man runs up with one, there is a tiny whinny behind us, and the thud of small hooves. My colt, Indus, bursts through the men, bucking and shaking his head, making some of them laugh and others curse. Aura is close behind, carrying a wild-eyed Charm, and Prince Ochus is giving chase on Caspia.

"Get that mare and foal back to the baggage train, girl!" Leonnatus yells, trying to catch her reins as she rides past. "Didn't you hear the trumpets? There's going to be a battle!"

Obedient as ever to her rider's wishes, Aura swerves around Zephyr and gallops straight up to me. I nicker to my favorite mare, while Alexander gives Charm a distracted look.

"What in Zeus's name do you think you're doing, Charmides?" he snaps. "We're making battle formation! Get back where you belong, and take Prince Ochus with you! This is no place for grooms and children!"

"Please, sir, Alexander!" Charm gasps. "You have to listen to me! I've been trying to tell you for ages. . . . I had a dream about this battle! You can't ride Bucephalas against those elephants, sir. If you do, he'll die!"

Alexander presses his knuckles to his forehead and shuts his eyes, maybe remembering he once ordered her to tell him about her dreams. But that was a long time ago. His whole body is so tense that I tremble as well. Does he want me to charge the elephants from all the way back here?

I get ready to attack. But he holds me back. A shudder goes through him. He eyes the advancing Indian line, waves back the Guard who are at a loss to know what to do about Charm, and grips her wrist.

He takes a deep breath. "All right, Charmides! Tell me what you dreamed. And make it fast."

Charm trembles even more. But she whispers, "Bucephalas fell, sir, fighting an elephant! He had javelins sticking out of him, and he was covered in mud. He didn't get up again. I didn't see — I'm sorry, sir, but I didn't see what happened to you."

Her wrist is still imprisoned in Alexander's fingers, and her spring-grass smell is sharp with fear. Indus stops playing and trots across to nudge Aura's hind leg, looking for milk.

Alexander stares at Charm with narrow eyes. He says very softly, "And is this a true dream, Charmides?"

"Yes! I swear it on the name of Zeus, your father!"

He nods and lets her go. "Mud . . ." he says thoughtfully, looking down at the dusty plain. He looks a bit happier. "Then this is not the battle you dreamed of, Charmides! Take that mare and foal back to the baggage train and don't interrupt me again at such a crucial moment, not even if you dream the sky falls on our heads. I've made allowances for you because you can handle Bucephalas. But if you show me up before my men again, I'll be forced to punish you as I would any one of my slaves who disobeys me."

Charm rubs her wrist and stays silent.

Leonnatus raises an eyebrow. "Do you want someone to escort her back to the baggage train, Alex?"

Alexander shakes his head. "The girl will go." He glares at Charm until she turns Aura and rides back through the phalanx, her shoulders trembling. Indus gives me a bold little squeal and follows his mother.

Alexander stares after them. Then he sees Caspia, who lay down when she got close enough to smell the elephants, and frowns at Ochus, who is trying to make her get up. "What's wrong with that filly?"

The Guard laughs nervously. "Look! The Mardian filly's doing proskynesis before the king!"

Hephaestion winces. "She kept doing that when we put the elephant skin on her, Alex. I think we've trained her to play dead when she smells elephants. I'm sorry, I thought it would help. Prince Ochus is too young for battle, anyway, and at least Bucephalas and Petasios have learned not to fear them."

"And Apollo!" Perdiccas says, stroking the palomino's neck. "He's being really brave, Alex, see?"

Alexander gives them an exasperated look. "We can't win a battle with just three horses! We'd all better hope Charmides' dream *isn't* true." He strokes my neck and squints at the advancing elephants. He seems worried, even though there is no mud. The members of the Guard glance uneasily at one another. Then a small band breaks away from the enemy herd and trots toward us, leaving the elephants behind.

Alexander relaxes slightly. "Is that a messenger coming to talk?" he asks, and the Guard all shade their eyes.

"I think it's Prince Ambhi himself, Alex!" Leonnatus says in relief. "Just his personal guard. No elephants!"

Alexander nods and waves away the man with the pike. He wipes the sweat off his brow and leans across my neck to untangle my tassels. He straightens with a grim smile. "All right, gentlemen. Keep your swords loose and come with me."

He clamps his legs against my cloth and trots me to meet the Indian boss, his chin tilted and a tough expression on his face. I make myself huge. The Indian horses are wearing bright cloths, and their tassels glitter with gold threads. But as soon as they see me, they arch their necks and clap their lips in submission.

Prince Ambhi bows his head to Alexander and offers him a fancy sword, hilt first. "My city of Taxila is yours, King Alexander," he says through his interpreter. "These elephants and the treasure they carry are also yours, since I heard the last ones I gave you met with unfortunate 'accidents.' I hope you weren't alarmed by the size of my army. I apologize for any misunderstanding. I wished merely to welcome you to my city in the proper style, as befits such a great king as yourself."

Alexander accepts the fancy sword. But he narrows his eyes at Ambhi and snaps, "You were stupid to bring your entire army out to meet us like that! We could have slaughtered you."

Prince Ambhi smiles. "I will send extra gifts to make up for scaring you, King Alexander. Please accept my humblest apologies."

I don't know if the interpreter got the word *scaring* right. If so, he was a bit stupid to translate it so accurately.

Alexander's hand tightens a little on my rein. But he is no longer the hot-blooded man-colt who threw the gold crown back at the Tyrians in Phoenicia and started a six-month siege. He passes the fancy sword to Hephaestion, controls his rage, and says, "Go back to your army and open your gates to receive me. I'll enter your city in person to receive your gifts. The son of Zeus-Ammon fears no man."

"As you wish, King Alexander." Ambhi bows and leads the other Indians back to his herd at a gallop.

Alexander watches him go with narrowed eyes. "Keep battle formation until we're sure it's not a trap," he orders. "And when Ambhi sends
his gifts, double their value from my treasure chests and send them straight
back again. I'll show this proud Indian ruler that the son of Zeus and
emperor of the known world doesn't need his gold!"

"Do you want us to kill him for insulting you like that, Alex?" Ptolemy
says, dropping his hand to his sword. "We can easily take his city *and* his gold."

But Alexander shakes his head and runs a hand down my neck, staring
thoughtfully after Prince Ambhi. "No, we need him until we've dealt with this
troublesome Porus and the other Indian rebels in the east. I want to avoid doing
battle with elephants until I'm confident we're absolutely ready to face them."

The Guard looks relieved, and so do all the men behind us, when the
news ripples back that there isn't going to be a battle, after all.

If you ask me, Prince Ambhi had it about right when he claimed to
have scared us.

THE WISE MAN

We camped on the plain outside the walls of Taxila, while Alexander and
his friends went into the city to meet Prince Ambhi and the other Indian
bosses who had accepted Alexander's invitation to come and surrender.
Needless to say, Prince Porus was not among them. After a few curious
stares at our army, everyone else in the city got on with what they had
been doing before we came.

I had never seen such a busy place! Thousands of humans thronged
the streets, barefoot, with dirty cloths wrapped around their heads. The
bosses rode on elephants decked out with tassels and had funny-colored
whiskers — red, blue, snowy white. They wore jeweled feathers in their
head-cloths. The air smelled of dung and unfamiliar spices, and the noise
was *awful*. All day, we heard the cries of humans, sheep, oxen, and the horrid sound elephants make with their long noses. And at night, millions of
mosquitoes took over.

Although the cavalry trained with special long javelins, lighter and
easier to carry than the pikes, their horses still would not go near the elephants. I couldn't show my herd how to be brave, because Alexander
stayed in the city talking to the Indians. Charm got quieter and quieter as

she and Tydeos watched the chaos on the parade ground. Then one evening, when the sun was sinking into red fire over the mountains, she brought a wrinkled little Indian man to the horse lines.

He wore a white rag tied around his waist, and his skin was nearly as dark as Hades' coat. He smelled strange. I gave him flat ears to warn him to stay away from my herd. But he stood very still and quiet, watching me with his black eyes.

"This is the horse," Charm said, stroking me. "Bucephalas, behave yourself. This is a very wise man. His tribe knows the answer to every question. He's going to tell us more about the horse bond."

The little man's eyes crinkled. He walked right up to me, put his hand on my tether, then waved his other hand on my blind side.

My heart thumped. But before his hand could turn into a pike, he rubbed it behind my ear, whispering in his own language. His voice was soothing, and although Borealis's ghost came closer, I lowered my head and rested it on his shoulder.

Charm stared, amazed. "Bucephalas never lets strangers touch him like that! How did you know about his blind spot?"

"The horse told me."

I did?

Charm smiled. "He seems to like you."

"I think this horse sees things men do not," said the wise man, still watching me. "Why do you want to break the bond that links your lives?"

Charm's face tightened. "So I can take Bucephalas somewhere safe, and King Alexander won't come after us. I've been a slave all my life. Now I want to be free!"

The wise man gently let go of my head. It drooped to the ground, I felt so sleepy and warm. It was a very nice feeling. I didn't even mind when Borealis rested his ghostly teeth on my withers.

"Ah," said the wise man. "Freedom — that is a much bigger thing."

"If the bond is broken, I'll be able to buy my freedom with the bonuses King Alexander has given us. As it is, I can't leave the king. Neither of us can."

"There is no bond, except that in your own heart."

Charm looked worried. "But the Amazon queen said there was! She said only death could break it. But there must be some other way, surely?"

"Hmm, death. I am not sure the Amazons understand death. Some say that in their country, the dead ride with the living. I do not know if that is true. Here in our world, the dead outnumber the living. But since we cannot see them, only the living matter. I think this horse bond you talk of, my child, is just another name for love."

Charm glanced at the city, where Alexander was staying, and said, "That's not true!" But she flushed as she spoke.

The wise man smiled. "Do not be ashamed. I've seen how your King Alexander makes people love him. Even those who fear him, love him so much they will die for him. It is hard for you, because he is a king and you are just a groom. But when we are dead, it will not matter what we were in life. Every one of us is the same — we will have just the small piece of earth where our bones rest. You, me, the horse, King Alexander. Where our ghosts go I cannot say, but I know they do not make war on other ghosts, because they all have the same amount of earth and do not need more. But until then we must make our choices and feel the love and pain that arises from them. That is the joy and the curse of life."

Borealis's ghost stared over my withers at the wise man, ears pricked. As the Indian peered closer at the place where he stood, I felt a big drop of rain fall on my back.

Not noticing it, Charm shook her head. "What about the edge of the world? Is it close, like Alexander says? Will it make him immortal?"

The wise man held out his hand to catch a raindrop and sighed. "I think it is a different place for everyone. Your king says the oracle promised him immortality when he reaches it, so maybe it is close for him. Certainly, no one will forget Alexander's name after the things he has done. Maybe you, too, will find your freedom at the edge of the world. It is said to be a place where all dreams come true."

Charm stared through the campfires into the darkness of the east and whispered, "That's what I'm afraid of! I dreamed Bucephalas would die there . . . in the mud." The next raindrop fell in her mane, and she looked up with a terrified expression.

"Then you will be free of your horse bond, won't you?" the wise man said gently. "I think the time is coming when you will have to choose between the horse and your freedom. You cannot have it both ways, my child."

RIVER
JHELUM

SUMMER 326 B.C.

A MISERABLE MARCH

In the morning, the trumpets sounded for us to break camp. The rain had stopped. But the air smelled moist, and it was hotter than ever.

Alexander was in a hurry. He urged me into a trot as soon as he was mounted. I instantly broke into a sweat. Behind me, the other horses of the Guard were sweating, too. Their riders wiped their foreheads and frowned at the sky. Prince Ambhi, the boss of Taxila, rode with us on his brown Indian horse, accompanied by his interpreter on a mule. I squealed at it as we set out.

Things are getting bad, if we have mules in the Guard.

"We have to get there before the river swells," Alexander muttered. "Porus has been playing games with me, sending all those messages pretending he wanted to reach a peaceful settlement and promising to come to Taxila. He was just delaying us until the rains came and he had a chance to march his army here. Faster!"

Alexander kept everyone moving as fast as they could. But by the time we reached the ford, the rain was falling in sheets, and the dust had turned to the mud Charm had dreamed about. My hooves squelched and slipped. I tucked in my tail and flattened my ears to stop the water from getting in them. The men pulled their cloaks over their helmets to stop them from turning rusty and stared miserably at the fast-flowing brown water.

The Guard stopped around Alexander, silent. I nickered in sympathy to my steaming friends, who were all trying to turn their tails into the rain. Worse still, on the far bank a line of elephants awaited us with Indian spearmen and archers sheltering under their massive legs. When they saw us, they shouted excitedly. The enemy soldiers ran to the edge of the trees and bent their long bows. Arrows flew toward our bank but fell short and were whirled away in the flood.

Alexander snapped at Ambhi, "Are you sure this is the only way across?"

"This is the ford we normally use," Ambhi said through his interpreter. "It's the only safe crossing during the monsoon. That's why Prince Porus has brought his army here to stop you. Are we going to charge him right away? He is not so confident. He doesn't have as many men as we do. Once we get across the river, you should be able to beat him."

Normally, this would be true. As I've explained before, the herd with the most men and horses usually wins. But this enemy has elephants. Also, this river reminded me of the Granicus. I shivered as I remembered how I lost my rider there and nearly drowned.

Alexander frowned at the stamping elephants, which were barely visible through the rain, and looked down at the rushing water. I felt him shiver, too. "I'm not taking my horses across that, not with those elephants waiting for us! Tell the men to make camp. I'm going to ride along the bank and find somewhere else for us to cross."

We left the Indian boss to pass on the order and squelched along the riverbank. Electra, Apollo, Hades, Harpinna, Hoplite, and Zephyr followed me in a miserable line, trying to tuck their heads under one another's tail. On the far bank the elephants made their horrible noises among the trees and kept pace with us.

"How many do you see?" Alexander said.

"Looks like quite a few, Alex," Laomedon said, bringing Electra up next to me. "They're watching all the places where the river narrows."

"How many?" Alexander snapped. "You can count, can't you?"

"About fifty?" Laomedon ventured.

"Even I can see more of the beasts than that!"

"At least a hundred," Perdiccas said. "And there are probably more of them back at Porus's camp."

Alexander closed his eyes. "Right, that's what I feared. I'm going to have to think about this. Attacking across that ford will be suicide, so we'll have to wait for my boats to come over from the Indus. Meanwhile,

I want you to keep the men occupied. Patrol in both directions and make a note of all possible crossing points. I want to know exactly where Porus has stationed his troops, and how many men and elephants he has at each."

As he spoke, his fingers played with my mane, faster and faster. His voice became shriller as the old excitement shone in his eyes.

"I want a parade every day on the riverbank in full sight of Porus's men, horses as well as the phalanx. Keep all weapons polished, and whip any man who complains. Ptolemy, you'll do the same at night. Work out a rotation so the men and horses all get their share of rest. I want Porus so nervous by the time we're ready to attack, he won't know which direction we're coming from! If he thinks I'm going to sit on this riverbank and wait two months for the rains to stop, he can think again. We'll show this proud Indian prince we're not afraid of his elephants!"

We shifted our hooves in the mud, and our riders looked at the monsters on the far bank. No one spoke.

Alexander turned on the Guard with a scowl. "What's the matter? We're going to win this battle, like we've won all our other battles. Fear is a disease, and I don't want it infecting my army. You must set a good example to the men. Understand, gentlemen?"

The others nodded, as miserable as their horses. On the way back, I let Electra put her head under my tail.

Our grooms rigged up a tent cover between baggage carts in an attempt to keep our hay and cloths dry, but it didn't work for long. The rain got everywhere. Our barley was soggy. Our bits tasted of rust. Our cloths clung to our backs. Our bridles smelled of mildew. Everyone — humans and horses — splashed through the mud with their heads low. Even rolling in it was no fun after the first few times, because it stayed wet on our coats so our grooms couldn't get us clean.

Alexander was the only one who didn't let the rain dampen his excitement. He rode me every day and insisted Charm put on all my tassels and my parade-cloth. He wore his Troy helmet with its soggy plumes, the Achilles armor, and his blue-and-white Persian cloak. The coming battle took his mind off Borealis's ghost, and he stopped looking over his shoulder so often. When he mounted me, we looked so good my heart lifted. But by the time we got back, my bit was rusty again, my cloth spattered with mud, and my legs tired from cantering up and down the bank so Alexander could talk to the men and give speeches. Don't ask me what he said. It was boring stuff about glory and honor and immortality and the edge of the world. But his words made the men cheer and work harder, so I suppose he knew what he was doing.

It didn't stop raining, though. Not even Alexander could control the weather.

CHARM PLEADS WITH ALEXANDER

Charm grimaces as she picks up my feet to scrape out the mud. My hooves have not been dry since we got here, and I'm not the only one. She prods a sensitive spot, and I flinch. "Half the horses will be lame soon," she mutters. "Bucephalas's feet are rotting away!"

"Then King Alexander won't be able to ride him in the battle, will he?" Tydeos says, doing the same for Apollo's. "Isn't he going to take him out today? He's usually down here before now."

Charm looks at the sagging, dripping tents. The men are busy farther along the bank, calling instructions to one another. I see part of Alexander's white pavilion being carried toward the river's edge.

Charm sees it, too, and stiffens. "Something's going on. They're moving the king's tent."

Tydeos puts down Apollo's hoof. "Not only the king's tent . . . the men are arming for battle, look!"

The grooms have all noticed the unusual activity in the camp, and their tension infects us. All down the line, horses throw their heads up and whinny. The rain is easing slightly. Men in full armor are picking up their weapons and running to form up in columns out of sight of the river. Unlike other days, when they shouted continually as they paraded and galloped their horses up and down, they are being as quiet as possible.

Hephaestion comes to the lines, his helmet dripping, and calls softly, "Battle-cloths, everyone. Rough bits. No tassels. And when the king comes, no proskynesis. We don't want Porus's men to see where he is."

Charm sucks in her breath. She runs to me, picks up my hoof with the sensitive spot, and pulls out her dagger. I don't know what she is going to do, but I trust her so I nibble her damp mane.

"I'm sorry, horse," she whispers. "This will hurt a bit, but I can't let him ride you in this battle." She presses the point against my hoof, then gulps and sets down my leg, shaking her head in horror at what she nearly did. She blinks up at Hephaestion. "Sir, Bucephalas has a touch of foot rot from all this mud. Can't you persuade the king to ride another horse? Xanthus, maybe?"

Hephaestion makes a face. "I'm afraid not, Charmeia. Craterus needs Xanthus, and you know as well as I do that Bucephalas is the only horse here who will face elephants. Alex needs him for this battle more than in any before. Come on, quickly now, get his cloth on him. We've had news of another Indian prince coming south to join forces with Porus. If that happens, we'll be outnumbered, never mind the elephants. We have to get across this river tonight."

Charm shakes her head and grips my mane. Everything is wet, but I think there are tears on her cheeks.

Hephaestion sees them, too, and lowers his voice. "Try not to worry. The king has a clever plan. We're going upstream to meet our boats. There's an island in the middle of the river there, so the channels are narrow. Porus's troops don't know we've explored that far. By the time he finds out what we're up to, we'll be on the far bank behind his army. Craterus is staying here with half the men, and he'll cross the ford as soon as Porus is distracted. Porus hasn't enough men to send against us both, and his elephants move slowly. We'll trap them between us. Alex won't take any unnecessary risks with the horses."

"But my dream!"

Hephaestion frowns. "In school, Aristotle told us if we're not careful we make our dreams come true, the bad ones as well as the good —"

Before he can say any more, I smell Alexander.

The grooms do not notice him immediately. He is wearing a plain Macedonian helmet, so at first glance he looks like a normal cavalryman. But his chin is tilted up, his eyes are gleaming, and he strides through the mud with energy shining around him as if he owns the world. Even if they can't smell him, I don't understand how they could not know Alexander.

Then one groom gasps and drops on his face in the mud, and the others quickly follow. Alexander waves an impatient hand at them. "Get up out of that muck and get the horses ready! Hephaestion, didn't you tell them I'm supposed to be in disguise? Where's Bucephalas? Why isn't he ready? Charmides! Get *moving*."

Charm stands protectively in front of me, her arms spread. "No," she says in a brave voice. "I won't let you ride him today."

Alexander glares at her.

Tydeos's eyes widen. "Charm!" he hisses. "What are you *doing*?"

Hephaestion's eyes widen, too. He says quickly, "I'm sorry, Alex, the girl obviously doesn't know what she's saying. It's this weather. No one's used to it . . . maybe she's got a fever."

"Charmides!" Alexander snaps. "If you don't get my horse ready this instant, I'll have you put under arrest."

Charm falls to her knees in the mud at Alexander's feet. "Please, sir," she whispers. "Please don't ride Bucephalas in this battle! I told you about my dream. It's muddy today."

Alexander starts to breathe faster. Hephaestion grabs hold of Charm's arm and shakes her. "Don't be stupid!" he hisses. "Get up and obey the king!"

Alexander looks as if he is about to say something to Charm, then shakes his head and mutters, "Oh, I don't have time for this! You, Tydeos! Get my horse ready at once."

"Don't you dare, Tydeos!" Charm shouts.

She struggles against Hephaestion's grip and tries to reach her dagger. Hephaestion takes it from her and tightens his lips. "Be sensible, Charmeia!" he says. "What's gotten into you today?"

Tydeos casts a stricken look at Charm and avoids her eyes. He puts my battle-cloth on me. I shiver as he fumbles with the straps of my bridle. Although Alexander has ridden me every day we've been here, I know very well this is not going to be another trot by the river. I toss my head, impatient to get on with it.

"*No*, Tydeos!" Charm yells, still struggling. "Don't! Bucephalas is going to die in this battle! I dreamed it!"

I dance anxiously as Tydeos leads me out. When Alexander taps my shoulder, I am far too upset to settle to my knees for him. He makes an impatient sound and leaps onto my back. He gathers up my reins and glares down at Charm.

"When I return, I expect you to have come to your senses," he says in an icy tone. "All right, Hephaestion. Let the girl go and get on your horse."

Hephaestion relaxes his grip. But Charm has not given up. She stumbles after me, flings herself at my rein, and hangs on, making me throw my head up. Sobbing and pleading, she clutches Alexander's ankle.

This is VERY upsetting. Has my favorite groom gone mad?

The king fends her off with his foot and shouts for his men. Two Macedonians come running, seize Charm, and drag her away from me. They force her to her knees in the mud and hold a sword at her throat, looking questioningly at the king. Charm stares up at Alexander with terrified eyes. Her sobs stop, and her spring-grass smell sharpens with fear.

Tydeos and Hephaestion both take a step toward her but hesitate when Alexander raises his hand. The other grooms watch in horror.

"Lock her in one of the empty cages," Alexander orders, giving Charm a peculiar look. "Make sure she stays there until after the battle. I'll deal with her when I get back."

The Macedonians haul Charm to her feet. Again, she begs Alexander not to ride me and struggles fiercely. But Hephaestion has taken her dagger, and she is not as big or as strong as the men.

"Bucephalas!" she cries as they drag her away. *"Bucephalas!"*

Upset, I plant my forelegs and whinny to her. Alexander loses his temper and swears at me. He grabs a spear from one of the men and brings it down on my hindquarters with a sharp whack. I squeal and give a small buck. But before it can turn into a battle like the one we had in the high pass over the Caucasus Mountains, Charm stops struggling and calls, "No, Bucephalas! Don't fight him. They haven't hurt me. See?"

She gives me a final anguished look, then bows her head to Alexander.

Since she is no longer fighting, I calm down. Alexander mutters something under his breath about crazy females and trots me over to his pavilion. The last I see of Charm is her tear-streaked face as the soldiers march her away through the mud.

ROXANNE PLEADS WITH ALEXANDER

At the king's pavilion, Iolaus is waiting for us dressed in Alexander's blue-and-white cloak and the Troy helmet, which is too big for him. This is very strange, but Alexander doesn't seem to mind.

He puts his hand on Iolaus's shoulder and says, "Make sure Porus's men can see you clearly. Craterus is briefing all the men and the grooms. They'll know they're supposed to do proskynesis before you. Don't stand for any nonsense, now! And keep that helmet on whenever you're outside. Our plan won't work unless Porus believes you're me."

"Just as long as he doesn't try to stick an arrow into me," Iolaus says, fingering the cloak nervously.

Alexander laughs. "Believe me, Porus is going to be far too busy coping with us to bother shooting at you!"

Iolaus still doesn't look happy. He mutters something under his breath about getting all the rotten jobs. But Alexander doesn't hear, because just then Caspia trots up with Prince Ochus sitting very straight on her back.

I whinny a greeting to the filly, and she nickers to me. She is wearing a battle-cloth. Ochus has a long Persian sword thrust through his sash, and a spiked helmet glitters beneath his yellow turban. He looks grave and determined.

Alexander frowns at the sword. "Ochus, what do you think you're doing? I told you, no training today."

"I'm coming with you," Ochus says, raising his chin. "I'm not a child anymore, and I'm good with my sword now. I can help watch your back."

Alexander's eyes flicker with surprise. He leans across, puts his hand on the man-colt's shoulder, and says more gently, "That's very brave, Ochus. But I didn't fight my first battle until I was sixteen, and believe me this battle isn't going to be suitable for a thirteen-year-old boy who has never killed a man. Go back and look after Roxanne for me."

Ochus bites his lip and glances back at the camp. He whispers, "Please, Uncle Alexander. I know about Charmeia's dream, and you must not die in this battle. You're short of Guard members. Please take me with you. I am your heir, so I should learn what battle is like. When you asked me to cut off Bessus the traitor's ear, I was afraid and ran away. I am afraid today, too, but I will never run away again."

Alexander gives him a closer look, admiration replacing the surprise. "Seems you've grown up faster than I thought. But you can't come. It's too dangerous. And don't you go spreading any rumors in the camp about me going to die in this battle, or I'll have you whipped, prince or not! I haven't worked so hard and come this far to have my men spooked by a silly groom's dream. The girl probably made it up, anyway. She's done that before."

He wheels me around to join the others. Ochus bites his lip, checks his sword, and tightens his chin strap. With a stubborn expression, he turns Caspia to follow us. But Roxanne runs across his path, the hem of her red dress dragging in the mud. She flings herself at Caspia's reins, just like Charm had done at mine, and speaks very fast in Soghdian. Ochus leans down and whispers something to her. Roxanne shakes her head, tears in her eyes.

Alexander gives the girl-filly a look of frustration. "I told you to keep my wife away from the riverbank!" he snaps at her two guards, who arrive panting from the chase. "Take her back to her pavilion at once, and make sure she stays there! What's wrong with everyone today? If we don't get going soon, we'll never even make it out of camp before Porus realizes something's up."

Roxanne glares at the men, who had moved closer to take hold of her arms. She catches her breath and pushes her long mane behind her ears. "Please, my husband," she begs. "Please not take Prince Ochus into this battle!"

Alexander frowns at her, then at Ochus. Something changes in him, like a cloud covering the sun.

"Oh, I see!" he says, narrowing his eyes. "I let the prince teach you Greek, and the next thing I know you two are exchanging kisses behind my back!" He laughs and gives Ochus a twisted smile. "So, my brave prince, do you still want to see what a real battle is like?"

Ochus nods nervously.

"Good! Then you can join my Guard and get a close-up view. But I can't be looking out for you once the fighting starts. If you get into trouble, you're on your own."

"*No!*" Roxanne wails.

But Ochus straightens his shoulders and trots Caspia after us, his expression hovering between pride and fear.

Out of the corner of my eye, I see Roxanne standing between her guards, staring after Alexander and the prince. She looks more terrified than when I found her hiding in my stall back at Balkh.

OMENS

We marched upstream as fast as we could. When it grew dark, Alexander passed an order back that no one was to speak, in case Porus's lookouts heard us. Only the squelch of our hooves, the creak of damp leather, and the heavy breathing of the foot soldiers could be heard above the whine of the mosquitoes. The rain stopped, and steam rose from the leaves. The air made our coats prickle.

Suddenly, the sky cracked with a white flash. Several horses bolted past me, Caspia among them. I reared up in shock. But Alexander held me on a firm rein until the others pulled up and trotted back, shamefaced. The storm crashed above us and lightning forked into the ground on all sides, leaving smoking holes. Back in our column, men shrieked. We horses smelled burnt flesh and flickered our ears uneasily.

"Zeus is warning us not to fight today," Peucestas whispered, staring over his shoulder. "He's aiming at the pikes! It's a bad omen."

Alexander laughed, in a better mood now that we were finally on the move. "It's a *good* omen, gentlemen, not a bad one! Remember how the moon went out before the battle against the Persians at Gaugamela? My father Zeus-Ammon is helping us. With all this racket going on, Porus's lookouts won't hear a thing. Take off your helmets, if you're worried about Zeus striking you."

He urged me into a canter. The Guard tugged off their metal helmets and followed. There was no more talk of omens, good or bad, because at our faster pace they had to concentrate on avoiding the trees.

Past midnight, when the lightning had given way to more torrential rain, we boarded the waiting boats by torchlight. It was not easy and took some time because every horse had to be coaxed on board. On our boat, we found a very soggy and miserable Zephyr. Demetrius, wrapped in his cloak, was crouched at her head. Alexander patted him on the shoulder and thanked him for saving his life in Soghdiana. It was good to see Demetrius back with a horse. But considering Zephyr's record of losing her riders, I thought he should be very careful today.

We doused the torches and used the current to take us along the shore of the island. We were so quiet, no one spotted us until the first ten boats had cleared the headland and were heading for the far bank. Then an Indian horse appeared on the other side of the river, stared at us, and galloped off downstream with its rider yelling a warning. Somewhere in the darkness, Indian trumpets blared.

Alexander gave the order to land, and our boats made for the bank in a hiss of dark water. We jumped out, thankful to have solid ground under our hooves again, even if it was mostly mud. Our riders mounted, our herds formed up, and we set off at a smart trot to find the Indians.

Before I'd gone ten strides, the ground crumbled under my hooves. I scrabbled back in terror. Alexander jerked forward on my cloth and slammed his hand against my withers. He sucked in his breath as I came to a snorting stop at the brink of a black torrent.

"Zeus!" he cursed, shaking his fist at the sky. "I thought we were across. Where did that come from?"

The Guard stared in horror at the flood. "We're cut off, Alex!" Leonnatus cried, looking up and down the bank. "We'll have to get the boats again."

Alexander glared at the new channel, gripped my mane tightly, and dug his heels into my sides. "No time! It can't be that deep. Follow me!"

FIRST BLOOD

I jump because I trust him. But it IS deep. For a moment I think there is no bottom and panic. It is like the Granicus all over again. Ghosts whirl around me. Then my hooves feel mud, and I struggle up onto higher ground. Alexander is still on my cloth. He looks pale. But it is all right because I am strong.

Caspia is among the first to follow me. The little filly's head disappears. Then she works out how to swim and reaches the higher ground beside me with Ochus clinging to her mane. Caspia's eyes have white rings around them. But Ochus grips her reins firmly and urges her after me. After seeing us disappear, the phalanx find a shallower place farther upstream, and the men wade across chest deep, their pikes held over their heads.

We scramble up the far bank and hurry inland before any more channels can open up. Alexander whirls me on the spot with his sword in the air, urging them on, and the men cheer when they see how confident he is.

Then we are galloping!

Behind me, I hear the splashing of twenty thousand hooves. The Macedonian battle cry echoes from fifteen thousand throats. My blood throbs. Caspia is right behind me, racing flat out. The rain glitters on Ochus's long eyelashes, and part of his turban has come unwound. His teeth are bared in excitement. My head whirls with excitement, too. I forget the mud and the rain.

Some enemy chariots and cavalry gallop out of the trees toward us. But they don't have as many horses as we do, and their boss is a very young Indian, not much older than Ochus. They hesitate when they see us.

Alexander grins and draws his sword.

We charge them without even stopping to form a line. Alexander heads me straight for the leading chariot, and his blade flashes down. The man-colt inside ducks, but his driver falls out and the first Indian ghost shimmers into the rain. As the chariot lurches past us, the man-colt drops to one knee and bends his long bow. The arrow flies at Alexander. It is a good aim, and I have to leap to avoid it. My hooves slip in the mud, and my old injury from Chaeronea gives a wrench of pain. The arrow misses Alexander, but as I land it pierces the soft skin behind my elbow just in front of my girth.

It goes in deep. Pain shoots through me, and the ghosts fleeing from the battlefield take on a strange solidity.

Then an Indian horse careers into me, and the feathered shaft of the arrow snaps off. The man-colt in the chariot abandons his bow and grabs the reins. He is heading straight for Caspia and Ochus. Alexander leans down, pulls a javelin out of the mud, and throws it at the enemy cavalryman, then he whirls me around, his sword ready to kill the next. I don't think he realizes I am wounded. There is too much mud on me.

The enemy chariots are in trouble on the riverbank. Their wheels get stuck in the mud. Their drivers fall easily to our javelins and swords, until the bank is littered with enemy dead. Some horses are in the river, struggling in the current. Their ghosts shimmer in the rain before disappearing.

Out of the corner of my good eye, I see Ochus fighting the man-colt who leads the Indian herd. Both of them look terrified but determined. Caspia lays back her little ears and bares her teeth at the Indian horses. Ochus's long Persian sword flashes, and the man-colt's ghost ripples away as his body plops facedown in the mud, pooling blood. As Ochus stares down at it, another Indian gallops up behind the prince and raises his sword. Hephaestion yells a warning and gets the Indian in the neck with one of his javelins, while Ochus gallops Caspia back to us. Seeing this, the rest of the enemy flee.

Alexander claps the prince on the shoulder. "Well done," he says. "I think that was one of Porus's sons."

Ochus stares at all the dead bodies, leans over Caspia's shoulder, and is sick in the mud.

Alexander grins, his eyes still glittering with the excitement of battle. "Don't say I didn't warn you! I was sick in my first battle, too. It gets easier. Stay close to Peucestas. He'll look after you. Everyone else, form up. That was just a taste. We haven't met the elephants yet."

As the others gather around me, stamping and snorting, I whinny to check that they are all right. The familiar whinnies come back. Caspia, Electra, Petasios, Apollo, Zephyr, Harpinna, Hoplite, Borealis . . .

BOREALIS?

My arrow wound sends a shooting pain through me, and I shiver in the rain. That is the first time I have EVER heard a ghost whinny.

OUR LAST BATTLE

It was nearly midday before we found the rest of the enemy. We caught the smell of the elephants long before we saw them. Every horse in our herd flickered its ears nervously. I forgot the pain of the arrowhead buried behind my elbow and broke into a trembling sweat.

Alexander smiled grimly and tightened my rein. "Don't let me down now, old horse," he whispered. "One last effort, and you'll be back with your groom before evening."

He seemed to have forgotten that he'd ordered Charm put in a cage.

I shivered all over as we came out of the trees, and I wasn't the only one. The men fell silent. Facing us in an unbroken line across the plain was Prince Porus's army. Foot soldiers in the middle with their long bows and javelins, cavalry and chariots on the wings . . . and, spaced along the line of men like towers in a battlement wall, elephants carrying huts stuffed with Indians on their backs. As Perdiccas had said earlier, a lot more than a hundred of the monsters.

While we waited for our phalanx to catch up, Alexander dismounted and examined the land, exactly as he'd done back at Gaugamela. His Guard followed him tensely, eyeing the elephants. But Prince Porus made no move to attack us. He sat in his hut on the biggest elephant at the center of his line and waited patiently for the rest of our herd to come out of the trees. He'd obviously heard how we had dominated his son earlier, and he wasn't going to let us do the same to him.

My wound hurt, but the arrowhead was hidden in the fold of skin behind my elbow under a crust of blood and mud, and Alexander was too preoccupied and excited to notice I was lame. He muttered to himself and eyed the enemy line over little rises in the land and from behind trees. Finally, he was satisfied. He vaulted onto me and called his officers across.

"I'm dividing the cavalry into three," he announced. "Demetrius, you hide your men behind this hill. The phalanx can hide behind that one. Perdiccas, stay in the trees over on the right. Hephaestion, you bring your men with me. We'll attack their left wing first. Hopefully, Porus will think I'm too scared to bring many of my horses against his elephants and believe that's all we have. When he sends his cavalry and chariots across to finish us off, Perdiccas can join us from the trees. That'll force Porus to bring the rest of them across from the right, so Demetrius can go around the back and attack them from behind. As soon as we've put their cavalry out of action, the phalanx can attack the center. You all know the best techniques for killing elephants now. Take out as many of them as you can, then we'll help you with those archers. But wait for my signal. I don't want you going in with enemy cavalry on your heels. Ochus, you ride for the ford and find Craterus. Tell him where we are, and tell him to hurry. Peucestas, you go with the prince." His eyes sparkled. "It isn't going to be easy, gentlemen. But we're going to win this battle!"

Thunderous cheers greeted this speech. I made myself huge and forgot the pain of my wound. Ochus tightened his reins and whispered something in Caspia's ear. Peucestas gripped the big shield of Achilles and stared anxiously after Alexander.

Alexander drew his sword and looked around at the Guard with a man-coltish grin. His eyes shone with excitement, as they used to back in Macedonia. His legs trembled, hard and tight against my cloth. His breathing quickened. "Right, everyone ready? Keep your formation, gentlemen. . . . *Charge!*"

Oh, it is wild! It is exciting! It is slippery!

Petasios and I gallop side by side, our riders knee to knee. Most of the horses are wary of the elephant at the end of the line, so our charge isn't as straight as usual. But the Indian horses don't like the elephants any more than we do, so they are waiting for us well out of reach of the monsters. They hold their formation until an Indian trumpet blows. Then they charge us in a ragged, whooping herd.

Our javelins hiss through the rain, and several horses and riders roll over in the mud and give up their ghosts beneath my hooves. I leap to avoid them, and Alexander's sword flashes as he dispatches more ghosts. The Indian riders grin at him. They think they're going to win, because they believe they have more men than us. They haven't seen the Macedonians hiding in the trees. More enemy chariots stream toward us from the other side of the plain. Alexander waits until the last moment, winks at Hephaestion, and waves to our trumpeter.

The blast sounds a bit damp, but it is loud enough, because a great answering cry sounds from the trees.

"ALALALALALALALAI!"

Brave Apollo appears at full gallop followed by his herd, with his pale tail streaming through the storm and Perdiccas yelling on his back.

The Indians whirl in alarm to face this new threat, and Alexander cuts down another enemy from behind, making another ghost. He waves his arm again as the chariots from the Indian right wing race across to help their struggling herd, and another damp trumpet blast brings Demetrius on Zephyr with the rest of our herd splattering behind them, their faces covered in mud but grinning because the king's plan is working perfectly.

But Zephyr is scared of the elephants, and the charge goes wide as the others follow the silly mare. The Indians realize they've been tricked and reform their line to bring the elephants into the battle.

"Where's Craterus?" Alexander yells, cutting down another of the enemy. "Watch those elephants! They're breaking out of the trap!"

One of the biggest elephants is lumbering straight toward me, followed by several desperate enemy foot soldiers who have broken away from our phalanx.

"Porus!" Alexander hisses. He leans down and plucks a javelin out of one of the dead Indians. "Come on, Bucephalas, this is our chance to finish it!"

He digs his heels into my sides, and we charge the elephant.

I am not afraid. The tall Indian boss in the elephant's hut looks down at us with astonished eyes and grabs his spear. I leap as high as I can, though it tears my wound. At the top of my leap Alexander hurls his javelin.

It pierces Prince Porus through the shoulder, and the enemy boss cries out in pain. Several javelins fly down at Alexander from the guards in Porus's hut. This never happened in training so I am caught unawares. I twist to avoid them but catch two on my hindquarters and one in my shoulder. It feels like being thumped by a bad-tempered groom. They don't really hurt, but my legs wobble as I land.

"Alex!" Demetrius cries, fighting to get Zephyr closer to us so he can protect the king with his little shield.

The trees around me blur, and I can barely feel Alexander on my cloth. I am aware of my friends leading a wild, brave charge against the elephants. Then Zephyr bumps into me as an Indian arrow hisses into Demetrius's thigh, knocking me off balance.

Just when it looks like we are in real trouble, a trumpet sounds in the woods behind us, and Craterus comes galloping out of the trees on Xanthus, leading his herd. Our phalanx advances on the elephants with shields locked and pikes lowered. Yelling battle cries, our men slash the long noses of the monsters, stab their legs, and do all the things they've trained for. One of the elephants falls with a crash that shakes the ground, and its huge ghost whistles past me, making me shiver all over.

"Porus is getting away, Alex!" Demetrius shouts, pressing a hand to his wounded leg and pointing after the biggest elephant, which is lumbering off into the trees on its own.

Alexander plucks out the javelin stuck in my shoulder, grips it in a determined fist, and puts his heels into my sides. I make a huge effort, but my legs are getting wobblier with each stride, and every breath hurts. I can't even see Porus's elephant through all the ghosts, so we soon get left behind.

At last, Alexander realizes something is wrong. The battle fever leaves him, and he pulls me up. He strokes my trembling neck. "What is it, Bucephalas?" he whispers. "What's wrong, old horse?"

I can't tell him. But my knees give way. Darkness closes around me. I see only ghosts, ghosts, ghosts.

Alexander jerks my head up in alarm and digs his heels into my sides. "No! I won't let you die! I *won't*. You're my immortal horse. Those little Indian spears didn't go in very deep. You've had worse wounds. You need a rest, that's all. You'll be fine when we get back to camp. . . ."

Hephaestion rides up to report the capture of Prince Porus, but Alexander waves him away impatiently. "Take the prisoner back to camp. Give him something to eat and treat him with respect. I'll discuss the surrender of his lands later. I've got to see to Bucephalas."

He slips off me and takes my reins over my head. I stagger after him through the piles of bodies and the mud, past the dead elephant, and back downriver to the ford. It is still raining. We are followed by a trail of weary, mud-spattered horses and men. On the way, we meet more of Craterus's herd finishing off the Indians and elephants that fled the battlefield. Alexander does not stop. One hand holds my bit in a tight grip, and his other hand holds my mane, keeping my nose off the ground so I don't trip over it. When I am not sure I can take a step farther, he whispers in my ear and I do.

When we reach the ford, Alexander clutches my withers as if *he* needs the support, not me. A small golden horse is lying on its side in the mud. Caspia! Hoplite stands beside her, head down and flanks heaving. Peucestas kneels nearby, covering something with the big shield of Achilles. I can see a strip of muddy yellow cloth coming out from under the rim. I can hardly raise my head far enough to check, but it looks like Prince Ochus under the shield.

Peucestas leaps up when he sees the king. "Alexander, I'm sorry! There was an elephant! The filly lay down, and the prince's leg got trapped beneath her. One of the Indians put an arrow in him. . . . He died bravely, poor boy. But I can't get the filly off him. I think she's dead, too."

Some of the men rush across and try to move Caspia, but she is heavy even if she is small. I summon the last of my strength and nicker to tell her the elephants have gone. She opens her eyes and scrambles to her feet at once. Under the shield, Ochus lies motionless.

Alexander stares at the dead man-colt with a peculiar expression. "Don't just stand there!" he snaps. "Take the prince's body back to camp, and someone let my groom out of her cage. Bucephalas needs her."

The men lift Ochus onto the Achilles shield, and we follow them. I try my best to make myself huge for Alexander. But the ford finishes me. Long before we reach the horse lines, my legs give way and I lie down in the mud. It is strange, but there is no pain anymore. Dark clouds fold around me, and I see Borealis standing before me, solid as a real horse with his brown ears pricked.

Alexander takes off my bridle and cloth. I hear him shouting for the horse doctor, but my eyes are dark. When feet splash toward me, and a warm human lies across my neck and strokes my face, I know from her smell it is Charm.

"Bucephalas . . ." she whispers. "Bucephalas, don't die, oh, please don't die!"

I nicker softly as her tears fall into my mane.

More feet run toward us, and I hear Roxanne's voice screaming at Alexander.

"You've killed my Ochus! I *hate* you! I'll hate you forever! . . . Oh, Ochus, wake up, please wake up. . . ."

But Prince Ochus's ghost is gone.

Alexander must be all right, because back at the camp the men are chanting his name and cheering. I think that means we dominated the Indians.

Only Charm is crying so much, I hear nothing more.

31

BUCEPHALA

326–324 B.C.

VICTORY?

I do not like the horse doctor. Every time he comes to see me, he does something to me that hurts. I want to tell him to go away. But my legs won't work, and I can barely make flat ears. He's still scared of me, though. He makes Charm put my muzzle on me and sit on my head while he's treating me. Also, he's useless, because he hasn't found the arrowhead buried behind my elbow. It's trapped beneath me, and it hurts all the time.

I think I am lying on a flattened tent. There is another tent stretched over poles and tied down at the corners to form a makeshift stall around me. The rain splatters noisily overhead, and drips hit my legs. I can hear my friends whinnying in the distance. But I do not have the strength to whinny back.

I can still smell the river, though I am no longer by the ford where I collapsed. I can remember sliding through the mud behind two mules, who complained at my weight but dragged me behind them all the way up the hill. Before they were led away, they lowered their noses and blew at me in sympathy.

Mules aren't so bad, after all.

Charm has not left my side since Alexander brought me back to camp. Tydeos brings her food and my medicine, while she strokes my nose and whispers to me. She keeps it up all day and night, which is a bit annoying because I am very tired.

Charm says this is how we dominated the Indians at the river Jhelum:

Indian dead: 23,000, including Porus's son

Macedonian dead: 14,000, including Prince Ochus

Horses dead: 3,000, almost including ME!

Elephants dead: 120

Prisoners: Prince Porus, and 10,000 Indian slaves for building work

I do not care. I'd like to leave my body and mutual groom with Borealis, who is waiting patiently beside me. But every time I start to drift through the dark clouds toward his ghost, Charm's voice tugs me back.

"As soon as the men have recovered from the battle, Alexander's taking them to find the edge of the world," she tells me. "It's not far from here. Then he'll bring back some magic water from the Eastern Ocean to make you better. He's building a city here to celebrate our victory over the Indians, and Demetrius is going to be left in command of the garrison, so we'll be all right. . . ."

Did she say city? It *must* be my city this time!

". . . and Craterus is building a fleet to take us all home when Alexander gets back. The scientists think the river Jhelum might take us back to Egypt, because they've found some Egyptian reeds growing on the bank. So even if you can't walk by then, we can put you on a boat and sail you to the big Alexandria in Egypt, and from there across the sea to Pella. We'll be home before you know it, Bucephalas, and Alexander's promised you can retire in the mare pasture. . . ."

I am too tired to think about mares. What's my city CALLED?

". . . So many men died here, Bucephalas! Everyone's sick of the fighting. Roxanne says Alexander took Prince Ochus into the battle on purpose to get him killed. I don't know if that's true —"

A corner of my shelter blows loose in a sudden gust, and Charm breaks off to stare at it. Borealis is standing out there in the night, looking in.

I manage a small nicker, and Charm jumps up at once. She brings me herb-smelling water and holds the bucket under my nose so I can drink.

"Are you thirsty, Bucephalas? Are you hungry? You must eat!" She takes away the bucket and brings me a handful of barley mash soaked in honey, which I lick from her palm to please her.

She gulps down a sob and strokes my cheek.

"Oh, I know Prince Porus is Alexander's prisoner, and the new city's going to be called Nike, which means victory, but it feels like we lost! None of the men are partying. They're just drinking to forget the battle. I think those elephants frightened them almost as much as they frightened you poor horses. And Caspia got poor Ochus killed! It's my fault. It was a mistake to teach her those silly tricks. Even Alexander's Guard has had enough. They're going to try to talk Alexander into going home. But I hope he finds the edge of the world first, otherwise you won't get your magic water to make you better. . . ."

I hear no more. My eyes have closed and my head is back on the ground, surrounded by dark clouds.

Alexander called his new city Nike!

What do I have to do to get a city named after ME?

MY OWN WORST ENEMY

The next time the clouds clear from my head, everything is much quieter and Charm is not with me.

I am still lying under my shelter, although the sides have been tied back. It has stopped raining. The sun steams in a golden haze. I can see barefoot Indians piling up mud-bricks to dry. Boats ferry them across the river to build the foundations of the new city.

Borealis is grazing nearby. When he sees I am awake, he whinnies and trots over. He sniffs my nose. As he does this, something black charges out of my blind spot and I hear Indus's brazen little squeal. The colt rears and strikes out at Borealis with his small hooves. His ghost vanishes. Indus comes back to earth and paws my shoulder. I raise my head and flatten my ears to tell him to leave me alone, and pain shoots through me. In the distance, Aura whinnies anxiously.

Indus will not give up. He nudges me with his nose and keeps pawing the ground, shaking his mane. Charm comes running back. "Shoo!" she says, waving her arms at Indus. "Go back to your mother, you silly colt! Bucephalas is sick. He doesn't want you bothering him."

Indus keeps trying to get his nose under my elbow, where the arrowhead is buried. It has been swelling for some time now, and it feels hard and tight. I move, and a shooting pain goes through me as the wound explodes, splattering my colt's nose with pus. He leaps back with a squeal, raises his head, and curls his upper lip. Charm stares at him in amazement. Then she lies down and pushes her hand under me. She brings it out smeared in pus and blood.

"Oh, Zeus . . ." she whispers. "Oh, Bucephalas! You're wounded, and it's infected. That horse doctor's useless! I'm going to get help. Wait here!"

I'm not going anywhere, believe me.

She races off, and I drift back into the dark clouds because moving took all the strength from me. Men come back with Charm and tie lead reins around my fetlocks. She takes my tail and pulls. Between them, they roll me over. More pain shoots through me, and I neigh in terror. Borealis is watching me again, his ears pricked. But at least Indus has gone back to his mother. There is a horrible smell. It think it is me.

When the clouds clear once more, Charm is sponging my arrow wound, and I hear Demetrius's voice.

"Looks like it's gone deep. It could have hit his lung, which would explain why he's having trouble breathing. This climate's bad for wounds." He pauses and says gently, "The horse is thirty years old, Charmeia. That's like one of us being ninety. It'd be kinder to put him down."

"No!" Charm spreads her arms across me. "Alexander will be back soon with the magic water from the edge of the world. Bucephalas will get better then. He *will.*"

Demetrius sighs. "Charmeia . . . you must know this immortality thing is just a story? Alex is extremely unlikely to find the water of life in India, even if such an elixir exists. It's just something he told the men, to make them follow him farther east."

"The Amazons were supposed to be a story, too, weren't they?" Charm says stubbornly, her eyes glittering with tears. Her hand drops to her dagger. "I won't let you kill Bucephalas!"

Demetrius shakes his head. "Maybe if we'd seen his wound earlier . . . Sometimes this horse is his own worst enemy. The horse doctor was obviously too scared to examine him properly. I don't know who you're going to find to remove the arrowhead. I've just had one like it dug out of my thigh, so I know how much it hurts. But it'll have to come out, or he hasn't a chance of surviving until Alex gets back — if he comes back. I have a feeling the edge of the world is a lot farther than he's told everyone it is."

I can't see their faces. But when Charm speaks again, her whisper sounds scared. "He's *got* to come back. He promised! He'll come back for Bucephalas. We can't let him die so far from home . . . we *can't*."

Demetrius says softly, "I'll help you, if you're determined to try. You'll need something to sew up the wound afterward. These Indian arrows are barbed like a spiny leaf, so you have to cut deep, you can't just pull. . . . I'll show you the one that came out of my leg, so you know. Bucephalas isn't going to like it much. He's still got a spark of life in him, the brave old horse!"

"He'll let me do it," Charm whispers, stroking my nose. "He's got to."

It hurt more than you can imagine. More than being branded. More than a spiked bit. More than a whip. More, I imagine, than the Scythian thing the Persians did to poor Zoroaster — No, maybe not more than that.

But Charm whispered to me all the time, and Demetrius sat on my head to keep me still. The arrowhead came out with lots of pus and infected flesh. Then Charm sewed up the wound and put herb paste on it. As she cleaned her dagger, Borealis's ghost breathed down her neck. Charm frowned and looked around. I tried to warn Borealis to keep away from her. But the effort was too much, and the dark clouds smothered me once more.

Demetrius ordered the slaves to build a stable for me on this side of the river. At some stage, I assume the mules dragged me into it. I don't remember that part. But I know I am out of the heat and lying in a deep bed of straw when I smell Alexander's sherbet sweetness again.

THE EDGE OF THE WORLD

I flare my nostrils, which is about all I can manage now. Aura and Indus are munching hay in the next stall. Caspia is next to them, thrown out of the army in disgrace, her mane shaved off in mourning for Prince Ochus. Borealis stands in the empty stall on my other side. He doesn't need hay, because he's a ghost. Charm is curled up in her cloak next to me, sound asleep. She has been awake all night talking to me, and she is exhausted.

Outside, men shout and laugh, trumpets blare, and horses whinny to their friends — all the familiar noises of our huge herd making camp. It sounds as if they have won another battle. But when Alexander walks into the stable, there is no light of victory shining around him. His mane is stuck to his head where his helmet has squashed it. His white cloak is grubby. His eyes shift nervously from side to side as if he's looking for Borealis's ghost. He peers over my door, pauses a moment, then lets himself in.

"Bucephalas," he sighs, stroking my cheek. "So it's true you waited for me. Oh, old horse! Where did it all go wrong?"

Charm starts awake. Seeing Alexander, she scrambles to her feet and bursts out, "Did you find it?" Then she blushes and kneels in the straw to kiss the king's dirty toes.

Alexander gives her the same sort of look he gave me. "Get up, Charmides," he says in a weary tone. "There's no one to see you do proskynesis here except the horses, and who are they going to tell? The edge of the world is farther than I thought. My men are cowards! We found another river as wide as the Jhelum, and they got scared they'd find more Indians and war elephants on the other side. They refused to follow me across. I'd have gone on alone, if they didn't need me so much. I am their god and their king, and kings and gods are not free to do things like that. You don't know how lucky you are, just being a groom."

"Sir?" she says, staring at him wide-eyed.

"I'm telling you I didn't find it!" Alexander snaps. "Don't you understand? There is no magic water. There is no immortality. The oracle in Siwa lied to me. My army wants to go home. I've shown them the wonders of the world, and all they want to do is crawl back to their pathetic little farms and families! Their ambitions are so small, Charmides, so small. . . . One of Parmenio's old officers led the revolt. He dared tell me that the sign of a great man is knowing when to stop! I should have gotten rid of all the old guard when I got rid of General Parmenio. Now it's too late. I can hardly execute my entire army, can I?"

He presses his knuckles to his forehead. "I'm not taking them back to Macedonia, if that's what they think. I'm going to make another court out here in the east, perhaps at Susa or Babylon. Somewhere I can keep a careful eye on my empire. And I'm going to replace Antipater back in Macedonia. I know he's been plotting behind my back for years. I'll just have to rethink things a bit. . . ." Energy glimmers around him again as he starts planning his new empire, but Charm is not listening.

"No magic water?" she whispers, looking at me. "But Bucephalas —"

Alexander takes a deep breath. "I know. The old horse is dying. I'm surprised he held on this long, after what the horse doctor told me. An arrow in his lung. He didn't dare take it out. Said it would kill him for sure, at his age. The Amazons might have helped him, but they've gone home." He mutters something about the edge of the world, then says, "Did you know there's a Queen Penthesilea in the *Iliad*, too? In the very last line, she comes to help Troy and does battle with Achilles, who is supposed to have killed her. I've been wondering about their country and whether the tales about them being immortal can be true. But I expect Amazons pass the same names down through generations just like we do, and the reason no one can find their land is because it's so small and insignificant." He shakes his head at me and says more gently, "I'll mount an expedition when we get back as far as the Caspian Sea. But even if the Amazons do know the secret of immortality, it's too late for Bucephalas now."

"I took out the arrow," Charm says, so quietly the king doesn't take it in at first.

Alexander keeps muttering about the *Iliad* and the edge of the world perhaps being in a different place from where he'd thought. But Charm's words finally get his attention. "You took it out?"

Charm bites her lip. "Me and Commander Demetrius. Bucephalas is no better, though." She pauses and asks in a small voice, "Will you let me go and find the Amazons, sir? If Tydeos stays here to look after Bucephalas, I could maybe take Aura and some of your men . . . ?"

Alexander's face softens. He fingers Charm's mane. "Ah, Charmides . . . Charmeia. You're so faithful. I know you'd go to the ends of the earth to save the old horse, if you could. You've got more loyalty in these few hairs than most of my men have in their entire body." He lets the curl fall against her flushed neck. "But it's out of the question. I need all my men, and I need Tydeos to look after the other horses."

Charm's face twists. "What about me?"

Alexander sighs. "I'm not going to make you leave Bucephalas, don't worry. The old horse deserves a friend at his side when he dies. But he obviously can't travel in that state, and we're leaving as soon as the fleet is ready. We won't be back this way, so I release you. You're free. I'll give you three talents to help you start your new life and papers to say you are a free citizen of the empire, under my protection. When the old horse is gone and you want to go home, show them at any Macedonian garrison, and they'll give you food and shelter for as long as you need and an escort when you're ready to move on."

Charm stares at him. "You're freeing me?"

The king smiles. "Can't have my half sister remain a slave all her life, can I?"

Charm sucks in her breath. All the blood drains from her face. Then, although Alexander has told her not to, she does proskynesis before him.

"Forgive me, Your Majesty! I didn't know how to tell you! I wanted to, but there never was a right time. I thought you'd be angry with me and make me leave Bucephalas . . . oh, please forgive me!"

She's facedown on the ground beside me, so she doesn't see Alexander's expression, which is a cross between puzzlement and sorrow. He gives Borealis's ghost a quick look. "Get up, Charmeia," he says in his weary tone. "It's hardly your fault my mortal father raped your mother after the battle at Methone, is it? I've known who you are ever since I captured the horsemaster in Soghdiana. General Parmenio knew as well, apparently, but he kept it from me. I was right to have him executed. If I was going to punish you for lying to me, I'd have done so long before now."

"It's worse than that, sir," Charm breathes, trembling as she peers up at him. "You still don't know why I went to Pella. I hated King Philip for what he'd done to my mother! I had poison in a mule's hoof —"

"Enough," Alexander says, cutting her off with an impatient hand. "I know all about that, too. Queen Ada told me in her last letter — I think she was worried what I might do if I found out from someone else. Demetrius has asked to stay on here, so he'll look after you. I'm also going to leave the old horsemaster with you, since you've been so reluctant to let me kill him. That's how I know you weren't involved in my mortal father's murder. You can't bear to see anyone suffer, can you, not even your worst enemy? But I'm sure you'll decide a suitable fate for him eventually, even if it's just leaving him to rot in his cage. Tell Demetrius, when you do, and he'll carry out your orders as if they were my own. Before we leave, I'm going to give Bucephalas a funeral grander than any horse has ever had. This stable looks good here, so I'll build a new city around it in his memory. Call it Bucephala, so no one will forget how brave he was."

Charm's eyes fill with tears. Borealis looks questioningly at me over the partition. I find a sudden surge of strength and give him flat ears.

BUCEPHALA!

My city. Mine!

Borealis is going to have to wait a bit longer for me to join him. I want to see what my city looks like when it's finished.

Hᴇᴀʟɪɴɢ

I didn't see my funeral, although the smell of burning flesh got every-where, even into my stall. Charm said they used the pyre to burn the bodies of all the horses and men who had died from their wounds while Alexander was off looking for the edge of the world, so no one noticed that mine wasn't among them. There were guards around my stable to keep everyone away, and the men were too excited about going home to take much notice of the building works. Tydeos had not forgotten us, though. The day the fleet set sail, he came into my stall and stroked my cheek.

"He's no better, is he?" he said. "Are you sure you want to stay behind, Charm? You can still travel home with us, even though King Alexander has freed you. I wouldn't want to stay here. It rains too much."

"You dolt! That's only a couple of months a year. It's sunny now, isn't it?"

Tydeos made a face. "I'll write to you with all the gossip. You'd better wait till we get somewhere more friendly before you write back, though, or your scrolls might never reach me. Can you remember the letters Prince Ochus taught you?"

Charm smiled. "I'll practice. I won't have much else to do." She gazed at him, and he gazed back. "Tydeos . . ."

"No soppy stuff!" Tydeos stood up with a grin. "This isn't good-bye. You can come after us as soon as Bucephalas — when it's over. And if you don't, I'm coming back here to find you just as soon as I've saved up enough money to buy my freedom and some mares to start my horse farm. King Alexander might've let you go, but you can't escape from *me* that easy!"

Charm started to laugh, caught her breath, and rummaged in her bedroll. "You can have the gold Alexander gave me. I don't need it."

"Nor do I." He fended her off, still grinning. "The king's still giving out bonuses. I'll be rich soon. You keep it till you've got enough to buy a decent stallion, and we'll start our horse farm together!"

Then, finally, it was peaceful again. At least, as peaceful as it could be with a city being built around us.

When Alexander had gone, Charm tried everything she could think of to make me better. She brought a procession of local wise men to my stable, and they gave her foul-smelling pastes to put on my wound and weird things to put in my food. None of these cures worked, mainly because I would not touch my feed if it smelled suspicious. I grew weaker because I wouldn't eat. Eventually, in desperation, Charm went to the only knowledgeable person in Bucephala she had not so far asked for advice.

By now I am too far gone to realize what she is doing and lie on my side with my eyes closed. But when the old horsemaster limps into my stall and his smell reaches me, my body does a strange thing. It breaks into a sweat and twitches, and one of my hind legs kicks out. I haven't done that for a long time. It hurts.

"Now, don't worry, Bucephalas," Charm murmurs, coming to kneel at my head. "The horsemaster's here to help you. I've promised him his freedom in exchange for making you better. He knows a lot about horses. Be sensible and let him examine you."

Charm has brought my enemy into my stall!

My hind leg twitches again. In my heart, I am rearing and kicking to keep him away from Charm. But my body remains lying in the straw.

I roll my eye at him. The horsemaster leans on his crutch and stares down at me. He is dirty and thin, and his whiskers have grown even longer than before. He wears a good cloak, though, over his ragged tunic.

"Well?" Charm whispers, looking up at him. "Can you cure him?"

"What if I can't?" growls my enemy, sending more sweat washing over me. He glances at the two guards in the passage. "Are you going to order me locked back in that cage and tortured to death as punishment?"

"No," Charm says quietly. "I told you. Alexander said it's my decision, so you'll go free, whatever happens. Even if Bucephalas dies. But you've got to try. Look at him! He's fought this long, and he's so brave. I have to try everything I can to save him."

The horsemaster looks at me with narrowed eyes, making me tremble with bad memories. He prods me with his crutch and grunts. "This horse is suffering. You should have put him down months ago."

"You haven't even examined him!"

"I don't need to. Anyone can see he's dying. He's thirty years old, for Zeus's sake! You're crazy, keeping him alive so long. The king's already led his funeral procession. He's a lost cause. I'll do it for you, if you can't stomach the deed yourself, which you obviously can't. That's the trouble with letting a girl do a man's job."

Tears spring to Charm's eyes. "Are you sure he's suffering?" she whispers. "Is there nothing we can do?"

The horsemaster makes a face. "Nothing, except a sword through the heart."

Charm bows her head and strokes my sweaty neck. "Then I'll see to it," she whispers. "You can go."

The horsemaster shakes his head as his guards escort him to the door. He keeps looking back at Charm and me, as if afraid it is a trick. I relax slightly as his smell fades.

But just as my enemy reaches the door, there is excited shouting outside. A Macedonian sentry races past, shouting, "The king's dying! A messenger just arrived from one of the rebel fortresses downriver! King Alexander led a charge over the wall, and only three men followed him. The scaling ladders broke. An arrow pierced his lung! Peucestas covered him with the Achilles shield, but the king's dying. King Alexander's dying!"

The horsemaster blinks at his guards, and a slow smile spreads across his face. They look at each other, wide-eyed, and hurry off after the sentry. Charm stares after them in dismay, while I look around nervously for Alexander's ghost. I don't see it, though.

Charm takes a trembly breath and continues to stroke me. "No," she whispers. "It can't be true. We'd know if the horse bond broke."

The horsemaster limps back to my stall and looks down at Charm. "Hear that, girl-groom? Alexander's finally gone and gotten himself killed! When this news spreads, there's going to be no safe place this side of the Hellespont. I'm getting out of here, but I'm going to need a horse and someone to look after me. My health hasn't improved any in that cage the king kept me in, so you're coming with me."

Before Charm realizes what he intends, he seizes her wrist and wraps the lead rein around it.

She gasps. "Stop it! What are you doing? I'm a free citizen now! King Alexander's not dead! When he hears of this, he'll come back here and kill you —"

"I doubt it," the horsemaster growls, lashing her wrists together. "And you're not free anymore. That document the king gave you isn't worth the papyrus it's written on now that he's dead. You owe me for wrecking my career back in Pella. Who's going to care what happens to a common groom, when the world's falling apart around them?"

"No!" Charm cries, struggling, frightened now. "I know I made you lose your job, but I made up for it. I stopped Alexander from executing you, and I've set you free! You *promised* to help Bucephalas... you *promised*! Help! Guard!"

But the guards have gone to spread the awful news and do not hear her cries. The horsemaster tears a strip off his ragged tunic and stuffs it into Charm's mouth.

Charm tries to reach her dagger with her bound hands, but the horse-master snatches it away from her and holds the point at her cheek. "Shut up and stop struggling, slave!" he hisses. "Or I'll mark this pretty cheek of yours with a permanent scar. Now, Bucephalas obviously isn't going to be much use to us. So we'll take that gray mare. Nice colt. It can run behind us." He drags Charm to her feet and marches her out into the passage where he loops her leash around a hook. Then he seizes Aura's bridle and opens her stall.

There is so much noise outside now, no one can hear what's happening in the stables. The horsemaster is trying to get the bridle on Aura, who thinks he has come to threaten her colt and gives him flat ears in the fierce way of a mare protecting her foal. Indus squeals and rears bravely. The horsemaster growls and hits him with his crutch. Indus squeals again, this time in pain, and races back behind his mother. Charm makes a muffled sound of protest and tries to get her gag off.

My colt and my favorite groom, hurt! My favorite mare about to be stolen!

Something stirs inside me. I make a huge effort and roll over, put my forelegs under me, and sit up. Borealis's ghost stares at me in surprise and fades a little. With a massive heave, I am on my feet. My legs tremble. But I am much thinner than I was, so they just about support me.

I stagger out the open door of my stall, make myself huge, and squeal in rage.

The horsemaster looks around. His eyes go wide.

"Impossible!" he breathes.

That is the last word he ever says.

Aura, furious because he hit her colt, rears up and hits him on the back of the head with her hoof. He stumbles out into the passage, dazed, and I take a chunk out of his neck with my teeth. He tastes HORRID. The effort of making myself huge finally catches up with me, and I crash down on him with my full weight. Bones crunch. He thrashes a little. Then his ghost shimmers away from under me, and he lies still.

I am puffing as much as if I had carried Alexander into a battle. Charm finally gets her leash free of the hook and tears off her gag. "Stay there, Bucephalas!" she cries, stumbling out into the night. "I'll fetch help!"

Aura calms down. She whinnies, first to her colt, and then to me. Indus whinnies back. Caspia neighs to me, and I manage a tiny nicker to tell them I am all right. Aura's door is still open. She walks around and sniffs me to check that I am not dead. I can see her more clearly now. Indus sniffs me, too. I raise my head and reach for a mouthful of hay.

It is good. I am hungry again!

That is how Charm finds us when she comes back with the guards. They look at the horsemaster's broken body and shake their heads. Then they look at me and shake their heads again.

"I'd never have believed it," says one. "The old horse has come alive again!"

"I don't reckon King Alexander's really dead, neither," says the other. "I reckon we should wait till we have proof. You know how he always looks like he'll never recover, then comes out of his pavilion laughing at us all for being so worried about him. Zeus only knows what he'd do to us if he heard we'd abandoned our posts."

Charm is not listening. She kneels beside me with her arm over my neck, pushing Indus's curious nose away and patting me so hard I am afraid she'll knock me over again.

"The horsemaster *did* heal you!" she says, laughing and crying at the same time. "He really did! You hated him so much, you came back to life to save me! Oh, Bucephalas! Oh, old horse! Don't you ever, *ever* scare me like that again!"

GOSSIP FROM TYDEOS

My city, I have to admit, proved disappointing. It was brown and crowded, with small mud-brick houses and narrow streets and the usual noise and smells. But on the riverbank the men had built a big statue of me with Alexander on my cloth, rearing into the Indian sky. Ha! They won't forget us in a hurry.

The rumors of Alexander's death proved false, as the horse bond had already told us. Over the next year, Charm received regular letters from Tydeos and read them to me while I was recovering. Most of them were soppy nickers and whinnies. But he wrote some groom-gossip, too:

Alexander recovered from his arrow wound and dominated all the Indian fortresses on his way downriver to teach them he was still the boss.
The river didn't lead to Egypt, like the scientists said it would, but to a horrible desert where 60,000 people and 3,000 horses died (including poor Xanthus), and the men had to eat mules because they ran out of supplies. They must have been desperate, that's all I can say.

When the army eventually reached Susa, the Macedonians took Persian
wives in a mass marriage. King Alexander married one of Ochus's sisters,
which made Roxanne hate him even more.
Tydeos got promoted to horsemaster.

Charm gripped this last letter tightly, a big smile on her face. "Hear that, Bucephalas? Tydeos has been made royal horsemaster! He says the army's on its way back to Ecbatana. You're strong enough to travel now. We can meet him there!"

Tydeos? Royal horsemaster? It's a good thing we are going back, because I am getting seriously worried about my rider's sanity.

32

BABYLON

323 B.C.

A MULE'S HOOF

We left my city in the spring before the rains came. Aura led the herd carrying Demetrius, and Charm rode Caspia so she could lead Indus, who was not yet old enough to be backed. She let me run free behind, since I was still a bit weak after nearly dying in India. She knows now that the horse bond links us too strongly for me to run off and leave her. Borealis's ghost followed us, hiding in the shadows of my damaged eye.

Alexander had already dominated all the cities and lands we marched through, so there was no fighting. We went slowly with plenty of rests, which was just as well, since my legs were wobbly at the end of every day. We left India through the Khyber Pass, then took the lowest pass over the Caucasus Mountains, so Borealis did not have to see his skeleton, then took the direct road back from Balkh. As we marched farther west, we heard more news of Alexander — disturbing reports of massacres that made Charm go quiet and the men frown. At the Caspian Gates, Zoroaster's ghost shimmered out of the shadows and trotted up to Borealis's ghost. They greeted each other joyfully and began to mutual groom.

By the time we arrive in Ecbatana, it is spring again. But outside the walls, we find only patches of yellow grass, blackened earth, smoking funeral pyres, and hoofprints in the mud. Alexander and his army have gone.

Charm drags us straight to the stables. "Tydeos!" she calls. "Tydeos!"

Even though I am exhausted after our long march, I can sense something is wrong. I flare my nostrils, disturbed. Hay blows everywhere. Leather buckets, left in the passage with water in them, have turned moldy. Most of the stalls are empty and smell of stale dung. But out of the shadows at the far end comes a desperate, lonely whinny. Aura and Caspia prick their ears. Indus gives a little squeal and shakes his head. I neigh in joy and trot down the passage.

Petasios! My faithful red friend!

Charm catches up with me and sucks in her breath as she looks over the door of Petasios's stall. His mane has been hacked off (which, as you know, is a bad sign for his rider) and his tail cut too short for him to flick away flies. His coat is dusty and his ribs stick out. His water is dirty, and he's wearing his muzzle so he hasn't been able to eat his hay.

I stretch my head over the door and nicker to him in sympathy.

Charm whispers, "Oh, you poor horse. How did Hephaestion die? Was there another battle? Why are you wearing your muzzle in your stall? Where's Tydeos?"

But if Tydeos were here, he would never have let Petasios get so thin and dirty. His smell lingers on the rake, but it is faint.

Charm shoves Indus into the stall across the passage, puts Aura next door to him and Caspia on the other side, and lets me into the stall next to Petasios. The red horse immediately pushes his nose over the partition and tries to mutual groom with me. Charm takes his muzzle off, pats him, and whispers, "You'll be all right now. I'll look after you."

Hearing our whinnies, a groom finally appears. He sees Charm in Petasios's stall and hurries across, eyes wide. "Watch that horse!" he says. "He's crazy."

Charm shakes her head. "Don't be silly. Petasios is one of the nicest stallions you'll ever know. I'll do him — he knows me. You go and see to that gray mare. She won't bite you. What happened to Hephaestion?"

The groom makes a face. "Caught a fever at a party, didn't he? Died a few days later. The king went crazy! He crucified the doctor, then led his cavalry off into the hills and killed everyone he could lay his hands on."

Charm goes pale and whispers, "I thought all the killing had stopped."

"You have no idea!" the groom says. "King Alexander ordered us to cut off the chestnut stallion's mane and tail in mournin' for Commander

Hephaestion, and said he never wanted to see nobody else ridin' that horse, not ever. We didn't dare take him out of his stall while the king was still in the city. And then when the king went off to Babylon, the horse got so crazy we couldn't handle him, not even on a lead rein."

"I'm not surprised," Charm says. "He's a warhorse, not a mule! He needs proper exercise and care."

She collects the dung from Petasios's stall in a bucket and comes to take the stale dung out of mine. I nibble her mane as she works, but she pushes my nose out of the way.

"Where's Tydeos . . . the king's new horsemaster?"

"Said he had somethin' important to do." The groom frowns. "He went off to Babylon with King Alexander. They're goin' to give Commander Hephaestion a big funeral there. They took all the best horses and most of the grooms with them. That's why this place is so dirty. Can't be expected to do it all myself, can I? I've still got all the garrison horses to see to, and the commander here is one of General Parmenio's old grumps. Always complaining about somethin' or another . . ."

The groom grumbles on, but Charm is no longer listening. She has been watching me nose around my stall and lift my tail to dominate the stale smells. In the corner of my stall, under some moldy hay, is something particularly foul — a mule's hoof. It has been hollowed out and fitted with a metal lid and has an interesting sweet smell. I push my tongue inside to explore.

Charm freezes. She stares at the hoof and goes very pale. "Poison," she whispers. "Hephaestion was poisoned!"

The groom stares at the mule hoof in confusion. Charm drops it into her bucket with a tight look and orders him to help her clean out the stalls.

Over the next few days, the stables were a whirlwind of scrubbing and sweeping and polishing. Charm put a bridle and cloth on Petasios and took him out to exercise, much to the garrison groom's admiration. After that, he still grumbled, but he worked harder when she was around. Charm made him help her back Indus and begged Demetrius to take us to Babylon. But Demetrius said the king had not sent for him, the heat would be bad in the south at this time of year, and we should wait until Alexander came back from the funeral. He promised to send a message saying that we were waiting for him in Ecbatana, so Charm had to be content with that.

She chewed her lip and exercised us every morning along the road to Babylon, staring hopefully across the plain. But still the army did not come, and she turned us back to the stables with a sigh. "At least the king's still alive, Bucephalas," she said, patting me. "I can feel it. He'll be back for you soon, don't worry. Then Tydeos will come, too, and maybe we'll find out what's been going on."

We did find out. But not quite in the way Charm hoped.

GHOSTS

One night, when I am lying in my stall dozing, I feel a sharp pain behind my elbow where the Indian arrow wounded me. It is like the arrowhead piercing my lung all over again, and my heart gives three rapid thuds and stops. Sweat bathes me. I neigh in terror. All the horses scramble to their feet and neigh in alarm. Borealis and Zoroaster shimmer out of the shadows and whinny to me in joy.

Charm is curled up in her cloak in a corner of my stall, exhausted after a battle with young Indus on the training ground. But our frantic neighs wake her.

She sits up with a start and stares at me. "Oh, horse, I was having such a dream! Alexander drank some poison at a party and collapsed like Hephaestion did, and then — *Oh!*" She puts her hand over her heart and turns very pale. "*It's going!* I can hardly feel it anymore!" She grabs my head and hugs it hard to her chest, trembling all over like a horse before battle. "It's just like the Amazon queen said. I think the horse bond's breaking! Stay with me, Bucephalas, don't you leave me, too. . . ."

She begins to cry like she will never stop. It is all very puzzling, because my heart has started beating again, so the bond isn't broken yet. When the pain fades, I am warm all over. Even the stiffness from my battle scars has gone. I still have a lump on my forehead where the Macedonian pike hit me back before everything started, but my eye seems better. I nicker softly and nudge Charm to tell her I'm hungry and want my breakfast.

She gets up, looks at me for a long moment, then shivers and wipes her eyes. "Oh, old horse, I have to go to Babylon! You understand, don't you? I think something very bad has happened to Alexander."

Charm runs to tell Demetrius about her dream. In the morning, she puts on Indus's bridle with trembling hands and leads him out into the yard, where the men are already mounted. She leaves my door open so I can follow them, as I did on the way back from India. Borealis and Zoroaster come, too.

Demetrius trots Aura to the front of the herd and gives Charm a steady look as she scrambles up on Indus. "This had better be a true dream, Charmeia," he says. "Because if it isn't, we're going to be in a lot of trouble."

We take the road to Babylon. We go faster than we traveled back from India, but I feel fitter than I have in years. After we've been several days on the road, a herd of Macedonian soldiers gallop past us in the opposite direction. Recognizing Demetrius, their boss pulls up his sweaty mare and shouts, "You'd better be quick if you're hoping to talk to the king! He's got a terrible fever. The doctor thinks it's his old arrow wound from India, gone bad inside, but rumors are already going around about poison. Everyone says he's going to die this time for sure! Can't stop — got to get the news to Ecbatana!" They gallop off in a cloud of dust.

Charm puts a hand to her mouth and closes her eyes. Demetrius glances at her, gathers up his reins, and shouts to his men, "Charmeia's dream is coming true! Hurry! We have to hurry."

Arion's ghost is waiting for us at the ford across the Tigris, gray ears pricked. When he sees me, he trots up to blow a greeting. His breath is warm, and his lips feel like lily petals. Borealis and Zoroaster whinny to him in delight. Several caravans are waiting to use the ford. But none of their mules and camels will go near it because of the three ghosts, so we get to cross first. It is fun to gallop through a river without a rider, and I make the most of it, splashing Aura until my favorite mare squeals and gives me flat ears.

We canter across the recently harvested fields and along the lush banks of the Euphrates. Finally, the huge blue-and-gold gate of Babylon shimmers in front of us. There are bulls and monsters on the walls, glittering in the sunset. But the gate is shut. A crowd of angry people is shouting at the Macedonian guards, and several caravans have given up trying to get in and have set up camp outside. We trot through them all. Aura throws her head up and pricks her ears at the archers on the high wall.

"Halt!" a guard calls down from the battlements. "No nearer, or we'll shoot. Identify yourselves!"

"Open up, you idiots!" Demetrius calls. "I have to see the king."

The Macedonian guards peer closer at him. "Commander Demetrius!" one says. "I'm sorry, sir, we didn't recognize you. We have strict orders not to let anyone through tonight. The gate will open tomorrow at sunrise for official business only."

Demetrius shakes his head. "Open this gate at once! I've brought King Alexander's groom with me. He left her to nurse his horse, and he'll want to see her before he dies."

The Macedonians look uncertainly at one another. "You mean that girl he freed back in India?"

"Yes, Bucephalas's groom! The king will be furious if he discovers you kept her out of the city."

"If the king's dying, it won't matter who we keep out," mutters one of the men.

Charm rides Indus to the front of the herd, and I follow her. Aura nickers to me. The guards fall silent and take a wary step back.

"That's *him*!" one says in an awed whisper. "That's the king's horse, back from the dead!"

"Don't be stupid! It's one of his colts, that's all. The old horse never looked so good, even when he first came to Pella."

I give flat ears to the guard who said that. He jumps as my teeth snap near his ear.

Their boss squints at me and shivers. "Open the gate," he says.

"Sir?"

"Open it! I'll take responsibility. If we can't trust Commander Demetrius and the king's own groom, who can we trust? Move!"

"General Perdiccas said while the king's sick we should trust *nobody* —"

I lift a hind leg and swish my tail in the guard's face. This time he goes pale and shuts up. The others run to unbar the gate for us.

We trot through an echoing passage under the wall and emerge in a wide avenue of blue walls decorated with more monsters. At every junction, we find a roadblock of overturned carts guarded by grim Macedonians. Demetrius has to repeat his story at each one, and I have to give them flat ears to make them let us through. A half-built pyramid of steps looms against the stars, covered in scaffolding.

"The ziggurat," Demetrius says. "I heard Alex was rebuilding it. At least he still respects the gods."

It is dark by the time we reach the palace. The guards at the bridge make Demetrius leave his sword with them. "Turn left for the stables, then go straight across and join the line," they tell him. "You'll see where. Half the world's in there, waiting to see the king before he dies."

The stable walls are blue in the dusk. As Demetrius hurries off, another ghost ripples out of the shadows to greet us. It is Xanthus with his scarred head. He must have followed the army back from the desert. I nicker to him, and he trots joyfully across to join us. Grooms hurry back and forth, carrying armfuls of hay and slopping buckets of water. Torches burn in the passages. Hundreds of horses neigh and bang their doors, impatient for their feed.

Charm looks around desperately. "Where is he?" she whispers. "I'll never find him among this crowd."

For a moment, I think she means Alexander. Then there is a choked cry behind us, and Tydeos races out of the dusk. With a look of intense joy, he throws his arms around Charm. They hold each other tightly, ignoring us horses.

"King Alexander's dying," Tydeos whispers to her.

Charm bites her lip. "I know. I dreamed it, and when I woke up the bond was breaking, and Bucephalas . . ." Her voice falters, and she takes a deep breath. "How did it happen?"

"Bucephalas looks well," Tydeos says, changing the subject and eyeing Indus in admiration. "I knew you wouldn't let him die."

There is a heartbeat of silence.

Then Charm gives a little laugh. "You dolt! This is Indus. I've backed him. Don't you even know the difference between an old warhorse and a newly broken colt yet? What sort of horsemaster are you?"

I whinny, but Tydeos does not hear me. He gives Indus a closer look. "Really? He's the image of his sire! Like Bucephalas must have looked when he was younger, anyway." Then he realizes she is blinking back tears, and sobers. "Oh, Charm . . . I'm sorry. Did the old horse suffer much?"

Charm shakes her head and wipes a hand across her eyes. "Never mind that! Just tell me what's been going on, and how I'm going to get in to see Alexander. They even made Demetrius join the back of the line."

Tydeos lowers his voice to a whisper. "Iolaus gave the king poisoned wine at a party. I don't know how many people were involved, but the plan was to blame it all on Antipater if anyone got suspicious, say he wanted to keep the Macedonian throne for himself and panicked when King Alexander came back from India. Roxanne never forgave Alexander for getting poor Prince Ochus killed in that horrid battle at the Jhelum, but I don't think she knew. She's pregnant now, you know? She slept with the king after he married Ochus's sister, but her baby isn't born yet so no one knows if it's a boy. We tried the poison out on Hephaestion first to see how much we'd need and started with just a small amount so it would look like the king died of fever. The doctor had more poison to put in his medicine. We never thought he'd last this long, but Alexander always was stronger than other men, wasn't he?"

"What do you mean, *'we'*?" Charm breathes.

Tydeos makes a face and puts his arms around her again. He says very quietly, "You must have found the mule's hoof? I left it in the stable under the muck where the garrison groom would never see it. You're the only one who ever mucks out properly under all the mangers."

Charm stares at him in horror. "Oh, Tydeos! You can't mean you were part of a plot to kill Alexander? And poor Hephaestion! What did he do?"

Tydeos puts a finger to her lips. I have to prick my ears to hear his whisper. "Hephaestion did his share of torturing and killing, you know that. They needed someone to get hold of the mule hooves." He gives her a pleading look. "I did it for you, Charm. Soon it'll be over. The bond will break for good, and you'll be free. Indus will make an excellent stallion to start our horse farm, and —"

As he speaks, a gust of wind lifts my mane, and I catch a whiff of Alexander's sherbet sweetness. It is very faint and nearly smothered by sickness, but I would know his smell anywhere! My groom is paying no attention to me. Something tugs at my heart. The four ghost horses prick their ears at the palace and whinny. They are impatient to leave the world. Aura neighs sadly as I whirl away from her and gallop into the night, and Charm looks around with a shiver. Her eyes go wide. *"Bucephalas?"* she whispers, and starts after me. I almost go back to her. But she's got Tydeos now. She doesn't need me anymore. My rider does.

Babylon's gardens are the size of pastures. I jump a wall and gallop through trees hung with lanterns, where herds of humans are sitting around the fountains talking in hushed voices. Someone calls, "Hey, isn't that the king's horse?" But the others laugh at him and tell him he's seeing ghosts. Borealis, Zoroaster, Xanthus, and Arion are galloping after me, so maybe he is. At the far side of the garden, an archway guarded by two Macedonians with crossed pikes leads into the palace. A line of people is slowly filing through.

I give them flat ears and push my chest against the crossed pikes. The guards' eyes widen. For a moment, they struggle to hold me back. Then the barrier gives way, and I am through. Before they can recover, several people from the line follow me.

"Hey!" the guards shout. "Come back here!"

But the whole mass of people surges forward, and the guards have to draw their swords to keep them out. I leave their shouts and screams behind me as I trot down the blue-and-yellow corridors, following Alexander's smell.

I have never seen Alexander looking so small and weak. He lies on a couch in a darkened room hung with cloths of glittering Persian monsters. His tangled mane lies on a blue-and-white cushion. He's dripping with sweat. The Guard stands around him, tense as spears. Hephaestion is missing, of course. So is Iolaus.

Perdiccas kneels at the king's side, holding the royal seal. A nervous doctor is mixing medicine in a golden cup. Roxanne sits on a little stool at Alexander's feet, her black mane loose around her shoulders and her belly swollen under her robe, clearly in foal. She is staring intently at her husband's face and doesn't notice me.

Darius's brother kneels on the other side of the couch, kissing the king's hand. Alexander's eyes are closed and his skin glistens with sweat. He doesn't answer when Oxarthes speaks to him. His ghost hovers just above the couch, holding on to the edge with white knuckles. It looks scared and angry.

I whinny and settle to my knees. A wind lifts the cloths, and everyone in the room glances around.

Alexander's ghost stares at me. A look of puzzlement crosses its face, followed by relief. A fierce joy lights its eyes. It lets go of the couch and drifts toward me.

"Alexander!"

Charm has caught up at last. She darts past me to the couch and throws herself across the king's body. "Please don't die! I've trained Bucephalas's colt for you to ride in your next battle, and everyone's ready to follow you again. They were scared in India, but now that you're back it'll be just like it was in the old days. . . ."

Alexander's ghost smiles at Charm, though she doesn't see this because she is crying over his body. With an effort, it climbs on my back and clutches my mane with ghostly hands. It is very light. I rise gently to my feet, afraid it might float off.

Perdiccas grips Charm's arm and pulls her away. "Leave him, Charmeia," he says gently. "The king's gone."

A deep hush fills the room as everyone stares in disbelief at the couch. The torches darken, and thunder cracks over the palace as the hole in the world opens one last time. The Guard looks up in alarm. Roxanne lets out a terrible wail and throws herself across the king's feet, and all the people in the room — slaves and soldiers alike — begin to wail and tear at their clothes in despair.

Their misery fills me. I have lost Alexander! Now my mane will be cut, and I will have to find a new rider.

But Alexander's hand runs down my neck and pulls my ear. "Come on, Bucephalas," he whispers. "Let's get away from these idiots, shall we?" And with a shiver of joy, I realize his ghost is still sitting on my back.

I make myself huge and carry him back through the corridors and out into the garden. No one tries to stop us. Everyone is too busy running, wailing, and shouting, while lightning crackles around them and thunder rolls around Babylon's walls.

"The king is dead!" they cry. "King Alexander's dead!"

The news travels faster than we do. By the time we reach the garden, all the people waiting to see the king are sobbing, too. Torches and lamps all over the city have been blown out by an unnatural wind. People stumble out of their houses with bundles of belongings and make a run for the gates. Others raise their arms to the half-completed pyramid and call on their god to help them. In the space of a heartbeat, the streets are filled with darkness, disbelief, and panic.

Still on my back, Alexander gives them a bewildered look. "It's all falling apart, horse, falling apart so quickly. Am I dreaming? I can barely feel you under me. It's like riding a horse made of air. It must be the potion that doctor's giving me. It's poisoned my brain! I wanted to die after Hephaestion left me, but it's about time I got up. I have so much still to do. . . ."

I don't think he realizes he's dead yet. It's a good thing he's got me to look after him.

To escape the confusion in the streets, we turn into another garden. This one is deserted and rises up into the stars. A wind rustles the leaves of the trees as I trot through the shadows. We find another river, though I don't think it is the Euphrates. I'm not sure where it came from, but it flows across our path, reflecting the stars, wide and dark and fierce.

Alexander stares at it. "More water," he whispers. "It looks like the river that Achilles fought in the *Iliad*. You'll have to jump it, Bucephalas. One last time, horse, for me?"

He trots me back a few strides and turns me to face the river. He tightens his knees and leans forward. A golden glow of energy surrounds him, like it used to back in Pella when he was a man-colt. He shouts the Macedonian war cry for courage.

"ALALALALAI! ALALALALAI!"

It still has the power to stir my blood. I spring into a gallop and fix my good eye on the far bank to judge the distance. It is the biggest leap I have ever made. But I'm not just any horse. I have Alexander on my back, and I trust him. If he thinks we can do it, then we can.

As I take off, lightning flashes across the sky. It reflects from the water beneath us, and I catch a glimpse of little Psylla, who died at the Granicus, on the far bank waiting for us with the other dead horses from my herd. Alexander must be able to see all the humans he killed waiting there, too, because he gasps, "Oh, Zeus, Bucephalas, so many! I never knew there would be so many ghosts. . . ."

The wind goes silent in my ears. Together, we fly.

THE
FINAL HOOFPRINT

The hole in the world opened by Alexander's death is fast sealing itself around us, and when it closes this time, I will be on the other side with the ghosts. So I must tell you the rest very quickly.

Since the Guard no longer needed its horses for battles, Charm and Tydeos took all the surviving members of my herd back to Anatolia to start their horse farm. They saved:

> AURA, *my special mare, now white with age*
> PETASIOS, *my faithful red friend*
> CASPIA, *who still does silly tricks*
> HADES, *not as quick as he used to be*
> HARPINNA, *battle-scarred and stiff in the joints*
> APOLLO, *still a bit vain*
> ELECTRA, *my huge filly, now a beautiful black mare*
> HOPLITE, *my tough colt, who will always be rather bad-tempered*
> ZEPHYR, *who kept losing her riders*
> INDUS, *who is the image of me*

As for their riders . . . Poor Iolaus, who got all the rotten jobs, was executed for poisoning the king, and Charm cut Hades' mane in mourning. Ptolemy took the king's body back to Egypt and placed it in a fancy tomb in the center of his big Alexandria so everyone could see it lying there. Perdiccas tried his best to keep the empire together, but it wasn't long before everyone started fighting again. Roxanne gave birth to a healthy man-colt and called him Alexander, though he never lived up to the name, and when he was thirteen someone assassinated him and his mother.

It is time for you to slip off my back now and return to your own world, where I understand warhorses are no longer needed because men have other ways of dominating one another. It must be a very strange place.

Go on! Don't argue, or I'll buck you off! I feel great, though I am older than any horse has ever been. I think I must be immortal, for I am growing a horn like the horses in Queen Penthesilea's herd. I will know soon enough, because Alexander says we are going to find the Amazons so we can dominate them.

I am Bucephalas.

I have a city named after me, and Alexander's ghost rides on my back.

No one will ever forget us, for we have journeyed to the edge of the world and dominated death.

HA!

AUTHOR'S NOTE

Most of what we know about Alexander the Great was propaganda written by his royal historian or by his friends and admirers several years after his death. Being a horse lover, I wondered what his warhorse Bucephalas, who carried Alexander for thousands of miles from Macedonia to India, would have thought of it all. And being a fantasy writer, I wanted to write Alexander's story in the magical spirit of the *Iliad*, which was the king's bedtime reading when he was on campaign. This book is the result.

Many of the characters you meet in it were real people, though I have allowed the Persian Prince Ochus a bigger part than the historians traditionally give him. I have also added the following fictional characters (naturally, I like to think they *might* have been real):

Bucephalas's groom, Charmeia, and her friend Tydeos
The evil horsemaster
Demetrius the Guardsman
The Amazons

The horses Alexander's men rode would have been real enough, but we know nothing about them except for Bucephalas himself, so I have invented their names and characters. As for research: I am too young to have served in Alexander's army, but I have been a racehorse groom, so I know what it is like to send a horse into danger (be it a race or a battle), desperately hoping — like Charmeia — that my charge will return unhurt.

I would like to take this opportunity to thank Barry Cunningham, self-confessed "old warhorse" of children's publishing, for having the vision to take on such an ambitious work, my editors Helen Wire and Imogen Cooper for asking all the right questions, and the whole Chicken House team for their enthusiasm and support.

Sometimes a book comes along that an author feels she was always meant to write. Such was this one for me, and I hope you enjoy Bucephalas's version of history as much as I enjoyed helping him tell it!

Katherine Roberts, Stroud, England, February 2005

SELECTED BIBLIOGRAPHY
of some of the books I used for research

Budiansky, Stephen. *The Nature of Horses*. London: Weidenfeld and Nicolson, 1997.

Clayton, Peter A., and Price, Martin J., eds. *The Seven Wonders of the Ancient World*. London, New York: Routledge, 1988.

Church, Alfred J. *A Young Macedonian in the Army of Alexander the Great*. London: Seeley and Co., 1890.

Green, Peter. *Alexander of Macedon 356–323 b.c.: A Historical Biography*. Berkeley: University of California Press, 1991.

Homer. *The Iliad*. Translated by Robert Fagles. New York: Penguin Books, 1991.

Humble, Richard. *Warfare in the Ancient World*. London: Guild Publishing, 1980.

Lane Fox, Robin. *Alexander the Great*. London: Penguin, 1986.

Nemet-Nejat, Karen Rhea. *Daily Life in Ancient Mesopotamia*. Westport, CT: Greenwood Press, 1998.

Roberts, Monty. *The Man Who Listens to Horses*. London: Arrow, 1997.

Stoneman, Richard, trans. *The Greek Alexander Romance*. New York: Penguin Books, 1991.

Wood, Michael. *In the Footsteps of Alexander the Great*. London: BBC Books, 1997.

Xenophon. *The Art of Horsemanship*. Translated by M. H. Morgan. London: J. A. Allen and Co., 1962.